Thanks, Dad!

"Snakes! Help!" Bart screamed.

Mikhail raced toward his son.

Ahead, a huge snake, thick as a man's waist and black with age, rippled along a tree branch toward the center of the stand of kenarda trees.

Mikhail sliced through the last drape vine and pushed it aside. His son was wrapped in snakes, their combined weight dragging him down. He struggled weakly, gasping hoarsely for breath.

Now Bart would turn! Now!

But his son fell to his knees. More snakes dropped from the trees to almost cover him. He struggled to pull them free, but they only wrapped their coils tighter. He tried to relax suddenly and slip out of their hold in the split second that they lost their grip, but there were too many of them. Agony filled Mikhail's heart. Bart was not turning. He was dying—a lanker!

Mikhail reached his son. Four blinding slashes and Bart lay limp in the midst of the writhing parts of a dozen or more snakes. Blood from the snakes and black mush from their intestines smeared his body. Mikhail grabbed Bart's shoulders and dragged him out of the nesting area. As Bart sucked huge gulps of air into his lungs, Mikhail sagged against a nearby tree—weak with relief that Bart lived, but sick with disappointment.

Bart had not turned. He would never turn. He would never be a zerker, a pack leader, or a lieutenant. He was a lanker—a warrior in name only.

And what of himself? Would he never have a zerker son to help him as he got older? He bit his inner lip until it bled. Would he have to watch Bart die the way Drell had?

Mikhail's shette fell from his nerveless hand.

INTIATION

MARIAN HUGHES

BAEN

INITIATION

Copyright © 1995 by Marian Hughes

A Baen Books Original

Baen Publishing Enterprises
P.O. Box 1403
Riverdale, NY 10471

ISBN: 0-671-87640-6

Cover art by David Miller

First printing, January 1995

Distributed by Simon & Schuster
1230 Avenue of the Americas
New York, NY 10020

Printed in the United States of America

Dedication

In memory of my father, Floyd E. Dike, who always encouraged me in all my interests.

Acknowledgments

There are so many who helped me learn to write, and each one played a different yet significant part.

I would especially like to thank:

Judy, who convinced me that I really could write,

Dr. Michael Wosnick and Dr. Pari Basrur who solved the scientific logistics of the zerker physiology,

The Bunch of Seven, Terri, Steve, Tanya, Fee, Mike, Louise, Karen and Shirley who were my cheering section during my first years of writing,

The Ink Blots, Louise, Terri, Steve, Ted, Alison, and Jan who honed my writing skills,

Josepha Sherman of Baen who kept at me until I understood her editing and got it "right,"

and most of all my husband who has endured years of scowling glares while I mentally struggle with plot problems or choreograph fight scenes.

1

The Last Gifter Moon of Winter

When the fert coughed, the normal grunts and squeals of jungle life fell silent. The hunting pack of men froze, listening. Within the pack, Bart examined the worms of tension that crawled through his belly, leaving acid trails. He tried to amplify the unease and restlessness. Was this it? Was he finally turning zerker? Briskly he strode around a huge Bulbata tree, trying to look like a zerker.

Around him, half of his father's hunting pack waited for the signal from the men at the game trap that they were ready. Even at rest Bart could easily see the difference between the lankers and the zerkers. Lankers sat quietly, resting or playing pebble-match with tiny nesting game cups. But the zerkers paced the clearing or sparred with each other to pass the time.

Yearning churned Bart's abused gut. When was he going to turn zerker? When was he going to gain the incredible speed and invincible strength of a zerker? When was he going to be able to stride through the jungle, looking for a fight, glorying in the chance to rip apart a tigrog, a keld, or even the most dangerous animal of the jungle, the fert?

Another fert coughed, a younger one, maybe a

1

yearling. His father notched an arrow as he slid between the animal and the whelps under his care. Bart moved closer to his own protector, Volf, imitating his swagger. When Bart turned zerker, he was going to be as good a fighter as Volf and as smart as his father. And when he became First Spear, or Pack Leader, there were going to be some changes. He already had a few good ideas that would increase the number of pack kills.

He heard a familiar chuckle. Before he could turn, a body crashed into him as one of his best friends, Guntor, tried to get a secure wrestling hold. Grabbing Guntor's wrists, Bart got a foot in front of himself and twisted as he heaved his whole body backwards. Guntor fell under him onto the soft litter of the jungle clearing. Around them the men laughed and Bart could hear the warriors betting on how long it would take him to pin his friend. Guntor was strong, but he did the usual. He tried to hold on tighter while attempting to rock Bart back onto his stomach, but Bart suddenly slackened his hold on one wrist and then ducked under the other, twisted and ended above him in a cross-body pin. Guntor's stocky well-muscled body bucked and heaved beneath him. Bart laughed. "Give up," he said cheerfully.

Guntor shook his head. "Best two out of three?" he asked, his black eyes sparkling with fun.

Undergrowth crashed; Bart and Guntor surged apart as the ground shuddered. A female keld charged into the clearing, trying to gore two ferts who were circling her in an attempt to bring down the early foal at her side. The keld mare was safe enough. Her huge ponderous body was covered by folds of skin that would turn aside the sharpest knife, or the vicious curved fangs of the sinewy ferts. But the foal had been born too early—in the jungle instead of up on the plateau—and it was scrawny and weak.

In one stride Bart reached his weapons and strung his bow. He ignored the mare and foal. Instead, he watched the ferts. They were waist high and twice as long—every dagger length of them packed with speed and strength. As the keld lunged at the ferts, one of them dodged and raked her with his claws. The keld didn't even notice. When the fert came within a bow shot, Bart's arrow buried itself in the fert's chest. The animal roared and gathered itself even as other arrows sprouted from its body. Instinctively Bart lunged around the huge trunk of the Bulbata and crashed into another whelp who had dived for safety from the other side.

"Keld brain," Bart yelped.

"Grunkle bait," Dyfid retorted as they both peered around the tree. The other whelp jerked his head toward the fight. "You'd better get in there with your bow. The zerkers have gone berserk, and you're the best shot left." He squared his muscular shoulders. "I'll cover your back."

Bart nodded and slid around the tree, excitement roaring in his veins. Zerkers charged the keld mare and the harrying ferts with dizzying speed. The ferts left off their attack on the mare and took on the warriors with savage glee. The zerkers' battle cries mingled with the coughs and snarls as both sides charged, feinted and retreated. While the zerkers fought, the lankers and whelps hung back, trying to loose their arrows, but were hampered by weaving, screaming warriors.

Bart saw his father roll and come up on one shoulder, trying to stab the keld mare in her soft underbelly; then, almost as his spear entered the mare, he backhanded one of the ferts with his shette.

Bart readied his bow, but the zerkers were too fast and so erratic he didn't dare shoot. A zerker went down under the second fert. As they rolled on the ground, Bart's protector, Volf, grabbed the fert from behind and heaved it aside. In the split second the fert was separated from its prey, three spears buried themselves in its belly.

With the ferts disposed of, the men spread out in the traditional baiting circle and started to tease the keld. As they did, the lankers moved up for the kill. Bart sighted on the mare. "Gopa, freeze!" he screamed.

But Gopa was a zerker, and he ignored everything except his prey. Bart frantically sighted and, as Gopa crouched to spear the soft underbelly of the mare, Bart's arrow sped over the zerker's shoulder to bury itself in the keld's left eye. Immediately she swung around trying to protect her wounded side. As she did, Bart's protector, Volf, charged and buried his spear in the other eye.

The mare went crazy, roaring, screaming and thrashing, blindly groping for something—anything—to trample. She knocked her own foal aside and sent it rolling end over end across the clearing. The terrified youngster bleated with fear as it struggled to its feet. It was small, only a few days old, barely enough to feed one family for a handful of meals.

As the roars of the men rose over the dying screams of the keld mare, the youngster tottered toward Bart. Beside him, Dyfid raised his spear.

"No!" Bart cried.

"Why not?"

The young keld froze looking at them. It was so small—like a kitten before it could be fattened for the pot.

"Because . . ." Bart struggled with an idea that was

trying to surface in his mind. "Because it's so small. You know how fast these foals grow. Why couldn't we feed it up—like we feed up kittens? A month on the upper steppe by The Home and it would put on another two or three man-weights of meat." He extended his hand to the keld the way he would to a kitten. The keld stretched its neck forward to cautiously sniff his hand. Bart moved a step closer. The foal licked his finger tentatively, then tried to suckle on it. Bart held still, hardly daring to breathe. It would work. Somehow they'd get the foal up to The Home and fatten it up. By migration time it would be three times its present size.

A spear slammed into the foal's side. It grunted and slowly sank to the ground.

Volf bounded forward and slapped him cheerfully on the back, sending him stumbling into Dyfid. "You kill keld," he boomed cheerfully. "You don't turn into a woman and try to nurse them." He laughed and pointed at Bart's finger. "Besides, that's not where you get milk from."

Around him the other zerkers laughed, and Gopa peered in Bart's face, as if he were a near-sighted elder. "Going to have to marry you off, boy; you're getting some very strange ideas," he quavered.

Bart flushed at being called a boy. He wasn't a boy, but a whelp who had hunted with the men for almost three migrations. "But," Bart started after Gopa only to be hauled back to the yearling carcass by Dyfid. "Save it," Dyfid said shortly, pulling the animal straight so Bart could start skinning it.

But Bart had caught his father's eye. Mikhail raised an eyebrow and wandered over. He was a strong man, grizzled with years on the trail and muscles thickened with age. But his eyes held the fire of a zerker warrior, the fire Bart hoped would soon shine in his own eyes.

"Pack Leader," he saluted respectfully, then blurted, "Didn't you see? The foal was frightened and weak. We could have saved it and fed it up—just like the cats we breed for meat." His father frowned and he hurried on. "If we could fatten it up, think of how big it would be by migration time."

His father hitched his broad spatulate hands on his weapon belt and shook his head, "We need meat now."

"But there'd be more meat later on, lots more meat. Think of the number of foals we've killed in the last while. If we could somehow tie them or cage them—the way we do our meat cats—we could have lots more meat during migration."

Volf shouldered his way into the conversation. "What's my whelp spouting now?"

Bart's father pointed to the foal. "How would you like to give up your share of that foal in hopes of getting more meat someday?"

Volf snorted. "Don't listen to him. He's only a whelp. Give him one day on the barricades at migration and he'll forget all these stupid ideas." He lost interest and wandered off.

"But, Father . . ." Mikhail frowned and Bart corrected his error. "But, Pack Leader, it would work. I know it would."

"Forget it!" Mikhail snapped. "We don't need food in a month. We need food now. The women are getting weak and the babies' bellies are swelling with hunger. You try to take food away from their families and the men will spit you like a fattened meat cat." He gestured toward the foal carcass. "Shut up and do your work." He strode off.

Bart turned to his friend. "Dyfid, it could have worked. We could have hobbled it near the barricades. The warriors on watch could have protected it."

Dyfid started scooping out the entrails. "Stop daydreaming and help me."

Bart squatted down to help. There was no point in talking to Dyfid when he was butchering. Where Bart had been born into the best quarters of The Home, son of a zerker Pack Leader, Dyfid had been born to a field hand in steerage, and he took food very seriously.

Bart looked at Dyfid, comparing himself to his friend. Where Bart was fair, tall and built like the flexible ashflower tree, Dyfid was short, dark and shaped like an aged burlpine, knotted and scrawny, and furrowed with scars. But the greatest difference between them was their lineage. Bart came from a long line of zerkers. Soon he would turn zerker, like his father and grandfather. But Dyfid came from steerage. He would never turn zerker. Instead of becoming Pack Leader or First Spear, he would always be a lanker, a servant to warriors, a nobody.

Still, he was a steady whelp who always did more than his share of the work. As soon as Bart turned zerker he was going to become Dyfid's protector. He'd thought of taking on Guntor. But Guntor was given to temper tantrums and sulks. Dyfid, however, never sulked or shirked his work. Bart smiled. He could hardly wait to see his face when he offered to be Dyfid's pack brother.

Dyfid's elbow caught him in the solar plexus. Bart turned and playfully punched his friend back.

"You're going to dull your knife if you whack at the meat like a blind granddad," Dyfid said. "Wait till you're a zerker warrior and a pack leader. Not even your father will listen to you while you're still a whelp."

Mikhail watched his son help Dyfid butcher the young fert. The leaf-choked ground was stained red. The smell of blood must be charging through the jungle, broadcasting its message of death to predators and carrion eaters alike. He pushed down his impatience at the slowness of the lankers and whelps, and watched his son instead. Bart was sixteen, almost a man. Taller than most, his large bones were clearly visible, held together with metal-thin slats of muscle that accentuated his broad shoulders while emphasizing his lean build. Blond cropped hair and bushy eyebrows framed steady grey eyes that could spot a hiding ildenhorn five klats away. Strong, smart, an excellent hunter, Mikhail could not help but compare him to the other whelps in his pack. Guntor was more heavily muscled and looked stronger. But that last wrestling match had shown who was really stronger—and smarter. Dyfid was also smart. No doubt about that. But he was from steerage, and would never turn zerker. No, the best whelp in the whole pack was Bart. He would be the perfect heir to Mikhail's position as Pack Leader and Lieutenant of The Home—when he turned zerker.

Mikhail's fist clenched. *When was Bart going to turn zerker?* When was he going to get that blinding speed and hysterical strength that separated zerkers from the rest of the lanker warriors? Time was getting short: Bart *had* to turn soon—for his own safety if nothing else. Mikhail didn't know if he could bear to lose *another* lanker-slow son.

The sharp outlines of the jungle around him blurred slightly as he remembered Drell that last day of the fert migration. His son had stood laughing on the barricades of The Home, waiting for the next pack of ferts to pass by the valley entrance.

Drell had leaned on his spear, looking back over his shoulder to the fields of wheat, rye, oats, vegetables and root crops that crammed every finger-width of the flat, river valley between the cliffs of The Home. "Taizaburo! Look at all that ship food! We're going to get fat."

"You won't, not if you take Broawyn Edgar's daughter for your second wife." Mikhail laughed as he checked his arrows before slipping them into his quiver.

A pack of thirty or forty ferts humped into sight, long bodies undulating while they bounded forward on stubby legs. Down the trail they came, leaving their summer home on the high plateau of the Forbidden Heights and heading for their winter hunting grounds in the jungle far below. As they passed the opening to Waterfall Valley, one suddenly stopped and rose three times its height to sit on its haunches, sniffing the air.

"Thank Godwithin they don't fight like that," Drell said. "It's bad enough when they're only waist high."

The questing fert coughed and the rest of the pack veered toward the waiting men, increasing their pace as they came. Drell darted back to his position on the other side of Volf, his zerker protector. As soon as the animals came within range the warriors fitted their arrows and started shooting.

Fifteen or twenty ferts stumbled and fell, but their momentum took them right up to the wall. Some attacked their wounded who soon disappeared under a snarling feeding frenzy. Others leaped on the gory feast and used the bodies, alive and dead to reach the top of the stone barricade. Soon Mikhail was roaring his battle cry as he swung his shette, amputating limbs and heads and being showered in blood.

A shriek of agony sliced through his battle rage. He turned. Drell was down with an old scarred female at his throat. When blood drenched his chest, the animal went wild. Volf, Drell's protector, was toying with a young fert who was barely alive.

"Volf, guard Drell." Mikhail started toward Drell, but two yearlings reared over his section of the wall. Drell's screams rose above the battle cries of all eighty-five zerkers and ninety lankers. From the corner of his eye he could see Volf look up from his kill.

"Drell!" Volf called in alarm. Then: "Get a stretcher here!" But, of course, it had been too late.

A long muffled whistle drifted through the jungle foliage and into the small clearing. Mikhail blinked away his memories. The whistle was from the warriors at the game trap a half klat away; they were ready.

Mikhail saw his problem warrior heading out of the clearing alone. "Volf, where are you going?"

Volf ignored him and plunged into the tangled bushes. Mikhail heaved his spear. It landed just in front of the man. Volf grabbed it and stomped back into the clearing, eyes slitted with anger. He was short and muscled like a keld stallion—had a temper like one too, but didn't have the brains of a rock rat. The idiot had his leathers open to his waist, an invitation to flying daggerjaws who swarmed the creeks, or tree-climbing viper beetles who hung on the undersides of leaves that draped over game trails, waiting for hosts.

Volf strode to Mikhail and slammed the spear into the ground. "I was only trying to see if there were any more keld out there." The vein on his temple throbbed.

"And what about your whelps?" Mikhail asked.

Volf heaved a disgusted sigh. "They're safe. The rest of the pack are here."

Mikhail only just managed to keep from hitting him. "Safe? As safe as Drell was?"

Volf turned dark red. "It wasn't my fault. I was berserker. I didn't hear him until it was too late."

Mikhail ground his teeth. There was nothing to say to that. Every zerker fucked up sometime or another because he lost control. But every time Mikhail saw Volf, he saw the man toying with a fert while Drell died. Mikhail pushed the image from his mind and impatiently signaled for the lankers and whelps to finish butchering the game. Volf was an ever-festering sore in his pack. Discipline didn't agree with him, and punishment didn't improve his temper. Mikhail had tried to trade the man to another pack, but no one wanted him. Sometimes he even thought about killing him, but had to face bitter reality. They needed every zerker they could get. Besides, Volf was young, accurate with his bow, and deadly with his shette. Another thought occurred to him. Volf was the same age Mikhail had been when he'd killed his own pack leader, Wayneth, during the Pack War—and Mikhail was now older than Wayneth had been then.

But he could handle Volf. *And Wayneth had thought he could handle Mikhail.* He turned resolutely away from Volf and watched his son skin the fert. Bart glanced up and flashed him a warm smile. How like Drell he looked. His eyes were grey where Drell's had been blue, but he had the same warmth and bright intelligence of his older brother. Had the same crazy ideas too. Mikhail shook his head. Bart would learn as he grew older that the old ways were the best. He watched Dyfid and Guntor cluster around Bart, while the other whelp, Mariko, hung around them. Bart was already making his lifelong friends. As soon as he turned zerker, they would become the nucleus for his future pack.

"All right, let's move out," Mikhail called.

Volf took up his hunting position on Mikhail's left where his recklessness could be watched and controlled. Mikhail had also assigned him the best two whelps in the pack, Guntor and Bart. It meant Mikhail was actually responsible for four whelps instead of two; it also meant that Volf's heedless behavior could kill his other son.

Bart was wiping the sweat from his forehead with the sleeve of his mottled leathers when he saw his father's stare. He straightened, watchful. Mikhail gave a tight nod and made a tiny gesture toward Volf. Bart lowered one eyelid.

As soon as the lankers finished, Mikhail lifted his arm, signaling the beginning of the hunt. The left and right flank of beaters slipped into the heavy undergrowth. Mikhail felt the familiar excitement of the hunt begin to build.

His son, Guntor and Volf took up their positions to one side of him. His son, blond, tall and very thin— but then they all were; it had been a hard winter. Beside him paced Guntor. Black haired, and slightly shorter, he was twice as wide as Bart, with heavy muscles and a fiery energy that made him bounce with every stride. Of his own whelps, Dyfid walked with quiet efficiency, while Mariko hung back, fearfully, clearly waiting for Mikhail and Dyfid to clear the way.

As Mikhail signaled the beaters to spread out, Dyfid and Mariko automatically started to beat and shake their cymbal drums. Bart began to sing the "Song of the Ancestors" in a clear voice.

> *When the ships of Olarni all fell from the*
> *   skies*
> *Her people were filled with fear*
> *They crashed on the Heights so cold and so*
> *   dry*
> *And they knew that their death was near*
>
> *Long live the people who fell from the skies*
> *Long live the Warrior Way . . .*

Mikhail listened to Bart's voice, fear biting at his belly. *That sounded like a man. Was the boy too old to turn zerker?* Cold fear drenched him in a sudden sweat. Get yourself together, he ordered. Think. Left flank. He tried to ignore his fear for his son and plunged into the undergrowth. Taizaburo, but they had to get meat today—a lot of meat—otherwise they wouldn't have any in storage for when they were trapped behind the barricades during the fert migration.

He whistled for the left flank to report. "Left flank, damn you," he muttered when they did not immediately whistle back. Then he relaxed as both the right and left flank whistles sliced through the undergrowth. Both of them were in place and moving slightly ahead of the center.

> *The ships were afire, the planet was strange,*
> *The air was too thin and cold*
> *Their radio damaged, their friends out of*
> *   range*
> *They knew that their fate was told*
>
> *Long live the people who fell from the skies*
> *Long live the Warrior Way . . .*

Drops of dew splashed his face. Cobwebs caught on his eyelids, and briefly tangled them together. As he slashed with his shette, clearing the way for his whelps, the sharp scent of fern cut through the odor of decaying vegetation.

His back prickled with the feeling of danger. He did a quick turn, froze for a split second and listened. Behind them he could hear snarling. The carnivores and scavengers had found the bloody remains of the kelds and ferts, and were fighting over every scrap of sinew and drying drop of blood. He hurried on. When he passed a huge amphora tree he reversed his shette and drummed on the monstrous trunk, sending booming echoes into the undergrowth. As the hollow reverberations died away, he heard something rushing away into the bushes in front of him. Good. The men at the trap would be waiting for it.

Something moved through the trees above. He looked up. The massive trunks rose into the gloom of the canopy. Branches clustered with leaves or draped with air plants and vines shielded the ground from all but the occasional flicker of sunlight. He checked the lacy orange and black air plants for nador spikes, and ran his eyes down every vine to make sure that they held no snakes or viper beetles.

On either side of him the muffled drumming and chanting kept pace. If only the pack would stay together! Yesterday Gopa had run into a tigrog lair. By the time he killed the animals, and his lankers and whelps had butchered the carcasses, the line had been broken and the men at the trap had waited in vain.

Damn. His pack was falling apart. As food got scarce, his zerkers took more and more risks. They had to hold together at times like this. He wiped his brow. He was getting too old to act as the pack leader, the best fighter, the best tracker, and the best hunter, every single day of his life. As soon as Bart turned zerker and was initiated as a warrior, Mikhail was going to work his butt off.

"Keep up," he snarled at Mariko. "How can I protect you if you're halfway back to The Home?"

The slender whelp shuffled into a run and took his place on Mikhail's right. Dyfid was solidly chanting and marching on his left.

> But the Mother General assembled her band
> And told them they'd find a way
> To live and grow in this dangerous land
> To conquer and hold it at bay

Mikhail's feet caught on a ground vine; he jerked free. Just another quarter klat and their families would all be eating well tonight. Irritably he slashed at a spice bush, showering the pungent smell all over his whelps. While they sneezed and chanted he tried to control his thoughts.

Left flank, right flank, danger in front, danger behind, danger above. Sweat trickled into his eyes, stinging them. Wings buzzed behind his ear. He whirled, grabbed a daggerjaw just as it plunged toward his unprotected neck, and crushed the bright blue shell, enjoying the destruction of something he could get his hands on. Wiping his hands, he marched on. When the hunt was over, he was going to let Tekiri massage his aching muscles. He smiled. She was so tiny, so bright-eyed with her delicate pointed chin. When he had married her, she'd looked so demure, but in bed . . .

A triumphant whoop ripped through the jungle. Volf's whelps, then Mikhail's, fell silent. Undergrowth crashed and something heavy tore through the ferns and lakor bushes. Dyfid braced his spear defensively in front of him. Mikhail caught a glimpse of a black-and-white pinto hog, the flash of a spear and a scrap of mottled jungle greens as Volf ran back the way they had come. Mikhail grabbed his whistle and shrilled "recall," but Volf was berserker; only his prey existed.

"Keep in line. Whistle if you see anything dangerous," Mikhail said, running toward the hole in the line. But as he ran, first Bart's and then Guntor's voice picked up the chant again. He couldn't see them, but they were holding the line. Good lads. After this he could finally demote Volf from protector to solitary, and one of his problems would be solved. From now on Volf would guard the outer flank where he could take all the game he wanted without endangering the pack kills. But he'd be ugly about losing his portion of Bart's and Guntor's kills. Well, too bad.

"'Ware snake," Bart shouted through the jungle. "Nesters, dozens of them."

Shit. There went the line. "All right," Mikhail called. "Go around them."

"But it will leave too big a hole in our line. Guntor and I will try to run through."

"No!" Mikhail roared. The rotten odor of nester snakes drifted past his nose.

Guntor screamed.

Mikhail threw himself toward the sound. "To me!" he yelled over his shoulder. Behind him the "man down" whistle silenced the rest of the beaters. Damn Volf to Hell!

Mikhail's shette blurred as he slashed his way toward the frenzied crashing. Frantically, he scanned for the nesters.

There. His stomach turned. Not a nest—a whole colony. Ahead of him, dark woven twig-and-grass nests bulged like obscene tumors on every branch. From these nests hundreds of green and blue snakes slithered or fell toward the sounds of a struggle. Mikhail hurdled a waist-high log, gripping his shette more tightly, and saw Guntor staggering in circles, wrapped by a half dozen snakes. He'd lost his shette and was trying to get his small knife between himself and the coils of the constrictors. Another two snakes landed; he roared with pain as they bit deep to anchor themselves.

"Damn you. Damn you." Hurt turned to rage, and suddenly Guntor went crazy. He dropped his small knife and began ripping the snakes off, screaming mindlessly. His actions speeded up; his eyes flared with insane rage. He seemed to grow bigger. His skin flushed while his black hair appeared to stand on end.

Dyfid caught up to Mikhail. "Zerker," he whispered.

One larger snake held on and Guntor ripped its mouth in half pulling it off. He threw it away and hyperventilated: he was dangerous; he didn't know how to handle his energy.

Mikhail spotted Guntor's shette lying in the leaf mold and picked it up. "Guntor!" He heaved the shette at the whelp. Guntor whirled, snatched it in midair and started climbing a vine-covered trunk to get at another nest.

"Where's Bart?" Mikhail yelled.

Guntor ignored him and shinnied up a waist-thick vine to hack a nest off the nearest branch.

Dyfid nudged Mikhail and pointed. Above the dense undergrowth three snakes slithered forward and dropped over the same spot. Mikhail lunged.

"Snakes! Help!" Bart called hoarsely from somewhere in the next clump of kenarda trees.

As Mikhail tore to his rescue a children's rhyme echoed in his head.

> *Zerkers sleep in children waiting*
> *For fights to death or calls for mating.*
> *Either one can wake his ire*
> *Fan his rage and feed his fire.*

Guntor had turned; now, finally, Bart would turn too.

"Mikhail!" Mariko screamed.

Mikhail whirled, leaped backward and slashed off the head of the nester before it could get its jaws clamped. Dyfid jerked sideways and avoided another. "Stick with me." Mikhail raced toward his son.

Ahead, a huge snake, thick as a man's waist and black with age, rippled along a tree branch toward the center of the stand of kenarda trees.

Mikhail sliced through the last drape vine and pushed it aside. His son was wrapped in snakes, their combined weight dragging him down. He struggled weakly, gasping hoarsely for breath.

Now Bart would turn! Now!

But his son fell to his knees. More snakes dropped from the trees to almost cover him. He struggled to pull them free, but they only wrapped their coils tighter. He tried to relax suddenly and slip out of their hold in the split second that they lost their grip, but there were too many of them. Agony filled Mikhail's heart. Bart was not turning. He was dying—a lanker!

Mikhail reached his son. Four blinding slashes and Bart lay limp in the midst of the writhing parts of a dozen or more snakes. Blood from the snakes and black mush from their intestines smeared his body. Mikhail grabbed Bart's shoulders and dragged him out of the nesting area. As Bart sucked huge gulps of air into his lungs, Mikhail sagged against a nearby tree—weak with relief that Bart lived, but sick with disappointment.

Bart had not turned. He would never turn. He would never be a zerker, a pack leader, or a lieutenant. He was a lanker—a warrior in name only.

And what of himself? Would he never have a zerker son to help him as he got older? He bit his inner lip until it bled. Would he have to watch Bart die the way Drell had?

Mikhail's shette fell from his nerveless hand.

2

Day 40: Sixth Gifter Moon of Winter:
452 Migrations After Landing

Sanda lifted her head and lustily sang the "Song Of The Ancestors," hoping desperately that she would win her scholarship. She mouthed the words describing the horrors the settlers had faced on their new world without really being aware of them. Too much was at stake.

> But a child that wandered away from his
>   dam,
> Was eaten by animals wild.
> The horrified mother attacked with her man,
> But neither could save their child.
>
> The blood of the child drove the animals
>   mad,
> And others did come at their call.
> The settlers won but the cost made them sad,
> Ten people had given their all.
>
> Long live the people who fell from the skies
> Long live Olarni's Rule.

She looked around at her graduating class. Thirty-six girls sang in a light two-part harmony as they

21

celebrated their last day as schoolchildren. They looked so happy. But then none had her dreadful inheritance.

> *But the battle had given them kills right at*
>   *hand*
> *And they feasted all through the night.*
> *And awoke to a world where half of the band*
> *Were berserker with strength and might.*

Teacher Illana caught Sanda's eye and smiled. Sanda felt her heart lurch. Did that mean she had won? Or did it just mean that Teacher Illana was trying to be nice. She smiled brightly and threw herself into the song.

> *Sister fought sister and father fought son*
> *The whole camp was torn apart*
> *Olarni was crazy, her rule was undone*
> *The people had lost their heart.*
>
> *Olarni decided to tame her wild soul*
> *And left for a forty day quest.*
> *She wrestled with demons and fought for*
>   *control*
> *Till she stilled the wild beast in her breast.*
>
> *Long live the people who fell from the skies*
> *Long live Olarni's Rule.*

Sanda stopped singing. She just couldn't stand the suspense. Could she win? She felt her heart pounding in her chest. She *had* to win. It was the only way she could enter the guilds—the only way she could fulfill her life dream. There was no other way open for her. She had no wealth. Her mother was a drugged berserker, and her stepmother only had enough cards for her own daughter's dowry. No, her only hope was this scholarship. She listened impatiently as the other girls finished the song.

> Then she gathered the people and told them
> to leave
> The Heights where the women miscarried.
> She found us a Home where our warrior's
> seed,
> Was safe for the women who carried
>
> She ruled for ten seasons then gave up her
> throne
> To Taizaburo, her warrior son,
> Then worked with the women to save in The
> Home
> Knowledge from a faraway sun.
>
> Long live the people who fell from the skies
> Long live the Warrior Way . . .

The thirteen-year-old girls in the graduating class settled onto their floor cushions, waiting with breathless anticipation for Teacher Illana to announce the winning scholarships for apprenticeship in the guilds. There were only three open this year: one in the scholar's guild, one in the potter's guild and one in the healer's guild. Any other girls who wished to learn a craft would have to pay the apprenticeship fee and that would put their families in debt for migrations.

Sanda had been holding her breath for so long she felt faint. She *had* to win the scholarship for the scholar's guild. She just had to. She had no cards for a dowry, and in these days girls without dowries remained servants all their lives, or were married off to doddering old men. But if she won, she could study, and maybe marry someone nice, like Bart. If she didn't win, a young man like Bart would never be able to marry her. For he would need a good dowry, or a guildwife to pay for his weapons and household goods when he set up his first home.

Teacher Illana smiled at them and smoothed her long rust-colored shirt. "The healer's award goes to Gena." She clapped her hands. Everyone turned to look at the steerage girl who sat cross-legged at the back, nearest the door. No one clapped.

Sanda's breath got even tighter in her chest. Now that her stepsister, Ava, had lost the scholarship she coveted, Sanda's whole future depended on winning.

"But I got better marks than her," Ava protested, tossing her long brown hair back over her shoulder.

The teacher frowned at Ava who had risen to stand defiantly in front of her. Ava, who was a trim thirteen, with small firm breasts, a tiny waist, and flawless skin, refused to be silenced. "I got better marks than she did and I come from a decent Promenade Deck family. I don't know how you can choose steerage scum over me."

"I wasn't going to say anything," Teacher Illana replied, "but since you are so rude, I will tell you why you did not win the scholarship." She looked sternly at the girl until she sat down again. "Whenever you did chores for the healer, you were last in and first out. While you were there, you worked as little as possible and tried to get other students to do the dirtiest tasks. Gena, on the other hand, was first in and last out. She did everything she was asked, and more. Many times she even stayed the night, nursing the dying." She pointed at Ava. "You're smart enough to be a healer, but even if your mother offers to pay the apprenticeship fee, you'll never be admitted to the healer's guild."

Ava glared at the teacher, her pretty face flushed

with anger. "That's just fine with me," she snapped.
"I never did want to mess with stinking dying people
anyway."

The teacher's lips thinned, but she ignored Ava.
"The pottery award goes to Ullan . . ."

Ullan jumped into the air, clapping. "I won, I won,
I won." Her black hair swung wildly to her waist,
and her fair skin was flushed with vitality and happiness.
The rest of the girls laughed and cheered as she pulled
Sanda to her feet and hugged her. "Isn't it wonderful?
We'll be in training together."

Sanda's heart was hammering in her chest. "I haven't
won it yet."

Ullan pulled her back down on her mat. "Don't
worry, you'll win, I know you will." She hugged her
friend again. Sanda hugged her back. *Goddess Within,
let me win*, she prayed. For it wasn't at all certain
that she would win. She had the highest marks, but
she also had a zerker mother and father, and her
teacher and all her classmates expected her to turn
zerker any day now. Since zerkers were not allowed
in the women's guilds, she might very well not be
chosen.

The teacher stood waiting until the girls were properly
quiet, then she said, "The scholarship to the scholar's
guild is awarded to Sanda."

Ullan led the cheer. Sanda didn't move. She just
sat quietly while her fears slid off her, leaving her
feeling light-headed.

"Don't cry, silly," Ullan said, hugging her. "We made
it. We're in."

"Can I get her scholarship when she turns zerker?"
Ava asked loudly.

Sanda's happy laugh stuck in her throat.

✧　　✧　　✧

Entering the water-supply room Sanda lifted her bucket into the stone tub and placed it under the kiln-hardened clean water spout. She'd made it. She'd get to study with Scholar Jehanee. She would be able to read about the ancient heroines of The Home: Olarni, Baptutha, Maherbainee, and Khalsah. And maybe, just maybe, she could find a way to help zerkers like her mother live a better life.

As long as she didn't turn zerker!

With a twist of her wrist she turned the water cock and watched the water trickle into her bucket.

"Sanda, hurry up with that water," her stepmother, Assilla, called from the wardroom.

"I can't. Everybody's using the water right now. It's just trickling out."

"Well, bring what you have, or the stew will burn."

Sanda waited a few more seconds then turned off the water. Stew. Some stew. Mostly mushrooms and fern leaf. It filled you up, but gave you no nourishment. She picked up the bucket and lugged it into the wardroom.

The rays of the morning sun filtered through the slit window, brightening the pattern on the reed floor mats, and illuminating the wisps of grey hair that stood out around her mother's head. Her mother. A zerker woman.

"Thanks." Her stepmother added water to the stew, thinning it. Then she ladled the stew into a bowl. "Now, go and give some to your mother."

Sanda took the bowl and turned reluctantly to face her mother. Brianna was sitting on a mat in the corner of the room, out of the way, but in clear view in case of trouble. Not that she ever gave any trouble for, like all zerker women in The Home, she was drugged to keep her peaceful, and to protect the lanker women from her rages and her hysterical strength.

Sanda knelt down in front of her mother. Brianna was sharp-boned and grey-haired. Her body slouched slackly against the wall. Her eyes looked at Sanda as if she couldn't figure out exactly who was standing in front of her. Sanda took a breath and nearly choked on the smell of Peace—the drug her mother was forced to take every morning "for the good of The Home."

Her mother seemed to struggle to focus on Sanda. "Aaag." She glared at Sanda as if willing her to understand.

"Oh, age. Do you mean age?" Sanda counted on her fingers. "You're thirty-seven." She tried to smile brightly, but she couldn't help compare her mother to Assilla. Assilla was older than Brianna, but Brianna already looked like Assilla's grandmother—one effect of the drug that slowly stole her life away.

Brianna's bony hands flopped uselessly in her lap. "Nnooo." Her jaw muscles seemed to clamp around the word.

"Age? Is that what you said?" Sanda wanted to run away from her mother and scream at the horror of the fate of all zerker women. But lanker women didn't do that. They calmly and patiently served the needs of The Home. So Sanda forced herself to sit quietly and watch the wreck that was her mother try to communicate. Her mother's fogged eyes were fixed on hers. "My age?" Sanda asked. Brianna blinked a nod. "My Thirteenth Sort ceremony is next month. But you know that. And I won the apprenticeship to the scholar's guild, but then I told you that this morning."

"If you don't turn zerker," Ava said nastily as she came into the wardroom.

"Shut up, Ava," Assilla said wearily. "At least someone in this family won a scholarship."

Her mother's jaw sagged open and saliva trailed out of the left corner of her mouth. At the same time her breathing quickened—a sure sign of trouble.

Sanda leaned closer, braving the sharp smell of Peace. "Mother, please calm down."

But her mother's chest heaved harder and her claw-like hand reached for Sanda. In spite of herself, Sanda panicked. "Assilla, come quick."

Assilla, Haddim's First Wife, wiped a tired hand across her brow as she padded over the woven mats that covered the rock floor. This past winter had been hard on the lanker woman. Sanda's zerker stepfather, Haddim, was making fewer and fewer kills and, with six growing children in the family, his pack portion of meat was not enough. New worry lines seemed to grow on Assilla's face every day, and her gown hung loosely on her once thick frame. She bent over and studied her sister-wife.

Brianna glared at her, hatred singing through the drug-enforced calm.

Assilla touched her forehead. Brianna tried to shrink back, but could only close her eyes to block Assilla out.

Sanda cringed behind the two women. Why had she called for help? But she knew why. She was afraid of her mother. Afraid of everything she stood for.

Assilla shook her head "It's so hard to tell if she's really upset." She considered her sister-wife as if she were a daggerjaw that had somehow gotten into the stew. "Maybe I should give her more Peace— just to be sure."

Sanda grabbed Assilla's hand as she turned to go. "Please, First Wife, not more Peace. Momma can barely walk now, and she's getting harder and harder to understand." She bit her lip. She hadn't meant to call Assilla ever again. But somehow it had just happened. Why was she so jumpy?

Assilla hesitated. A tear ran down Brianna's cheek. The First Wife shook off Sanda's hand. "Look at those tears. She *is* upset." She looked at Sanda. "Why don't you get some more water?"

Sanda nodded and went into the bathing chamber. But she didn't turn on the water. Instead she crept to the door and opened it a crack, listening.

"Inara, where are you?" Assilla called nervously.

"What's wrong?" Although younger than either Brianna and Assilla, she spoke with the assurance of a guildwife. Sanda lay on the floor and peeked around the door. Inara had come out of the bedchamber holding a stack of fibercloth towels.

"I'm going to give Brianna some more Peace. Will you watch, just in case?"

"Hasn't she already had her Peace?"

"She asked Sanda her age." Behind the door Sanda felt as if she'd been doused with cold water.

"That's harmless enough," Inara said, comfortably. "She must lose track of time drugged like that."

"Yes, but when Sanda told her, she started to cry."

Inara tossed the towel over one shoulder. "Do you think Brianna is afraid that Sanda might turn zerker?"

"Afraid! Of course she's afraid. Almost all daughters of zerker women turn. I expect Sanda to turn any day now, and I've got the initial dose of Peace all ready."

"Good," Ava said savagely. "Then maybe I can get her scholarship."

Sanda curled up behind the door stuffing her hand in her mouth so they wouldn't hear her whimper. No. Please, Goddess Within, let me be lanker. Let me be a scholar. *And let me find a way to help my mother.*

But there was no message from her Goddess Within. Sanda's blood pounded in her ears, as she struggled to keep from shrieking in terror. Finally, when she got control of herself again, she watched as the women advanced on her mother. She hoped her mother would not refuse. But if she did, they would call Bridd, the old watchguard, and he would pry her mouth open while Assilla poured down a double dose— "just to be sure." And her mother would be half conscious for days.

"Open your mouth," Assilla ordered.

Brianna opened her mouth. Assilla tilted the drug down her throat. Seconds later Brianna slumped back on the mat, her jaw slack and drool slowly sliding down her chin.

"Someday," Sanda silently promised the still form, "someday, I'm going to help you."

Assilla turned and slapped her daughter across the face. "From now on you be nice to Sanda," she ordered. "Let the poor girl enjoy her dreams as long as she can."

The door stood wide open, letting in the cool spring air. Sanda stood guard beside the door with her flail, watching to see that nothing dangerous got into quarters. Brianna tried to focus her eyes.

As Sanda raised her flail she moved with the grace of a hunting rockcat but looked as slender and delicate as a porcelain stem vase. Her brown tunic draped softly over small breasts and her sash defined a tiny waist above hips that were rounding with womanhood.

Brianna fought the drug that kept zerker women placid while it slowly froze their bodies. When had Sanda grown up? She got her mouth open. Her lips were numb and her foot was asleep. What had she been upset about this time? She struggled to remember. But all she could think about were the might-have-beens.

If only her first husband, Jaspaar, hadn't died. He'd ignored the custom of drugging zerker women. Probably because he'd enjoyed her laughter and turned their fights into passionate love. And his First Wife, Jant, had not been afraid of her, so she never insisted on giving Brianna any more than the basic calming dose.

She wrenched her mind away from happier times. She had to do something . . . but what? Everything was fuzzy: the Peace urged her to relax, forget. It seemed to affect her more and more every time she took it. Either that or . . . Fear cleared her mind. Was Assilla increasing her dose?

People moved around in front of her, cooking, weaving, mending and cleaning. Gradually their presence sharpened and Brianna was distracted by Assilla's daughter, Ava, who carried firewood to the hearth. She was wearing a brown child's tunic with a sash tied tightly to emphasize her young breasts. Her shining brown hair was held back by a polished horn comb. She dropped the firewood by the hearth and turned, pouting. "It's not my turn. I cleaned the head yesterday."

Brianna watched the girl complain. It *was* Ava's turn. The carefully polished grey rock walls of the wardroom dimmed as her vision narrowed to the spoiled girl who had her health and her freedom but didn't appreciate it.

Slowly she turned her eyes toward Sanda who stood poised to strike any intruders. Her daughter was taller and thinner than Ava and she quivered with energy and vitality. Beside her Ava looked like a meatcat, just fattened for the Mid-Winter Feast—lazy, sleek, and self-satisfied. Fear drenched Brianna, leaving her weak as well as numb. Sanda was too vibrant, too alive. She remembered Sanda saying she was thirteen. Had it been a dream? She looked at Sanda's tiny breasts. No: it was real.

"I don't want to clean the head: it smells like Sanda's mother," Ava whined.

Brianna saw Sanda's flail start to tremble in her hand.

Assilla threw down her mending and bore down on Ava. "Mind your manners. How can we find you a husband if you're a shrew?" She slapped her daughter soundly.

Ava staggered back, her hand on her face. "Why are you always beating *me*? Sanda never gets beaten. Let her clean the head." She skipped back out of reach.

Assilla's lips thinned. "Ava, you *will* clean the head. And Sanda will watch her mother. I think Brianna might be pregnant, and we can't have her aborting another male child."

Brianna relaxed in satisfied memories of her success in aborting Haddim's hated seed. Her husband had been furious. He'd beaten her and both his lanker wives and then broken every pot in quarters. It had taken the women months of work to earn the cards to replace them. Every time Assilla had looked up from her weaving, or her sewing, she'd glared at Brianna and increased her Peace. But Brianna hadn't minded. She might not be able to refuse Haddim, but she could refuse to carry his seed to term. And *that* was what Haddim wanted more than anything—guaranteed zerker sons.

"But, Mother," Ava was whining, "Brianna has a son up in the nursery. You have my two sisters, and Inara just had a boy. We're short of food as it is. We don't need any more babies."

Assilla shook her daughter. "How can you say that! We need every baby we can bear so there will always be enough warriors to feed us and protect us . . . besides, Haddim wants zerker sons."

Ava pulled herself free. "Yes, but if Brianna has a girl we'll be stuck with another crazy woman zerker." She sneered at Sanda.

Sanda's face went dead white. "I won't turn. My older sister Kayella never turned."

The older woman's eyes softened but she squared her shoulders. "Time will tell."

"Well, Sanda should turn, shouldn't she?" Ava said in her little girl voice that always preceded something really poisonous. "After all, when the mother and father are zerkers, boys always turn, and girls usually turn too. Kayella was just lucky."

Assilla grabbed her daughter and shook her. "How many times must I tell you to leave Sanda alone? Clean the head. Now!"

"You're always picking on me," Ava whined. "It's Sanda this and Sanda that. Nobody ever cares about me. Nothing I ever do is good enough. I was in the top three in my class, but I didn't get a scholarship. I wash nappies until my skin breaks out but you're never satisfied." She pulled out of her mother's grasp and ran sobbing toward the companionway leading up to the children's gallery. Brianna would have shaken her head if she could. The child was pulpy rotten.

Ava's mother started after her and collided with Inara who was coming out of the women's bedchamber.

"What's gotten into her now?" Inara asked.

Assilla sighed and rubbed her forehead with a calloused and chapped hand. "This time? I think she's jealous. But we have a problem. We have to keep her bad temper to ourselves—if it isn't already too late. Now that she's lost the scholarship, all she can be is a wife. But if word gets around that Ava is disobedient, no one will want her to marry into their household."

Inara put her hands on her hips and pursed her lips "I could take a loan out for Ava's apprenticeship fees."

Assilla shook her head. "We can't afford it. Besides, Teacher Illana told me privately that she could not recommend Ava to any guild. If word of *that* gets around, Ava will never marry anyone, no matter how pretty she is." Suddenly Assilla realized that Sanda was there. "And don't you say anything about this either," she snapped. Sanda shook her head. "Go out and pick some spice pods for dinner." Sanda disappeared.

Assilla sighed. "Ava is so unhappy. She competes with Sanda for everything, and Sanda always wins. Even Haddim gives her more attention than any of his other children."

Haddim! Brianna struggled with the grip of Peace. What did Haddim have to do with Sanda? She wasn't even his daughter; she was Jaspaar's.

"It's not my place to tell you what to do," Inara said, "but, if I were you, I'd keep Sanda away from him."

Assilla turned abruptly and started pulling bowls down from the shelf. "You're imagining things."

"Yes, First Wife." Inara stood quietly, waiting.

Assilla banged some wooden spoons down beside the bowl. Suddenly she stopped. Her hands rested on the table and her head drooped. "That's all I need."

Goddess Within, not Haddim. Brianna struggled to fight the Peace. She couldn't let another day drift by before Sanda was warned.

" 'illa." Brianna's voice cracked as it pushed through the drug that froze her tongue and slurred her words.

Assilla turned and waited.

"Wata . . . see . . . K'lla."

Assilla sorted out the words and then abruptly nodded. "Good idea. Sanda will take you." She raised her voice. "Sanda, come and take your mother to Kayella's."

Inara grinned. "Wonderful, I'll help you finish up here and then we can go to the Women's Gathering Rooms."

The Gathering Rooms. Brianna wondered what went on there. All the women went at least once a day—everyone except for the zerkers. They were forbidden—for the harmony of The Home.

Sanda came in and reached to help her mother get up, but Brianna glared her down. If she let Sanda assist her, someday she would be totally helpless. She awkwardly rose, managed to get her legs straight under her, then wobbled, waiting for her balance to feel secure. When she felt safe, she shuffled through the door Sanda was holding open, and stepped onto the Promenade Deck, blinking in the dazzling sunshine that reflected off the opposite cliffs.

"Sanda, take your flail," Assilla called.

Sanda grumbled and disappeared for a moment.

Brianna stood, waiting. The deck was like a square tunnel cut into the side of the cliff hundreds of meters above the narrow, flat valley. On one side of the deck, lavishly carved doors led into the quarters of the warriors. On the other side, huge pillars of stone supported the overhanging cliff face. Between the pillars, woven vine netting hung, protecting the people of The Home from dactyl or cliffcats. Just within the netting were planters and boxes of earth that in summer would grow fresh greens for the families of the Promenade Deck.

Sanda returned with a small flail tucked into her

belt. The handle was worn smooth by years of use.
The cord was made of the toughest keld hide and
the swinging paddle was of aged ironwood. Sanda
was good with the flail. Brianna prayed they'd see
no danger—not now, not when Sanda was so close
to maturity. Usually Brianna stopped to enjoy the view
of the grey-white and brown banded cliffs opposite
that rose from the valley floor to the snow-capped
Forbidden Heights thousands of meters above. She
liked to follow the ribbons of color up the cliffs to the
blue sky. Either that or she would wander to the head
of the valley and watch the waterfall that changed from
black to green and then to white, as it plunged from
the plateau above, over the water-smooth rocks, down
to the flat river valley below. But today she took Sanda's
arm and shuffled straight off toward Kayella's.

Sanda and Kayella. They reminded her of happier
times—when she was married to Jaspaar. If Jaspaar
hadn't fallen in the jungle, what a different life she
would have had. Her eyes blurred as she pictured
Haddim. Thick set, black receding hair, beak nosed,
and selfish. She knew he had only married her for
the zerker sons she would bear. When he'd tried to
breed her with the brutality and speed of a fert, she'd
fought him to a standstill. That had been a mistake
because he'd ordered her Peace increased, and Assilla
had been quick to obey. Since then Assilla had often
increased the dose, even for the smallest show of
temper or unhappiness. And each increase slowed
her down more.

"Momma, come away from the wall. You don't
want to bang your elbows." Sanda urged Brianna closer
to the women hoeing endless rows of planters, getting
ready for the spring planting. Along the pillars, other
women sat with their backs to the rock wall, mending,

weaving, or just gossiping in the early spring sun. As she trudged by, they all fell silent. She looked at the deck, trying to tell herself that they didn't exist. But she could still feel their eyes as she stumbled along. She knew they saw her as a crazy, disheveled, old zerker. But she wasn't really. Her hair was coming loose because Ava had tied it so carelessly that morning, and her clothes were always askew because she was slowly freezing up from Peace. If she had been able to, she would have combed her hair and kept her clothes clean. She wanted to. She died inside whenever she spilled food or drooled. Nor was she crazy. Sometimes the drug froze her mind for hours, even days, and at times she even welcomed its numbing presence, but always, in the end, she became aware of the world, her helplessness, and the fear and contempt that surrounded her on every side.

Suddenly Sanda pressed down on her arm. "Warrior," she hissed. "Curtsey." Brianna managed to get her knees bent a little and waited, eyes lowered, till the *slap slap* of a man's sandals faded.

They passed from the Old Cloisters to the New. The Old Cloisters had been built soon after The Landing. The deck was six meters wide and three meters high. Using machines that were only legends now, the ancients had square cut the walls, ceiling and floor and then polished them until the white and grey banded rock sparkled in the sun.

The New Cloisters were much more extensive than the Old. The ancient chronicles said they had been started in the fourth generation. During times of plenty the stone masons continued to chip a few more quarters out of the solid cliff face. When times were good—like right now—the quarters were all crammed. But the chroniclers said there were times in the past when they had stood half empty: when there had been a pack war, or after the ferts had breached the Barricades and destroyed all the ship crops.

With each generation the newest cloisters and quarters became smaller and rougher. Near the old cloisters the rock was rough split and the quarters were only a little smaller, but at the end of the Promenade Deck, the cloister was a chipped path behind pillars that had turned into walls with only two slits in front of each tiny home. Naturally the lowest ranks lived in the newest quarters while officers, pack leaders, and senior zerker warriors lived in the spacious quarters of the Old Cloister.

Brianna tried to duck as the deck narrowed and the rock ceiling lowered.

"It's all right, Momma, the ceiling is still way above your head."

Brianna slowly straightened, wondering when she had become the child and Sanda the parent. What did Sanda think of her? Did she still see her mother? Or just a drooling wreck?

"Oh, there's Kayella."

There's Kayella. Did Sanda think she was stupid too? Her soul bled as she trudged her weary way toward her older daughter. Kayella's long jet-black hair was caught in a looped knot at the base of her neck. Her face was flushed and relaxed from nursing. She was the picture of the perfect wife as she sat cross-legged, weaving mats for her home. She wore a navy blue gown gathered in smocking around her waist, and tucked neatly over her bare feet. Her flail lay with the handle touching her mat and just in front of her, Reena, her three-year-old daughter, played with a doll fashioned out of dried jungle grass. Brianna's vision blurred as tears formed in her eyes. If only her life could have been like that . . . free of the drug, ordered, and harmonious.

Kayella rose gracefully and settled Brianna on her own mat. Brianna wanted to shout that she was only thirty-seven, not a doddering old great-grandmother. But there was no use trying. Besides, she had to keep her mind on what she wanted to say. So she waited patiently as Kayella disappeared into her quarters and came out with two more mats.

"How are things at home?" Kayella asked, picking up her work.

Brianna dropped a limp hand in Kayella's lap. "Tell'ur," she rasped. "Sanda, thir'een." Goddess Within, but she'd give her life to talk clearly for a few moments.

"What do you want her to say, Momma?" Sanda asked.

"Sanda, go into my bedroom and get a jacket for Reena," Kayella ordered crisply. "I think it's too cold for her."

"I'll be glad when I'm married," Sanda said, getting up. "Then people won't *always* be sending me away when they want to talk."

Kayella waited until the door shut behind Sanda. "Momma, I can't. You know I can't. Sanda is only a child."

Brianna groaned in frustration. How could she convince Kayella with only one or two words? "Did . . . it . . ." She bit her lips, ". . . for . . . you."

"Yes, but you were already drugged. You had nothing to lose. I'm happy. I'm safe. What if Sanda says something?" Her breath came faster. Her terror surrounded her and reached out to join with Brianna's own roiling emotions; they combined giving the older woman more energy.

"She won't tell." Brianna ran out of words so she

fixed her pleading eyes on her daughter's face and waited.

Kayella dropped her eyes. "You're right. If I hadn't been warned, I would never have been able to hide what I am. I've actually tried to tell her before, but each time, I freeze. What if she unwittingly betrays me? I couldn't bear being drugged." Kayella slowly crumpled up the stiff half-finished mat as if it were flimsy paper. "How can I be sure, Momma?"

". . . have . . . to . . . your fault . . . if . . . she . . . drugged."

After a long silence Kayella bowed her head and nodded. "I'll tell her."

Both froze as they heard Sanda open the door. "I couldn't find it," she said accusingly.

"Never mind. I have something to tell you." Kayella looked around. There were three or four wives within hearing and a dozen children raced up and down the deck, freed from the long winter months of being cooped up in their quarters. "Let's go inside."

It took them a few minutes to get Brianna up. But she didn't mind. Kayella would warn Sanda, and Sanda would have a fighting chance.

"Hello, Ava," Sanda said clearly, as Ava strolled in, loathing dripping from each word.

Ava smoothed her tunic over her breasts and tugged her sash tighter. "Assilla's sister is sick. She wants Sanda to come back and brew some fever root tea."

Brianna growled deep in the throat. No! Not now! They might not get another chance before it was too late.

Ava paused and stared at her. "What's wrong with the old zerker?"

"Nothing," Kayella snapped.

"Did Brianna do something terrible?" Ava asked eagerly.

"No, Brianna didn't," Sanda said shortly.

Brianna felt tears gather in her eyes. She'd worked so hard. Now, with Ava there, no one could say anything. She lowered her eyes . . . and saw Reena. Kayella's baby had crawled to the dactyl net and was regarding a meter-long poisonous wall snake with grave interest. Brianna choked a warning. Ava screamed.

The greenish-black snake coiled around its lifted tail and raised its head, ready to strike.

"Pretty, pretty," Reena reached a chubby hand toward the glittering milky scales.

Ava screamed again and ran into Sanda. Brianna lurched forward—fell—tried to crawl over Reena to throw herself between the snake and her granddaughter, but her arms wouldn't move.

Kayella jumped over them—grabbed Reena and tucked her daughter under her arm. The snake ground its fangs onto the deck where Reena had been. Kayella leaped back across the deck, and grabbed her flail. The snake twitched into another coil and struck again. Kayella caught it with her flail in midair. It writhed mindlessly first on its stomach and then on its back, exposing its green-white underbelly.

Brianna stared at her daughter. Power surrounded Kayella like an aura of thick winter fur. Her stomach sickened; Kayella was clearly zerker.

Doors crashed open and men tore out of quarters, clutching their wives' butcher knives.

Men. Zerkers. They would feel Kayella's power.

"Calm," Brianna gasped.

Kayella gave her a startled look, picked up and cuddled her daughter, then closed her eyes and began to slow her breathing.

The men charged through women still frozen over their tasks. Radnor, a senior zerker, was first to reach them. He slashed the head off the snake with a woman's butcher knife. "Actually, it's already dead." He laughed, pulling fleshy lips back in a huge guffaw. "Who should I give the killer portion to?"

Brianna managed to get to her knees. Sanda helped her the rest of the way up.

Ava smiled with pretended shyness. "Kayella killed the snake." She sank into a graceful curtsey. "She hit it in midstrike."

Brianna stopped breathing.

Radnor laughed. "Hardly in midstrike. Wall snakes are faster than ferts. Only a zerker could kill a wall snake in midstrike."

"But she was fast—faster than my father, and he's a zerker." Ava's roving eye paused on Sanda for a minute and her mouth curled in a self-satisfied smile.

Brianna felt a fist start to close around her heart. She glared at Ava wishing her silent. Wishing her dead.

Kayella's face paled to a deathly white. "Don't be ridiculous. Any woman can move quickly when her child is in danger."

Be calm, Brianna wanted to whisper, but her tongue would not work. She watched Ava flush and toss her hair, loving every bit of the attention. Hatred roared in Brianna's veins.

The women who had crowded up behind the men started muttering and edged closer. "Test her," someone called.

"Yes," Ava said eagerly, "test her." She curtsied again with a smug smile on her respectfully inclined face. The smile drove Brianna crazy. The perfect teeth. The perfect skin . . . the perfect cruelty. Her heart was beating so hard she could hardly hear it over the murmuring of the women.

When Ava rose from her curtsey she sneered at Sanda. "You're next. I'll get them to test you too."

Brianna's heart exploded. "Nooo!" She launched herself clumsily at Ava. The girl ducked out of her way and stuck out a foot. Brianna fell heavily.

"Stinking zerker," Ava hissed under her breath. Brianna tried to reach her, but Ava danced away, laughing.

Kayella jumped a planter to land in front of Ava. She held Reena with one hand and slapped Ava with the other so hard that the girl reeled into two women, knocking both off their feet.

In dreadful silence Brianna whispered, "No. Please." But no one paid her any attention. They all stared first at the stunned girl on the deck and then at Kayella who stood still. Reena wriggled in her mother's arms, whimpering.

"Well, that proves it," Radnor said.

A murmur drifted through the crowd. Nystra, Mother General to The Home and speaker for the women, hurried into the circle. She was tiny, with eyes that sparkled with humor and interest. In a Home where olive skin was the norm, her fair complexion contrasted sharply with her jet hair. She curtsied deeply, then raised her head and spoke. "Are there woman problems here?" she asked softly.

Radnor grinned, gesturing toward Kayella. "We've found another zerker."

Nystra stiffened, the rosy glow in her fair cheeks faded.

Ava got up from the deck. One side of her face had a white hand print on it. "Kayella killed a wall snake in midstrike, and then she attacked me." She smoothed her tunic over her breasts, giving sidelong glances toward the men.

The women pressed closer, their hard eyes intense with fear and hatred. The men were inspecting Kayella with new interest.

Nystra's hand on her gift necklace trembled for a moment then her shoulders slumped. "I guess she must go to sickbay to be tested for the correct dosage." The Mother General took Reena from Kayella and gave her to Sanda. Then she led a stunned Kayella away.

Brianna crumpled to the deck.

Radnor's words, "We've found another zerker," echoed and reechoed in Sanda's head. Kayella. Zerker? She couldn't believe it. Kayella was so strong. So calm. So normal. It had to be a mistake.

She turned to the women for help, but they watched her as if she were a fire spider threatening a baby. Some even had their hands on the flails stuck in their belts. Sanda took a step backward and almost tripped over her mother. Brianna was slumped against a planter. Her belt was undone, her gown had twisted at her waist, and her wife's knot looked like last year's rock rat nest. From her clawlike hands to her clamped jaw she looked old, wrinkled, and disgusting.

Feeling guilty, Sanda balanced Reena on one hip and reached down. "Come on, Momma, we have to go home."

Her mother's breath stank of Peace, and her skin smelled old. She tried to get up and failed. Sanda put Reena down. Ava rushed over and picked her up, acting very motherly. Sanda was too shaken to be angry. She got one of Brianna's arms over her shoulder and heaved. Brianna staggered and got up.

Sanda took her arm to lead her home, and saw that a path had been cleared for them. Her neck prickled as they slowly walked down the pillars of multicolored gowns. No one moved or said a word. She could hear the sound of their own skirts as they shuffled along. Once, when she glanced up, she saw a woman study her, then compare her to Brianna. Sanda looked down at cracks in the rock deck. I'm not going to turn, she promised herself. I'm not going to turn. She drew a deep breath to steady her fears.

The smell of Peace almost choked her.

3

Water splashed on Bart's face, wakening him. He gasped for air, and choked on what smelled like vomit and shit. Opening his eyes he saw the dark crowns of trees high above, and beyond them the rich blue of a cloudless day. Below the canopy, heavy boughs were draped with spiky green, purple and red air plants. Nearer the ground, thick trailing vines drooped to the tangled undergrowth.

The jungle!

He gasped in pain. What was he doing in the jungle? His shoulder throbbed and burned. Agony stabbed him with every breath. He tried to breathe less deeply. Shouts of victorious warriors filled the clearing. Again he smelled something foul—and identified the sharp oily tang of snake.

The nesters! He struggled to get up. More pain sent waves of agony through him.

Dyfid leaned over him. "You're all right. The snakes are dead."

Again Bart tried to get up. Waves of pain radiated out from his shoulder, drenching his mind. The world wavered. He lay back and gasped until his vision steadied, then looked around. The seven zerkers in the pack were hooting and shaking the tangled drape vines, trying to dislodge more of the stinking nests. Dyfid, the steerage whelp, stood over him, bow at the ready, guarding him.

47

Guarding him! Why? He fumbled at his shoulder. His tunic was torn, wet and sticky.

Taizaburo! His worst nightmare! Bleeding, and in the jungle. Immediately he looked for Mikhail.

His father was in the thick of his zerkers, urging them to find every single snake. Almost forty migrations old, he was as muscular and as fit as his younger warriors. The only signs of age were the traces of grey in his brown hair and a multitude of squint marks around his eyes. Bart tried to attract his attention but, although Mikhail had the far sight, his gaze seemed to slide over Bart every time he glanced in his direction.

Bart struggled to raise himself up on one elbow. His patterned jungle leathers were smeared with blood and stinking, black snake gore. "What happened?" he whispered.

"Volf fucked us up again," Dyfid said bitterly.

Bart stared blankly ahead; he couldn't remember.

"He left the line. Then you and Guntor were attacked by a whole colony of nesters."

"Guntor . . . ?"

"He's okay—turned zerker."

Zerker? Guntor? He twisted to look for his friend and saw him striding around the clearing, his chest stuck out and a grin splitting his face from ear to ear.

Guntor. Zerker . . . Bart felt an insane urge to cry. Why couldn't it have been him? He was so tired of waiting. He pounded his fist on the leaf litter and nearly passed out from the pain in his shoulder.

He breathed slowly, willing himself not to lose consciousness. There was blood in the air. He had to be up and walking—soon.

The ferns beside them rustled. Dyfid stiffened. A huge snake's head poked through the grass, twisting this way and that.

Bart struggled to his knees, nearly blacking out for a second time.

Familiar laughter came from the brush behind the snake.

Guntor jumped to his feet, waving the head that was impaled on his spear. "Here's your sweetheart, Bart. Want to give her another bite?" He roared with laughter as he shoved it in Bart's face.

Bart forced a smile, pretending to appreciate the "joke." The blue-black snake's head was huge. Fear churned Bart's guts even though he knew it was dead.

Guntor dropped the head and danced around Bart, his black eyes flashing. "Did you hear?" He straightened and puffed out his chest. "I'm zerker! Now I'll always win against you. Of course I can't fight you any more— 'cause of the lanker-zerker fighting ban—but it doesn't matter. I'm better than you—finally."

Bart strained to keep his false smile in place. "We'll fight again, Guntor. When I turn zerker too."

His friend snorted. "Not from what I hear." He jumped to his feet and strutted to join the other zerkers as they pulled down the last few snakes. Bart swallowed a lump in his throat. Why couldn't it be him there, laughing and speaking to the zerkers as equals?

Dyfid nudged him gently. "Better get up. Meat's almost packed." He ducked to peer into the undergrowth. "We'll be moving and you need to be bandaged."

Bart reached for his fieldpack, watching the other whelp stalk back and forth. Thank Godwithin for Dyfid. If anything attacked him now, he would be easy prey, especially when his protector didn't seem to be anywhere in sight. When Bart turned zerker he was definitely going to let Dyfid become his pack brother. Meanwhile . . . he looked for his father, hoping to catch his eye.

"I wouldn't talk to him right now," Dyfid warned him. "He's in an ugly mood."

"Why?"

The other whelp avoided his eyes. Finally he spoke to a fern beside Bart. "You might as well know. Your father took it real hard when you didn't turn zerker."

"But they caught me by surprise," Bart protested. "I'll turn. You'll see."

"Sure you will," Dyfid agreed, but he didn't sound as if he believed it. He pulled a mirta-soaked bandage out of Bart's fieldpack, flooding the tiny clearing with the rich, heavy smell of distilled mirta. He opened Bart's jungle tunic and slid it off.

Bart bit his lips as Dyfid eased the dressing onto the large bite that had punctured the skin on both sides of his shoulder. Waves of pain threatened to drag him back down into darkness. "I must have been knocked unconscious when I fell down. That's why I didn't turn," he grated through his agony.

"No . . . I watched. You were conscious. They were squeezing the life out of you and you were fighting with everything you had. But you never turned." Dyfid gently tied the dressing in place.

With a crash Volf barreled into the clearing. He was bent double under the load of a pinto hog. The zerkers fell silent and the lankers stopped their butchering.

Volf didn't seem to notice. He slung the hog at Mikhail's feet. "Well, it's a good thing somebody got *quality* meat," he said, sneering at the snake carcasses. He stretched his arms. "Send some lankers back along my trail. I have another two hogs hanging from vines."

Mikhail's lips thinned. His eyes were killer cold.

Silently he signaled. Four lankers and two zerkers hurried away for the meat. Then he turned on Volf. "You left the line," he said quietly. The rest of the pack drew closer, watching.

"Yes, but *I* got meat."

"You also left your whelps without protection."

Volf rolled back on his heels, trying to look unconcerned. "You were there. They weren't in any danger."

Mikhail gestured toward Bart.

Volf's eyes bulged as they took in Bart's bloody shoulder and shredded jungle leathers. "But you were right there," he protested. "How could he get so—"

"And you ruined the hunt."

"But I got three pinto hogs."

"The pack can only survive through cooperation . . ."

"Sure, sure," Volf interrupted, trying to look bored. But he stole a worried glance toward Bart.

"So if you don't want to cooperate, you can leave."

Volf's face went slack. He swept his eyes around the circle. The older zerkers gave him tough grins, while the lankers turned their backs. "But . . . but I got three hogs!"

"So? We could have lost four whelps today. I'd prefer four whelps who obey orders to one zerker who doesn't."

"But . . . but—" Volf started to bluster.

"Leave or obey." Bart could hear Dyfid suck in his breath. Mikhail had always jollied Volf along— kept him working—and kept him supervised. He'd never brought it to this.

Volf glared at Mikhail. The pack leader smiled like a fert—all teeth and death. Volf's eyes dropped. His broad chest seemed to crumple inward and the scars that crisscrossed it suddenly seemed like badges of failure rather than success. "All right," he muttered.

Astounded, Bart stared at Volf's chin. It had quivered! He couldn't believe it!

"All right, what?" Mikhail's voice was relentless.

"All right, I'll obey," Volf muttered in an even lower undertone. Bart saw a glint of moisture in Volf's eyes. How did his father do it? Volf would charge a raging pack of ferts and laugh, but his father could reduce him to tears.

Mikhail snorted. "We'll see. Meanwhile, you'll get no meat from today's kills."

"But my hogs . . ."

"Will go to the pack as compensation for what you did today."

Volf's face took on a desperate sheen. "But my family needs meat."

"Maybe you'll think of that the next time you're tempted to break the line." He gave a humorless laugh. "Mind you, it won't matter as much now." He turned to the other men. "Volf is now a solitary hunter. You can't look to him for help, so you have no duty to help him either. What he kills he shares. What we kill we share only if he is pulling his weight." Mikhail looked around. "Get ready to move out."

Volf stood in the center of the clearing, opening and closing his mouth and turning a deep angry red.

Gopa, Mikhail's First Spear, bore down on Bart. "You!"

"Yes, First Spear." Bart tried to straighten up, but his spine seemed permanently kinked, and his shoulder had throbbed to twice its usual size. He waited, sweating with pain.

Gopa was zerker, a competent officer and an intelligent

hunter, but he hated extra complications. He looked over Bart's bandages angrily, assessing how much of a problem Bart would be on the way home. "Fert shit! You really did bleed. And it's still coming through your bandages. The mirta won't cover the smell of all that blood. We have to leave right away."

A short whistle pierced the clearing. Guarded by Samay and Kittu, the lankers staggered through the screening undergrowth, panting and red faced from jogging through the steamy jungle loaded down with Volf's kills. While they redistributed their loads among the other lankers and whelps, Mikhail shouldered his way into the group around Bart.

"What's going on?"

"Look at all that blood," Gopa complained. "We're going to have company on the way back."

Mikhail seemed to look through Bart without seeing him, or his wounds. "Then let's get out of here!" He stalked away, leaving Bart staring stupidly after him.

Tev, Bart's lanker uncle, hurried over to him. "Can you walk?"

"Yes, sir!" Bart spoke smartly, even though he was swaying with pain. His eyes tracked his father, hoping that Mikhail would turn and notice his courage. But his father moved to the head of the column and left the clearing without a backward glance.

"Who's my zerker protector?" Bart asked Dyfid. "He didn't assign anyone."

Dyfid propelled him forward. "Godwithin, with the blood you're broadcasting on the wind, it will take all of us."

Pain stabbed through Bart's shoulder. He stumbled. His pack was off-center, and dragged against his bandaged shoulder.

"Do you want help?" Mikhail's lanker brother, Tev, straightened the pack gently.

Bart shook his head. He wanted his father, not his Uncle Tev to help him.

His uncle kept pace with him for a few more strides. "Walk carefully, Bart. Zerkers are most dangerous when they feel angry, disappointed or guilty. Both your father and Volf are so upset anything could trigger a berserker rage in either of them."

Before Bart could answer, Tev dropped back.

Ahead of him the pack started singing the "Song of the Ancestors."

> But a child that wandered away from his
>   dam,
> Was eaten by animals wild.
> The horrified mother attacked with her man,
> But neither could save their child.

Bart groaned aloud. That was all he needed to hear. He wanted to shout at the pack to stop. No one who was bleeding needed to hear about how blood lusters went wild when they scented a man's blood. But the pack sang on relentlessly.

> The blood of the child drove the animals
>   mad,
> And others did come at their call.
> The settlers won but the cost made them sad,
> Ten people had given their all.

Bart tried not to listen. Instead he attempted to figure out where they were. Somehow they had left the steamy jungle behind, climbed up through the stumps of the old needle forest and ascended into the cooler climate of the true steppe. Winter-dried grass and tough shrubs crackled under their feet. As they rounded a bend in the valley, the chilly wind, funneled by the cliffs that rose on either side, made the climbing even harder. The men pulled out their overtunics and slipped them on. Bart shivered. He should do the same, but he only had enough energy to put one foot in front of the other. Luckily, it was spring and they didn't have to brace themselves against the numbing gales of winter.

Wiping the sweat from his eyes, he looked up. Ahead, Mikhail scanned the cliffs that rose steeply into the sky on either side. Usually the Forbidden Heights were hidden in the clouds, but today the white rims of the plateau sparkled in the afternoon sun. Between the Heights, dactyls rose in endless spirals on the warm air currents from the jungle below. Would they scent his blood? He studied their wing membranes and green scaly heads. Godwithin, he prayed, don't let the wind change and carry my blood smell to them. He plodded on, trying to keep his feet moving in time to the warriors' marching song.

> When Taizaburo took over our lives
> The women put down their arms
> The warriors swore to protect all their wives
> And keep their families from harm
>
> Oh, Taizaburo knew well what we lacked
> To save us all from hell
> He divided his men into warrior packs
> And gave us laws to tell
>
> Long live the people who fell from the skies
> Long live the Warrior Way . . .

His father suddenly let out an oath and stopped.

Immediately, Bart slid his pack off and dropped to the ground, wanting nothing more than a few moments of rest, without the persistent rub of the fieldpack.

"Will you look at that!" his father roared, pointing up toward the tops of the Forbidden Heights, which gleamed a soft white against the deep blue.

The unburdened zerkers drifted toward Mikhail, leaving the non-zerkers exposed. The lankers and some of the whelps threw their packs toward Bart, formed a protective circle around him and strung their bows. Nakano, a young whelp fourteen migrations old, bounded after the zerkers.

"Another would-be zerker," Dyfid sneered. Bart stared at him astounded. He had never heard Dyfid speak this way when Bart had hunted with the zerkers before.

"Keep those farseeing eyes open," Tev called to Bart. "We don't want to be ambushed."

Bart dully scanned the trail while his father drifted further away, pointing toward the top of the Forbidden Heights where the huge dactyls looked like reptilian rock mites against the sky.

"Look, there's someone up there!" his father bellowed, pointing to the Forbidden Heights.

The zerkers all looked up. The lankers around Bart gasped and looked down. Bart knew he should look down too. Only ghosts lived on the Heights. If you met a ghost or saw one, you were his soul slave forever. But, in spite of his fear, his curiosity dragged his eyes upward. Just below the cliff edge something moved. Bart shuddered involuntarily. Sangirs . . . the ghosts that had driven his ancestors off the Heights and down into the valley. He watched in breathless fear as a black ghost, holding one end of a squared log, backed to the edge of the ledge, then braced himself while the hidden end of the log lifted. Finally he moved forward staggering under the weight.

"There, do you see it?" Mikhail called. "Somebody's up there."

The zerkers shook their heads. None of them had the far sight. But they feared the ghosts of the Heights. They backed away from Mikhail, lowering their eyes and inspecting the ground as if their lives depended on it.

Tev nudged Bart. "We've been stopped too long. Do your great eyes see anything on our back trail?"

Bart twisted around, almost breathless with pain, and looked through the dry grasses and shrubs on either side of the trail.

Something flickered through the weeds near the base of the cliff. With a hoarse yell he tried to leap to his feet, but only made it to his knees.

The ferts gave up their attempts at stalking, and lunged, noses still questing for the smell of human blood that had drawn them out of the jungle. One huge male and three younger ones led the way, their short, broad noses perched on gleaming rows of teeth. Half as high as a man, and longer than a warrior is tall, their sinewy bodies humped for the final leap that would take them into the midst of the whelps and lankers. Behind the males came the four females, bodies heavy with young. Further back, Bart saw some tigrogs bounding up the trail, attracted by his blood. The first male fert roared a challenge as it launched itself toward him. He was so weak he could only hold his shette in front of him like a weanling cub.

An arrow sprouted in the fert's neck. Its momentum carried it onto Bart's shette, soaking him in hot blood.

The heavy fert knocked the breath out of him, and musk-drenched fur choked him. But the animal was dying, its nose twitching on the blood it craved. All around him men shouted and bow strings hummed. He half pushed, half rolled the fert off him, and staggered to his feet. Beside him, Dyfid drew his bow string back, swearing and ducking as he tried to get a clear shot.

A familiar killer yell rent the air. Mikhail leaped forward, howling and slashing with a speed that made his arms seem to blur. He sliced the head off a pregnant fert, whirled and streaked toward a silver-frosted male who was launching himself at Mariko. Tev loosed an arrow at the male. The animal twisted in the air, snapping the shaft in its flank, then shrieked as Mikhail slit its belly. Mikhail dodged as the fert dropped to the ground, twitching among its tangled guts.

Bart's father whirled again, eyes alight, looking joyously for another prey. He patted Nakano casually as he ran by. The youngest whelp watched his leader with worshipful eyes. Two of the yearling ferts turned tail and bounded down the trail.

Behind and above Dyfid, a huge reptilian dactyl with a leathery grey wing span of at least three spear lengths, dove for the kill, yellow eyes glittering with anticipation, nose slits wide open, drinking in the sweet smell of blood. Bart called hoarsely. "Above! Dactyl!"

Dyfid twisted, but before he could loose his arrow, a shette sliced through the air, transfixing the reptile. The dactyl coughed, its membranous sails rippled, lost the air, and it luffed to the ground. Guntor whooped, "That's mine! That's mine!" and tore around in circles, searching for more sport.

Only one small dactyl still circled above them. Ten arrows hit it almost instantaneously, knocking it upward, before tumbling it down to join the bodies of the ferts, dactyls and woolly tigrogs on the ground.

Bart sagged back on the fert carcass, glad that there were only ten or twelve animals, and not the thousands that attacked The Home during migration.

Volf strode over to Mikhail. His chest was heaving. Now that the danger was over, he didn't relax, but seemed strung tighter than during the fight. "I hope you saw that I stayed with the pack." His voice was half defiant, half pleading.

"So?"

"So, don't you think I should get my killer and pack portions for today?" He watched Mikhail, his chest thrown back, hyperventilating, as if before a fight. But his eyes were worried, not angry.

Mikhail nodded. "You can have pack portion from this fight."

"But the hogs I got in the jungle?"

"No."

Volf stalked away. He grabbed a tigrog carcass and heaved it at Bart who only just managed to roll over and avoid it. As he rolled the world faded to grey. He looked to his father for help, but Mikhail ignored him, and started to clean his shette. His rhythmic strokes were relaxed: he was over his killing rage, and his anger. Bart forgot Volf. Now was the time to talk to his father, just after he had spent most of his energy. Getting up gingerly, he approached him, hoping to talk about raising the keld as meat animals.

"Shouldn't you be working, whelp?" His father's voice was cold.

"But I'm wounded," Bart protested, his smile shattering.

Mikhail finally looked up. His eyes reminded Bart of crystals of ice. "That never stopped me."

Bart floundered. Rage he could handle, but icy disinterest was something he had never seen before.

Mikhail examined his shette for nicks.

Bart didn't have to look to know that the whole pack was watching. Shame weakened him like fear. He turned, as if nothing had happened, and walked toward the lankers, who were already finished with their hurried butchering.

Tev picked up Bart's fieldpack, and put some meat inside. It was a small load, a boy's pack really, but to Bart it looked huge.

"I kept it light." Tev eased it onto Bart's back, and adjusted it carefully. "You shouldn't be carrying, but Mikhail's too dangerous to cross right now." He slipped a pad of moss between the straps and Bart's wound. "He'll come around. Just give him time."

Bart nodded. He didn't trust his voice. No one else spoke to him as the men took their positions and started up the Migration Trail. When Bart leaned into his load, the straps pulled on his wounded shoulder, and the world yellowed around the edges.

Dyfid put the flat of his hand on Bart's back and pushed him along.

"I can manage on my own," Bart insisted as the ground kept shifting under him. Surely his father would stop, and order the packs redistributed. He watched Mikhail's back, willing him to turn around. His father scanned the Heights, the trail before them, and the trail behind them, but he never looked at his son.

Suddenly Bart bumped into Mariko. Looking over the other whelp's shoulder, he saw that they had caught up to another pack. Good. More protection.

"Move the wounded whelp to the center," Mikhail roared.

Dyfid put his hand on Bart's good shoulder and pushed him forward to the center of the line where two lankers stood with a litter. Shock cleared his brain. It was a body—he couldn't tell whose because the face was covered in gore, the throat had been ripped out, and part of the arm had been eaten.

"Move out," Mikhail called.

Bart trudged behind the swinging litter, his mind so fogged with shock and pain that he couldn't think.

Someone in the other pack started a marching song. Slowly, with bitter humor the others joined in.

> When I die and go to heaven
> Taizaburo, he will say.
>
> You have served The Home most nobly
> Now your limbs you'll get in pay.
>
> Here's the finger that was chopp'd off
> Infected, poisoned, on the trail.
>
> Here's the eyeball that was gouged out
> By a fert who feasted well.
>
> Here's the knee bone you are missing
> Men don't limp in heaven now.
>
> Here's new skin to cover burn scars
> Taken in a drunken brawl.
>
> Here's a ball cut off so painf'ly
> By your zerker wife so wild,
>
> When you woke her passions fully
> When you planted your first child.

He silently plodded on, mesmerized by every gaping hole in the body ahead. Between the two of them, they must be sending a clarion call to any blood lusters within scenting range.

"Come on," Dyfid urged him. "We're falling behind." He put Bart's good arm over his shoulder and they broke into a shuffling trot, to catch up with the litter that had somehow pulled ahead. Fresh sweat broke out all over him, followed by a chill. He stumbled on, wishing he would hurry up and turn zerker: so he could defend himself, so he'd have his father's respect and love again, so he'd be safe.

But he didn't feel safe, and the macabre chant he used to laugh at sent further chills down his spine.

> *When I die and go to heaven*
> *Olarni she will say to me.*
>
> *Let me care for you most carefully*
> *Let me give you wives for frce.*
>
> *All you have to do is feed them*
> *All you have to do is fight.*
>
> *All you have to do is lose blood*
> *Fighting for them day and night*
>
> *We will watch and we will praise you*
> *For each wound you take in pain.*
>
> *Now your body's new and healthy*
> *You can serve The Home again.*

Involuntarily he raised his eyes to the gory mess in the litter in front of him. . . . What if he didn't turn?

4

Day 21:First Gifter Moon of Spring:
452 Migrations After Landing

Sanda looked down at her mother. Brianna lay huddled
under her bed fur. Her eyes were closed, her skin
was the color of parchment, and her damp, greying
hair stretched in snarled strands across the pillow.
From her body rose odors of unaired bedding, sweat,
and stale Peace. "Momma," Sanda pleaded again.
"Talk to me. I know you're awake. It's been two tendays
since you've eaten anything."

But her mother did not move.

Sanda set some mirta pudding on the bedshelf.
It was hard to do, she was so hungry herself that
her mouth watered just being near food. Surely she
could just have one spoonful. No one would ever
know. . . .

She slammed the bowl down, feeling guilty for
her wish to steal from Brianna, feeling worse for
not being able to stay and endure the presence of
the dirty, smelly bundle that was her mother. Dashing
the tears from her eyes, she fled from the bedchamber.

Assilla paused as she stirred up the fire. "Did she
eat anything?"

Sanda shook her head, without looking at Assilla.

63

It wouldn't do for Assilla to see that she was upset. "I left it there. Maybe she'll eat a bit."

"I'll check her later. If she hasn't touched it, we'll eat it ourselves."

Sanda knew better than to protest. Food was too important to ever waste. Taking her place at the fire she stirred the mushroom and fern-bone stew. "If only she would eat just a little. But, ever since Kayella turned, she seems to have lost the will to live."

"I am sorry about Kayella, Sanda," Assilla said softly. "I've never heard of anyone turning when they were so old."

"If Ava hadn't pointed her out, nobody would have noticed." Sanda stirred angrily.

"Nonsense, child. Ava just did her duty—for the good of The Home. Who knows, she may have saved someone's life."

Sanda looked toward her mother's locked door. Assilla had cut Brianna's dose, then cut it again, but her mother seemed to have lost all interest in life. "Isn't there anything we can do?" she pleaded. "Couldn't we call the healer?"

"I did," Assilla snapped. "I saw Leeorah in the gathering rooms, and she said that sometimes old zerkers just fold up and die."

"But couldn't you get her here to look at my mother?"

Assilla gave her a level look. "We don't have the cards. I'm trying to pay for ship bread for our children and save up for Ava's dowry." Sanda looked startled, and Assilla hastily added. "You won't need a dowry. If you're a scholar, men will pay good green cards for you."

Sanda gave Assilla a bitter look. She knew the real reason why Assilla wasn't figuring on paying her dowry. If Sanda turned zerker, men would pay *gold* cards to breed her. She could feel the familiar pain in her stomach and pushed it aside, trying to help her mother. "What about the scholar? Maybe she knows something. After all, Olarni was originally a zerker, and not only did she rule The Home for ten seasons, but she also lived to be eighty-five."

"Olarni was a *star* woman. That was different."

Sanda cast around for something to say that might get Assilla to help her mother, but could think of nothing. She felt angry, frustrated and helpless. If only she were already a scholar, she would pay for the healer and comb the old stories to find a way to help her mother—and Kayella.

The outer door opened. Sanda stiffened, but it was only Second Wife Inara, and not Haddim, whose recent kindness inexplicably made her back crawl.

Inara bustled in, and dropped a heavy iron lock and a leaf-wrapped package on the table. "I got that lock to stop whoever is stealing food out of the storage room."

Assilla nodded grimly, but her eyes were on the leaf-wrapped package. "Is that Olarnite bread?"

"Yes. The Daughters of Olarni charged me fifteen green cards."

Sanda's mouth watered as they unfolded the large dried leaf. The bread was tasteless: the elderly Daughters of Olarni cooked it without spices or sweetener, and dried it to a jaw-creaking flat patty, but it was made of ship crops and it satisfied hunger in a way that no jungle food ever did.

Assilla fingered the lock. "Better fit that up to the storage door right now." She shot Sanda a stern look. "Now, all that pilfering of food is going to stop."

Sanda stirred resentfully. "I didn't steal any food," she protested.

Assilla ignored her and spoke to Inara. "How is everyone in the Gathering Rooms?"

"I didn't have time to go. The miner's guild is getting ready for the trek to the iron mounds, so I had to work late."

Sanda tried to stir quietly, so she could hear everything. Imagine, women going outside The Home and travelling into the jungle.

"When will you be leaving?" Assilla asked.

"As soon as migration is over. We're out of iron ore, and the charcoal has been all used up; we can't even remelt broken implements. We'd be going now, except that it's too close to migration time." She took a mason's bit out of its fitted nest in the tool box and started to drill into the rock beside the door. "And speaking of migration, I've been worried about Haddim . . ."

"Don't even think about it." Assilla sat down at her loom and picked up her shuttle.

"Well, I can't help it. There have been three whelp funerals in the last Gifter month, and two more whelps were so badly injured that they've already been sent to steerage. I saw Zorava, Bart's mother, on my way down. She nearly lost him two tendays ago."

Sanda turned her head to hear better. So that was why she hadn't seen him on Assembly Day! She wanted to pounce on Inara and ask about Bart, but dared not. If she so much as mentioned his name, Assilla and her sister-wife would watch her the way they had watched Ava after she started talking about Guntor. Assilla was determined that both girls would get good husbands—difficult enough when there were so many women and so few men, but impossible if either girl had a bad reputation.

"Did the ferts get to him?" Assilla asked.

"No, nester snakes. Volf's wife told Zorava that Guntor turned when he was attacked, but Bart didn't. Mikhail took it real hard," Inara said as she leaned against the bit, twisting it deeper into the rock.

"Was Bart badly hurt?" Assilla had sorted out her fiber, and was rhythmically sending the shuttle back and forth.

Sanda strained to hear.

"No. But his shoulder was torn, and became infected. He couldn't hunt for days."

Sanda's knees went weak with relief. She didn't know what made her happier—that Bart was better, or that he was lanker.

"But that isn't what was really bothering her. After all, whelps get mauled all the time. What's got her terrified is the Sangirs." Inara made a protective circle with her fingers. "Mikhail says he saw a ghost that day. And he's been talking about it."

Assilla turned and saw Sanda listening, her spoon forgotten. "Run outside and watch for Haddim, so we can have everything ready for him when he arrives."

Sanda pulled the stew from the fire, and took a flail off the hook as she headed for the door.

"You know, Zorava looked pretty bad today," Inara said. "Her hair wasn't combed, and she was practically shrieking when she talked. Something's really upset her. I hope it's Mikhail's new wife, or even Zorava's change of life. The last thing we need is ghost trouble."

"Then don't talk about it," Assilla hissed. She glared at Sanda.

"I'm going, I'm going." Sanda slammed the door. How she hated being excluded. Ghosts! The last time The Home had been ghost ridden, her father had been claimed by the Sangirs, and his spirit had gone to serve them on the Heights. She remembered her

mother crying with Jaspaar's other wives, and the
misery of the first moons in Haddim's quarters. Ghosts!
Assilla was right. It was best not to even think of
them, even in the safety of The Home. She made
the Holy Circle on her chest as she crossed the deck
and looked through the dactyl netting.

The afternoon sun had passed behind the Forbidden
Heights, casting inky shadows across the valley and
half way up the opposite cliffs. Above the shadows,
sunlit bands of white rock glittered between duller
layers of ocher and brown. Below, the rock turned
various shades of grey that darkened to black along
the valley floor.

In the fields on either side of the river, steerage
hands were leaving their tiny stone-bordered plots,
heading for their homes carved into the base of the
cliffs. Along the hunter trail, warriors headed home
for the night. Sanda took a deep breath of the crisp
evening air and leaned against the pillars, letting
the tranquility of the scene soothe her. She watched
the sky as the deepening sunset above the Forbidden
Heights turned it to a deep rose that reflected on
the banded grey and white cliffs, turning them into
a wonderland of red, lilac, and mauve. Finally she
remembered her duties and squinted into the gloom.
She could usually identify Haddim because he rolled
as he walked and, even when with his pack mates,
tended to be separate and alone. Bart was harder to
spot because there were so many whelps in every
pack. She leaned her forehead against the dactyl netting
and looked down the valley, past the barricades built
to keep the ferts out during migration, past the opening
to the larger valley of the Migration Trail, to the
spot where the hunters disappeared behind the cliff
wall every morning and returned each night.

Something tickled her ear. She brushed it off. It tickled her neck. She slapped the mite, heard a familiar breathless giggle, and turned, laughing.

Ullan put her hands on the netting, and shook the ropes. "You're no fun at all." She tossed her long black hair off her neck. She had been Sanda's best friend ever since that day in school, when Ullan had dumped a spider down the back of Ava's neck. Ullan was short, with an hourglass figure and flawless olive skin that all the girls envied. But what made her special was her lively mind that concocted endless jokes, and the way she dove into her work with the intensity that would one day make her a great potter.

She tested the ropes. "Want to go climbing? My back's stiff from bending over the potter's wheel." She pulled on the ropes, stretching her back muscles. "You should see the pitcher I threw today. It's perfect. Bassarra said if it were on a shelf, she would think it was made by a guildwife."

Something twined around Sanda's ankles. She glanced down to see her aged meatcat, Mirta Blossom, purring in circles around her. "Oh no, he left the cave!" She scooped him up. "Keep watch for me, Ullan. I'm going to take him back, before anyone sees him and pops him into the nearest stew pot."

"Someone's coming," Ullan hissed.

Jungle boots thudded on the deck. Both girls started to curtsey, then Ullan laughed. "It's only a whelp."

A whelp? Sanda looked up.

Bart strode along the deck, carrying a bloodstained bundle of pelt and meat.

For some reason Sanda seemed breathless. She had no idea why. Bart was a perfectly ordinary whelp— tall, big boned, but very thin. He looked tired clear through and there were grim lines around his eyes.

She felt warm and realized that she must be blushing. Ullan prodded her.

"Why don't you say hello?" she giggled.

The dactyl ropes creaked as Ullan started to climb. While Sanda stood there tongue-tied, a couple of brown-clad children, happily free from winter's long confinement in the children's gallery, chased a meatkitten. The kitten, wearing a breeder's collar around its neck to protect it from the stew pot, let the cubs get almost within arms' reach, then scampered off again.

The two barefoot cubs saw Bart, and stared up in awe. He looked like a man in his jungle greens and heavy boots; the cubs were too young to notice the lack of pack insignia on his shoulder.

Sanda stepped out from the shelter of the pillars. He'd saved Mirta once before . . . would he do it again? Her heart hammered as she dropped the full curtsy of a woman to a warrior, then lowered her eyes to the scrawny meatcat who lolled comfortably in her arms. She waited for Bart to give her leave to rise. Instead he took her elbow with a calloused palm and urged her up.

When she rose, she had to look up to meet his gaze. He was taller and broader than she remembered, but his grey eyes had the same steadying strength. Before she lost her nerve, she blurted her request.

"Bart, could you save Mirta Blossom again? It's spring cull; Assilla wants him for the stew pot, and I'll die if they butcher him."

Bart took her by the arm, and tugged her toward the other side of the pillar—out of sight of Ullan and anyone else on the deck.

She followed, feeling deliciously wicked and thinking up excuses at the same time. After all, he wasn't a man, only a whelp: they'd never warned *her* against whelps.

"Could you hide Mirta in the whelp's dormitory again?"

"No! Everyone's too hungry. He'd be meat in seconds." He looked at the cat. "And, scrawny as he is, I'd be tempted, too."

"But you're the only one who can save him!" She put a hand lightly on his arm, the way Assilla did when she was wheedling Haddim.

Bart rubbed his cheek thoughtfully. "I might make a cage," he said, "but you'll have to hide him and find something to feed him. I need every scrap I can get." He hitched his sagging jungle trousers up tighter.

"I'll get some food somehow. . . . Please?"

For the first time, he looked straight into her eyes. "Are you going to hide him in that cave under the deck where you and Ullan play?"

Sanda froze, and clutched Mirta so hard he yowled.

"Don't worry, only my father and I have good enough eyesight to see you climbing down the fissure to the cave, and once he's inside the barricades my father drops his guard, and never looks up."

Sanda leaned against the rock, and breathed out shakily. "You won't tell?" Could she trust a man?

"No." He watched her steadily. He seemed so calm and safe.

Her heart thumped unevenly in her chest as he edged closer, sharing her secret. His gaze was clear and direct: surely she could trust him. For the first time, she noticed a tiny scar that puckered one eyebrow.

"But you should be careful," he warned her. "That crevice is narrow, but a small dactyl could land on the ledge. After all, why do you think the ancestors built The Home halfway up a steep cliff?"

"I know, I know. To protect us. But I always carry my flail, and I never miss."

"Then why don't you come down to the cave tonight. I'll show you how to make a cage, so you could save your meatcat during every cull."

Sanda gasped. "That's forbidden!"

A door slammed behind them.

Sanda and Bart jumped apart as Assilla bustled out onto the Promenade Deck. She didn't see them: she was glaring at Ullan.

"What are you doing up there?" Assilla threaded her way around the planters on the deck, waving a wooden spoon. "Get down this instant!" As she approached the net, she disappeared from view behind the huge stone pillar.

Sanda started around the column, but Bart put an arm out, blocking her way. "Will you come tonight . . . just after Fee rises?"

"Ullan!" Assilla's voice rose to a shriek.

Sanda pulled free, and rounded the huge square-cut pillar.

"Get down! What if a warrior saw you? Your mother would die of shame." Assilla tugged frantically at the netting, jiggling the girl around and exposing a lot of thigh.

Ullan clung stubbornly to the net, and glared down at Sanda's stepmother. "You aren't from my quarters. I don't have to do anything you say." Her glare turned to a giggle, and she threw back her head, letting her long black hair swing free. "It's spring, Assilla. I've been cooped up in the children's gallery all winter!"

Assilla gave up, and put her hands on her hips. She saw Sanda and Bart. For a second her eyes narrowed, then she was distracted by Ullan again. "Sanda, get the Mother General."

"All right, all right," Ullan yelled down at them.
"You don't have to send for my mother. I'm coming
down."

As she stretched a toe for a lower loop in the net,
the wind whirled around the pillar and whipped her
hair and skirt high in the air, revealing both plump
buttocks.

Bart leaned forward, eyes widening. For the first
time in her life Sanda hated Ullan. Where Ullan was . . .
well . . . shaped like ripe mirta gourds both top and
bottom, Sanda knew she was tall and thin. Ullan's
thick black hair hung to her waist; Sanda's light brown
curls only twisted and tangled to her shoulders.

Something shifted in Bart's pants. Sanda watched,
fascinated, wondering exactly what was happening.
Baby boys were no mystery to her, but men's spears
were supposed to be different. At least the girls in
her class thought so.

"You shameless creature!" Assilla screamed, "Get
down!" She jumped up and grabbed Ullan's foot.

"Let go! Goddess Within, I'll fall!" Ullan tried frantically
to hold onto the netting, but with Assilla pulling her
and shaking the net, Ullan lost her grip and fell—
right on top of Assilla.

Sanda darted in to help.

Bart followed.

"This is not your affair," Assilla hissed at him—
he backed off hurriedly. Assilla pulled Ullan up by
her hair. "You're disgusting! What if a warrior had
come by? You'd be there for the taking, wouldn't
you?" She slapped Ullan on the face, rocking the
girl back against the protective netting.

"You . . . you fert!" Ullan's scream ripped through
the air, bounced off the cliff walls, and faded into
the distance.

Sanda felt a chill run down her back. Only her mother screamed like that.

Assilla slapped Ullan harder. "Mind your manners, child."

"Mind my manners! Mind my manners!" Ullan screamed even louder than before. "All I was doing was climbing the spearing net!" Her eyes were shining; her words were beginning to slur. "A'll show ya." She attacked Assilla, her nails clawing the older woman's face and neck.

Assilla went down. Ullan's flail clattered to the deck, but she ignored it, scratching, biting and kicking. Bart lunged, grabbed Ullan's arms, and pulled her off. Ullan beat her fists against his shoulder; he turned white. She twisted in his arms, and ripped at his face with her nails.

Sanda backed away. Not Ullan, not her, too! It was a nightmare. It had to end. Beside her, Assilla started screaming, "Zerker! Zerker!"

Bart stopped trying to grab Ullan's flailing arms, and tackled her, sending them both crashing to the stone deck.

Sanda wanted to rush in and stop them and, at the same time, wanted to run away. First her mother, then Kayella, now Ullan. Who would be next? Dread made her vision fuzzy.

Doors slammed open all along the deck. Bart wrapped his arms around Ullan, and locked his hands together.

"Taizaburo, who's zerker?" a man yelled.

Assilla practically threw herself on him. "Help me, she's turned!"

But the man drew back, laughing. "Turned, has she? Well, I wouldn't want to spoil the whelp's fun."

Ullan bucked, screamed, tried to bite, and nearly freed her arm several times. Her screams ground their way into Sanda's brain and down her spine, rasping her nerves. She took a deep breath to steady herself as the world seemed to rush at her: the wind, whispering around every rock outcropping; the waterfall, roaring at the head of the valley; light and dark patterns on the deck, the pillars and the walls; and Ullan's open mouth as she screamed and screamed. Sanda's gaze shifted from Ullan to Bart. His eyes were glazed with pain, and he grunted every time she jarred his shoulder.

Suddenly, Ullan went limp, tired and sweaty, like all zerkers after a rage. Bart struggled to his feet, twisting her arm savagely behind her. No wonder the Supreme Guardian forbade fights between zerker and lanker men on pain of death. Bart was almost a warrior, but he looked as if Ullan had nearly finished him off. New blood was seeping through the shoulder of his jungle tunic; his face and neck bled along deep scratches, and one of his eyes was swelling shut. Sanda wiped her sweaty palms on her dress.

The clatter of heavy boots announced Bridd, the old watch guard. From his belt pouch he took a vial. "Hold her," he told Bart. "This will knock her out."

Ullan came alive. "No! I'm not zerker."

Bridd paused, looking short-sightedly at Assilla.

"I'm not zerker! Honored First Wife, tell them I'm not." Ullan's chest heaved, her black hair was disheveled. Her body seemed to thrum with wild vitality, and her eyes held that strange light that marked all zerkers.

Assilla braced her shoulders. "She's zerker."

"Right. Snap to it, whelp. Get her head back."

"Noooo!" Ullan wrenched herself one way, then jerked another, trying to get out of Bart's grip. Her eyes were fixed on the vial Bridd held. She kicked and squirmed and shrieked wordless curses. When they did her no good, she threw herself to one side, jerking his shoulder. Bart swore and twisted her arm, viciously.

A sound like a breaking pot echoed along the Promenade Deck. Her screams cut off and she curled around her arm, whimpering, her power vanquished as if it had never been.

Sanda shoved her fist into her mouth to keep from screaming. She'd never truly understood how dangerous men could be. She *never* thought of Bart as being anything but kind.

Beyond the watching men, the women crept closer, studying the limp girl with grim satisfaction. It reminded Sanda of when Kayella had been taken away. She wanted to run from their merciless faces, but couldn't leave her friend.

"Okay, now let's get that Peace into her." Bridd pulled Ullan's head back and poured the medicine down her throat. "Hold her for a moment," he instructed Bart, "and then I'll take her back to her family."

The heavy smell of sedatives and Peace drifted over to Sanda. Her saliva turned to acid in her mouth. She swallowed, and backed away.

While Ullan hugged her arm, gasping for breath, Bridd eyed her. "Good looking!" He turned to Assilla who was edging away. "Isn't she the Mother General's daughter?"

Assilla nodded, and curtsied deeply, eyes carefully lowered.

"She'll be a fine prize—the only one of her age group to turn so far." He tilted Ullan's head, so he could see her better. "What luck for her family. She'll bring wealth into her family, not take it out!" He sighed, and rubbed his puckered cheek scar, tracing it absently around to the back of his head. "Six daughters I had to find a bride gift for, six!"

Assilla gave a refined snort, and Sanda knew why. Bridd didn't have to do anything. His wives were the ones who earned the cards that paid the bride gift.

Ullan started to snore. No longer a demon, she was now an unconscious outcast who would live her life under the sentence of Peace—valued for her zerker sons, but ritually locked in her own room every night to keep her family safe from her unpredictable rages.

Sanda felt dizzy. Ullan had always been so carefree. How would she bear this? And her dreams of becoming a potter . . . Zerkers were barred from the guilds. Suddenly, Sanda saw herself, and not Ullan lying drugged on the floor. Her stomach backed into her throat. She edged out of the circle, and made a dash for the cliff, where she threw up until she had dry heaves. Finally she leaned weakly against the stone pillar. A booted foot came into sight and swept the mess off the edge of the deck. Bart hunkered down beside her.

"Are you ill?" he asked.

Sanda darted a look at the crowd of men and women, but no one was watching. She brought her shuddering breath under control and shook her head. Her mouth tasted sour, and the saliva she swallowed urged her to gag again.

"Was it Ullan?" he asked.

She nodded.

"I didn't mean to break her wrist. I just wanted her to stop hurting my shoulder." His voice lowered with shame and he avoided her eyes.

"It's not that," she said. "It's the turning. My sister

turned; now Ullan has turned. I'm terrified I'll be next."

His breath came through his teeth in a soft hiss. "I'm sure you won't turn," he said soothingly. "Very few women do."

She hugged herself with her arms. "But girls with zerker mothers do. Assilla's already watching me for the first signs."

He shifted uncomfortably and looked over his shoulder. "Bridd's taking Ullan away; I have to go before anyone notices us talking." He cleared his throat. "Uh, I'll build that cage for Mirta. And if you want to talk, I'll be at the cave tonight, soon after Fee rises." He touched her hand briefly, rose and went to get his meat.

Sanda looked numbly after him.

Bart held his wounded shoulder stiffly when he lifted his slippery bundle. Beyond him, Bridd picked up Ullan, her black hair flowing in shimmering waves down his back. As the grizzled lanker walked between the cliff wall and the cloister pillars, the women turned aside, as if from a polluted carcass, but the men walked closer to look at the new prize—a woman who would *always* produce zerker sons if married to another zerker.

As Bart left he gave Sanda an encouraging but lopsided smile—lopsided because the bruise under his eye was darkening and swelling.

5

Bart walked past huge, square-cut pillars toward his father's quarters, thinking about the new zerker. Girls! He'd give anything to turn, but Sanda threw up at the very thought. He tried to imagine Sanda drugged, but couldn't. She was too intelligent, and too alive to be reduced to vague stupidity.

Poor girl. She was so alone—terrified of her future, but afraid to discuss it with anyone. His walk slowed. But he could help her. He knew what it was like to feel alone, and tonight, if she came, he knew he'd be able to ease her fears, and help her to smile again. His lips curled in a nostalgic grin as he remembered the last time he'd saved her mangy old meatcat. She'd still been a kid then, and she'd thanked him by stealing a couple of jam pitas for him.

Suddenly he stiffened as he saw Dyfid coming toward him. He drifted to the center of the deck. Dyfid nodded neutrally and eased around him.

"I haven't got jungle fever, you know," Bart said, moving to block the other's way. "What is it with you anyway? After the nester incident you guarded me with your life, and then suddenly you won't even talk to me."

"Ask Guntor," Dyfid snapped. Darting around him, the steerage whelp hurried away.

Ask Guntor? Bart watched, puzzled as the other

whelp disappeared around the bend. He shook his head, feeling lonely. Ever since the nester incident, his life had been turned upside down. His father had been in an ugly mood and spent his time either shouting at his men, or studying the Forbidden Heights and frightening his pack out of their wits. These days the men were walking carefully, afraid of Mikhail's temper, and of the ghosts he might bring down upon them.

As for Bart, he had been almost universally ignored. When no one had been assigned as his protector, he'd asked Gopa if he could walk with his whelps. Gopa had agreed, but not very enthusiastically. The only one who had remained his friend was Guntor. In fact, Guntor had even snarled at Volf when the older man had casually shoved Bart aside. Volf had laughed, but he'd left Bart alone after that.

But—his steps quickened—tonight Mikhail was in a good mood. He'd ordered Bart to bring the day's catch up to his quarters—just like before. Once home, his mother and her sister-wives would praise his father, fuss over Bart and invite him for evening stew. He and Mikhail would talk and sort things out. Tomorrow everything would be all right. He hurried along the darkening deck, forgetting his shoulder. He'd talk to Mikhail about that keld foal, and tell him how they could keep young animals in the side canyon near The Home. He had it all worked out. Not only would they be growing their own meat, but they wouldn't have to pack it ten to twenty klats home from the jungle. His father would see that he was right. All he needed was the time to explain his ideas.

When he stopped at the familiar burl oak door, he could still see a crude carving dug into a knot in the wood grain. He had tried to turn it into a fert

head when he'd been a cub. His mother had screamed
at him for dulling her meat knife, and then had hugged
him, crying because the next day was his Sixth Sort,
and he would leave family quarters to live in the
boys' dorms, and learn warrior ways.

His father's newest guildwife, Tekiri, answered his
knock. He tried not to stare at her small, thin body.
What did Mikhail see in her? She had ordinary dark
hair, brown eyes, a pointed chin and an expression
that always seemed either intensely interested or
very remote. Her hands on the doorway caught his
eye. They were calloused—as thick-wristed as a man's—
results of her work as a stonemason.

She lowered her eyes, and curtsied.

"My father asked me to bring this meat." It was
hard to think of her as one of his mothers. She couldn't
be much older than he.

"Bart, get in here!" his father bellowed.

Cold fear drenched him. What had gone wrong?
Mikhail had left the armory in great spirits.

"Are you frozen solid?"

Bart cautiously edged into Mikhail's quarters, blinking
in the dim light. The wardroom was one of the best
in The Home. Light filtered through high slit windows
covered with tiny panes of puddle glass. Rows of
cooking pots and utensils hung on the polished stone
walls, cut migrations ago by the ancestors. Herbs
and spices hung from the great hooks set in the rock
ceiling, filling the quarters with the rich fragrance
of spices, mirta, lenpic and feffer. In a corner, on an
outside wall, was a huge fireplace, blackened by
generations of cooking fires. A preparation table,
its top warped and scarred by the hundreds of wives
who had used it since The Landing, dominated the
room. When his eyes finally adjusted to the dim light,

his stomach knotted. Mikhail leaned back against his warrior's chair, but his muscles were taut with anger.

His mother came over to take the meat, her face tear-streaked, her body trembling with emotion. Bart's heart sunk. His mother and father had been fighting again. Why did the only woman in The Home who ever stood up to her husband have to be *his* mother?

Mikhail shifted in his seat and glared at Bart, his thick-muscled body rigid with anger. Verdi, his Second Wife, stood by the door of her bedchamber, ready to run inside the moment she dared. She was the perfect wife, always courteous, always deferring to Mikhail, but always irritating him by cringing whenever he was angry. Fiaranna, who usually cuddled the cubs and provided them with sweets, fussed over the meat Bart just brought in, cutting it with painstaking care. Tekiri was looking at the stone grain in the wall, as if it were the most interesting thing in The Home.

Mikhail leaned forward, staring. "Taizaburo! What happened to you!"

"A girl went zerker," Bart explained, trying to keep his voice soft and soothing—the way everyone did with angry zerkers.

"All that blood?" his mother whispered, coming closer. "Verdi, get a cloth; it must be cleaned."

"I don't need anything." Bart shrugged her off. "My wound just opened a little in the struggle." He stood straight and tried to seem indifferent to the pain.

Mikhail's eyes narrowed. He uncoiled, and glided forward. "And how did you enjoy the tussle?"

Bart shrugged. Why was his father so interested? "She was just a girl."

"But you're so slow you couldn't even avoid her nails."

"When I turn, I'll be faster."

Mikhail cuffed him. Bart gave with the blow, but his head still rang. His father leaned forward. "Bart, you have to accept facts." He deepened his voice and chanted. *"Zerkers sleep in children waiting— for fights to death or calls for mating."* He gave Bart a shake that snapped his head back. "Well, you've had your fight with the nesters, and you didn't turn. Now you've rolled around with a screaming girl. If you'd been within a migration of turning, you'd have raped her and had to marry her." He smashed a stack of wooden bowls off the table.

Fiaranna flinched, looking down at the meat as if it would vanish if she took her eyes off it. Verdi slipped into her bedchamber. Tekiri went to a corner and settled in the shadows in meditation position.

A growl rose from Mikhail's throat. "Bart, you're lanker; you'll never turn. You've got to accept that, or you'll die."

"But—"

"Do you think it's been easy keeping you alive this last tenday?" Mikhail shouted. "Volf wants my hide for the way I shamed him the day he left the line. He doesn't dare touch me, but you're a helpless target. If he gets you, he gets me." He kicked one of the bowls aside.

"But you haven't even talked to me, or assigned me a protector. I've been the one who's kept myself alive in the jungle, not you."

"Stupid. Who'd I assign you to? You're a fight waiting to happen. With Volf. With Guntor who is circling you, licking his chops and waiting to pounce. With Mariko who is as jealous as hell. Or with some lanker who gets tired of your zerker airs."

He swung around to face Bart, eyeball to eyeball.

"You have to make a choice. You have to choose your place in the pack. Either you are going to be a zerker's lover, or a lanker. So make your dammed choice. Find protection with your own kind or with a zerker lover. But don't wander around pretending that you're going to be zerker. It only irritates the lankers, and the zerkers aren't interested because they've decided you'll never turn."

"But I will turn. I will."

Zorava caught at her husband's sleeve. "He'll turn. He's still young; it's too soon to tell."

Mikhail jerked his hand free, knocking her aside. She stumbled, and fell to the floor. "Taizaburo, I can't stand this!" he shouted at his crumpled wife. "Do you think I like accepting that he's lanker?"

Bart hunched his shoulders. He wanted to stand over his mother and protect her: he also wanted to please his father.

Mikhail rounded on Bart. "I asked you to come up here to tell you that you have to choose. You're screwing up your life, and mine as well, because Volf is using you to get at me."

"But couldn't you throw Volf out of the pack?" Bart asked. "You nearly did the day he left the line."

Mikhail kicked his chair half way across the room. "Damn you, Bart. Don't you think I'd like to? But of my seven zerkers, three are my age. We *need* that bastard."

"You're the bastard," Zorava whined. "Abandoning your son. This is all because you talked about that ghost. The curse is already working."

With a roar Mikhail overturned the central food table. The crash of broken storage pots echoed off the walls and the fruity smell of lenpic wafted around the room. "Shut up. I wouldn't let my pack treat me this way. Why should I let you?"

Zorava's face was ugly with old memories and distilled anger. "Because I'm right. Because everything you touch, you destroy . . . starting with Wayneth."

Mikhail lowered a hand that was lifted to slap her. "Taizaburo," he said wonderingly, "that was eighteen years ago, during the Pack Wars. And I did the right thing. I took you to wife, and looked after you."

She drew herself up. "You still killed my husband just so you could be pack leader." She sneered, her wrinkles twisting into uglier lines. "I hope you're not too surprised when Volf tries the same thing."

In one easy motion, Mikhail knocked her across the room toward the door, leaped after her, and dragged her to her feet, his slaps knocking her face to and fro. Zorava tried to cover her head, but he knocked her hands aside.

Bart stood rooted with horror; he knew better than to interfere. Tekiri ran to Mikhail's side. As she did, she opened the top buttons on her dress, letting Bart see a hint of tiny breasts.

"Husband." She slowly ran her tongue along her upper lip. "Come to bed."

Mikhail blinked, rage struggling with sudden lust. Lust won. He carried the half-unconscious Zorava to the door, and threw her out onto the Promenade Deck. "Don't come back." He turned toward Tekiri and saw Bart.

"Get out. Stay away from me."

"But, Father . . ."

Mikhail advanced on him. "I'm warning you, if I start to beat you I might not be able to stop." Bart ducked around him and ran for the Promenade Deck. Behind him the door slammed.

✧   ✧   ✧

Was his father right? Bart thought about his fight with Ullan. Maybe he'd been in too much pain to turn. *But pain spurred zerkers on to greater speed and strength.* He rubbed his head, wishing he could think clearly. Surely he would turn zerker.

He turned into the tunnel and headed for the armory door. After all, his father was zerker. His grandfather had been zerker. He pulled open the armory door, and looked down into the sand-covered training arena. Along the outer wall, open slit windows showed the grey of the evening sky. The floor of the cavern, where the boys, whelps and men trained, was covered with fine sand. Around the walls, racks and chests held weapons or training devices for the men of The Home. Over by the weapon check racks, cabin fetches were cleaning and inspecting weapons. Since it was already early evening, the warriors had left the armory, but the large cavern was still full of whelps and boys, cleaning up, repairing leathers and harnesses, or raking the sand that covered the floor.

He walked stiffly down the forty steps the ancients had carved from the Promenade Deck entrance near the roof of the armory to the floor of the huge cavern, trying to counter his father's arguments. Peering through the flickering shadows cast by a few lamps along the stairs, he saw Guntor sitting by the far wall cleaning his weapons. *You're a fight waiting to happen.* Well, not with Guntor. After the snake fight his friend had been the only pack member who had ignored Mikhail's dark looks and had been friendly with him.

The scent of mushroom stew drifted past Bart as he walked over to the rack where he had checked his weapons before going up on deck. Mushroom stew again. Weren't they ever going to get any meat?

He forgot about the stew as Guntor grinned and came forward to meet him. When he saw Bart's face, his muscular arm froze in their familiar poke-in-the-shoulder greeting. His black eyes narrowed as they inspected Bart's scratched face, his scuffed clothes, and finally his shoulder. "Taizaburo, what happened? You didn't have a mark on you when you went up there. . . . Has your shoulder reopened?"

Bart touched the wet patch. "A girl turned zerker," he explained. "I had to subdue her." He straightened up, and tried to look indifferent.

Guntor grinned evilly. "Hey, I bet you wanted to get your spear into that one." He slapped Bart cheerfully on the back, jarring the wound on his shoulder.

Pain sliced into Bart, and sweat broke out on his brow.

"Oh, sorry, I forgot," Guntor casually apologized, "but why so gloomy. I'd think you'd enjoy rolling around with a young zerker."

"My father threw me out of quarters. He and my mother were already fighting. Then he said things that made no sense. I mean, he is a pack leader, isn't he? And he can do what he wants, can't he?" He lowered his voice when two boys went by carrying wood for the mess hearth.

"You want to talk in private?" Guntor jerked his chin toward one of the storage caves under the stairs to the upper decks.

Bart shook his head, but the other whelp put a friendly arm around his shoulder, and propelled him toward the other side of the armory. As they crossed the dark cavern floor, whelps and boys clustered around a few of the younger warriors who were lighting torches for the evening watch. Snatches of conversation drifted past.

"I got a four-point ildenhorn, but Ontu's pack didn't get anything today. Don't even look sideways at *them*. Ever since Ontu's pack mate died, they've been catching mighty little."

Self-pity wrenched at Bart. Who cared about Ontu's pack? *They* at least had their pack brothers and their families. But he had only Guntor. Once Mikhail made it clear that he was through with Bart, the rest of the pack would never talk to him.

Mariko shoved between them. "Gun, let's go to steerage and scare up some fun."

Guntor pushed him away. "Later, Mariko."

"But you promised." Mariko shot an angry look at Bart.

You're a fight waiting to happen. Bart snorted. Ridiculous.

Guntor pushed past the slight whelp. "Ignore him, Bart." He steered his friend toward a storage cave, and shouldered aside the old hide that covered the entrance. Once inside the dark cave Guntor felt his way over to the wall, where he lit a wick lamp with his pouch flint. "Now, what happened?"

Bart sat down and put his head in his hands. He didn't answer. Guntor's sympathy unnerved him. He felt that if he started to talk, he would end up crying like a cub.

"What did you do to get him so mad?"

Caution suddenly invaded Bart's self-pity. Guntor was open with his and everyone else's secrets. He couldn't tell him about the threats his father faced— of Volf or the Sangirs.

"Was it about the nester fight?"

Bart looked at the sand that had drifted in from the armory. "That was part of it." He took a deep breath and tried to distance his mind from the pain of his father's dismissal. "He seems to think I won't turn zerker."

"So? Everybody knows that."

Bart's carefully maintained shell of tough indifference broke. Tears blinded his eyes. He lost control of his chin. Sobs overwhelmed him, and he fought them silently. Through clenched teeth he said, "How long do you think I'll last? In the last watch cycle you were the only one who didn't treat me like a tenday-old carcass."

All the dangers of hunting without a protector flooded his mind: that tigrog who had stalked him, the way the trees seemed to close in on him when he knew that no one was watching his back, and how nobody seemed to see him until they needed a porter. And Volf . . . always Volf . . . tossing carcasses at him, calling him "keld brain" and laughing . . . always laughing. Bart's sobs overwhelmed him.

Guntor patted him awkwardly on the shoulder. "Hey, I'm sorry. But your father will get over it."

"Maybe when I turn zerker."

"Don't be a dreamer!"

Bart buried his face deeper in his hands. Not even Guntor believed in him.

"But don't worry. I'll help you." Guntor sat down and put one arm around him. "You can team up with me." He squared his shoulders. "Yes, I'll ask to be initiated before migration, and I can get you assigned to me."

Hope flared higher than a harvest fire. If he and Guntor paired up, his worries would be over. He'd carry for his friend and rely on Guntor's zerker strength and speed for protection in the jungle till he turned zerker himself.

"We'll arrange to get you initiated right after me."

Guntor squeezed Bart's shoulder, sending waves of agony through him. "We'll find you a tall isolated tree, clear of animals and flyers during the day. All you have to do is climb it and stand guard till morning." He jerked a thumb toward the armory. "That's what Mariko's going to do."

"But I don't want to get initiated until I've turned."

Guntor snorted. "That again. Listen, you're sixteen. If you aren't initiated by the fall migration, you'll be sent to steerage as a field hand."

Bart swallowed. He'd do anything to avoid *that*. He decided there and then to be Guntor's lanker. "I'd be a loyal pack brother," Bart promised. Guntor gave his shoulder an encouraging pat. "We'll have good times together, won't we?" Bart said.

"The best."

Bart closed his eyes in the total relaxation that only safety and friendship can bring. . . . Hands gathered him gently, then lips brushed his.

The shock froze him breathless. His eyes flew open to see Guntor's half-lidded eyes unfocused with passion. Guntor's tongue sought entrance through his frozen lips. Bart tried to wiggle away. Guntor's tongue slipped in between his teeth. He almost retched. With a push that seemed to rip his shoulder apart, he shoved Guntor away. "Fuck off." He hunched over in his pain, feeling the world fade and return.

Guntor's breath rasped in his ear. When Bart could see, he found himself staring at the bulge in Guntor's jungle pants. A wild light flared in his friend's eyes as his harsh panting quickened.

Ducking, Bart lurched painfully toward the door, but Guntor blocked him like a rockcat playing with its kittens. "Come on, Bart, we'll be lovers, too." His arms opened as he advanced.

"But, Guntor, you know I'm not a man lover. We've talked about it before."

"That's because you haven't tried it." Guntor lunged and caught Bart neatly.

Pain slashed from his shoulder to every part of his body. The tiny room turned red, then yellow, then grey. He sank to his knees.

"That's right," Guntor said, misunderstanding. "We'll be happy." Guntor got behind him; his hands were everywhere. Bart felt his belt come undone; his pants were loosened and slid partway down his hips. As he tried to twist away, Guntor's little finger slid into his mouth. Panic and revulsion overwhelmed him; he bit down as hard as he could.

Guntor screamed.

Bart put his fading energy into his teeth and ground them through skin and muscle to bone. Hands grabbed his head and pounded it into the sand floor, driving grit into his eyes and ears. His head spun; all his muscles became weak; he curled away from the other whelp.

"Okay, lanker, you want it rough, you'll get it rough." Guntor drove his fist into Bart's kidneys.

He doubled in agony, his mouth tasting sand and blood.

Warm light flooded into the storage cave as the hide curtain flicked aside.

"What's going on in here?" Guntor's stepfather, Radnor, stood blinking in the gloom, his wide fleshy lips drawn back from crooked yellow teeth.

Bart rolled over to see Guntor rocking on his knees, cradling his hand.

"He bit me." His face was slack with astonished outrage. "That Taizaburo-damned whelp bit me!"

"You buggering a helpless lanker?" Radnor asked

softly. He shook his head disgustedly. "Just like your birth father."

Guntor glared at the warrior, his black eyes seemed to have a red cast. "It wasn't like that," he protested, "I offered to be his pack mate—to protect him."

Radnor raised an eyebrow and looked at Bart. "Do you want this?" Bart couldn't even speak; he was still gasping for air, but he managed to shake his head. "Are you sure you're all right?" Radnor came and hunkered down beside him. "Taizaburo! You're bleeding!" He turned on Guntor who was sucking his finger like a cub. "You stupid pile of fert shit! You know the rules. No fighting or forcing lankers." He slapped his stepson. "Godwithin, how can you be so stupid? We nearly had a pack war over the last lanker beating." He cuffed his son again.

Guntor blocked the blow. "I was berserker! He led me on; I had no control."

"You can't claim berserker status for rape, stupid. It takes any man at least six heartbeats to get it up, and that's time enough to put a lid on it." Radnor slapped him again.

Guntor lost his temper and tore into his stepfather. The air was filled with grunts and punches. Bart wriggled into the furthest corner, where he crouched, shivering with pain, praying that they wouldn't crash into him. Within seconds Guntor sprawled on the floor.

"See if *you* like being beaten." Radnor grabbed Guntor by the scruff of his neck and dragged him out into the armory. "Don't worry," he said over his shoulder to Bart. "I'll send the healer to you."

Outside, the babble of voices stilled, then was replaced by the mushy thunk of fist on flesh.

Bart pulled himself to a sitting position, and tugged his pants up. He touched the shoulder of his jacket;

it was soaked with blood and crusted with sand. Outside, the thuds and groans continued. He tried to ignore it. The whelp was getting what he deserved.

Bart cursed Guntor, Radnor, his father, Ullan, and all zerkers as he struggled to his feet and wobbled out into the armory.

By the time he got past the hide curtain, Guntor's nose was spurting blood, and one cheek had that white look that is always followed by a jet-black bruise. Around them, the boys, whelps and men watched in fascinated silence. Both Radnor and Guntor were berserker; they stood toe to toe, slugging it out. The blows came faster and faster. Neither man noticed his own pain as they punched and kicked.

Five warriors came running in from the night watch. Grabbing buckets of water kept full for just that purpose, they drenched the fighters, then hauled them apart.

Radnor recovered almost immediately. He forced a laugh. "I'm not berserker," he insisted, trying to calm his breathing. "I'm just giving him the beating he deserves." He waved toward Bart who stood clinging to the doorway. "Tried to rape a lanker." He turned to Bart.

"Do you wish to press charges?" he asked.

"No, I'll handle him," Bart gasped, trying to force his wavering vision to clear.

Radnor laughed. "You'll handle him, will you?" He looked back at Guntor whose bloody hand was holding his nose. He laughed. "From the looks of both of you, I'd say you were evenly matched."

A murmur of laughter ran around the watching men. "These whelps aren't too bright," a warrior said, "but they're gutsy, I'll give you that."

Bart watched in dazed fascination as Radnor's fleshy lips curled back off his long teeth. "If he bothers you again, you tell me." The warrior licked his lips in anticipation.

Bart tried to think of something tough to say, but couldn't. He looked away from Guntor right into the eyes of Uncle Tev.

"I see you're making a mess of things again," his uncle said softly.

"But he tried to rape me."

"Sure. You're *so* wronged. *You* didn't lead him on. *You* haven't seen him watching you since you were caught in the nesters, courting you, waiting for you to turn to him. *You* haven't noticed him cold shouldering Mariko for his new love?"

Bart stared at Tev numbly. "No."

Tev spat in the white armory sand. "Wake up. You're lanker. If you continue trying to act like a zerker, you aren't going to survive."

Bart looked at the uncle he had always ignored. Tev watched him gravely, thoughtful brown eyes taking in every scratch and bruise. With his father and Guntor out of his life, he was terrifyingly alone. Tev was only a lanker, but he was a fair man. Bart cleared his throat. The words came hard. "Will you help me?"

Tev raised one bushy eyebrow. "Do you accept that you will never turn zerker?"

Bart knew this was his last chance. He had to say yes. But the words stuck in his throat.

Tev nodded. "I see." He turned and walked quietly away.

A harsh laugh jerked Bart around to face Guntor.

The whelp was on his knees. His shoulders were hunched with pain, and one eye was already swollen shut. But the other still burned into him. "I'll get you," Guntor promised him. "Just wait."

6

Sanda huddled in the corner of her sleeping platform, stroking Mirta Blossom, and letting the meatcat's rumbling purr soothe her ragged nerves. It was first dark, before the moon Fee rose to chase away the black emptiness that swallowed cliffs just across the valley.

Over and over she saw Ullan's laughing eyes blaze with zerker rage, then dull as the sedative took effect. She tried to think of other things—her mother. No, not her mother. The image of Ullan fighting Bart flashed back into her mind; she heard her friend scream as she clawed Bart's face.

Goddess Within, she couldn't stand this.

She jumped up, dumping Mirta, and paced the room. Think of something else. Think of . . . of . . . Bart. Yes, Bart. Her stomach settled a little. His steady grey eyes had always soothed her and he had always been good to her—from the day he had rescued her grain-husk doll from a group of older cubs until last migration when he had hidden Mirta in the whelp's quarters. But, in spite of herself, she again heard the sickening crack of Ullan's wrist.

How could she ever have agreed to see Bart tonight—especially after he had broken Ullan's wrist? But then Ullan had ripped his shoulder open . . . and he'd been ashamed of hurting her. Sanda relaxed. It had been an accident; he would never hurt *her*.

She'd go. She grabbed her flail and tied it to her sash. Mirta grumbled a bit when she folded the bony meatcat into her spare tunic and tied the hem and arms over her shoulder like a baby carrier. She petted him, and he settled down to purr. For the thousandth time she wished that meatcats were not ship animals. As ship animals their meat was far more valuable than fert, or keld meat: young children could digest meatcat only months after birth, but keld, fert or any jungle meat gave them diarrhea and vomiting fits until they were about four.

She eased her bedchamber door open. By the light of a flickering wick lamp near the head she could see that the eight bedchamber doors along the cliff side of the long children's gallery were closed. She ran for the head, slipped inside, padded past the ceramic washbowls and drainage plugs, and stepped on a ledge to get to the slit window.

Fee was rising, easing the pitch black of the night; it was time to go.

Bracing herself, she wrestled the crusted, iron catch of the window grill open and stuck her head out. By the light of the small moon she could see dark shadows that marked outcroppings and deep cracks. She checked her flail and backed out onto the cliff. Her bundle shifted and she nearly fell. Dizzy with fear, she dug her fingers and toes into every available crevice. Mirta squirmed once and continued to purr so loudly she could hear him over the roar of the waterfall at the head of the valley.

Sanda remembered those first few climbs when she had been terrified, but unable to refuse, because Ullan had been below her saying, "Isn't this great? Isn't this fun? Granny Deraga thinks I'm being punished in my room." A lump grew in her throat. If Ullan had been with her, they would have laughed at her fear. She took a deep breath of the damp spring air, and started feeling her way down the rock face.

Down she climbed, wedging fingers and toes in gritty cracks, settling each hand and foot securely in the next notch before she shifted her weight. Within seconds she could feel the wild exhilaration that always came to her when she climbed. The wind teased her hair and the music of the night beetles lifted her spirits. With each step her arms and legs grew more tired and Mirta became heavier. But with each new toehold her spirit became more free. Her ears strained through the cliff breeze, trying to hear unusual sounds. She had no idea what she could do if something attacked. Her flail was securely tied to her belt, and both her hands were stretched out above her. But she didn't care. The only time she felt really alive was when she was climbing.

Below the level of the children's gallery she came to the massive square-hewn cloister pillars, and felt along them till she touched the dactyl net. Cautiously, she peeked around the pillar. The Promenade Deck was dark and the huge door to Haddim's quarters was closed. Quicker than a rock rat, she swung onto the netting and scampered along to just above the crack that marked the fissure to her cave. She wriggled under the netting, and started climbing down into the crevice. Goddess Within, but Mirta was heavy. Grunting with effort, she slowly lowered herself down the rock face. When she reached the sand-covered ledge she collapsed, easing her burning muscles. Slowly she stretched out and relaxed on the soft sand. Here she was completely free from the rules and regulations of The Home. She giggled, imagining the horrified look on Assilla's face. If the

First Wife ever knew that her well-ordered household had a nightstalker . . .

Not, of course, that Sanda was doing anything *wrong*. She wasn't sneaking out to meet a man—Bart was only a whelp—and he would never ruin her—whatever that meant—but still . . .

She wriggled her toes in the fine sand, looking across the valley to the Starboard side of The Home. The gloomy Promenade Deck was free of lights and the tiny windows were black slits against the grey cliffs. No one was up: no one had seen her.

As she stood watching, a fiery ball spat up from the Heights across the way, rose high into the night sky, and then sputtered out as it started to arch down again.

Ghostfire! Cradling Mirta, she ran for safety. The ghosts were out; evil was coming; the only safe place was in the caves of The Home. The cliff breeze followed her into the tunnel, and then, at the first turn, left her in a blanket of safety and silence. She relaxed; the Sangirs had never taken a soul from inside The Home. As she leaned against the safety of the enclosing rock, her fear slowly left her to her thoughts.

The silence that closed around her echoed with memories of happier times when she and Ullan had hidden from the wives, the chores and the babies. She smiled, remembering Ullan laughing as she imitated her mother chastising a sloppy wife. Pain stabbed her heart. Ullan would never come down here again. She would be carefully watched during the day, and locked, drugged, in her room at night, so she could hurt no one. Sanda blinked away a tear in the darkness and felt her way further into the tunnel.

When the floor of the tunnel angled sharply upward, she felt around in a small crevice till she found a cracked wick lamp, a fragment of flint, a broken iron hinge, and a small pile of dried grass. Working slowly in the darkness she struck a spark onto a bit of grass and blew till she had a tiny flame. Then, carefully holding the cracked bowl, she lit the lamp. The small wavering flame warmed the rocks around her, showing round glass-smooth tunnel walls that twisted away into blackness. She walked into the cliff until the walls brushed her arms and the roof grazed her head.

Finally she squeezed into *their* quarters—a tiny cave only two meters by three. In one corner she and Ullan had gathered sand and heaped it on the bumpy floor. Over the sand they had made a "bedcover" by stitching a couple of ragged skins together. In the center a chipped pottery bowl and two worn rush mats from the children's gallery furnished their wardroom.

But there was no cage: Bart hadn't come.

She collapsed on the "bed." Mirta spilled out of his carrier with an angry grunt. Tears prickled her eyes. How was she going to keep him in the cave? Although the crevice down here was steep, she knew from past experience that Mirta could somehow climb out. She couldn't block the entrance; there was nothing to put in front of it. And even if she could keep Mirta in, how would she feed him? The storage room had a new lock on it and, when the food was out, Assilla watched every scrap. She tugged Mirta onto her lap for comfort. What was she going to do?

A soft scuff brushed through the entrance to the cave. Sanda stopped breathing. Was it Bart? Or was it something else? A dry rustle whispered along the walls of the passageway and into the cave as something came closer and closer. Sanda grabbed her flail, but couldn't seem to untangle it from her sash.

Another scuff! It sounded like a meatcat landing

at the end of a huge pounce. She wanted to call out to see if it were Bart. But what if it weren't?

The thing scraped closer. Fear robbed her strength and she shrank weakly up against the wall, her flail forgotten.

Bart loomed around the last corner of the passage blinking in the soft light of the wick lamp.

"You did come." Sanda plopped down on the floor in sheer relief. "I should have known you'd come. You've never let me down yet."

Bart smiled. One eye was closed and the other was bloodshot. Black bruises like ripe grassberries decorated his face and neck. Across the whole mess were the tracks of Ullan's nails.

"What happened?" Sanda asked. "Your face is even worse than before."

He jerked upright, his cheeks flaming. "Nothing." He slid his bundle into the room. The dry rustle that had so frightened her, turned out to be a load of ashbend sticks tied with a rawhide lash.

Bart avoided her eyes and examined the cave. The back of Sanda's neck prickled as he inspected the sadly tattered "bed" covering, but he didn't say anything. Instead he put the bundle of sticks down, favoring his bandaged shoulder.

He *was* hurt. Why didn't he want to talk about it? She knew that Haddim loved to have his wives fuss over his wounds—except when he'd gotten beaten up. She leaned forward, looking at the welts, scabs and bruises. Of course. That's what had happened. But who would fight Bart? He was so good, so kind. She sank back on the bed furs— which she suddenly realized were *bed* furs. Her heart beat faster but she felt very grown up, almost like a wife dealing with a husband. When Haddim was in a terrible mood Assilla always tried to distract him.

"Did you see the ghostfire?" she asked, then swallowed nervously and made the Holy Circle with her right forefinger. Bart pretended not to hear. She bit her tongue. How stupid could she get? Ghosts were more dangerous to men than women, because men left The Home every day. She quickly prayed to the Goddess Within that the Sangirs had not heard. If they took Bart too . . . Her father's face, faded by time, suddenly became clear, and she remembered him as he tossed her in the air that last summer he'd been alive. That was the summer her father had planned to follow the keld up to the Heights when they migrated. He'd ignored everyone's warnings about breaking the ancient taboos, and so the ghosts had taken him.

Suddenly she realized that the two of them were standing there, staring at each other. Her ears heated up and she fixed her eyes on the finger-thick sticks. "You're going to build Mirta a cage," she said brightly. That was dumb! Of course he was going to build Mirta a cage. That's why he was here.

But Bart relaxed and smiled at her. "Well, I'm not nightstalking," he joked. He realized what he had said and slapped his forehead. "I should have my tongue cut out."

Sanda giggled. "Why? We are nightstalking . . . aren't we? Sort of?"

He smiled down at her. "Not really, but you wouldn't understand that. You're only a child."

"I am not," she protested. "I'm a woman! I've started . . . I mean . . . I'm going to the upper decks to take wife training in less than a Gifter month." She looked down, feeling her face go very red, and stopped petting Mirta. Her meatcat stretched, wandered over to the focus of their attention—the pile of sticks—curled up on top of the whole pile and went to sleep.

"I didn't know you were that old." He pulled a stick out from under Mirta without disturbing him. "What kind of a wife are you going to be—quarters or guild?" He began forming a frame with the largest ashbend sticks, and his hand just happened to touch hers. It was hard and warm. A little thrill went through her.

"Guild. I've won an apprenticeship into the scholar's guild because my maths and sciences were the best in my age sort. I plan to study the old scripts—maybe retrieve some of the ancient skills. I even promised Ullan I'd try to find a better blue dye for her pottery . . ." She suddenly stopped. Ullan would never be a potter now. "And I want to see if I can find some way to help the zerker women of The Home."

"What's science and math?" Bart stopped his work and stared at her as if she had spoken gibberish.

"Well, you know, the study of natural laws, reading about biology, doing math problems, that sort of thing."

"Reading?"

"You know," Sanda said airily, feeling very wise. "The learning texts set out by Olarni, and the chronicles of The Home."

Bart sat back and shook his head, looking at her thoughtfully. "Do these texts say anything about the Forbidden Heights? After all, we were supposed to have fallen from the stars and landed there."

Sanda circled her breast and shook her head. "I only know the songs that we sing on Assembly Day—the ones about the air being too thin and cold. We learn that in physical science, too. The higher you go, the colder the weather. But you already know that. All summer long my stepfather, Haddim, constantly complains about the heat of the jungle."

She caught him looking at her with a longing expression. "Is something wrong?"

He shook his head. "You women have it all. You're protected and can choose your future, while men have to fight to stay alive every day." His hands snapped a stick in two.

"But that was Taizaburo's gift to Olarni and to The Home," Sanda protested. "When Olarni gave up her rule of The Home, she put down her weapons, left the jungle and the valley and went up to her quarters in the Promenade Deck so that she could safely have children, and so that she could protect the knowledge that we had brought from the stars." She shook her head. "You are the ones who have it all. We have to study for hours on end and then come home and look after the babies while you get to have an exciting life."

"Exciting? Exciting to walk into the jungle every day and not know if you're coming out? Exciting to have your life depend on people who will judge you entirely by whether you turn zerker or not? Exciting to find out that your very best friend wanted . . . Never mind, you wouldn't understand." He pulled a stick savagely from the pile, disturbing Mirta who gave him a dirty look and moved off. "But it *will* be exciting," he said, sounding more determined than sure. "When I turn zerker, I'll be faster and stronger. The lankers will call me 'sir,' and carry my packs. It'll be great!"

"It isn't great for *girls* who turn zerker." *Goddess Within*, she prayed for the hundredth time. *Don't let my feelings get too strong: don't let me turn.*

Bart laughed bitterly, tossed one woven panel aside and started working on another. "You don't want to turn, and I'd give anything to turn."

"Not if you were a woman."

"But zerker women get paid a bride price. Their families can pick and choose husbands, while lanker women have to pay a man to take them."

She stared at him, openmouthed. "Yes, but zerkers are drugged!"

He blinked. "Well, yes, but they're dangerous, aren't they?" He cocked his head thoughtfully and started lashing the frame for the second side of the cage.

"Would you drug me if I turned?" she demanded.

"But . . ." His eye met hers and her breath stuck in her throat. He looked down and concentrated on his weaving, thinking seriously. Finally he cleared his throat. "Sorry, Sanda. I never thought about it that way." He tied several crossed sticks together. "I'm glad you didn't turn."

"It's all right." But it wasn't. He hadn't answered her question.

"Besides, I'm sure you'll never turn. You don't act or talk like a zerker at all."

His answer made her fluttery-happy. She watched him work. It was like weaving—only the warp and woof were stiff. She selected some slender branches and started another panel. They worked quietly side by side. Sanda only partially concentrated on her weaving. His body was so close she could feel its warmth. Being alone with a whelp who was almost a man should make her feel awkward. But it felt so— so right. She studied him surreptitiously as they worked. His close-cropped blond hair caught the wick light and glinted red and gold. His lips were slightly pursed as he concentrated, and she could see a couple of soft curling hairs on his chin, the beginnings of a beard.

Once Sanda and Bart both reached for a piece of

ashbend. Their hands touched. Warm shivers chased themselves up her arm and she felt strangely dizzy.

When all six sides were done she helped him strap them together. As they worked she always held the ashbend near his hands so he had to touch her again and again. He could have avoided it, but somehow he didn't. Her warm shivery feeling increased. And oddly enough, she was short of breath.

For the first time in her life she thought it might even be fun to be married—to someone like Bart who smelled clean and did kind things. She pushed unpleasant memories of her stepfather out of her mind. Tonight was too nice to spoil.

As Bart finished tying the last knot, he patted her hand, hesitated, gave it a squeeze—and didn't let go!

Her hand seemed to belong to someone else. Her whole consciousness centered on her palm and fingers that were being held so warmly and gently.

"It's done," he said. "We can use that little bowl for water and I'll give him grizzle or old soup-bone splinters till hunting gets good after migration. After that people will probably leave him alone till next winter."

He still held her hand.

With his other hand he scooped Mirta up and popped the surprised meatcat into the cage. He let the top fall shut.

Mirta padded curiously around a couple of times, then shoved his nose against the top panel lifting it open.

Their hands parted as they both leaped to tie the top shut.

Sanda felt silly, but Bart was grinning. Suddenly they both burst out laughing while Mirta butted the top of the cage with his head.

"I like you," Bart said. "You're honest. Not like most women who lower their eyes and block you out."

"But they're only practicing *enryo*."

"*Enryo*?"

"You know, putting a respectful distance between you and someone whom you must live with . . . so you can avoid arguments."

"I guess someone forgot to teach my mother that. She and my father fight all the time."

"People say," Sanda spoke carefully, "that she's upset because Mikhail no longer takes her to his bed."

Bart gave her a startled look. "Well, whatever is bothering her, it got her kicked out of quarters today."

"That's terrible. What will she do?"

"Oh, after he's cooled down, she'll probably crawl back and be good for another couple of migrations. She's done it before." He took the extra length of rawhide and started to cut it viciously with a small knife that he pulled out of his belt sheath. "Women!"

"Don't you like women?" Sanda asked. "I've heard that some men don't." *Goddess Within, why did I say that? Next I'll be talking about pack lovers.*

"Of course I like women. I've always liked them ever since my first."

"Your first?" Uneasiness shivered down her backbone. What had she done coming here? What did he expect? Was he a man? Had he done *it*? Whatever *it* was.

Bart squared his shoulders and looked down his nose at her. "Of course."

Sanda wanted to ask him what it was like—why it could only be told to a girl when she entered wife training. It had to be very strange. It couldn't be like what Mirta did. That was too ridiculous. She stared wide-eyed, wanting to ask question after question, but not quite having the nerve.

Bart's eyes wavered then dropped to his hands. He took a small block of wood out of his pocket and started to whittle. "Well, actually it was only once, and it wasn't a real woman."

"What's not a real woman?"

"She was from steerage. Just someone my father bought for a hunk of meat—said he wanted to fix good habits in me." He took the blade between his fingers and used the tip of his knife to make tiny indentations. "But I never went again. All she did was lie there and look at the meat."

Lie there? So women lay there while it happened. She thought of Mirta again and was positively revolted. No wonder women protected girls from this knowledge until they were older. She started to imagine her and Bart. . . . Her face heated up and she hastily averted her eyes.

"Are you looking forward to being grown-up and married?" he asked, obviously trying to change the subject.

Sanda suddenly felt more shy than a sixth sort girl in her first class. "Well, maybe, maybe not." The fire in her face spread to her neck. Why did she have to blush at all the wrong times?

"Why maybe not?" He leaned forward and then winced as something in his shoulder hurt him. She felt the silliest urge to trace the scar in his eyebrows with her fingertips. Lowering her eyes, she locked her fingers together. This was getting ridiculous.

"Oh, don't go practicing that *enryo* on me, Sanda. We're friends."

Sanda looked up, startled. She wasn't doing that at all.

"After all, didn't I risk a month of night watch just to sneak up here and help you save Mirta?" He slammed his small knife back into its sheath. "If you don't want to talk about being a wife, just say so. Don't disappear into yourself. My father hates it in his wives, and I hate it, too. For all your talk about my mother, I think he always takes her back because she speaks her mind and he knows exactly where he stands."

"I wasn't blocking you out. I just didn't know what to say." She got up and started to pace around. "I don't mind the idea of getting married . . . I suppose. But I pray to the Goddess Within that I don't get claimed by a man like Haddim."

Bart flowed to his feet. "Sanda, most men aren't like Haddim." He led her over to the "bed" of tattered furs. "Sit down. Relax."

She let him support her arm while she settled on the furs with her back against the rock wall. Bart sat beside her, hesitated, and then carefully put his arm around her.

There was a breathless pause as he waited to see what she would do. She stiffened. His arm was warm on her neck. His hand brushed her shoulder. They sat silently while the lamp chased shadows of the cage across the entrance. Bart sighed and the light weight on her shoulder eased.

No! She didn't want him to take it away. Her muscles stiffened as she tried to lean slightly toward him without shifting her weight. Immediately, Bart's hand closed warmly around her shoulder. "Am I like Haddim?" he asked.

Sanda shook her head. He wasn't at all like Haddim. Where Haddim was frightening, Bart was exciting— in a reassuring way.

He squeezed her shoulder and gently pulled her closer. "Haddim is an old zerker. He's tired . . . afraid . . . and he drinks too much."

"Haddim afraid?" Sanda found that hard to believe.

"Well, old zerkers tend to either fall apart, or learn to handle themselves—like Sair, the Supreme Guardian. He's as cool as a lanker—except in a fight, of course. But men like Haddim can't handle growing older. They get ugly and totally unpredictable."

Sanda thought of Bart's father. "Like Mikhail?"

Bart stared into space. Almost absently he took his hand off her shoulder and hunched with his arms around his knees. "I never thought of my father as an aging zerker." He leaned back against the wall and closed his eyes. His face was drained of color and his scar was a faint slash of purple across his eyebrow. He opened his eyes. "I've been a fool. I've been so caught up in my own problems, I never thought about my father's."

Sanda wriggled apart from him, to see his face and read his expression.

"Don't move." He looked a bit uncertain. "Or don't you like me, either?"

"Of course I like you." She sank back and he put his arm around her, making her feel protected. Yes, she did like Bart. He was calm, soothing and safe. She snuggled comfortably against him.

His arm tightened. Her breath caught. He might be a whelp, but he had been with a woman. He pulled her even closer. Her heart fluttered. She shouldn't be doing this. She should run home right now. Assilla had warned her about this sort of thing again and again. But this wasn't dangerous. This was Bart. She lay breathless, waiting, wondering if she would learn the great mystery of "women's service."

He gathered her in his arms, then went rigid, listening. "Did you hear something?"

They both faced the tunnel entrance. Sanda was petrified: someone was going to catch them alone! But all she could hear was the faraway echo of a whistle. "Oh, it's only one of those silly old whistles the men use." She leaned tentatively against his chest.

"Those whistles are signals, and midnight isn't the time for anyone to be piping down orders!" He surged to his feet, grabbed her wrist with his good arm and hauled her into the dark tunnel toward the faint shrilling that went on and on.

"Bart, the lamp!"

"No time."

"Yeaoowwww!" Mirta screamed as he realized he was being left.

"Duck!" she called, "The ceiling is low."

"Shit! My forehead!"

He jerked her around another corner and onto the moonlit ledge. The second moon, the Gifter, was high above the valley, illuminating the rocks opposite with a silvery sheen. Immediately Sanda looked toward the Forbidden Heights just above the waterfall, searching for ghostfire. But now there was no ghostfire in the sky. Only the Gifter which flooded the valley with its light.

Bart dragged her to the edge of the cliff. She took comfort in the warmth of his arm alongside hers and moved a little closer; but Bart remained tense, waiting for the next whistle, which sounded first above them, and then echoed across the valley, until it faded slowly into the sky. Doors slammed on the opposite cliff. Torches flared as men ran for the swing bridge that joined the Port and Starboard sides of The Home.

"General alarm!" He took her shoulders. "I've got to go! But we've got to get you home safely first."

"Never mind me." she said bravely. "I can climb up to the window in the children's gallery and get in there." She tried to sound like Ullan, brave and fearless, but her mind saw the ghostfire arch into the sky again and she shivered.

He didn't seem to notice her fear. "So that's how you got out!" He peered up into the darkness. "But you could have fallen. Taizaburo, the winds alone . . ."

A woman's shriek rent the air.

They froze. The scream bounced back and forth between the cliffs, becoming more pitiful as it faded.

Sanda pointed over the Heights. Far above them there seemed to be a slight rosy glow along the rim of the plateau. "Ghosts," she whispered.

Bart gave her a frightened look and ran for the crevice. He started to climb, then paused. "Are you sure you'll be all right? You could wait until I come back. Then I'll watch out for you as you climb."

Her relief overwhelmed her and she could only nod.

He climbed quickly up and out of sight.

7

Bart practically threw himself up the cliff. If he were found missing when the packs formed, there would be hell to pay. But he couldn't be caught sneaking out of this cave either; whelps had no business on the Promenade Deck at night. When he reached the top of the fissure, he peered cautiously over the lip. The back of a large herb planter blocked his view of the deck, but he could hear people shouting and doors slamming.

Another whistle cut the air: stand down.

Relief soothed the knots out of his stomach. Maybe he wouldn't be missed; he didn't need punishment detail, on top of everything else. Slowly, he eased himself onto the deck, and crouched behind the planter. If he could just slip down to the armory . . .

The babble of women's voices dashed his hopes. Taizaburo, why didn't their men keep them at home? As two women hurried into view, Bart hunched lower behind the planter, listening.

". . . broke her contract," he heard.

Broke her contract to The Home: suicide. He hoped it was no one in their pack. They had enough troubles without the shame of suicide.

He risked a look, then ducked again. It seemed as if every wife in The Home was on deck. As they bustled by, asking questions no one seemed able to answer, he forced himself to relax and wait. While he waited, he noticed that there were no men with them. His stomach churned with impatience. Were the men already in packs? Had his absence been noticed? He forced himself to wait until no more women went by; then he casually followed the last group, fumbling with his trousers, as if he had relieved himself over the cliff.

The cloister pillars cast pitch-black shadows across the silvery moonlit deck. The valley was a sooty hole unplumbed by the moonlight of the vanishing Fee or the just-risen Gifter. Ahead the ever-present roar of the waterfall grew louder as he approached the oldest part of The Home. When he rounded the last cliff bend before the waterfall, the glow from hundreds of torches warmed the ghostly white light of the Gifter. In front of him was a canopy of hair, long unbound women's tresses, mixed with the cropped round heads of warriors. All were gathered near Mikhail's quarters, staring at something hidden by the stone pillars.

Bart craned his neck. His father stood in front of the crowd. The torchlight, which emphasized the frown lines on his face, and the hollows of his cheeks, made him look old . . . and vulnerable. Bart searched for his mother, but although Tekiri, Verdi and Fiaranna were all clustered around Mikhail, his mother was not there.

Bart lost his breath, as if punched. He started to push his way through the crowd. No, it couldn't be. His mother was probably staying with someone until his father cooled off.

"Get your hands off my wife!" A man grabbed him, but his wife pulled at his sleeve, and whispered in his ear. Bart heard the words "Mikhail's son . . ." and the man let go.

Daggerjaws burrowed into Bart's stomach. He pushed past the last man and entered an open space in front of the dactyl net. Two men, Volf and Tev, climbed the net. Above them, a woman dangled from a noose tied to an empty planter hook. Bart swallowed. The woman's back was to him, but he knew that slight frame as well as he knew his own bow. He knew the bare toes he had played with as a cub, and the hands that had soothed away his hurts.

Volf and Tev climbed higher. Tev's face was expressionless—the way it always got when the zerkers around him were upset. Volf was trying unsuccessfully to look dignified, but he was eyeing one of the women in the crowd. Clad only in trousers, he flexed his muscles to show off his fighting scars, and looked meaningfully at a woman who, suddenly, was gone, pulled away by her angry lanker husband.

Zorava slowly twisted around on the rope.

Bart's stomach heaved; her face was puffy—a horrible purple black; her bulging eyes seemed to stare directly into his, and her protruding tongue was obscene. Something fluttered on her chest—a square of paper covered with women's writing.

Volf reached the body. He made a face. "Godwithin, what a smell!" Bart suddenly identified the sharp scent on the breeze: urine and shit. Volf steadied Zorava across his shoulder. Tev cut the rope and the dead woman flopped limply across Volf's scarred back.

Bart swallowed heavily, and bit hard on his tongue to stop his tears. Turning away, he looked through the dactyl net to the swinging bridge that crossed to the Starboard cliffs. The protective webbing over the bridge looked like a spider web wrapped around the people, who still scurried across the dark planking.

By the time Bart had himself under control, Tev

had lowered Zorava to the deck. He watched the piece of paper on her frail chest, expecting to see it rise and fall. But it lay still. He swallowed. With her eyes staring like that she looked just like a carcass ready to be butchered.

For a horrified moment Bart actually visualized how he would make the opening cut. He groaned aloud, and forced the image away, only to have it pop back into his mind even more vividly. Godwithin, was he going crazy? Hope struggled with grief. Was he turning zerker? Damn, how could he think of that, when his mother lay dead in front of him? But a tiny voice in his head whispered. Test yourself, maybe you're turning.

Bart looked around the crowd of faces staring toward his mother. Sure, run around like a singed meatkitten to see if you've got zerker speed. If my father doesn't kill me, Tev will pack me off to steerage for sheer stupidity.

He looked at his father who stood woodenly, face grey, square shoulders rounded, and capable hands hanging loosely at his sides. His wives clustered around him, hair loose, wearing unbleached night robes under their hurriedly belted kimonos. Fiaranna was comforting Verdi. Tekiri stood slightly apart in her jet kimono, her face a blank mask—was she practicing *enryo* or was she really that uncaring? Around her, the watching crowd was so quiet Bart could hear every one of Verdi's sobs above the background roar of the waterfall.

Mikhail leaned forward, ripped the paper free of its securing broach, and held it up to Fiaranna. His wife tried to turn back to Verdi, but Mikhail jerked her away from her sister-wife. "Leave Verdi alone, and read this crazy scribbling to me."

Fiaranna murmured something.

Volf edged forward, obviously listening.

"What do you mean, 'Not here'? Read the damn thing."

Fiaranna lowered her head, and murmured softly again.

Volf guffawed loudly.

Mikhail jerked upright, his bushy eyebrows meeting in the middle of a furious frown. "You got something to say?" He reached for his shette, remembered it was in the armory, and opened his arms in a ready stance.

"Me?" Volf backed up hurriedly and saluted him with overcareful respect. "No, Pack Leader. I honor your sorrow."

Mikhail clenched his fists. Bart knew his father wanted and needed a fight, to clear his veins and make him feel better. But Volf wasn't going to give him the pleasure.

Mikhail transferred his glare to Zorava. Someone coughed. Bart's father whirled around. The women immediately dropped their gazes; the men found the dactyl net extremely interesting.

Mikhail turned, hustled his wives through the crowd, and pushed them inside his quarters. The night bar fell with a muffled thud, sealing them in.

Volf tried to look grave. But his eyes sparkled with malicious glee. He coughed for attention. "It's a sad day when a pack leader has no honor." He sighed dramatically, then strode off. He didn't get very far. Sair, Supreme Guardian of The Home, blocked his way.

"You and I are going to talk. Now," the slight, grey-haired killer said, with menacing calm. Volf tried to look innocent as he meekly followed Sair toward the armory, but he watched his grey-haired leader worriedly.

"What's going on?" a man behind Bart demanded.

"The note said Mikhail has no honor," a woman murmured.

"No honor? Mikhail? It was she who had no honor. She broke her contract to The Home. He fed and clothed her and her children for twenty years. While all she has done is caused him trouble. And him one of the best pack leaders in The Home." He took his wife by the arm. "This isn't our business." He cast a worried look toward the Heights and made the sign of the Circle. "I saw the sky tonight. It's more likely that 'they' got her." He hustled her away. Other men agreed, and led their families home.

Slowly the crowd thinned. The concentrated glow of torches dimmed, until only a few sent thin tongues of light up to the ceiling of the cloisters. Bart continued to stare at his mother's body, unable to accept the reality of her death. Gradually he became aware of someone beside him. The tiny Mother General waited quietly, respecting his grief. Behind her, Tev stood in the gloom with his two wives. Everyone else had gone, leaving the cloister almost black. Only the strengthening light of the Gifter made it possible to see them.

When she had his attention, the Mother General curtsied. "What would you like us to do?"

Bart shook his head dumbly. "What?"

Tev came forward. "Nobody dares ask your father what should be done with Zorava's body."

Bart looked blankly at his uncle.

Two more women joined the circle—strong stonemasons who carried a stretcher between them. They set it down, and carefully eased Zorava on. The older one looked at the Nystra. "Where is she to go?"

The Mother General curtsied to Bart. "May we take her to sickbay until your father's wives can make her funeral arrangements?" He tried to say yes, but the words stuck in his throat, so he nodded. The women picked up the stretcher, and left. The Mother General followed. Tears blurred Bart's eyes and he turned away.

Two strong hands gripped his shoulders briefly. "Try to understand."

Bart wiped his eyes angrily. "Try to understand what? She's dead. If she was so unhappy, why didn't she go to the Daughters of Olarni?"

"I think she wanted to hurt Mikhail." Tev held up one hand. "Listen."

Bart only heard the ever-present roar of the waterfall. "Listen to what?"

Tev pulled him over to the window under Mikhail's bedchamber. Just over the sound of the waterfall, he could hear hoarse breathing, mixed with the splintering of wood, and a sound that was a cross between a sob and a howl of anger.

He looked at his uncle, astonished.

"Don't look so surprised. He's got problems. He's worrying himself sick about you—terrified you'll die like Drell. His pack is unbalanced—he has too many old warriors. Volf is nipping at his heels. And now this."

Bart remembered his talk with Sanda. "Do you think he's losing it?" he asked, making the clawed sign for "crazy old zerker" with his fingers.

"No, but he's not having it easy." Tev straightened up. "Anyway, you've firewood detail early tomorrow. Get to bed. And tomorrow, leave your father alone. If you bother him with some of those crazy ideas of yours, he's liable to break your neck." He turned and escorted his wives toward their quarters.

Bart moved away from the unnerving sounds coming from his father's bedchamber. He sank down in the gloom of a pillar, and buried his head in his hands.

Sanda watched Bart disappear up the cliff. Suddenly, she realized that a torchlit crowd of people was hurrying along the Promenade Deck on the Starboard side of The Home. She scrambled back into the cave entrance, and watched the torches bob, disappear, and reappear behind the cloister pillars, as people hurried toward the swinging bridge that joined both sides of The Home. She'd never seen so many women running in her life and curiosity made her want to know why. As soon as Starboard was clear, she climbed to the deck and hid behind a planter.

". . . a shame really."

She pressed herself flat against the cool rock.

Women's voices drifted by. "Poor Zorava, I wonder what finally pushed her over the edge?"

Zorava! Bart's mother!

She strained to hear more. Another voice said clearly. "Maybe it was punishment to him for talking about *them*." There was a pause and Sanda knew they were warding off the ghosts. Then a man muttered. "Ghostfires always mean death. Now they've got their slave we can relax."

Had Zorava died? She must have heard wrong. She strained her ears, but those voices faded and others took their place.

"But why didn't Zorava join the Daughters of Olarni? She didn't have to kill herself to get away from Mikhail."

Killed herself! Bart must know by now. Sanda wished she could be with him—to help somehow.

After a while the voices stopped. Sanda waited. Bart didn't come. His mother was dead; he wouldn't be coming. She'd have to climb alone. The sky above her was free of ghostfires, but that didn't make it seem less deadly. What if the ghosts were still there and wanted another slave? Suddenly she wanted to get home more than anything in the world. She jumped to her feet, raced for the pillar, and started to wriggle under the dactyl netting. A hand came out of nowhere and jerked her backward. She bit down a scream as she sprawled on the deck.

"Taizaburo, are children nightstalking too?"

Sanda went limp with relief. Not a ghost: her stepfather. Then dread curled her up in fear. Caught nightstalking! What would he do to her?

Haddim pulled her to her feet and brushed her hair away from her face. "Sanda!"

The moonlight shone off his receding forehead, making his long bony nose look like a beak. He lurched; he was drunk.

"Sanda."

She flinched away from the sour smell of sweat and mirta wine. He pushed her against the pillar. "So you can't wait for wife training before you service a man?" He threw back his head and laughed.

Sanda ducked under his arm and ran. But Haddim was zerker. He caught her by the hair and brought her close again. The roots of every hair on her head screamed as she tried to wriggle out of his grasp.

Haddim swore, and shoved her against the rock pillar. "So you want a little spearing, do you?" He shoved his leg between hers. His foul breath made her want to gag. "Come on, kiss me!" As his gummy mouth came down on hers, he let go of her hair to fumble at her buttocks. Sanda tried to scream, but his wet stinking mouth covered hers.

She struggled, but he held her easily and stuck

his awful tongue deep into her mouth. His legs got tangled in hers and they fell to the ground.

"That's more like it." He rolled on top of her. *It* was going to happen. She couldn't stop it; she could feel him pulling her tunic up. She frantically tried to writhe away.

"That's it! Keep moving!" His breath got harsher and more foul.

He wasn't going to do it. He couldn't! But he got his other leg in between hers. She could feel terror and rage rise and meet. Her fingers hooked into claws. She'd kill him first! She started to scream, and found her mouth stuffed with her own tunic. But that didn't matter, for suddenly her arms grew strong. As she raked his chest, she pushed him away. His bleary eyes flickered in surprise. She wriggled half out from under him before he grabbed her again. Her fury overwhelmed her; she wrenched one hand free, and clawed at his face. Joy battled with rage as she saw his blood welling from her deep scratches.

His face suddenly vanished as he was dragged off her. She caught a brief glimpse of Bart, his lips pulled back in an insane snarl. "Get off her." He kicked Haddim halfway across the deck.

Sanda followed Haddim. She'd kill the bastard. As he charged Bart, she attacked her stepfather. The men's flailing arms knocked her sideways into a pillar. Her head hit rock, stunning her. She blinked, trying to see. The rage drained out of her. Goddess Within, what had she been doing? How could she even think of attacking a man? Dazed, she watched the struggling figures.

Drunk as he was, Haddim moved with dizzying speed. His fists flashed, but he staggered and lost his balance, missing Bart completely.

Bart dodged, caught Sanda, and sent her flying across the deck. She tripped as she tried to skip over the planters, and ended up on her hands and knees in the freshly hoed loam. "Run," Bart hissed, never taking his eyes off her stepfather.

The nearest door banged open. "What the hell is going on!" A warrior stood in the lighted doorway, peering into the gloom. Behind him, his wives gaped over his shoulder.

Sanda pressed herself into the dirt. If she were caught here, Assilla would send her to steerage.

"Just a friendly argument," Bart called out, his stance suddenly casual. Haddim tried to bow, lost his balance, tripped over the planter edge, and stepped into it. Bart hiccuped and staggered sideways.

"Take your drunken fights to the armory." The warrior slammed the door.

In the echo of the slamming door, Haddim tackled Bart. They both went down, splintering a wooden planter. Sanda tried to force herself back toward the opening in the dactyl net. That was the safest thing to do. She must run. Hide. But Haddim's rage sparked her own, and drew her like a starving weanling to ship bread. She edged forward. Vitality and anger radiated from Bart's stern face. But Haddim's raw fury was even stronger. No wonder zerkers ruled.

Bart waved her away. "Run, Sanda!" He grunted as Haddim tackled him, knocking him to the ground again. While Haddim tried to pound Bart's head into the deck, Bart managed to roll on top, and hit him, on the cheek, jaw, and stomach. "You won't hurt her. You won't, you won't," he panted with each blow.

Sanda edged closer, the excitement making her breath short. Haddim's rage flared in her own body. She jumped, as Haddim clutched Bart's hair and yanked him sideways. They rolled over and over again, grunting and snarling. Haddim kneed Bart in the ribs. Bart curled around his sore side. Haddim grabbed his throat, squeezing with all of his drunken strength. Sanda could no longer watch. She pounded on Haddim's back with her fists, but he took no notice. When she clawed for his eyes, he half rolled on one knee, and kicked her legs out from under her. The deck smashed upwards, dazing her. Then, right in front of her, she saw a clay watering jug. She seized it, and brought it down on Haddim's head, shattering the jug into a dozen pieces.

Her stepfather slumped on top of Bart.

Sanda threw the broken handle down and started pounding Haddim's head with her fists, feeling powerful and alive. Her stepfather's body heaved as Bart pushed him off and took her in his arms. "There, there. It's all right." She turned to beat off this new horror, and found herself looking into Bart's worried face.

What was going on? What had she done? Her mind howled and tried to break free, but horror drenched her rage. No, she screamed silently. But she knew better. She'd gone berserker. It had finally happened.

Had Bart noticed?

She pressed her face against his leathers, shaking in terror. Would he order her drugged?

"It's all right. You knocked him cold." He felt his shoulder gingerly. "That was rough." He looked thoughtfully at her. "I owe you."

His eyes crinkled in a smile. Her heart soared. He hadn't noticed. He didn't know. Sanda felt her face almost split in a relieved grin.

"You should have been a whelp," he said. "You're so fast."

Cold fear shocked through her. She hugged herself, frightened.

Bart struggled to his feet and put his arms around her. Sanda slowly relaxed. If he knew, he'd be on guard, not holding her. She felt like jumping up and down and screaming with relief. He didn't know. He *didn't*.

"Did Haddim recognize you?"

She nodded. She turned in Bart's arms and looked at Haddim. He lay twisted on the deck; his jaw was slack, and a trickle of blood ran out of his hair.

"Don't worry." He turned her face up to look at him. "What can he do? Accuse his own daughter . . ."

"Stepdaughter."

"Accuse his own stepdaughter of refusing to be raped? Hardly. He'll probably hope that you're too frightened to tell." Bart gave her a reassuring squeeze. "Any man who has to stoop to taking his pleasure with his own daughter could never face his pack mates again."

"But what about you? He saw you too."

Bart stiffened, then he snorted bitterly. "He probably doesn't know who I am. Warriors don't bother to learn whelps' names unless we're in their pack, or are related." He shrugged and gave a little laugh. But Sanda could feel that his arms were still tense with worry. She closed her eyes, and leaned against him, wrapping his comforting presence around her like a cloak, feeling him begin to relax.

A groan distracted them. Haddim straightened a leg, and reached out weakly. His eyes were half-open. The pupils were almost turned up into his head, but he was struggling back to consciousness.

Bart kept his arm around her as he rushed her to the net. "Better hurry."

The moonlight picked up the little puckered scar in his eyebrow.

Haddim snorted, and rolled on his stomach.

"Stay away from him," Bart whispered, and shoved her toward the gap in the netting. "And if you can, meet me tomorrow night in the cave."

As Sanda skimmed up the cliff, fear giving her strength she never knew she had, she heard the thud of Bart's boots as he ran toward the armory.

8

Sanda's eyes softened. Her lips parted and she leaned forward to kiss Bart. But as he reached to touch her tangled waves of hair, its light brown strands turned dull grey, the skin on her face darkened and her tongue protruded. Then her teeth grew fangs as she turned into a Sangir Slaver.

"Bart!" The Sangir's dead lips peeled back from his teeth and his head changed into a skull. "Bart!"

Sweat bathed him. He tried to back away, but her arms became ropes and wrapped themselves around him. The ropes turned into snakes that coiled and started to squeeze his life away.

Suddenly he was awake. He pried open gummy lids. Dim light. Shadows on the rough-hewn rock above. He was in the whelps' dormitory. Relief thudded through him. He lay still, letting his terror-weakened limbs slowly gain strength. But instead the nightmare came to life: his mother was dead. Never again would he sneak up for some fruitbread, or sit talking to her while she mended his clothes.

And his father—what was his father to do? He stood accused of having no honor and would never be able to challenge the accuser to clear his name. Thank Godwithin Sanda wasn't like Zorava. Sanda would confront him face to face and deal with any problems in a straightforward manner.

Beside him, he could hear a grunt as someone heaved himself up to his bed slot. "Wake up, please!" a boyish voice begged.

"All right, Pineor, I'm awake." He didn't move. What was the point of getting up? He closed his eyes and burrowed into the bedclothes. Every muscle screamed in agony, and every joint seemed fused. Suddenly he remembered his fight with Guntor. His humiliation and angry frustration overwhelmed him. When Pineor shook him, sending sparks of pain through the wound in his shoulder he growled angrily and opened his eyes. Pineor, his solemn-faced cabin fetch, clung to the climbing notches cut up to Bart's second-level bed slot, watching him warily.

"You have to get up. Mikhail wants you to stack a full load of wood before he finishes his staff meeting."

Suddenly, Guntor's battered face loomed up beside Pineor. "That's not the way to be a good cabin fetch." Guntor grabbed Bart's legs and heaved him out of his second-level slot. Muscles tearing in agony, he scrambled for a handhold, found none, and twisted, to land painfully on all fours on the deck.

When Pineor jumped down beside Bart, Guntor slapped the boy on his back, sending the small cabin fetch stumbling across the dim whelps' dormitory. "That's how you wake a lazy whelp. Got to stay on top of him, you know. His mother's a contract breaker."

Bart got up, shaking with fury, wishing desperately that he wasn't naked. The zerker whelp leered at him. "What's the matter: can't you take a joke?" Guntor's black eye sparkled with malice—only one eye, because the other was swollen shut. He had a large bruise on his cheek, a lump on his forehead, and a nose as big as a plum melon. Although he bounced on his toes, ready for a fight, he also held himself stiffly, and crouched slightly, as if to protect a sore rib.

All talk in the dorm stopped, and the other whelps watched, motionless.

Bart's lips stung with the memory of Guntor's kiss. If only . . . but there were no "ifs" in The Home. All that stood between Bart and a really ugly beating was the law against zerker-lanker fights.

The zerker danced forward and shoved him roughly against the wall. "Are you deaf as well as lazy? Mikhail wants us to have a full load of wood stacked before he joins us to hunt." He grinned evilly. "You don't need to hide in your bed. The ghosts have their slave. It's safe to go out of The Home now."

The world froze as Bart's breath stuck in his throat. His fingers burned with the desire to feel his shette and his muscles ached to slash the fat-lipped grin right off Guntor's face. But . . . Guntor was zerker. Bart breathed out slowly, trying to push away his hatred. Zerkers *always* won; he couldn't fight. He turned toward his cabin fetch. "Get my clothes."

Pineor shot across the dim room toward the clothes hooks, passing under window slots that were lightening to grey. All through the dormitory, cabin fetches started moving again, waking whelps and bringing them clothes. But few people spoke. Bart knew they were all listening.

"That's right, lanker," Guntor sneered. "It's time you learned to walk softly around *men!*"

Bart's face burned. He half turned back.

"Yes?" Guntor asked, hopefully.

Bart's stomach churned with frustration. "I'll take you on the day I turn zerker. I always beat you before, and I will again."

Guntor laughed contemptuously. "I'd wait for you to turn, but I'd die of old age."

"Guntor, where are you?" Mariko peered into the gloom, looking at the shadowy figures. "Gun, I've got some special liniment from one of my mothers."

Guntor waved and Mariko jogged over. He saw Bart and scowled. But when Guntor put an arm over Mariko's shoulder, the slender whelp stood straighter, and gave Bart a triumphant look. "Let's go down to the baths," Mariko said. "I'll rub your sore muscles before we go out this morning."

Guntor spat at Bart's feet, and allowed the other whelp to lead him away.

Bart stood in the center of the dormitory. He was shaking—from rage, frustration, or fear—he didn't know which. Quiet talk resumed. Whelps and cabin fetches hung their bed furs to air and drifted out to breakfast.

Dyfid approached him, warily. "You all right?"

Bart nodded. "I'd like to beat his brains out."

"Well, you can't, and you're lucky he can't either."

Taking his hunting leathers from Pineor, Bart wrung them, as if trying to kill the keld that had originally worn the skin. "It's going to be hell out there today."

Dyfid threw Bart his belt. "Welcome to reality."

"Reality?"

"Yes. Why do you think I'm covered with scars, and you only have one or two?"

Bart flushed. "What?"

Dyfid's lips thinned. "Until the nesters, no one dared bully you." He glared at Bart, then pivoted and walked away.

Bart gawked at his retreating back. "Dyfid!"

As the other whelp turned, Bart saw the end of a scar on his neck. A scar he knew extended to Dyfid's lower ribs. Suddenly he felt like a fool. "I always thought everyone liked me."

Dyfid grinned gently. "They do. But you were also Mikhail's son. If you had turned zerker, you would probably have been one of their officers. So they always walked carefully around you."

"And they will again," Bart blustered. "When I do turn zerker."

Dyfid took a step forward. "Feel your chin."

Startled, Bart touched his chin, and felt a soft down and a few longer hairs.

"See, you're growing a beard! You're a man."

"Boy's fuzz."

"Boy's fuzz would slip through your fingers." Dyfid reached forward, pinched, and jerked, sending tiny prickles of pain into Bart's chin.

"What do you think you're doing?" Bart knocked his hand away.

"Boy's fuzz can't be pulled. Face it. You'll never turn. You've got a man's voice and the beginnings of a man's beard."

Bart touched his chin again. The few long hairs caught on his callouses. He tugged, and felt them pull his skin. Then, he felt around his chin and found more. Numbly, he dropped his hand. A beard. Somehow he'd known it since the nesters, but he'd refused to admit it. Now he had to face reality.

He was a man—and he was still lanker. His legs suddenly shook with weakness. He'd have to be initiated as a lanker, and go into the jungle alone, without the zerker speed or strength. And all his dreams of changing things in the packs. His ideas about raising keld in the side canyons near The Home. All over. All gone. Nobody listened to lankers. Nobody who counted.

Dyfid's look softened. "Finally. I was beginning to think you were stupid as well as stubborn." He cleared his throat and looked at his feet. "Once you get used to being lanker, you can be initiated. Then you'll be a man."

Lanker. Forever. "Or I'll be dead."

Dyfid smiled. "You'll live. You have the best eyes in The Home. Men who hunt beside you will always find game, and see danger before it hits them. You'll live . . . and you'll have to marry."

"Taizaburo, Dyfid, let me survive this watch first." *Lanker. Servant. Never to be a pack leader. Never to help change things in the packs. A servant. A nobody.*

Dyfid rested his calloused hand on Bart's shoulder. "We were friends before Guntor set his claim on you. We could be friends again—as pack brothers."

Bart didn't say anything. The oath of pack brother was for life. Pack brothers watched each other's backs, fought each other's fights, and shared their weapons and food. He'd dreamed of grandly offering to be Dyfid's pack brother after he had turned zerker . . . but now . . .

Dyfid took a deep breath. "I have an older sister who is widowed and needs a home." He paused, and searched Bart's eyes intently. "I could help you as your pack brother, and you could help me."

A lanker home. Dyfid would never have dared ask Bart if he'd turned and been in line for pack leadership. But now he was nothing . . . like Dyfid. Bart didn't know whether to laugh hysterically, or punch the other whelp out.

The last mess bell clanged. "Food!" He frantically scrambled into his clothes. "Taizaburo, but I'm hungry."

Dyfid nodded—content to wait. But then weren't lankers always content to wait, Bart thought bitterly as he finished dressing. He avoided Dyfid's eyes and ran down the tunnel to the mess, his footstep thudding a refrain. Lan-ker, for-ever. Lan-ker, for-ever.

Bart jogged down the Migration Trail. Lan-ker, lan-ker. His boots pounded out a steady refrain, and the throb in his shoulder echoed his boots. He felt old. His muscles were either stiff with pain or fever-weak.

The sun outlined a few puffy clouds in the brilliant gold of dawn, but grief for his mother and sheer physical misery cast a pall over the land. Not one person had spoken to him after he left Dyfid. But he had seen them whispering and pointing—whether they were talking about his mother, or Guntor, he didn't know. Several lanker men had started toward him, looked at his face, and then veered off uncertainly.

He followed Tev across a stone bridge over the Waterfall River, and started through what used to be the needle forest. All around them, old stumps poked their rotting heads through the shrubs and undergrowth. Small firs hugged the ground, but anything taller than waist high had been cut for firewood. While he jogged, hunger gnawed steadily at his belly, weakening his thighs and making every step an effort. Lan-ker. Ser-vant. Lan-ker. Would the day never end? He shifted his pack trying to ease his shoulder. Maybe he should have reported to sickbay. But he knew he'd die before he admitted how much Ullan, Guntor and Haddim had hurt him. Fear soured his stomach. Had Sanda's stepfather recognized him?

Ahead of him, Dyfid darted out of the pack and ran a hundred yards, to jerk a yern root from the ground. He came back, stuffing it into his field pack. Bart snorted in self-contempt. Well, now he was lanker, he would have to do that, too. When he had a family to feed, there'd be no great kills for him. He swallowed. And, as a lanker, he would need friends. But who was his friend? Not his father. None of his father's zerker friends. Certainly not Guntor.

He turned to look thoughtfully at Dyfid. Even though Bart would never be a zerker, the other whelp still wanted to team up with him. Bart shook his head. He needed time to think.

He almost trod on Tev's heels. His uncle had stopped and was looking up at the cliffs where Mikhail had spotted the stranger. Bart made a circle on his breast as he followed his uncle's gaze up the terraced cliffs to the top tier. "Be careful," he whispered, "ghostfires in the sky last night."

His uncle nodded as he traced the Holy Circle over his heart. "Yes, but they have their life, don't they?"

A spear prodded Bart's shoulder. "Move it," Volf demanded. "You're holding up the rest of us."

Tev didn't move. "How's your son?" he asked.

Volf's hard stance softened and lines of worry overwrote his scowl. "Not good. My wife's milk isn't enough for him, and he throws up every bit of other food we give him." He slashed viciously at a shrub by the path. "He's my third son, and he's going the way the others did. If only there was more ship food available . . ."

Something moved in the sky. A dactyl dove out of the sun. " 'Ware above!" Bart called.

Volf was instantly distracted. He whooped with glee and started to limp away from the pack. The zerkers and most of the whelps followed behind, yelling encouragement. Bart noticed young Nakano imitating Volf's fake limp. He even carried his weapons the way the zerker did.

When Bart heard something behind, he whirled

to see Guntor charging down the trail toward him. It was obvious that the young zerker was not going to give way so Bart jumped off the trail. Guntor sneered at him and waved Mariko to his side, just the way Guntor had waved Bart to his side only yesterday. The slender whelp leaped forward, grinning idiotically at his hero. Bart flushed. During the last tendays had he ignorantly responded as eagerly as Mariko?

He turned away, and saw his uncle nudge Norv and wink toward Guntor and Mariko. Norv tapped his head with his spear: prick for brains. Crude chuckles rippled through the lanker pack. Crude, but quiet; the chattering zerkers never noticed. Nor did they notice the lankers drift off the trail.

As the lankers moved away, Bart followed them, hesitantly. He had always joined the zerker games. But now he was too hungry and battered—besides, he was lanker, too. The lankers watched him with hard faces. He nearly turned back; clearly, he wasn't welcome. But Dyfid waved and moved over to make room for him in the group, so he sat with a sigh of relief, easing the pack from his shoulders, watching while the zerkers cheered each other on, laying bets as to how many dactyls they could lure down.

The dactyl circled, its membranous wings stretched to their widest to catch the updraft of hot air, its yellow eyes watching the "wounded warrior."

Volf took two more staggering steps, and collapsed on the ground. But he fell so that both hands were free; one hand held a shette, while the other held his spear. The dactyl gave a raucous shriek that echoed off the cliffs, folded its wings and dove. Just as it stretched out its talons for Volf's throat, the zerker twisted and jumped away. Guntor tore across the ground, and fouled the dactyl's wings with his spear.

Suddenly, Guntor dropped his spear and retreated, holding his side and cursing Mariko viciously when he rushed to help. The other zerkers took over the fight, keeping the enraged dactyl grounded. While Gopa and Volf played with the flyer, Nakano darted in, plunged his spear into the dactyl, and howled in triumph. One of the lankers snorted.

"Some kill. They almost held his hand."

Bart flushed. How many times had his father let him have an easy kill? A hundred? A thousand?

"Are they coming?" Volf yelled. "Are they coming?"

Gopa shaded his eyes with his hands, and scanned the sky.

Tev nudged Bart. "What do you see?"

"Fifteen or twenty are already diving."

Tev gave a signal. The men moved closer together, crouched and set up their spears, so the group looked like a giant woman's pin cushion. Bart set his own spear solidly in the packed earth of the trail, feeling a tremendous sense of security in the iron spear tips that surrounded him.

Norv ground his spear deeper into the ground. "I'll never understand zerkers as long as I live."

Bart looked curiously at Norv—a lanker who kept to himself and talked only to other lankers. The man's hands were thick and scarred with hard work, his face furrowed with perpetual anger. "They'll turn up their noses at berries and roots; then waste time on dactyls that taste like hell and are more bone than meat."

"Sh," someone hissed: Bart sensed that the men were looking his way.

Norv grunted and shut up. Bart hunched his shoulders, and pretended he didn't care.

Beyond them, the dactyls were circling. The zerkers

below shouldered their bows and spread out, ready for the fun.

As if on signal, the dactyls folded their wings and dove.

"Stupid," one of the lankers muttered.

The zerkers twisted and turned, slicing and stabbing. One of the reptiles shrieked as Volf broke its wing bone at the last joint.

"Now," Tev said, "let's go stack wood."

"But we can't. The zerkers . . ." Bart abruptly shut up. If he was lanker, then Tev was his leader—after Mikhail.

"The zerkers will keep the dactyls busy. But right now, our families need wood."

"But who will butcher the carcasses?"

"They get the same training we do. They'll butcher, or they'll carry them whole—at this time of year they're too hungry to leave them lying there."

"But you can't do that. They'll kill you." And me.

"No, they won't. We'll just say that Mikhail would have sent us on for fuel. He would have, you know."

"But he would have sent you on with zerker protectors," Bart protested.

Tev nodded. "Gopa isn't your father. He's forgotten all about us. But don't worry, Gopa won't make trouble. He remembers the old days. He'll soothe things over. They'll have meat and we'll have firewood by the time Mikhail gets here. And results are all that Mikhail cares about."

As they descended toward the jungle, the zerkers, and then the circling dactyls, gradually disappeared. The battle cries faded, and the men relaxed, shifting into a different formation. Instead of the long line that Mikhail used, they bunched up in groups of three or four. One group would guard the others until they stood far to the rear. Then they would trot forward while the next group guarded them.

His uncle noticed Bart's amazement. "Never seen this before, have you?"

Bart shook his head. He'd always been glued to his father or to his zerker protector. As he shook his head something far down the valley caught his eye. "Tev, ildenhorn." *Food. Red meat.*

A soft chirp froze the whole pack, instantly. "Where?"

"There, at the edge of the jungle, they must be gathering for their migration."

"I can't see anything. It's too far away. But . . ." he chirped again. The pack oozed into motion, but slowly. So slowly that the grass bending in the down-valley breeze seemed to move faster. Down they went, finger-width by finger-width. The slow stalking was harder on Bart's aching body than the jogging. Muscles seemed to stick and then jerk painfully forward. He envied Dyfid's fluid prowl. Tev stiffened. Bart knew he had finally seen the ildenhorn. But still he didn't hurry his men.

"Aren't we going to rush them?" Bart whispered. Tev snorted softly and didn't reply. Fuming, Bart followed them until they reached the last small rise of land before the herd. Then two men stayed behind, bows strung, whistles in their mouths, guarding the rest of the pack.

The ildenhorn grazed on the undergrowth and young trees near the edge of the jungle. The herd was protected by three large, sharp-horned bucks. One snatched the occasional mouthful of food while the other two junior bucks paced around the does, guarding them. The does, heavy with young, were tearing into the lush ferns and small bushes at the jungle's edge. Their yellow, striped bodies blended into the ferns around, making them difficult to spot, but Bart counted twenty-two animals. Twenty-two! His mouth watered and he swallowed heavily. It had been months since he'd eaten well.

One of the does threw up her head. Bart gathered himself to lunge; Tev's hand pushed him down. Bart wanted to pound his uncle. They were going to lose them if they didn't move fast. But the men froze, and waited, and waited. They waited long enough to drive a zerker mad. The doe dropped her head. Still the men waited. Finally at some signal Bart could not see, they began to ooze forward, spreading out to encircle the herd. Closer and closer. Bart had never gotten this near to ildenhorn that weren't in a trap. The men were so silent and so slow that even the flyers and treebores in the jungle continued their calls and shrill cries.

The guards behind them whistled. Bart heard someone running down the path. Treebores screamed alarm; bow strings hummed; five fat does went down. The herd leaped for safety—leaving another two wounded behind. The men ran forward, shooting as they went, wounding more does. One of the lame animals went down. Another, near Bart, stumbled but kept on going. Bart sprinted into the jungle after her, ignoring his aching muscles and sore shoulder in his desperate need for food. He shot again; the doe went to her knees; he threw himself forward on top of the struggling body, immobilizing the horned head. She wasn't that badly wounded. If he tied her up with vine, maybe she'd heal. Maybe. But he was lanker now. No one would listen to him. And he was desperately hungry.

He drew his knife and cut her throat. Hot blood spurted and he clapped his mouth over the wound, drinking deeply. He could almost feel new strength flowing into his body. He drank until the heart stopped, then sucked frantically. He desperately wanted to eat a raw slice, but anything beyond first drink was forbidden.

Someone cleared his throat. "Well, well, what do we have here?"

Bart jerked upright. He'd been so hungry, he'd dropped his guard.

But it was only Movich, a zerker warrior from Ontu's pack. He was a long way from where his pack usually hunted. But since Ontu had lost his pack mate last spring, strange things were happening in his pack. Movich swallowed as he looked at the doe. Initiated only last year, he was young, and thin—painfully thin. "You shouldn't be drinking from *my* kill, whelp."

"But it was my kill," Bart protested.

Tev pushed his way onto the tiny game path, his bow ready. "Bart, did you get her?" Norv and Dyfid shouldered their way into the clearing, holding strung bows.

Movich bared his teeth. If he'd been an animal, his ears would have been flat. "That's my kill."

"It isn't his kill. I caught it, and I cut its throat. Look, *I'm* covered with the first drink, not him."

Tev pointed to the carcass. "Those arrows have the red stain of our pack," he said reasonably.

Movich jerked the offending arrows out. "Prove it," he sneered. "And don't try to hide behind Mikhail. I know all the leaders are at their staff meeting."

Bart mutely appealed to his uncle, but Tev gave a tiny shake of his head. Movich's snarl turned to an evil grin. "Thought you'd see sense. After all, it's a zerker's word against yours." He picked up the carcass and slung it over his shoulder.

The men around Bart lifted their bows. Movich

looked up to see the arrows released. "Damn you!" He leaped for Tev, pulling his shette with blinding speed. Two arrows slashed into the bushes beside him, but one caught him full in the chest. His leathers instantly soaked with blood; he came on, growling, like an animal. Tev shot again, hitting his neck. He staggered, and slowed down to lanker speed. Another arrow thudded into his liver. He grunted; bright red blood sprayed down his chin. His eyes glazed; he flailed weakly for balance and finally toppled backward, his face still a mixture of surprise and anger.

"You killed him!" Bart wondered if he were coming down with jungle fever. This couldn't be happening.

"He was stealing our meat," Tev snapped, fitting another arrow to his bow. Bart gasped as his uncle raised his bow and pointed it right at him.

"But . . ." Bart looked at Dyfid who met his eyes squarely; Dyfid wasn't surprised. Dyfid reluctantly lifted his own bow, to cover Bart. Then Norv did as well. Suddenly he was surrounded by killers. But they didn't shoot. They were waiting—for what?

"Well?" Tev said with deadly calm.

Well what? He desperately tried to think of how he could get them to lower their bows. Then he heard something moving through the forest. " 'Ware!" he whispered, pointing toward the sound of someone running.

Nakano, the youngest whelp in their pack, burst through the undergrowth.

Tev moved his arrow so it could cover the young whelp, but Dyfid and Norv kept theirs trained on Bart.

"Tev, Gopa wants you back. You've got to butcher the dac—Taizaburo!" He gaped goggled-eyed at the dead warrior, whose body bristled with arrows bearing

Mikhail's pack markings. "Godwithin!" He stared at Tev's raised bow, cringed, and whirled to plunge back into the jungle. But Dyfid jumped ahead of him, blocking his way.

"What do you think you're doing?" Tev's words slashed as if with a shette.

"Reporting. We need *zerker* protection—our own zerkers."

"No, we don't. We can get rid of the body. It will cause a lot less trouble."

Nakano rolled his eyes. "You can't kill a *zerker* and forget it." He half turned away. Tev drew his bowstring. Nakano gaped, then turned and bolted down the trail. Tev's arrow buried itself in his back.

Nakano was not zerker. He dropped like a stone, hands clawing at the ground as he half rolled onto his side. One hand reached toward them, pleading. But no one moved to help.

Tev lowered his bow. Nakano lay where he fell. His hoarse breathing was becoming weaker, but his terrified eyes were very aware.

Dyfid asked. "What are you going to do about him?"

Tev stowed his bow. "What we have to do." He pulled his shette.

Nakano grunted in terror and tried to scramble away, but Tev swung once and cut the whelp's head half off, jumping aside to avoid the spray of blood. Then he cut his arrow from the corpse, went over to Movich and cut the arrows out of him. Finally he turned to face Bart, his eyes like frozen mud.

Bart went cold. "I won't tell." He would, though; Mikhail should know his lankers were out of control.

Tev sighed. "Not good enough, Bart. You'd do anything to please your father." He cleaned his shette of the human blood, and sheathed it. "I'm real sorry, but you can't even accept you're lanker." He raised his bow.

They were going to kill him. Not the ferts, not the zerkers—the lankers, the servants. He felt dizzy.

Dyfid pushed between him and Tev. "But he's accepted he's lanker. This morning. Hit him pretty hard."

"Don't interfere. We can't afford to let him go."

"Wait," Dyfid moved to stand beside Bart. "He agreed to be my pack brother—and to marry my sister, Wahiri. Once sworn, what can he do? If he betrays me, his pack brother, he's as good as dead. No pack will have him, and he'll be outside the law. Guntor will finish him off within a day."

Silence fell as the men considered this.

"I'll swear," Bart pleaded. "I'll swear."

In the terrible silence Bart could hear Tev breathing. "I don't know. He's a good whelp, but forced oaths don't always hold."

"Tev, look at me. Have I ever gone back on my word?"

"You've never been called on to give it." Tev looked distinctly unhappy. Unhappy, but determined.

"You say I'll do anything for my father. But my father is finished with me." Tev raised his eyebrows and Bart stumbled on. "If you let me live, I'll be loyal to you, not him, and I'll be silent."

As Tev weighed what he'd said, Bart was terribly aware of the smell of blood in the tiny clearing. And his chest prickled in anticipation of an arrow.

A fert coughed and howled in the distance. Already the human-blood scent was drifting through the forest.

Tev waved him down the trail. Bart was given the ildenhorn carcass, and shoved in front of Dyfid and Tev as they jogged toward safety. He wanted to run, but knew two arrows covered his every move. When they came to where the light from the jungle edge made the leaves a bright, almost fluorescent green, Tev stopped and faced Bart. "Swear. Now."

Dyfid came forward with his knife.

"Just a prick," Tev warned. "We can't have any more human blood attracting the blood lusters."

Bart pricked his palm. *"In mingled blood are we born as brothers. In friendship and trust will we endure. In purpose will we survive."* He raced through an oath usually intoned ritually at ceremonies more solemn than marriage.

As Dyfid repeated the oath that would bind them for life, Bart stared at a flowering orange airplant behind Dyfid's head, wondering that the jungle still seemed the same. He barely felt Dyfid's handshake that sealed them into a lifetime partnership.

Tev stepped forward. "Now swear to me."

"What should I say?"

"I swear to obey Tev, before all others. I will be loyal to my lanker brothers, before all others. And I will never speak of this again."

Deeper in the jungle, harsh snarling erupted as several ferts fought over the carcasses of Nakano and Movich.

He babbled the oath.

9

Bright shafts of sunlight stabbed through the puddle glass windows into Mikhail's quarters, illuminating thousands of sharp dust particles and reflecting their light off the grassy sheen in the floor matting. Mikhail squinted. The glare seemed to rub sand into his eyes with every blink. His head ached, his mouth tasted like carrion meat, and all around him he saw Zorava: in the clothes he wore, the arrangement of her pots and pans, and a set of carving knives she'd brought to his home when he'd taken her in. Damn her! He'd been more than fair: he'd made her First Wife. She'd eaten well and seen her daughters married to good warriors. How could she say he had no honor?

Tekiri approached him and curtsied. Behind Tekiri, Verdi crouched over her loom, looking as if she would like to weave her black curls right into the blanket and out of his sight. Fiaranna bustled about, doing nothing, looking determinedly cheerful.

"Get up." He jerked his sash tight, and settled his ceramic lieutenant's disk on his neck. Taizaburo, but his wives' apprehension hurt worse than the sun glare. "You don't have to curtsey in quarters."

Tekiri rose with slow grace. "I wanted to know about Zorava. Are we having her funeral feast?" Her eyes were carefully lowered.

His jaw muscle twitched. A funeral feast—with

his pack members thinking about that damned piece of paper. He glared, hating her for backing him into a corner.

"May I make a suggestion, husband?" She had risen but her head was still lowered.

He nodded, warily.

"We," she gestured toward his other wives, "wondered about having a quiet family ceremony—just ourselves and Zorava's children. It's the wrong time of year for a feast; we don't have any extra food. We all know that Zorava was getting stranger as she got older. Everyone will understand."

Mikhail nodded tightly. He didn't even want a private ceremony, but as lieutenant he couldn't afford to show any sign of weakness to anyone—especially Volf. He headed for the door. How *could* Zorava accuse him of having no honor? They could say she was not right in the head, but in truth she was a bitch. It was she who had no honor, not he.

As he stepped out onto the Promenade Deck, he faced the cut rope where Zorava had hung herself the night before. Taizaburo, what was happening to him? He'd never thought to make arrangements for her body—not even when Tekiri was talking about her funeral. But somebody had taken her away . . . and he didn't really want to know who.

He took a deep breath and marched through the cloisters toward the armory entrance. Let anyone so much as smirk at him, and there would be blood on the deck. A woman working in her planter garden dropped her hoe and curtsied deeply. Damn women for their infernal writing. He stood accused and couldn't fight back.

Two warriors suited in hunting leathers stopped talking as he passed. The back of his neck tightened the way it did in the jungle when he knew he was the prey.

When he entered the safe tunnel to the armory, the flickering shadows from the torches leered at him. The scents of damp rock and old blood clogged his nose. The narrow passage constricted his chest, and the ceiling seemed too low. He ducked his head and walked faster. By the time he got to the door of the armory, his blood was roaring through his veins; he felt strong, ready.

If anyone says anything . . . He nearly ripped the door to the armory off its hinges, took a deep breath and stepped onto the top of the armory stairs. The familiar smell of lamp oil, leather and sweat enfolded him as he looked down on the sand-covered armory floor where he had spent so many years, first training to be a warrior, then proving over and over to his men that he was the best fighter in the pack.

Right now there were only boys and trainers below. Most of the men and whelps were all out gathering wood. He watched Edgar, the training officer of the boys, limp among his charges, organizing their duties for the day. Some were carrying packs to bring in more firewood. Others, stripped to loin cloths, bent and twisted in the warm-up exercises for weapons practice. A group of young boys was gathered around a carcass, learning how to butcher game. Usually he enjoyed watching their eager competitiveness, but today he was struck by the numbers. There were about two dozen in squads of twelve, each commanded by an older boy. There were only six age sorts there, but they outnumbered the living warriors of all ages. He watched. Which ones would survive? There were only three left from his own sort, so that would mean all but eighteen or twenty would die young.

He stomped down the stairs. Some of the boys looked up, then turned away as if stung by daggerjaws. So they'd heard about his "honor." He bore down on them, pretending to glance casually around. In reality, his farseeing eyes were watching their faces, and the tension around their mouths. The boys took their cues from the warriors. If one boy smirked, he was in for it. Down he stalked toward the sandy floor, nerves alive, eyes seeking prey. But no one smiled. Slowly, his breathing eased. As he walked through the boys, he even managed to nod calmly to one of the old warriors who assisted Edgar. But his heart sped up again in the tunnel that joined the armory to the staff room. He flexed his muscles, prepared to act on the first raised eyebrow. Lack of respect could swell faster than a puff mushroom on a hot humid day. As he pulled the door open, he took a deep breath and relaxed—supple but battle-ready.

The other eleven pack leaders looked up, nodded, and went back to their discussions.

Mikhail felt unbalanced. He had been so prepared for a challenge he felt almost cheated. He stalked to his place and sat down. As the other men talked quietly, Mikhail leaned back and fingered his ship chair. It was made of something that felt like bone, but was grey-blue and so hard that, even though it had come from the ship itself, it was as shiny and unchipped as a new ceramic disk. He leaned further back and put his feet on the table—another unscratched marvel of past times. Only this was the color of cooked egg white and supported by four ancient stumps of burl oak. He looked out the window. Instead of panes of puddle glass held together by wooden frames, it was one huge oval sheet half a spear-length high and three spear-lengths long. Unlike glass it bulged outward at the center. A man could lean into the hollow and look straight down to the fertilizer ponds built into the base of the cliff. Above the window were two crossed star weapons—bent sticks, shorter than shettes, sticks that could supposedly stop a thundering keld or pick a fert out of the air in midleap. Humph. Maybe. Or maybe it was just a story. Still, they were made of a strange grey-white metal. He studied the weapons trying to imagine how they might be used.

The door opened. Sair came in followed by the Mother General. The men rose as their leader limped to the head of the table, his bad leg dragging slightly on the floor. But maimed or not, he was a man to be reckoned with. His hair and clipped beard might be grey, but his body was as slim and fit as a boy's. And he still went out on hunts even though the twelve-klat climb down to the jungle left him foul-tempered and mean. He still fought, too. But he fought dirty and always killed his challenger. The Supreme Guardian sat down.

Except for the Mother General, they all sat. Nystra stood quietly beside Sair's chair, eyes properly lowered.

Sair nodded to Mikhail. "Before we start, I want to extend my personal support, and the support of all the Pack Leaders, in your difficult time."

Startled, Mikhail searched their expressions. Every one returned his gaze steadily. There wasn't a hint of laughter or contempt in their faces. His eyes smarted; he managed to nod gravely.

"Now, to work." Sair waved toward the Mother General. "As you know, both food and fuel are in short supply and migration is less than forty days away; so I've called in the Mother General to tell us the women's worries."

The Mother General looked up. She was a tiny

woman with gentle brown eyes and black hair caught severely in a wife's knot. Her fair skin was unmarked by scars, blemishes, or worry lines. Even though she managed the problems of over five hundred women, she radiated none of the anger or frustration of zerker warriors. Nor did she have the sullen strength of the lankers. But as passive as she looked, she still kept all the women in The Home under an iron grip.

"Honored warriors, we have a crisis. The countant's guild has gone into every quarters to find out how much food each family has."

"What the hell!" Ontu swore, baring his crooked, yellow teeth. "Since when did you have the right to go into my quarters?"

Sair glared him into silence.

Nystra bowed respectfully to Ontu. She never lost her look of serenity. "We had to, Honored Warrior. We've never had so many people in The Home. Our crops were good last autumn, but every year we run short of food earlier and earlier in the spring." She paused and slowly looked each man in the eye. Mikhail felt uneasy looking straight at a woman who was not his.

After this most unfeminine of stares she continued, "Most families in The Home are eating their last stores now. We're going to run out of ship food *before* migration, not after. Since you can't hunt during migration, we're not talking about a few people going hungry; we're talking about losing some of the children and aged in every family. Even if we share, we will run out of every scrap of food by the middle of migration. The Daughters of Olarni have a little ship food in their stores, but that is usually reserved for pregnant or nursing mothers and small children." She stopped and looked at each man in turn. "Unless you kill a whole herd of keld between now and the beginning of migration, you will have to make a decision. Will you continue to share your food with your families, and be hungry when you have to fight, or will you reserve all of the food for the fighting men?" She lowered her eyes, curtsied, and left.

Radnor, the other lieutenant, rubbed his scraggly beard. "She always goes for the jugular, doesn't she?"

Mikhail grunted in agreement.

Radnor snorted. "Thank Godwithin, Olarni gave up her rule willingly. If Nystra thought she still had the right to control us, can you imagine the battle of wills? She'd be always bowing her head, and always doing exactly what she pleases."

Sair cleared his throat. "What makes you think she doesn't do that right now?" Korv laughed out loud and nodded. Sair continued. "Anyway, this will have to be a common decision. We can't have some packs denying their families so they can fight and others denying themselves and then being too weak to fight effectively. It would tear the packs apart, to say nothing of killing a lot of people."

A chair scraped on the rocky floor as Ontu jumped up. "What are we standing around here moaning for? Let's hunt. I have children. I can't deny them, but I can't fight well on an empty stomach either."

"Sit down!"

Ontu sat, obedient, but still angry. Mikhail sneered at him. Ontu had to do more than hunt. Ever since his lanker lover had died of infected wounds, his pack's luck had been notoriously bad.

But Sair merely nodded. "I agree. We'll hunt until we drop before migration." Ontu relaxed and inclined his head, grimly. "But game is scarce this spring. We've got to do something else too."

The men sat in silence. Finally Korv cleared his throat.

Korv was the smallest, squarest man in The Home, but he had the rich full voice of a giant.

"What about the ferts?" he rumbled. "In migration they die in heaps right in front of us. Couldn't we somehow manage to get a couple of carcasses before they rot or attract more trouble?"

Every man stiffened.

Radnor snorted. "I'm not tired of living, yet."

Mikhail laughed. Sair glared at him, and he shut up.

Ontu braced his arms against the table. "We haven't the manpower," he protested, shaking his grizzled head. "We'd all end up dead."

Korv leaned forward pounding his hand on the table for emphasis. "And how long will we last if all our cubs starve? Fifteen migrations from now, when you'll want young men at your back, you'll find yourself struggling alone. Then how long will you last?"

Not long. Mikhail hadn't realized how much he had depended upon Bart turning zerker and helping him. He had another son, Kao, who was ten, but he needed a zerker ally, now.

Ontu cleared his throat. "That doesn't solve the problem. The barricades are so long we can barely defend them as it is."

Edgar rose. Mikhail groaned inwardly. Edgar was such an old fool. He had been put in charge of the boys' training because leg injuries had made him useless on the hunt. After years of teaching boys, he had become an insufferable authority. "There is another solution." Edgar's tall body leaned to one side, favoring his mangled thigh and hip. "You could put the whelps on the barricades with the men."

"Never!" Radnor yelled. "That would kill off half of them. We need them as warriors!"

"It wouldn't kill all of them," Mikhail disagreed. "I have some whelps who could manage—Guntor just turned zerker; he's good with his weapons. Dyfid could manage, too. He's steerage and tougher than any other two whelps put together. Why not initiate two or three of the best whelps from every pack? Then we'll have thirty more men on the barricades." Mikhail's stomach tightened. If they agreed, Bart's fate was sealed one way or another. He had hoped to initiate Bart and his other older whelps after the ferts had left the jungle for the Heights. Now Bart would have to take his chances with everyone else. Mikhail wrenched his mind away from his son and listened to the other leaders.

". . . before migration?" Ontu scratched his grizzled head. "With the ferts still in the jungle that's pretty desperate . . . but it might work. I've got two whelps who could probably hold their own, and another two who couldn't, but could provide good backup for zerkers."

The meeting broke into argument.

Sair rapped his heavy silver guardian's ring on the table. "Could those two backup boys survive initiation?"

Ontu rubbed his chin. "I can scout out a couple of safe trees and order them to get there and hole up." He paused. "They'd make it if they went together."

Mikhail leaped to his feet. "No. How can you trust a coward to guard your back? They *have* to go into the jungle alone." He sank back into his chair, wondering if he was helping kill his son. Well, better dead than dishonored.

Radnor pounded the table in agreement, and the rest of the men broke into violent arguments.

Sair stood, waiting for the men's attention. "I agree

with Mikhail. We can't change initiation. Our packs are built on trust, and without respect you have no trust." He looked at his ring and studied the blue stone clasped in the silver claws. "But we do need more men. Right now we mostly use the lankers as stretcher bearers, and weapons or water carriers. That's going to have to change. They may be slow but there's nothing wrong with their aim; we can use them as archers." He looked at Edgar. "Could you take the rest of the whelps from all the packs and organize them to do lanker work, leaving the lankers free to fight? It'll mean that the whelps are exposed, but we can always send them to safety if there's real trouble."

Edgar shot to his feet, then nearly toppled over as his bad thigh collapsed. But he ignored that and held onto the table. "I'll organize them. The warriors'll never have to leave the barricades."

Korv groaned.

Sair grinned. "Your newest wife will just have to wait, Korv."

The men laughed and the mood lightened.

Sair winked at the other men. "Or we could have a competition. Every man who brings in meat during the migration gets one whole watch to spear his wife."

Ontu jumped up. "Good idea." He grinned lewdly. "My pack and I will take every other watch off."

"You have to earn it, grizzle face," Korv yelled. "Five clouts of wine say I get the first watch off." His face showed he considered the bet already won. Ontu flushed.

Sair rapped on the table for attention. "Right! Now we can hunt. Does anyone here want to hunt outside their pack boundaries?"

Mikhail cleared his throat. "I'm thinking about heading down to the iron mounds. That hasn't been hunted since the last time we took the guildwives there for ore."

Sair looked around, saw no objection and nodded. "Any other changes? Good. Make your plans, but wait at least until the day after the Barricade Walk. Otherwise, all our wives will be down our necks" — he looked heavenward— "and our daughters will remain unmarried till Fall."

As Mikhail rose to leave, Sair caught his eye. "Wait a moment, will you?"

Mikhail slumped back into his chair. *What now?*

When the men left, Sair got up and closed the door.

Mikhail tensed, waiting.

Sair sat. "You know we need a unified fighting force during migration."

Taizaburo, here comes the unified Home speech. Mikhail relaxed and nodded. He knew this speech by heart, but he couldn't figure out why Sair was repeating it to *him*.

Sair pounded the table. "Then what in the hell is going on in your pack?" he roared.

Mikhail sat bolt upright. "What are you talking about?"

"I'm talking about trouble. Volf is getting out of hand. Guntor tried to mate with your son last night. Bart refused; Guntor broke the covenant against lanker-zerker fights and tried to rape him."

"Shit!" Mikhail rose half out his chair. "Wait till I get my hands on that stupid son of mine." He paused. "Did Guntor get away with it?"

Sair shook his head. "No, Radnor tore into Guntor. Really enjoyed himself. But, Mikhail, how come you didn't know? I knew all about it before I ate my evening meal." Sair clasped his hands and looked at them sadly. "You're slipping."

Mikhail ground his teeth. Tev would hear about this. He should have been at Mikhail's door the instant the fight started.

Sair continued, "Even Tev is causing trouble. Says it's time I kept my promise to allow the lankers a warrior vote in general meetings. Says you promised him after the last pack war that you would work for it and you haven't."

Mikhail felt an angry heat work its way up his neck. "You know why I haven't worked for it, Sair. The zerkers would never stand for it."

"Still, he says if the lankers can't have a vote, then they should be able to at least form their own packs. Says he'd feel safer if there were lanker packs again."

"Lanker packs! That's what started the last Pack War—when the lanker and zerker packs started fighting. Godwithin, Sair, you were the one who ruled that all packs had to be mixed."

Sair threw himself into his chair and rubbed his grey close-cropped beard. "We're up against it, Mikhail. We have to get more food, or our families will starve. You remember the Pack War, but I remember before it. The lankers always brought home more food than the zerkers."

"Sure," Mikhail sneered. "Roots, fungus, berries."

"Food's food, Mikhail. But there's more."

Mikhail ground his teeth. "What."

Sair looked over his shoulder and lowered his voice.

"The Sangir you saw." He traced the Holy Circle on his breast.

"But, Sair, it wasn't a ghost I saw. It was a person, someone struggling with a squared log. Ghosts don't do that."

"Don't they? We don't know what 'they' do." Sair paused and nervously traced the circle again. "You saw 'them' and look what happened." He looked around and whispered. "A ghostfire burned last night."

"A ghostfire? When?"

"Just before your wife broke her contract. People are wondering if the ghosts drove Zorava mad because you were paying too much attention to them. If that's what really happened, you're lucky they didn't go for you. But they will if you mess with Sangirs any more and you'll end up like Iduaor."

"Iduaor?"

"My great-grandfather. He wanted to follow the keld to the Heights and salt enough food up there for the whole winter. Figured it would stop the spring die off of weanlings and elderly."

"How did he die?"

"You know. He led the Lost Pack—the pack that passed the Sangir totem on the upper Migration Trail, rounded the bend and were never seen again."

Mikhail shivered in spite of himself and followed Sair in the age-old protective sign of the circle. "Don't worry. I don't plan on going past the totem. I figure I can go up a side canyon and climb to where I saw that person."

"No! You can't afford it! Hell, I can't afford it. Your pack has started to fall apart. The women fill the Meditation Chapel every night with their fears."

Mikhail snorted. "Who pays attention to women?" *Or reads their scribblings.*

Sair threw his hands up in the air. "The men who sleep with them, that's who." He pulled his chair up and leaned forward. "Now don't get angry with me. I'm behind you all the way. After all, you helped make me Supreme Guardian at the end of the Pack War. I also remember who fought all comers until my leg wound healed. So before you start bellowing, listen to me."

Mikhail shut his mouth and blew his pent-up breath through his nose.

"This is the hungriest year since the Pack War. I *need* you more than ever. But you've got to do something about 'them.' You've got to lift the curse. Go and see the Holy Circle priestess. Make amends. And drop this crazy idea of exploring the Heights." He held up his hand as Mikhail half rose out of his seat. "I'm on your side, remember. I want you to survive. So go to the iron mounds. But come back without your crazy ideas and with a unified fighting pack— even if you have to kill someone to do it." He rose and leaned forward, shoving his face toward Mikhail. "Clear?"

Mikhail growled an unintelligible reply. Sair had no right to shove his nose in another pack's business. *He had seen someone on the Heights.* He'd show Sair.

But first, he'd go on the hunt. Nothing like a long dangerous hunt to force a pack to rely on each other. After migration he'd climb the Heights, carefully, and during the day when the ghostfires didn't burn. He'd find that person or that squared log. Then they'd believe him. He nodded to his leader.

Sair grinned, came around and embraced him, ignoring the fact that Mikhail's body was as stiff as rock. "Good."

10

Day 22:First Gifter Moon of Spring:
452 Migrations After Landing

Sanda jerked upright. She had nodded off again!
Blinking the sleep from her eyes, she tried to concentrate
on her weaving. Goddess Within, she was tired. Last
night she had huddled on her bed, shaking, unable
to sleep the whole night.

What had happened during the fight between Bart
and Haddim? Had she really turned zerker? Or had
it only been a bad dream? And what about Haddim?
She stole another look at his bedchamber. The door
was shut. She didn't know whether he was already
hunting or still asleep. And she didn't dare ask. But
she didn't think he'd told Assilla anything about last
night, because her stepmother was acting as if this
was just another day. In spite of her fear, another
yawn nearly cracked her jaw. What would Haddim
do when he saw her? She heard Bart's calming tones
again. *He'll probably hope that you're too frightened
to tell.* It had comforted her last night. But today it
made her stomach climb into her throat.

When Assilla came from Brianna's room, Sanda
half rose, startled by her own terror as much as her
concern for her mother. Assilla shook her head in
answer to her unspoken question. "There's no change.

She won't talk, and she won't eat. She's been off
Peace almost since the day Kayella turned, but it
doesn't seem to do any good. I'm afraid . . ." She
trailed off, then walked heavily to the storage room.

Sanda bit her lip. If only she could help her mother—
and Kayella. There must be some way. There had to
be. The song she'd clung to all these years drifted
through her head again. It was part of a cradle song
that was mostly gibberish.

> *Olarni burned with fire and fury.*
> *Anger and hatred her soul did bury.*
> *But she faced this world with courage rare,*
> *And gave her throne into Taizaburo's care.*

Surely that described a zerker. Yet when she'd
questioned her teacher, the older woman had laughed
at her and said Olarni had been zerker, but that when
she had conquered her will she had become a good
lanker woman. She had given up her weapons and
her throne and had retired to the Promenade Deck
where she had five more sons and three daughters.
But there were other songs too, and they never described
Olarni as a woman like Nystra: quiet, gentle and obedient.
They talked of a woman who ruled The Home the
way Sair ruled it now. Sanda's head ached as she turned
the mystery of Olarni over and over in her mind.
Why had Olarni given up her throne after ruling for
ten years? Zerkers never gave up anything. Was saving
the knowledge from the stars so important that a
zerker would voluntarily give up her freedom to do
what she wanted and rule the way she wanted? And
when she gave up her throne, how had she turned
herself into "a good lanker woman"?

Sanda rubbed her aching forehead as she watched

her stepmother head for the storage room. Since times had gotten leaner, she'd lost her brisk efficient air, and dragged through the day as if she were carrying a fifty-kilo weight. When she unlocked the door, she gave Sanda a frustrated look. "At least no one can steal our food any more."

Sanda glared down at her loom. There was no point in denying she was the thief. Everyone in quarters had done that. She swallowed at the thought of food. She was so hungry. But she had never stolen food. She bet it was Ava who had been into the supplies. She watched hungrily as Assilla reentered the wardroom with dried lenpic pieces. She hoped that was for the evening meal; she was tired of fernbone and bitterleaf stew. It filled you up, but never satisfied you. She swallowed. Her stomach ached with hunger. Then, in spite of herself, she yawned. How was she going to keep awake long enough to meet Bart again that night?

Inara came out of the bathing chamber with some freshly washed clothing. Her blue sleeves were rolled up her muscular arms and several strands of black hair curled wetly away from her wife's knot at the nape of her neck. "Volf's wife says that Mikhail is going to climb the Forbidden Heights to prove he saw a man and not a ghost."

"Going up to the Heights!" Assilla circled herself. "If the ancients with their star weapons were driven off the Heights, who are we to try to go back?" She lowered her voice. "How are the wives of his pack members taking it?"

"The women think the ghosts took Zorava as a warning," Inara said darkly, "and that Mikhail is next. I thank the Goddess Within our husband isn't in that pack." She shook out Haddim's wet Assembly Day tunic and hung it on a line strung across one corner of the room.

Sanda slowed her treadle and tried to throw her shuttle with less noise. Tales of the Landing swirled through her head. "But what if he did see someone on the Heights? Maybe it was someone from the Sea Home, or the Steppe Home."

Assilla snorted. "Your head is filled with children's stories. Those Homes probably died out generations ago—killed by the . . . by 'them.' " She made a tiny gesture upward, then gave Sanda a severe look. "Why have you stopped weaving?" Sanda quickly threw her shuttle. Ava entered the wardroom. Her generous mouth was turned down in a sulky pout as she wandered over to the prep table. Hatred stiffened Sanda's fingers.

"Sanda, really, you're weaving like a five-year-old." Assilla leaned over and pushed the shuttle back through, undoing Sanda's last throw. Behind her back, Ava took a furtive look at Assilla, grabbed some lenpic from the bowl, and stuffed it into her mouth.

Sanda jumped up, pointing. "There. She stole some lenpic. It's been *her* all along!"

Her stepmother ran across the room and grabbed Ava by the arm. "Put it back."

Ava chewed frantically, tried to swallow, and gagged. So instead of slapping her, Assilla ended up pounding her back.

Inara rushed out of the bathing chamber. "What's wrong?"

"Ava got caught stealing food," Sanda said. She felt a savage pleasure in getting her stepsister into trouble.

Ava coughed up the fruit.

Inara rounded the table and slapped Ava hard. "How dare you? I'm breast-feeding. My baby and I have gone hungry because you've been stealing all this time."

Ava sucked in a ragged breath. "But I haven't. Honest, I haven't. I'm just so hungry. I only took one slice, and this was the first time."

"Don't lie to me!" Assilla grabbed Ava and shook her violently, whipping her hair over her face. "My own daughter! Stealing food! If this ever gets out, you'll *never* find a husband. *Never*." She shoved Ava toward the companionway.

"But, Momma," Ava cried. "It was the first time, really it was!"

Her mother ignored her protests. "I'm locking you in the head with the laundry. You can start with the Assembly Day tunics, go on to the fiber bed covers, and finish with the nappies. Then tomorrow, if you're good, you can start eating again." She disappeared upstairs, pushing the crying girl ahead of her.

Sanda hummed a little as she wove. *Served Ava right.*

A little while later Assilla reappeared. "Sanda, I'm sorry I even thought it was you," she said stiffly. She twisted her work-worn hands and then wiped them on her apron before taking it off. "And now that I know it's not you, I can leave this food soaking on the table and go up to the Gathering Rooms with Inara. I want you to weave until Haddim gets up and then give him his breakfast."

Sanda nearly dropped her shuttle. Haddim *was* still there. And Assilla was going to leave her alone with him. Sanda's vision narrowed to a blurred section of the warp. She had to get out of here! She couldn't be left alone with Haddim! What would he do? Would he beat her? If only Bart were here to help her. She tried to flog her brain into action. Maybe she could get sick. Yes, that's it.

But before she could make up a convincing story, Assilla cleared the table and left with Inara.

Sanda methodically pushed the shuttle back and forth through the warp. Maybe he would sleep in. Maybe he was too drunk to remember. Yes, and maybe the sun wouldn't set behind the Forbidden Heights tonight, either.

She worked slowly; the shuttle kept sticking halfway across the warp. Finally she gave up, and rested her head against the frame. In spite of her terror, her eyes closed and then the shuttle dropped from her hands. . . .

The door to Haddim's bedchamber creaked open. Sanda started awake. Haddim shambled in dressed in a loose unbleached night robe. His beady eyes were bleary with sleep, and his bony nose seemed sharper and more dangerous this morning.

Sanda found the shuttle and started weaving frantically, but she was more aware of her stepfather than the pattern Assilla had taken such pains to design.

"Where are Assilla and Inara?"

"At the Women's Gathering Rooms." Sanda hit the wrong treadle and kept on going. Look busy. Maybe he'll leave you alone.

"And Brianna?"

"Still in her room."

"So?" He licked his lips as if tasting something awful, went to the water jug and dipped himself a beaker of water. But the whole time his bloodshot eyes never left her. He paced by the fruit bowl, paused and took some lenpic and started eating it as he walked. Back and forth he paced, inspecting her as if he had never seen her before. Finally he came to stand in front of her.

Sanda paid particular attention to her weaving. Goddess Within, she'd lost the pattern. Hastily she threw her shuttle in a reverse of the pattern, concentrating with every nerve in her body. All the time she was aware of the bare feet with yellowed toenails that stood just beyond her loom.

"Who was he?" Haddim demanded, chewing noisily on the fruit.

Sanda looked at him warily. "Who?"

"The man you were with last night."

"I wasn't with a man." She looked him right in the eye, glad that she could be truthful. Besides, if Haddim thought Bart was a man, then her friend would be safe.

Haddim leaped forward, grabbed her hair and jerked her backward. She yelped as every hair on the top of her head strained to come out one by one. She tried to rise to ease the pain, but the bench blocked the back of her knees.

"Who jumped me?"

"I don't know." His breath made her feel faint. It was fresh lenpic underlain by rotten mash.

"Don't give me that, you little nightstalker. He called you by name." He pulled her hair harder and his other hand squeezed her throat.

"Don't know." She choked, struggling to breathe.

The hand on her throat suddenly slipped down into her tunic. She sucked in a great lungful of air. "Well, well, what have we here? All that food I gave you has been growing something." His hard calloused hand cupped her small breast. She wriggled backward, trying to get away, but his grip on her hair chained her to him.

His eyes. She'd seen the look on her mother once or twice when her dosage had been too low; there was a light behind his eyes that made her breathless with fear.

He put an arm around her waist drawing her toward him. She averted her face and he nuzzled her neck. "Sanda," he murmured. He shifted and suddenly trapped her face with both hands.

Panic made her legs weak. "I can't," she whispered. "I can't."

"Of course you can. It's not as if you were my real daughter. Besides, don't you think that you should pay me back for all the food I've given you?"

She tried to wriggle free.

He held her lightly, laughing. "Come on. You've already serviced others, why not me."

"But I haven't!" Her heart was hammering in her chest and her vision had narrowed to his smug mouth. "I was trying to save Mirta Blossom."

He paused. "Mirta Blossom?"

"Yes, my meatcat. Assilla wanted him for stew."

Instead of letting her go, he tilted his head and smiled like a guildwife on the scent of a good bargain. "So I'm to be the first?"

"No!" Sanda shrieked. She braced herself against his arms and kicked him in the stomach as hard as she could. He gasped in surprise and let go. She tried to run, but instantly his powerful hands trapped her waist and she was swept into his arms as he headed toward his bedchamber.

He couldn't. He wouldn't. But she knew he would—whatever it was that men did to women. The bastard. Fear turned to rage. It gathered strength as he entered his bedchamber and blotted her vision of all but his neck. She leaned forward and bit as deeply as she could.

His roar of pain fueled her rage with pleasure. He tried to drop her, but she hung on to his neck with her arms and her teeth. She'd defeated him once; she could do it again.

He jabbed his fingers into her stomach; she fell on the floor, winded. He stood panting over her. The light in his eyes was like the afterflash of lightning. But she was past thought. She struggled to her feet, still gasping for air, and attacked him with her fingernails. When he trapped her hands, she started kicking.

He laughed. "Go to it, Sanda. Fight, kick, scream!" His panting was louder than hers, and he hadn't been winded. "I thought you were zerker. But I was so drunk last night I couldn't be sure."

"No!" Her rage froze, still there, but chilled by fear.

"Yes. You're zerker, and you're mine." He pulled her to him.

She threw away all caution—tried to bite his arms, scratch his face, but he avoided her teeth and tossed her on the bed. She twisted in midair, landed on her feet and tried to dodge around him.

He got her by her tunic, twisted it in a knot and pulled her in. He was laughing, but his forehead was wet with sweat, and the front of his robe tented out strangely. "Nothing more fun than a pretty zerker," he said thickly.

A hoarse voice slipped between them. "Water."

Both whirled toward the door. Sanda's mother leaned against the doorjamb, looking dully at them. Her grey hair hung in a tangled mass down her back, and she still wore the sleeping robe she had put on the day Kayella had turned. The rage drained out of Sanda at the pain in her mother's eyes.

"Shit!" Haddim let go of Sanda's tunic. Released, she jumped off the bed and ran for her mother.

He snagged her as she went by. "You talk about this," he hissed, "and I'll report that you're zerker and see that you get drugged senseless—like your mother."

Brianna gave a hoarse sigh, and crumpled to the deck.

"Taizaburo." He lifted Brianna easily and carried her back to her room. "Get her water."

Sanda poured a beaker and brought it in. Haddim was sitting on the edge of the bed shelf, so she had to pass in front of him. An echo of her earlier rage made her tremble. It was followed almost instantly by despair. There was no hiding now: not from herself, or from anyone else in The Home. She might as well throw herself off the Promenade Deck. She'd never be a scholar, never be loved by her sister-wives, and never be free again. But, even as her mind sank into despair, her hands carefully lifted her mother's head and let her sip the water.

Haddim stroked her waist and hips with one meaty palm. She jerked away, spilling water on her mother's face. He chuckled, then surprisingly moved back. "Do you want to end up like her?"

Sanda shivered.

"You don't have to, you know. I won't tell . . . if you're a good fourth wife. You're one of the powerful zerkers, not one of the crazy ones. You and I could quench your fires in bed. Marry me after wife training and I won't tell on you until you lose control in front of Assilla. After that I'll make sure that you never get more than the basic dose."

"But I'm planning to apprentice myself to Scholar Jihanee."

"Forget that. I'm not waiting that long."

Brianna moaned and doubled slowly into a painful ball.

Haddim swore and started forward. "Assilla," he roared, then remembered that she wasn't there. "Get Assilla," he shouted.

When she hesitated, he grabbed the beaker out of her hands and pushed her toward the door. "Hurry up, Assilla thinks that your mother may be pregnant again, and the healer says that this is probably the last son I'll get out of her." He sent her stumbling across the wardroom. "Move!"

Sanda moved.

Brianna watched Sanda go through slit eyes. Be calm, she told herself. Be calm, be calm, be calm. You didn't play the dying zerker for the last tenday or creep around stealing food with the stealth of a warrior only to lose control now. Be calm. Look sick. They must think you're still frozen, that the medicine has not left your body.

But it was leaving. Although she felt as weak as a kitten, her muscles obeyed her now. She'd had no trouble stalking her disgusting husband and picking the right moment to intrude—when he was obviously guilty, but not yet out of control.

Haddim came back, and awkwardly patted her shoulder. She wanted to scream at him, to throw herself at his throat. The rat turd. So he wanted her daughter, did he? And his promise to keep Sanda's doses low? He'd made the same promise to her, too. And forgot it the instant she angered him. Rage rose singing through her body; she clamped her arms to her stomach to avoid tearing him apart. Be calm, she screamed to herself. Remember Sanda. You can't help her if they give you Peace again. She doubled up more and moaned.

Haddim got up and padded around the room. "Damn," he muttered, "damn."

So he wanted one more son out of her, did he? She'd see about that. Did he really think that she would willingly bear him another child? And then, when Peace finally froze her solid so that she could have no more children, then what? Why, off to the Daughters of Olarni, of course, never to be seen again.

She groaned again. They had to think she was sick so they wouldn't give her any more Peace. If only they hadn't locked the food room, she was getting so weak. But she couldn't give up. She had to warn her daughter—and somehow protect her from Haddim. Brianna gagged and clutched her stomach tighter. She couldn't let him destroy Sanda, too.

The outer door banged open and Assilla rushed into her bedchamber. Her grim face was lined with tension, but her freshly combed and scented hair hung loosely down her back, making Brianna wonder for the thousandth time what went on in the Women's Gathering Rooms.

Haddim pounced on her immediately. "Is she losing the baby? Is she?"

Brianna closed her eyes so no one would be able to see the hate in them.

Assilla spoke in the soothing tones she used when dealing with both zerkers in the family. "I'm not even sure she's pregnant. It could be her change of life, you know."

"No, it has to be another son, it has to." His voice rose.

Brianna risked opening her eyes. Haddim was shaking Assilla who was mentally retreating, using her *enryo* with the single-minded concentration she had achieved through years of practice. Sanda was behind Assilla, eyes wide with the wildness that was stirring and growing with every day that took her closer to maturity.

Haddim released Assilla. "Women," he cursed, and stormed out.

Assilla immediately shut the door behind him. "Sanda, stir up the fire and make some sleepy-fern tea."

Assilla felt Brianna's forehead, then turned. "Sanda, did you hear me? I asked you to brew some tea."

Brianna sneaked a look.

Sanda's face was blank, her eyes were on the floor. Brianna knew what she feared: Haddim was out there.

"This isn't like you at all." She gave Sanda a little shake. "Your mother will be fine. I'm sure it's just a tummy ache. Now go and make some tea."

Liar, Brianna thought. *You think I'm losing a baby and want to get rid of Sanda while it happens.*

Sanda never moved. Her face remained blank.

Assilla put her hands on her hips, thinking. Her jaw was clamped tight—the way she always got when she feared someone was going to defy her—only this time it was Sanda, and not Brianna.

"Do as you're told. I have to look after your mother. If you don't snap to it, you'll have to unlock Ava and do all her work while she makes the tea."

Before she finished speaking, Sanda was out the door and running up the stairs, leaving Assilla staring after her, astonished.

Brianna heaved a long deep sigh and ignored Assilla's fussing as exhaustion and famine weakness claimed her. Soon she'd find Sanda alone. Then she'd tell her daughter the secret. But what was she going to do about Haddim?

11

"Godwithin!" Mikhail cursed.

Bart watched his father take in the sad splintered bones and skulls that had been Nakano and Movich only a short while before.

"Taizaburo, there's two skulls! We're missing Nakano. But who is the other?" He swung around to glare at Gopa. His First Spear shrugged hopelessly. Mikhail's eyes searched out each man in his pack. The zerkers shook their heads in puzzlement. The stone-faced lankers just shook their heads. Mikhail's gaze turned to Bart.

Beside Bart, Dyfid shifted his position slightly and growled almost soundlessly in his throat. Bart gulped, tried to meet his father's eyes and finally shook his head while staring at his father's boots.

Mikhail blew up. "Godwithin, Gopa, I leave you for less than a quarter day, and you fuck up and lose one of our whelps."

Gopa turned purple. "Don't blame me for fucking up. If you were paying attention to your pack instead of 'them' this never would have happened. It's your fault they're dead. Not mine."

Mikhail exploded toward Gopa who met him with equal fury.

"Stop, both of you!" Tev shouted. But it was too late. Mikhail and Gopa were mindlessly pummeling each other.

"Jump them!" Tev screamed. "We've all got to stop them." He threw himself into the fight, followed by Norv and then a half-dozen more lankers. Bart jumped forward to help his father, but Dyfid held him back.

"Don't," was all he said.

The fight was like a log jam bursting in a spring flood; only instead of logs, men exploded from the center of the fight before hurling themselves back. The berserker anger of Mikhail and Gopa more than matched the desperation of the lankers and whelps who were trying to save their Pack Leader and First Spear. Around the whole mess the zerkers prowled. They knew better than to get involved, but they snarled at each other as they picked up their leader's fury.

Suddenly the two men were dragged apart. Each, held by about six or eight lankers and whelps, was turned so that they could no longer see each other.

Mikhail recovered first. He shrugged his men off, and turned to glare at Gopa. "Form up," he snarled. "Gather the remains, and then, by Taizaburo himself, we'd better find meat." He barely waited long enough for Norv to gather up the pathetic remains before he stormed off into the jungle in a towering rage. Gopa followed, sulking dangerously. The lankers fell in quickly. As Bart moved to take his place, Norv followed him.

For the rest of that day, Norv, or Dyfid, or Tev were always near him. Everywhere they went someone was practically breathing down his neck. He couldn't even piss without someone drifting by. At first he was frightened. Then he got mad. He'd given his word and promised his silence. What did they think he was?

✧   ✧   ✧

The deck tilted; Bart straightened his load and stopped for a minute to get his strength back. All he wanted to do was crawl into his bed slot and pass out, but he had promised to meet Sanda, and if he didn't meet her tonight, he might not see her before she went to the upper decks to be trained as a wife.

A young woman passed him. He looked at her under lowered lashes, wondering if she was Dyfid's sister, Wahiri—the widow Dyfid wanted him to marry. The woman was minding two toddlers. Dyfid hadn't said anything about children, but she did have a black widow's sash that outlined trim round breasts. Her glossy black hair looped down over her ears before being knotted at the nape of her neck. She glanced at his tunic, the same as a warrior's, but without any pack insignia.

He waited for her to turn away from a mere whelp. But instead she sank into the deep curtsey of a woman to a warrior.

"May I serve you?" she asked.

Bart turned around to look behind him. She *had* to be talking to someone else. But there was no one there. "I'm only whelp," he protested.

She remained in her deep curtsey. "But today, in the Women's Gathering Rooms, we learned that many whelps may soon be men." She looked boldly up at him and smiled. "Have you found your First Wife, Honored Sir?"

Bart grew inches taller at the "Honored Sir." But his ears started to heat up, too. Could he ask her name? Could he say, "Excuse me, but are you Wahiri? Are you going to be my wife?" Dumb, dumb. He tried to nod wisely and grandly gestured for her to rise. His bundle of firewood shifted and half the wood fell to the deck. He knelt down, gathering the logs frantically, wishing he were klats away. Suddenly a small hand thrust a log at him. Startled, he looked up. She knelt before him, like a wife, and handed him some more wood. He took it, hardly knowing what he was doing. Taizaburo, she was lovely. Each breast thrust firmly against her gown; her neck was a clear light olive color; her lips glistened as if with moisture; and the smell of summer flowers drifted toward him.

She rose gracefully. "I am Rassinna. When you are a man, you would find me a good wife."

He nodded again. Rassinna? Did he know her? Because he couldn't think of anything else to do, he secured his bundle and walked on . . . down the deck . . . and right into Tev.

Tev stopped him with a gesture. "Been trapped into yet another marriage?" he asked, grinning widely.

Bart paused as he settled the wood more securely on his shoulder. "Her?" Had Tev been spying? Did they not even trust him to deliver wood without watching him?

Tev looked soberly over Bart's shoulders. "Poor Rassinna. My wives say she's spent all day getting ready to meet any whelp she could and you weren't even interested in what she was offering."

"But, why?"

Tev shook his head at Bart. "She's desperate: she's a widow, living with her brother and his three wives. They haven't enough food for her and her children, and they've made it plain they want her out. If she marries you, she'll have more food, and she'll be a First Wife."

"Oh." Bart stared stupidly at Tev.

Tev snorted at Bart's confusion and walked on.

Another woman walked by, reminding Bart of his

future. What would Wahiri be like? Would she be like Sanda? He visualized Sanda's intent blue eyes framed by tangled waves of light brown hair. Would Sanda be there tonight? He was desperate for her bright-eyed chatter. He'd even offered to take Gopa's fuel up so he would have an excuse to get to the upper deck.

As he knocked at Gopa's door, his peripheral vision saw Tev stop and talk to Norv, then Tev went on and Norv leaned against a pillar. A woman appeared, then lowered her eyes. "Wood for your household," he said. He had always thought lowered eyes meant respect. But Sanda had made him realize that Gopa's wife was only practicing *enryo*. Somehow it made The Home seem colder.

She curtsied without saying anything and pointed to the ground. Bart dropped the bundle and left, carefully not looking at her. Not respect. Not *enryo*. Only plain prudence. Men just didn't look at other men's wives. Besides, she was old. She must be Gopa's First Wife, for she looked at least fifty.

With Norv watching, he headed obediently for the armory entrance. He got uncomfortable as he approached Rassinna, but saw that she was smiling at another whelp. Before she could notice him, he slipped by, nodded casually to Norv, as if Norv were his friend and not his watcher, and walked into the armory. Then he pulled off his belt and small knife sheath and fiddled with it, waiting to see if Norv followed. Several men from other packs passed him on their way home, but Norv didn't come. He waited until one of Radnor's zerkers approached, then slapped his forehead as if he'd forgotten something. When the man passed, he followed him out. Norv was gone.

He loitered along the deck out of sight of Rassinna

until everyone went in for their evening meal. Then, making sure no one was watching, he slipped into the shadow of the huge square-cut cloister pillars, slid down the crevice, and felt his way toward the ledge. On the loose sandy floor their tracks from last night were already half obliterated by the wind.

His stomach rumbled hungrily. He wished he'd been able to come up after evening stew, but the armory guard never let boys or whelps up at night. Entering the tunnel, he cautiously felt his way into the cave where he lit the lamp with his flint.

Mirta Blossom blinked and squinted in the warm glow. Pulling out a bloody scrap of pinto hog skin he had saved from the hunt, Bart untied the lid and shoved it into the cage.

"Meurrouw." Mirta sniffed the scrap cautiously, then attacked and killed it. Bart pulled out his water gourd, and filled the cracked bowl. Mirta left the meat shreds on the skin and lapped frantically.

Sighing, Bart eased his tired body onto the tattered bed furs. His struggles with Ullan and Guntor, his sorrow over his mother's suicide, a sleepless night, and the murders of Nakano and Movich overwhelmed him. He closed his eyes . . . and slept.

Poke. Black. Nothing. Poke. Sinking down. Warm. Poke.

"Bart." Soft voice. A new fetch? What had happened to Pineor?

"Go 'way," he muttered and pushed his nose into musty furs.

Musty?

"Bart, wake up. I have to talk to you." Sanda's voice dragged him out of his deep sleep.

He sat up, blinking in the dim light, his mouth

tasting foul, his stomach reminding him that he had missed evening stew.

The soft light of the wick lamp picked up the auburn highlights in her hair, but her eyes were red, and her skin was blotchy from crying.

He swallowed. "Did Haddim remember?" he demanded.

"Yes." She twisted her brown sash in her hands.

"Did he remember me, too?" he asked hoarsely.

"No, he thought you were a man." She crouched in a ball and held her knees with shaking hands. "He wants me for his fourth wife," she whispered.

"But he can't! He's your father!"

"Stepfather," Sanda said indignantly. "And he can." She cried harder.

"The bastard!" Bart put his arm around her. Sanda threw herself against him, sobbing wildly. Prickles ran down Bart's spine. This wasn't like his mother, sobbing in misery, or like the youngest boys in training who sometimes could be found crying in frustration or stifled fear. This was a despairing thing that shook her body with ever increasing sobs until the wildness of it frightened him. He wanted to back off from the terror coming from her in waves. At the same time her overwhelming need for him reached out to trap him. He held her tighter.

Sanda responded by burying her head in his chest and clinging to him. He found himself rocking her gently, like a mother might rock her cub. He felt powerful, protective. His spear hardened and shifted in his pants.

Godwithin, not now! But it had a mind of its own. Fire licked his groin as his spear hardened against her buttocks. He patted her back, hoping to distract her so she wouldn't notice. "What happened?" he asked her. The urge to pull her even closer and caress her almost overwhelmed his resolve not to upset her. His balls ached.

Sanda took a couple of long, shuddering gasps as she swallowed the last of her sobs. "First he wanted to know who you were, then, he wanted to . . . he wanted to . . . you know."

"I'll kill him." Bart jumped to his feet half dragging her with him. "I'll kill him!"

"But he's zerker," Sanda protested, wiping tears out of her eyes.

Bart stopped in midstride. Haddim was zerker. And he was lanker . . . forever. He could do nothing. He remembered seeing Tev shoot Movich. Could he do the same—to Haddim? His stomach churned. Not likely. It had taken three lankers to kill Movich, and Bart was alone. He pounded his fist against the rock wall. "Did he . . ."

"No, he didn't." She drew a shuddering breath, "My mother interrupted him." She looked as if she was going to fall in a faint. Bart put his arms around her again. She leaned against his chest and they rested there for a long time.

"Can he really take you to wife?" he asked.

She nodded her head. "He's not my real father, he's my stepfather. Next Assembly Day is the start of my Barricade Walk time. Once he claims me, everyone will assume that, since we live in the same quarters, I've already done wife service."

Her Barricade Walk time. He'd forgotten. Just before they went to the upper decks for wife training, girls were allowed to walk to the barricades with any warriors who might ask them. His stomach knotted at the thought of Sanda walking beside Haddim while the rest of the men nudged each other and made obscene gestures.

"I wish I were zerker, then I'd challenge him for you," he said angrily.

Sanda turned slowly, her red eyes were swimming in new tears. "I wish you were, too."

Bart's heart thudded with ridiculous joy. She wanted him. He thought frantically. There must be some way he could have her and also save her from Haddim. "Didn't you say you were going into training for one of the guilds?"

Sanda sniffled, "I was, before this."

"Go ahead. Don't change your plans. Maybe he'll forget you. A lot can happen in three migrations," Bart said, taking her limp hands in his. "Zerkers can't keep their minds on anything for very long; by then he'll probably have another young wife, and you'll be safe." He stopped.

Sanda was staring at the cave wall, shaking her head slowly.

"Forget it. Haddim said he wouldn't wait that long." She clenched her fist and tried to brush by him. "I don't know if he'll even wait long enough for me to get my wife training."

Bart caught her hand. "What?"

"Let me go! You can't help me, I don't know why I came!" She pulled out of his grip, so he leaped in front of her, barring her way.

"What will he do? Maybe I can help."

Sanda tried to push him aside. He braced himself and caught her gently. She tried to jerk free, but he held her easily. As if something snapped in her she screamed and attacked him, kicking and shrieking with rage. For the third time in two days he tackled a zerker. Sanda pummeled him and hit his chest and wounded shoulder. He groaned but still held onto her squirming shrieking body, his mind numb with pain . . . and confusion.

Sanda? Zerker? Why her? *Why not me?*

Slowly her struggles became weaker and weaker. Tearing sobs replaced her screams. He remembered her throwing up after Ullan had turned—throwing up in fear of her own future. And now it had happened. *And if I married her I might have zerker sons!* But zerker women were dangerous! Hadn't his great-grandmother stabbed his great-grandfather with a carving knife while he lay sleeping? Besides, lankers never got to marry zerker women. They were always snatched up by zerker warriors.

Beneath him Sanda went limp and covered her face with her hands. "Not again," she whimpered, "Not again."

So she knew! Bart suddenly felt an overwhelming sympathy for Sanda. Everything made sense. Her courage, her fear, her desperate loneliness.

Knowing the rage was over, he gingerly let her go. Part of him wanted to pull her close. Another part of him wanted to get out of here, away from her terrifying despair. But her need was so strong that he found himself reaching, and pulling her carefully toward him with his good arm. "There, there, it's all over."

"No, it isn't." Her voice was a hoarse whisper. "It's just beginning. You might as well report me and get me drugged. If you don't, Haddim will."

"Haddim knows?"

"Yes. He said he wouldn't tell and that I could stay undrugged until I lose control in public. Then, if I'm nice to him, he'll make sure I only get the basic dose."

"And if you're not 'nice' to him?"

"He'll drug me into stupidity, like he did my mother."

A vision of Brianna rose in front of Bart, sickening him.

"But it doesn't matter anyway. I've lost control three times in two days, I might as well turn myself in." She rubbed her eyes, reddening them even more.

"But if you've lost control three times already, you'll be worn out. Unless someone does something horrible, you'll be calmer than usual for another week or two."

Sanda pushed away and stared at him. "What do you mean?"

"Zerkers—men zerkers—will build up a rage. Anyone can see it coming. Intelligent zerkers try to drain off the energy, through a long gruelling hunt, drinking themselves blind, or spearing their wives and pack mates." He winced, remembering Guntor's advances. "Or through a rage. If you don't want to be caught, you should try to find ways to drain your energy before it builds to rage level."

Her blue eyes drilled into his with an intensity that convinced him more than anything else that she was truly zerker. But was she a strong one, like his father, or a crazy one, like Haddim?

"Aren't you going to tell?"

He laughed. "Tell what? That I found out you were zerker when we were nightstalking together? I'd like to stay alive. If Haddim didn't kill me, his brothers or cousins would." As if they had a will of his own, the fingers of his left hand traced the line of her collar bone. With warrior determination he kept his eyes from dropping lower—to the way her gown draped slightly over her high breasts.

She grabbed his hands. "Bart, help me. Tell me everything you know about how zerkers control themselves. I don't want to be drugged."

"But I did tell you. Of course every man, whelp and boy learns to read the signs, so if a warrior is getting snarly, we all stay away from him, and treat him with careful courtesy if we have to talk to him."

"Women won't do that. They'll just call for more Peace."

Bart nodded toward the tattered bed furs. "Let's sit down and I'll try to think." When she settled on the middle of the furs he sat beside her and put an arm around her shoulder. "Sair is the most controlled of all the zerkers, but that's because he's got nine wives and scuttlebutt has it that he uses all of them every day. Although I find that hard to believe, he does take every opportunity to go to the upper decks."

"Haddim said he'd quench my fires in bed, but I feel like throwing up when he gets within three paces of me."

Bart felt his arm stiffen. "Do you feel like that with me?"

She shook her head slowly, watching Mirta prowling in his cage. "You're the only good thing in my life." She sighed. "What else can you tell me?"

"Haddim gets drunk, but you know that. Then, there's my father," he said hurriedly, "and he usually keeps level by killing more game and working harder than any other man in his pack. I've seen him fall asleep while taking off his harness in the armory. You could try that. Work so hard you're exhausted all the time. Besides, once summer comes, zerkers calm right down. This is the worst time of year."

Sanda squirmed upright. "Why is this the worst time of year?"

"I don't know. Maybe it's because we're all hungry. During the first and second harvest, when everyone has more than enough to eat, zerkers can be almost placid." He laughed ruefully. "But it could be something else, too. After all there's a lot I don't know . . . as I found out today."

"Like what? Is it about zerkers? If it is, I have to know." She twisted in the circle of his arms to face him.

"It's about lankers and zerkers, and I can't tell you." At her hurt look he said, "I'm oath bound. I can't speak of it to anyone except my lanker brothers!"

She stared at him transfixed, her eyes wide, and her breath coming in shallow gasps.

"What's wrong, Sanda. Are you all right?"

"Lanker brotherhood! Are they starting that again? Goddess Within, are we heading for another Pack War?"

"Pack War? What do you know about a Pack War?"

"I know what happened. I'm already starting to study The Waterfall Home Chronicles. They have the histories of Nystra's time, and Rodetta, her predecessor's time."

"Histories? You know what happened?" He jumped to his feet in a ready position. "Tell me!" Seeing her shrink from his fists that he had unconsciously jabbed at her, he dropped to his knees and took her hands in his. "Please tell me. The older warriors know, but they won't talk about it."

"The chronicles call the last one the Marysa War because it started over a woman called Marysa. When her lover killed her husband, the husband's brothers attacked the lover's lanker pack . . ."

"Lanker pack! There's no such thing!" Bart shook his head.

"No, there were lanker and zerker and mixed packs then. The rule that enforced mixed packs was brought in by Sair at the end of the War to try to cement the two kinds of warriors together."

Lanker Packs. Bart's mind was reeling. How could the lankers cope without zerkers? Then he remembered this morning. Without zerkers Tev had managed to kill eight ildenhorn, as well as a zerker, a stupid junior whelp and very nearly himself.

Sanda continued, "Anyway, in the fight several men were killed. When the Zerker Brotherhood took sides against the lankers the war was on."

"But there is no Zerker Brotherhood!"

Sanda shrugged. "There was then. Anyway the war lasted five weeks. During that time the women and children put up the migration window bars and locked themselves in their quarters. The healer and her apprentices took their food and their children and went to the upper artisan decks where the stonemasons rolled the war stone into place. The first summer crop rotted in the fields because the warriors stopped protecting the steerage hands. By the end of the war fifty-seven men, almost a quarter of the warriors, were killed. Under Sair, the new Supreme Guardian, the packs and steerage worked themselves almost to death trying to bring in enough food for the next winter. There was no midwinter feast that year and over three hundred women and children died of starvation before the next keld migration."

"And the Zerker Brotherhood?" Bart asked, more interested in the men than the women.

"I forget, no, now I remember. They were broken up. The Samur society was formed in its place and it had to have both lankers and zerkers as equal members."

"Well, they're not equal now." Bart rose and started to pace the tiny room. "A month ago everything was simple and straightforward. Now I feel as if I'm climbing a rotting dactyl net. And when it collapses I'm going to die—of stupidity."

"I felt that way when I started reading the chronicles. Everything seemed different . . . more complex. But I stuck with it and learned. Mind you, I had Jihanee to help me." She bit her lip thoughtfully. "Why don't you find someone who knows a lot to help you?"

Tev's knowing eyes, capped by bristly eyebrows, drifted through Bart's mind. But he dismissed the idea immediately.

"Who were you thinking of?" she prompted.

"Tev, but I can't ask him. He thinks I'm so stupid he nearly . . . he almost . . . never mind," he snapped. His pacing speeded up.

"At least you can ask someone. You aren't the first whelp who didn't turn zerker. Up to now I've always learned things by asking teachers for the answers. Unfortunately, the only undrugged zerkers lived hundreds of years ago, so I can't ask anyone." She sagged against the rock wall. "For a moment you made me forget, but even if I keep myself tired, I still have to face Haddim, or he'll tell—maybe he'll tell anyway."

Bart almost stumbled as an idea hit him. "I have it. You can run to steerage. In steerage, women can marry or not as they please. After three months Haddim will have no claim on you and even if you lose control and let them know you're zerker, no warrior will want you; for you'll have the double taint of being untrained, and being a runaway. Then, after I'm initiated, I'll marry you."

"Steerage." Her lips curled in contempt.

"It's that or Haddim," Bart said simply.

Her face paled. "But don't they starve down there?"

"I'll try to sneak food to you while I'm a whelp, and after initiation I'll feed you openly."

"But my studies. The Mother General has offered me a scholarship!" She took up her sash and started twisting it, thinking. "Maybe I could keep myself tired and stay in the upper decks as long as possible . . ."

"Once you turn up there, I can't help you. You'll be drugged, locked up, and claimed by a warrior, probably before the watch is over."

Her shoulders sagged. "But steerage! What if I turn there? What will they do?"

"Steerage can't afford Peace, and I won't make you take it." There, he'd said it. Taizaburo, what if she were one of the crazy ones? What had he done?

Sanda sighed and squared her shoulders. "There's no other way, is there?"

He shook his head and pulled her closer. "Let me look after you," he said, pushing his reservations behind him. "But you'll have to run to steerage first. And you'll have to stay there unmarried for three Gifter months. After that Haddim will have no claim on you, in fact he'll probably pretend he never knew you. Then I can bring you up to my quarters." He ran his hands down her back. Fire burned through his spear; he wanted her. She was his, wasn't she? And if she was going to run to steerage, honor no longer mattered, to her or to him. He kissed her hair. The warmth surging through his groin drove away his exhaustion. He tilted her head back to kiss her, but she wriggled out of his arms and danced around him.

"I'm free, I'm free, I'm free. On my Barricade Walk Day, I'll walk right down to steerage and stay there." She gave him a brief hug and whirled around again. "I can't wait to see Haddim's face when he realizes I'd rather go to steerage than wed him. But . . ." She stopped, thinking. "I mustn't lose control before then. So I'll have to get tired." She turned and darted away into the dark tunnel.

He tore after her, remembering to duck his head this time. She was already half up the cliff. He caught a calloused heel. "What are you doing?"

"I'm going to climb until I'm exhausted, then I'm going to climb some more, and tomorrow, I'll be too tired to rage." She jerked her heel away and flitted out of sight in the darkness chanting, "I'm free, I'm free, I'm free."

Bart was left staring at a damp rock face. His spear wilted slowly, but his balls continued to throb.

12

Day 30: First Gifter Moon of Spring:
452 Migrations After Landing

"This is your first day of Initiation." Nystra, Mother
General to the Women of The Home, smiled down
at the girls sitting in two disciplined rows in front of
her. Her blue, smooth-weave gown shimmered from
the early morning light that slanted down from the
Assembly Hall windows. "From now until your Thirteenth
Sort Ceremony in two tendays you will be free from
school and from your household chores." She smiled
and fingered her gift necklace: three red stones for
living sons, two blue ones for living daughters. "Until
you make your life choice, you are free to go where
you like in The Home: to the Guildhalls, to any quarters
on the Promenade Deck and even to steerage. And
you may talk to anyone you like: anyone who might
help you decide whether you wish to live your life
as a quarters-wife, a guildwife, or a steerage field
hand." A couple of the girls gave muffled snickers.
The Mother General paused; the girls quietened
immediately. "Your initiation has another purpose,
too." She smiled warmly at them. "This is also your
Barricade Walk time."

Sanda sat tiredly on her mat. She'd been so afraid

191

of her reactions to today that she had climbed up and down the cliffs all night. Now she could hardly stay awake. Goddess Within, she prayed silently, let it work, let me not lose control until I am safe in steerage. Let the other girls go to their Barricade Walk. Let them talk and giggle with the warriors. *And let Haddim wait for me in vain.*

She looked around the Assembly Hall, waiting for the farce to end. She was in the second row of sixteen girls who sat facing the dais. Around them and behind them was a wide expanse of worn stone where more than five hundred adults and a thousand children crowded in for Assembly Day ceremonies. On either side, the walls rose ten meters to an arched roof blackened by centuries of torches used to light the hall on gloomy winter days. The voice of the Mother General echoed thinly in the emptiness of the hall as she described the life choices open to the girls.

Beside her Ullan shifted to a more comfortable position. She was sullen, weighed down with bandages and heavy wooden bone-splints. Was she mourning the end of her dreams, too? She'd wanted to be a potter as intensely as Sanda had wanted to be a scholar. And now both their dreams were impossible: guilds did not allow zerkers.

On Sanda's other side, Gena, the dusky steerage girl, sat twisting her sash. Sanda wished she could trust Gena enough to ask the questions that raced around and around in her head. But she couldn't. Not until she'd made her choice. Not until she was safe from Haddim. When she thought about him she could feel an increasing unease. Having Ava in front of her didn't help either.

She glared at her stepsister, wanting to reach out and break her neck. Brianna was still in bed. Kayella was still in sickbay, ill with a bad reaction to Peace. Goddess Within, Sanda whispered. Let me pay Ava back. Someday, some way let me pay her back.

Ullan started, and turned to stare. Sanda realized she'd been muttering aloud. She lowered her eyes and waited as Nystra lectured them on their behavior when meeting a warrior. As the rest of the girls got more fluttery, Sanda sank deeper into depression. She'd never be a scholar. While her friends were trained as wives, she'd be grubbing in the fields, waiting three Gifter months—a hundred and fifty days— until Bart could take her back to the upper decks. Fear lanced through her. What if he didn't come? What if he was killed during his initiation?

Nystra caught Sanda's eye. "You have three choices," she concluded, seeming to talk directly to Sanda, "and in the next three days you will visit each of the places you might choose." She grinned. "Today, you will go through the men's armory . . ." The girls giggled self-consciously and a few nudged each other. As they did, Sanda caught a whiff of crushed lenpic flower. ". . . to get to steerage where you can learn about them and, if you wish, choose their life."

Whispered denials erupted around her.

"Tomorrow, you will visit the guild decks." She looked around at the girls who were fluttering like newly emerged moths, drying their wings. "Are there any questions?" Nystra smiled gently at the whispering girls. Her eyes paused on her daughter, and the smile slipped for a moment; then her mouth curved again, but the smile was gone from her eyes. When no one asked a question, Nystra raised her arms. Obediently Sanda assumed meditation posture, straight back, hands on knees, eyes closed. But she couldn't relax into the familiar chant. The step she was taking was too terrifying. She didn't know anything about steerage. As she waited in her tired body, she felt as if she were being watched. When she opened her eyes a slit she saw Ullan's large brown eyes riveted on her. Nystra cleared her throat. Sanda hastily closed her eyes and endured until Nystra brought the silence of the meditation to an end with the familiar words:

"Sisters, let us think without anger," Nystra intoned. "Let us act without malice. And let us listen to our Goddess Within."

Sanda pretended to surface with the rest of the girls. But while her friends stretched, and smiled at each other, she stared straight ahead, pretending she didn't still feel Ullan's eyes on her. When the Mother General made the sign of the holy circle, she rose with the other girls and curtsied to Nystra as she left.

Sanda's friend Jessance headed toward the door where Teacher Illana waited for them. "Come on, Sanda," she cried, smoothing her soft, silky hair with tiny gestures. "I'll save a place for you in line."

Sanda started to follow, then felt a strange stab of resentment. She looked back and saw Ullan sitting all alone, cradling her cumbersome set of splints.

"Come on." She went back and held out her hand to help her friend up. "We'll be right with you," she called.

Jessance winced and signalled frantically with tiny negative gestures that she didn't want anything to do with Ullan.

Sanda stared. These were Ullan's friends, too. And none of them had seen her since she'd broken her wrist. *And turned.*

"That's all right, Sanda," Ullan huffed, "I don't want to go with them anyway." She turned away, but Sanda could see the tear sheen in her eyes.

Sanda tucked Ullan's good arm in hers. "Let them run down to the armory like meatcats in heat. We'll take our time." She glared at Jessance. Bitch. So that's what she could expect from her friends when they learned she was zerker, too.

Jessance tossed her hair and ran after the other girls who stifled their breathless chatter and demurely followed their teacher into the torch-lit tunnel to the armory. Sanda trailed behind, knowing she'd never trust them again.

At the end of the corridor was a small, sturdy door made of fire-hardened burl oak wood. Teacher Illana pulled the heavy braidvine that hung beside the wrought-iron hinges. A muffled clang drifted through the door.

With a groan from its heavy metal hinges, the door swung open. The old watchguard's scar twisted as he grinned and stepped back to allow the girls into the armory. Sanda took one last look behind her. When she came up here again it would be as a visitor, on feast days—until Bart claimed her.

The rank odor of stale sweat surrounded her. She choked, then tried to breathe shallowly. They were on the landing of a narrow stairway near the roof of a huge cavern that was almost as big as the Assembly Hall. The stairway, which had no railing, descended steeply toward the far corner of the armory. The girls stood at least twenty meters above fifty or sixty young men who practiced with their weapons on the soft, sandy floor. Light from dozens of arrow slits caught the twisting and darting figures in golden shafts of sun and dust.

As the girls filed in, the young men froze and watched, their bare chests heaving from recent exertion. Most wore only loincloths that emphasized their swelling muscles. Sensuality reached up and immobilized the girls.

Old Bridd waded forward to glare down at the men below. "What are you gaping at! A fert could have killed the lot of you in the last ten heartbeats." He puffed up and grinned at the awed girls. "Not a real warrior there," he said.

The young men lunged at each other. The girls leaned forward to watch, eyes glittering.

Ullan's fingers dug into Sanda's arm. "They're so lucky," she said tightly, "I turn zerker and all my friends act as if I've got jungle rot. They turn zerker . . ." She jerked her jaw at the men below, "and they're heroes."

Sanda could only nod. She wished she could edge away from Ullan, for the girl's anger was awakening her own, and she couldn't afford that, not today, not until she was safe in steerage.

Bridd cleared his throat. "Fourteen migrations ago the ferts actually got into the armory."

Sanda knew that the steerage people sheltered in the armory during migration. "What happened to the field hands?"

Bridd raised a grizzled eyebrow. "Got most of them to the Promenade Deck before the ferts broke through." He hawked and spat over the edge of the platform. "Lost about twenty prime field hands, though."

"Men?" Sanda asked.

"Don't remember."

She shivered. Maybe Haddim wasn't so bad. He did promise that he wouldn't tell, and that he'd keep Assilla from giving her more than the basic dose. Besides, if she married him, she'd be able to help her mother, too.

Her resolve weakened.

"Look at the fert head!" Ava cried, her sallow skin flushed with excitement.

One muscled, black-haired warrior carried a long wooden shette in his right hand. Another slight man held a battered fert head in his hands. He walked behind the dark warrior and drove the head at the dark-haired warrior as hard as he could. The dark-haired warrior wheeled and crouched in one motion to slash at the head, knock it aside, and hit it again.

Sanda gasped. He was fast! His standing image was still in her eyes when he had finished his last stroke. Could she be that fast?

"That's Guntor, one of Radnor's stepsons," Ava said importantly. "He's . . ." she looked down and giggled. "I just know he's going to claim me."

Guntor tossed the battered head at his slender partner and waved to the girls.

Ava waved back, daringly. "See, I told you so."

Sanda ignored her and searched the armory. She had hoped to see Bart: she was terrified she would see Haddim. But all she saw were thirty or forty bearded men dressed in Assembly Day tunics, looking over the girls and talking in low voices. They didn't have to show off. As senior warriors, they had first choice. The men on the floor would marry older widows, as their first and second wives. Young girls only went to established families. Her lips curved in a smile. Her only regret was that she wouldn't see Ava given to a man she didn't want.

"Come along, girls, it's time we went to steerage." Teacher Illana had to push the first two girls to get them started down the stairs. Sanda followed, feeling unsettled—glad that Haddim was not there, but bitterly disappointed she hadn't seen Bart.

They crossed the armory floor, entered a narrow,

smoky tunnel and filed through a thick door into another cloister. Fresh spring air cleared their nose of smoke, damp, stale sweat and crushed lenpic. Sanda looked around. Two fully armed warriors guarded the door. They carried spears. A bow hung from quivers filled with arrows while their belts seemed to bristle with knives and shettes. Men never carried weapons on the Promenade Deck. She couldn't understand, but the addition of a few bits of wood and steel made the men seem alien, and dangerous. She looked down the well-worn steps to the valley. The pillars were more like walls and the spaces between the pillars were barely a meter wide. And down at the first turn in the trail, two other armed men leaned against the walls talking— to Haddim.

Sanda looked away from the man who planned to claim her. Was it worth risking death to run from him? Could she trust Bart to claim her when she was disgraced by her stay in steerage?

Ullan patted her arm. "Calm down. We're almost there," she murmured.

Now what did Ullan mean by that?

"Won't the dactyls get us?" Ava asked the warrior, making eyes at him at the same time.

Gena, the tanned steerage girl, laughed contemptuously. Ava flushed. Gena said, "The spaces between these columns are so narrow a dactyl would foul its wings." She shook her head at the girls. "I come up here every day to come to school, and I don't have two warriors to protect me." She turned her sturdy body and started walking down the stairs. One of the warriors took his place in front her, the other waited for the class to go by. Ava bit her lips angrily, glaring at Gena's back. Somehow Sanda knew that Gena was now going to get special attention from her stepsister. She didn't envy the poor girl.

Ullan poked Sanda, and she started forward. The girls were ahead of them now, clinging to the cliff wall in fear of the un-netted spaces between the cloister pillars. Sanda ran to catch up, and as she left Ullan, her anger and fear seemed to fade and exhaustion made her mind dull again. Dull and safe. Goddess Within, was she picking up Ullan's feelings—the way zerkers did? She hurried faster.

"Wait for me."

Sanda waited, unwillingly, as Ullan and the boiling emotions she awakened came closer. It was true; she could feel Ullan's emotions, but could Ullan feel *hers*? She hurried after the other girls, fear hammering through her fatigue.

The line of girls descended steep steps carved into the cliff within the fortress-like cloisters. Sanda glanced back. Her stepfather was no longer alone. The older warriors were filing out of the armory and following Haddim down the steps cut into the cliffs.

Sanda faced forward and concentrated on the journey. Down they climbed. Twice they entered darkened tunnels cut into the cliff. In the center of each tunnel, the cloister narrowed to a meter wide, and strong iron-bound doors stood hinged open.

How did the ferts get by all this?

Four times the stairs twisted into the cliff, then back down in the opposite direction. The girls descended more and more slowly. Sanda could see some of them were actually panting from the unaccustomed activity.

When they came to one of the arrow slits, she looked up. The Promenade Deck of the Starboard side of The Home was now a line of tiny black squares set into the grey bands of the cliff. The women tending their vegetable planters were invisible. Involuntarily, she looked back at Haddim; he smiled greedily. She jerked away. She wanted to run down the steps, through the valley, onto the Migration Trail. Run and never stop. But her tired body numbly plodded on.

Finally the stairs ended at the valley floor. The cloister widened and became large and square-cut, like the Promenade Deck. The girls, no longer forced into single file, clustered against the cliff, away from the open fields.

Sanda buried herself in the crowd, as far away from Haddim as possible, and stared at the valley. After a life lived in small rooms off the Promenade Deck, she felt unbalanced to see flat ground extending in front of her for almost half a kilometer. The land looked different down here. Tiny lines of black she had seen from the Promenade Deck turned into irrigation ditches, black with water and plowed furrows of soft, dark brown earth. Further up the valley men and women in brown undyed, fiber-cloth garments bent over, planting seeds and carefully covering each one. She watched, mesmerized. Could she live like that? As they worked, their scrawny arms and legs moved with an almost sleepy rhythm. Every once in a while one of them would straighten and stretch their backs.

"Look," Jessance whispered, her eyes wide with delicious shock. Sanda followed her pointing finger. A hugely pregnant woman staggered through the fields carrying water to the hands.

"Look at what?" Gena snapped.

Jessance smoothed her dress, almost caressing her own slender body. "She's allowed herself to be pregnant in spring. Now she'll probably have a famine-stupid child." She took a black lock of her fine hair and pressed it back behind her ears in a tiny precise gesture.

"My mothers take womb loss every month during the hungry times." The girls around her murmured in agreement.

The steerage girl flushed. "Womb loss grows in the jungle. How do you expect us to get any?"

Ava chuckled. "Do what all steerage women do," she suggested. "Warm a whelp's bed. Then promise him more if he'll bring you some of the herb."

"You bitch!" Gena seized Ava's hair, but before she could do anything one of the warriors grabbed her hand. Immediately Ava curtsied, and smiled contritely up at the warrior.

"Apologize," Teacher Illana snapped.

"I'm so sorry," Ava said, gazing dreamily up at the warrior, whose face softened and relaxed in an admiring smile. Gena stomped off down the deck.

Jessance giggled to get some attention, then wrinkled her nose. "Does it smell this bad all the way out to the barricades?" she asked, lifting her skirts as if to protect her dainty figure from the sharp midden smell that drifted down from the fertilizer ponds.

Teacher Illana briskly herded her charges along the cloistered walk. "It's only fertilizer; you'll forget all about it when you're talking to your warrior."

Now that they were more in the open, the guards walked outside the cloisters, shettes held loosely in their hands, and eyes scanning the sky for dactyls. Sanda risked a look behind her. Haddim was leaning against the cloisters watching. When he caught her eye, he smiled and bowed slightly.

She practically dived after the girls ahead who were disappearing into a doorway carved into the base of the cliff. She crowded up against Ullan, her heart hammering with fear. As her eyes grew accustomed to the gloom she realized that it was set up like the

Assembly Hall on the Promenade Deck. But where their Assembly Hall was spacious and airy, this one barely reached a meter above their heads. Instead of smooth polished walls, you could see the chisel marks around and above them. Not only that, but part of one wall was covered by a rack of about forty straw-filled coops. Inside the coops ship hens clucked as they watched the girls.

Sanda sneaked a quick look behind her and breathed a sigh of relief; Haddim had not followed her in. Soon . . . soon she'd be free of him. She moved to the far side of the cave, away from Ullan. The palms of her hands were cold and clammy.

"Welcome." An old woman smiled at them, but her voice was tremulous and just a little defiant. She was narrowly built, thin, and weathered like a warrior. Her grey hair was plaited loosely down her back. "I'm Zella, First Woman of Steerage."

The girls watched silently. She was so thin her cheeks had sunken in. And they were flushed. She knew what the girls were thinking and didn't like it.

"You could choose to come with us, you know."

Ava snickered.

The woman braced herself and lifted her chin. The flush on her face turned to angry red blotches that spread from her cheeks down her neck. "I know what you're thinking. You don't like the smells down here. You think we're scum." She stopped and tried to look at every girl the way the Mother General did. As she did, each girl smirked or looked down. No one met her eyes or smiled back. Zella gave up halfway through. "You may think we're trash, but we're also a refuge. You may laugh at us today, but in a few years when you are a battered wife, or a widow whom no one wants, remember we take in all."

"The Daughters of Olarni take in all, too," Jessance corrected her primly.

The steerage woman shook her head firmly. "No, they don't. They only take in women who have gone through the change in life. And then they lock them in the upper decks so the women can never see their families again. We take *all*. And you can see, talk to, or marry anyone you choose. Think about that if you find yourself claimed by one of the crazy zerkers—the ones who beat and torment and sometimes even kill. Then you may, as I did, leave the upper decks for steerage."

"Were you a widow who no one wanted?" Ava asked maliciously.

The nut-brown woman grimaced then looked at the other girls as she answered. "No, I was a fifth wife. I had a place. But my sister-wives were already finding it hard to feed everyone in quarters when I arrived. They didn't want me; my warrior beat me, and I was glad to leave. But if you come down here, you won't be beaten. The work is hard, but you may find happiness that your meditations only hint at. For one thing, you can marry whom you wish."

Sanda raised her hand, the way she did in class. Zella nodded. "Do many steerage people die in migration?"

The woman's eyes widened. "Whatever gave you that idea?"

"Well, Bridd said they lost twenty field hands fourteen migrations ago."

Zella's eyes narrowed and her voice was bitter. "Our noble warriors thought migration was over and left the walls." Her lips thinned. "It wasn't."

Ava stepped forward, looking at the hens. "How

come you have food here?" she challenged. "We're hungry on the upper decks."

Zella gave her a long look. Her fists clenched and unclenched at her sides. "We're hungry, too. Those are breeding hens." Her voice got bitter. "The guards take all the eggs away every morning, and we don't see any of them."

Ullan cleared her throat. "If anyone chose steerage, who would feed them?"

"Every family would give a little. We'd feed them until they were assigned to a warrior's plot, and could earn their own food."

Sanda stepped forward. It was time to make her choice. Her heart hammered so loudly she could hardly hear Ullan speaking.

"Tell me." Ullan's voice shook a little. "Do you take in everyone?"

Sanda's mind did a tumble. Could Ullan be thinking of coming down here, too? That would be wonderful. They could still be friends—maybe even sister-wives. Perhaps Ullan could still learn to be a potter. Not like the guildswomen, but still, she'd spotted a stubby pot in a corner that had never been made on the upper decks.

Zella smiled warmly at Ullan. "Of course, child. Didn't you understand? We're a refuge, if you wish to come here, you may." Sanda took another step forward. Now, she had to declare herself; now, before she lost her nerve.

Gena hurried up to Zella and whispered something in her ear. Zella looked at Ullan again, her smile gone. "But we don't take zerkers." Sanda froze in the act of shouldering her way past Ava.

"But you said . . ." Ullan gave up a little dry whimper and turned her face to the wall. Ava snickered.

"You said everybody," Sanda snapped. She heard the snarl in her voice and felt fear freeze the breath in her lungs. *I can't lose control, I can't.*

"Well, almost everybody," Zella answered. "But not zerkers—oh, we do have a few zerker men, crippled before they became warriors, or cast out of the upper decks for other reasons, but they live in tiny caves by the barricades and keep to themselves. They know that if *we* cast them out, it's the jungle, alone."

Sanda tried to make her breath come more slowly, but the vision of Haddim's wet lips almost made her throw up.

Gena tugged at Zella's sleeve. "What about Elrida the Crazy? She was zerker, wasn't she?"

The First Woman gave Gena an exasperated stare and did not answer.

"What happened?" Ullan demanded. "Did you send her back?"

"We couldn't. Once a zerker woman comes down here, the Mother General won't let her back."

Sanda sagged against the wall. "What about steerage women who turn zerker?" she whispered.

Zella shrugged. "We don't. Our blood isn't tainted."

"But if she did? Why wouldn't you just drug her?" Ava asked

"We could never afford the cards. I guess we could turn her over to the zerker field hands who live near the barricades. But we wouldn't have her in our community."

Sanda's eyes blurred. Why hadn't Bart told her?

Ullan turned back. "So what happened to Elrida?" Sanda saw that she was holding her cast, and rocking. Ice slid into Sanda's stomach and she forgot Haddim in the face of immediate danger. Ullan's eyes looked like Brianna's had that night three years ago—when she'd tried to skewer Haddim with a fire poker.

Zella hesitated, then looked away from Ullan. "Elrida was crazy. She took over one family quarters just for herself. She ordered people around, and stole food from other quarters." She sighed. "We simply couldn't handle her. People tried to explain our ways, but she wouldn't listen. Finally she went too far. She took up with the guards on the barricades and while they were having their little parties, a flock of dactyls invaded the fields. They injured dozens of us and carried off two children before the warriors came to our rescue. That night someone took bricks and mortared her into the cave she had seized."

Ullan gave a little gasp and started rocking faster. "But I'm not like Elrida. I'm not one of the crazy ones."

Zella looked curiously at Ullan. "We can't afford to find out," she said firmly.

Ullan glared at Zella. "Trapped," she muttered thickly. "Trapped."

Sanda wanted to go to her friend, but the unhappiness that was radiating off Ullan only made her own bitter disappointment more painful. She couldn't handle Ullan's despair and her own terror as well.

Ullan took a step forward. "What right have you to bar zerkers? You're just a dirty field hand."

The girls around Ullan edged away. Ava turned and ducked out—to get one of the guards probably. Terrified that she would be discovered as well, Sanda slowly backed away from Ullan until she leaned against the rock wall. Several more girls ran for the door.

Ullan took another step forward. With every word her voice rose and gained more power. "You said you were a refuge for all. You said you take the beaten and the unwanted. But you won't take the people who really need refuge, the people who are imprisoned, locked up and controlled by Peace. Oh no, you're too nice for that, aren't you?"

The last girl bolted out. Sanda pressed herself against the rock. Ullan's rage reached out to her and revitalized her. But she couldn't, she wouldn't let herself go. Ullan advanced on Zella who had backed up against the hen coops.

"Now, child," Zella's voice shook, "don't get angry."

"Don't get angry!" Ullan lifted her heavy splints like a club. "I'll show you angry!"

Sanda couldn't bear to see Ullan hurt again. She rocketed across the room. "No!" She grabbed Ullan and pulled her away from Zella. "The Peace," she whispered urgently. "Remember the Peace! Remember Brianna!"

Fear flared in Ullan's eyes. Sanda pulled the unresisting girl further away from Zella. Fear she could deal with. It made you want to shrink within: it didn't spawn rages.

Zella ran for the cave entrance and collided with Teacher Illana. Seconds later one of the guards raced in.

Ullan whimpered in Sanda's arms. "No," she whispered, "not again."

"Now, now, Ullan," Teacher Illana soothed in a soft monotone. "Let me give you some more Peace."

"But I didn't rage, I didn't." Ullan's wild gaze swung around to appeal to Sanda. "Tell them I didn't rage."

"She didn't," Sanda said earnestly. She pointed scornfully at Zella. "That woman doesn't know how to deal with zerkers." She turned to look at Ullan, whom she still held tightly. "Are you feeling better now?" She made her voice fur soft but, out of sight of the teacher, she pinched Ullan's arm.

Ullan might be zerker. But she wasn't stupid. She nodded, then pointed her chin at Zella. "Make her go away," she said in a pathetic little voice. "Make her go away, Sanda."

Zella disappeared.

Ullan lifted her good hand within the circle of Sanda's arms and rubbed her eyes. "Make everyone go away, Sanda. I'll feel better if I could just talk to you for a while."

Sanda looked up. Her teacher was looking at her with respect. "Will you be all right?" she asked.

When Sanda nodded, the teacher waved the men out of the room. "Sanda, I have to apologize. Not only does it look as if you aren't going to turn, but I think you might have the natural talent of a handler." She smiled. "Call if you need me."

Sanda stared at her retreating back. Her? A handler? She felt a bitter laugh in her, but was too tired to let it bubble up. Zerker handlers were women who could live easily with zerker men, and who could control zerker wives.

The second the door flap fell into place, Ullan jerked free of her. "Sanda, you have to help me. I can't stand the thought of turning into another Brianna."

"What am I supposed to do?" Sanda asked, surprised.

"You've got to help me. Sanda, I've been locked up since I turned. First they locked me up because they were testing me for the right dose. Then my mother's sister-wives locked me up because they were afraid of me. I would have gone climbing, but this cast makes it impossible."

She walked over and banged the cast against the chicken coops. The hens clucked frantically as they scrambled for, then lost, their footing. Ullan bent over, clutching her arm. "Damn. Damn." She whirled to face Sanda. "Do you know what it's like being locked up with nothing to do? I nearly went crazy." At Sanda's alarmed look, she waved her hand. "No, not zerker crazy. Just crazy. And all the time I was thinking, what could I do? I went over everything I'd ever heard anyone say about zerkers." She recovered from her pain and started walking up and down. "I don't mind the Peace, really. It does calm me down. But then I think of your mother and I get the cold shudders." She stopped in front of Sanda and grabbed her shoulders. "I thought we might be able to hide down here. But now I know we can't."

"We," Sanda whispered.

"We," Ullan said firmly. "I know you're zerker, too. I could feel your anger and fear every time Haddim came near."

Sanda didn't say anything. Her throat literally closed in fear.

"Don't worry. I won't tell. But, Sanda, you have to help me."

"How can I?" Sanda whispered. How could she indeed? She couldn't even help herself.

"When I was locked up I had a lot of time to think. You were always talking about the old stories, about Olarni and Taizaburo? Remember, one of the old songs said Olarni fell first. I remember you saying you thought it meant that she turned zerker first."

"So?" Sanda wasn't interested in history right now. She felt as if a vial of Peace were hanging over her own head.

"But, Sanda, Peace wasn't discovered and used until the time of Papiri the Healer, about fifty migrations later."

"So." Haddim was waiting. Goddess Within. She'd have to face him!

"You always said you wanted to find out what happened to Olarni. You always said you wanted to find out how they lived. Sanda, Olarni ruled The Home for ten seasons after she turned zerker. She *ordered* men to do her bidding. Then when she had to take her women into the safety of The Home so that The Home could have enough children to keep our ways alive, she still ruled over the women and she was Mother General until she died. If she was zerker, and if they didn't have any Peace, what did Olarni do? The old songs talk about her strength and her wisdom, but they never talk of senseless rages, or having to lock her up. So what was her secret? And why can't it be mine, too?

"Sanda, you can help me. Be a scholar! Go to the upper decks. Read the old manuscripts like you always planned. And find out some way to help me." She paused, panting. *"Please?"*

Sanda stared at her friend stupidly. "But Haddim wants me for his wife."

"Be his guildwife. Then help me."

"But Haddim says he won't wait three migrations. He wants me now."

"Pretend to choose wife training, then after a couple of tendays, transfer to guild training. He might be mad, but there's nothing he can do when you're in the upper decks."

"He can tell them I'm zerker."

"He knows?"

Sanda nodded. "He knows and he wants me, now, or as soon as I finish wife training."

"Then give yourself to him now, and promise him anything if he'll keep silent and let you be a scholar."

Sanda thought of Haddim, and how his face sweated when he fought with her. "I can't. I just can't. I'm even afraid to go out there now. He's waiting to walk me to the barricades."

"Well, he can't. I'll insist you take me home." Her usually generous mouth twisted in a bitter smile. "They'll let me have my way in this."

Relief drained Sanda of energy, and she sat on the dirt floor like an overbalanced cub.

"But after that, you'll have to face him. I don't care how you do it, but you have to become a scholar." Ullan suddenly knelt beside her and gave her a desperate hug. "You have to help me. You're the only one who'll talk to me. Not even my mother will come near." She drew back and looked Sanda straight in the eyes. "You're my only friend. You're my only hope. Think, Sanda, you'll be helping yourself, too. For when you find out what Olarni did, you'll be safe, too." When Sanda didn't say anything, her eyes hardened. "Besides, if you don't promise to help me, *I'll* tell on you, and right now."

13

When Mikhail entered the armory to summon his men to the hunt he swore silently. The zerkers and lankers were separating again. The zerkers checked their weapons and gathered, arguing and boasting at the top of their lungs, while the lankers squatted along the sides, staying well away from them. Whelps and cabin fetches tore from one group to the other, bringing last-minute items to their warriors, or simply running wild with excitement. Mikhail sorted the warriors out and saw that it wasn't just his pack that was separating, it was all of them. Yet after that last Pack War lankers had clung to their zerker protectors, who had defended them from other zerkers, while other lankers had acted as witnesses, stopping lanker ambushes of zerker warriors. He shook his head. Not good. Not good at all. As he watched, pack leaders formed up their packs, and the two kinds of warriors mixed again. Not out of friendship, or teamwork, or loyalty. Just orders.

He searched the seething mob for his own men. A ray of sunlight slanted down from the arrow-slit windows, catching his son's blond hair. As his eyes traced its slight wave, Bart turned away. He hadn't

213

looked directly at his father since the day Nakano had died.

Nakano and Movich. Killed. By ferts they said. Not likely. Movich was too good a hunter. But what was Nakano doing with Movich? And why?

Tev knew. He'd bet his life Tev knew; but the stubborn lanker wasn't talking. None of the lankers were. Not even Bart who now walked with the lankers and let them guard his back . . . and linger around whenever he had to talk to his father. Bart was scared. If cornered, he would probably spill the truth. But then his new friends would turn on him. And by neglect or design, he would end up dead.

Frustration made Mikhail plough rudely through the mob, bouncing men aside as if they were cubs. What *had* happened to Nakano? He changed direction to avoid Nakano's father. Jarahd held him responsible for his pack's action—or lack of action in Nakano's death, and if he talked to him in his present mood, they'd end up fighting.

A loud whoop came from his group. Guntor, wearing his new pack insignia on his shoulders, was describing yet again how he had braved the jungle during his initiation, and killed a burrow sheep. His black eyes flashed as he acted out his kill. With a malicious grin, he charged into Bart, forcing him to jump aside. Guntor laughed and draped his freshly bandaged hand carelessly over Mariko's slender shoulders. The lanker whelp colored with pleasure—and the lankers of Mikhail's pack drifted farther away from their zerker protectors.

Mikhail's gut tightened. Pack discord, no matter how small, could cost lives. It was time to whip them into shape—quell them or kill them.

Gopa's familiar bulk loomed beside him. "Mikhail, you aren't still planning on going up onto the Heights, are you?" He rubbed his powerful square fingertips against his brow. In the dim light, Mikhail saw his beard was more white that black.

Mikhail was about to argue when he saw Leeorah, the middle-aged healer, standing in the door of the infirmary. Tall and black haired, her eyes were riveted on Mikhail, waiting for his reply. Women. Well, this was one rumor the women weren't going to start. He slapped Gopa's back cheerfully. "Let's worry about this hunt first."

Leeorah's expressive face showed her frustration as she backed into her infirmary.

Gopa frowned. It obviously wasn't the answer he wanted. He shuffled his feet uncertainly. "No, let's forget you ever saw anything." He looked like a two-century burl oak, thick and sturdy looking, but ready to fall in the first storm.

Mikhail glared at his lankers, who had gathered to listen. He squared his shoulders. "It's not as if I'm asking you to do anything. This is my business. I'll handle it." He glanced toward the infirmary. The hide door curtain swayed. Damn it, that woman was listening.

Guntor pulled Mariko through the gathering men, frantically waving for Volf to follow. His pale skin was flushed with excitement and his eyes danced with eerie fire. As he pushed forward, he elbowed Tev aside. The lanker half raised a fist, then stopped, remembering that Guntor was zerker now.

"Pack Leader," Guntor called, loudly enough to be heard down by the barricades. "Now that I'm a warrior, can I have Mariko assigned to me?"

Mikhail tried to gather his patience around him. This was too important a hunt to start with a sulking warrior—even one as young as Guntor. "You know you're not senior enough to have a whelp assigned to you."

Guntor shrugged, undampened by the refusal. "Then could you assign Mariko to Volf and let Volf and me hunt together?" Behind Guntor, Tev's grizzled eyebrows were pinched together in a disapproving frown. Volf tried to look indifferent, but his massive chest strained forward for an answer. This was the first time since the nesters that anyone had offered to hunt with him.

As Mikhail opened his mouth to squash the idea of putting all the bent arrows into one quiver, he suddenly saw its advantage. Almost before he knew what he was thinking, he nodded solemnly. "If Mariko agrees, I suppose we could try it—as long as you bring down lots of game."

Guntor puffed up his chest. "Mariko agrees." His lover nodded, but he still looked worried. Tev caught Mikhail's eyes, but he ignored his brother's guarded, passionate head shake. This was too good a chance to pass up. Whatever he managed to dump on Volf could also land on Guntor, pay him back for what he had done to Bart. As for Mariko . . . he lost interest. The whelp had no backbone.

He raised one eyebrow to Volf. "Are you willing?"

Volf shrugged, managing to open his hunting tunic down to his waist and exposing a few more muscles and scars. "No problem." His smile broke through as he said wonderingly, "They want to hunt with me."

Mikhail nodded and tried to keep the triumph out of his voice. "With Mariko gone I'll need another whelp besides Dyfid to run errands for me." He looked at Gopa who had picked up Bart when Volf had been declared a solitary.

Gopa caught his thought. "Take Bart."

Dyfid whooped, his dark face alight with pleasure. He slapped Bart on the back. "You can take first duty as hunt fetch." Bart grinned and Mikhail held back a satisfied smile. Now he'd get the chance to shake the truth about Nakano out of his son. As for Volf and Guntor . . . well, he'd plan something. He ignored Tev, who was making tiny gestures with his hands, asking to speak with him privately. His brother was not the pack leader. *How dare he go behind my back and ask Sair to let him form his own pack?* He controlled his irritation by biting his cheek until his tongue tasted salty blood. Once he got to the bottom of Nakano's death, and found out what Tev was hiding, his brother would be saying no more about lanker packs.

"Everyone is here and fit to hunt," Gopa reported, resting his massive hands on his hips and looking once more like the toughest First Spear in The Home.

Mikhail looked at the filthy bandage on Guntor's hand, the hand that Bart had apparently bitten to the bone.

Guntor shrugged it off. "I'm fine. It was just a bit sore."

"You're sure?" Mikhail asked. Guntor's wrist above the bandage was swollen and discolored.

"I'm great, and I wouldn't miss this for anything, not even for my marriage feast." He smiled, his white teeth contrasting sharply with his black eyes and hair.

Mikhail nodded. Usually he checked zerker wounds to prevent long and painful infections, but this time he rather hoped that Guntor would suffer.

Tev jerked his eyes to one side. Mikhail pretended not to see. "All right, let's go."

As the men sorted themselves out, and drifted toward the exit tunnel, Tev hurried to his side. "Mikhail,

you can't let Guntor go out. The healer wants to
keep him here and dress his hand every day. She
said if she didn't, the infection would get worse."

"So let *him* dress it every day." Mikhail glared at
his brother. Tev looked rugged in his leathers, with
his butchering knives slung everywhere. But, as he
spoke, his gestures were that of an old woman.

Tev shook his head in puzzlement. "What's gotten
into you, Mikhail? You know he won't and we don't
need a young warrior raving with fever when we're
days away from home."

Mikhail faced his brother squarely. "Are you
questioning my orders?" he hissed.

Tev jumped back as if he had just seen a charging
fert. "Of course not," he said soothingly. He looked
at the men. "I'll get in position." He practically ran
to his place.

Mikhail grinned savagely at his back. Soon, Tev,
soon. Once I find out what you're hiding, you'll be
mine again—my ears in the armory—my faithful shadow
on the trail.

He shouldered his pack and led his men into the
tunnel. Bart would deliver Tev—whether he wanted
to or not. Now all he had to do was figure out how
to force his two separate packs to mix again and act
as one. And while he was at it, settle a few scores
with Volf and Guntor. Maybe throw a scare into them,
put them in a danger they couldn't handle; then get
the rest of the pack, especially the lankers, to save
them. That wouldn't be easy. Volf might be a distractible
idiot, but he could fight. So could Guntor. Nesters?
No, that wouldn't work. It was too close to Bart's
accident. A daggerjaw nest? No. You could hear their
jaws grinding for spear lengths.

By the time they descended to the valley floor

and passed through the barricade gate onto the Migration
Trail, Mikhail had discarded the idea of trying somehow
to knock them into the river for the nurls to feast
on, and was considering doping Volf's fieldpack with
female fert musk . . . except that it was the wrong
season for mating. He sighed and adjusted his pack.
He had five days on the trail before they reached
the iron mounds. By then he'd have a workable plan.

It took much longer. They reached the iron mounds,
set up camp in the entrance to one of the mining
caves, and hunted for another eight days before Mikhail
saw a way to pull his pack together.

Guntor was bandaging a cut on Mariko's arm.
The slender whelp had been slashed during the last
determined charge of a keld Volf had finally brought
down. "Don't worry about a thing, Mariko," Guntor
said. "My mother double soaks the bandages. The
blood lusters will never scent your blood."

Mikhail smelled the heavy mirta, looked at Mariko's
bloody arm, and suddenly knew what to do. Just put
human blood on Volf's and Guntor's packs. Without
the covering mirta, the blood lusters would be all
over both men before they were a klat from the main
camp. Then, when the rest of the pack saved them,
the two zerkers would be cut down to size. And in
the confusion, Mikhail could separate Bart long enough
to shake the truth out of him.

Tev called from the cluster of lankers around the
keld. "We're ready to pack the meat, but we need a
few more hands."

The other zerkers drifted over, but Volf and Guntor
continued to entertain each other with boasts of exactly
how they had shot and then speared the huge keld.
Tev left his lankers and approached Mikhail. "More

of the zerkers are going to have to carry. That carcass has to have at least fifteen to twenty man-weights of prime meat on it. My men have been double loaded for almost a tenday, and they're tired out."

"We're all tired, Tev. It's only a klat or so from camp. I think we can get away with only two unburdened warriors. The rest can help you."

Tev nodded. "Just don't make the two guards Guntor and Volf. My men don't trust them."

Mikhail glared at his brother. "I run this pack, not you."

Tev's face smoothed out into a blank stare. "Of course you do." His voice was careful and quiet. "But you don't want your lankers unhappy."

Mikhail seethed as he waved Tev away. No, he didn't want his lankers unhappy. Unhappy lankers held up the hunt, refused to do any more than was defined by pack law, and . . . he thought of the pack war and shuddered. No, he didn't want unhappy lankers.

Angry shouting interrupted his thoughts. "I tell you I'm not carrying," Volf yelled at Tev. "I saw the keld, and Guntor and I brought him down. Killers never carry."

Guntor stopped in the middle of putting meat in his field pack and waited, his black eyes watching Volf, ready to follow his lead. The lankers clenched their jaws and yanked pack straps angrily.

Mikhail stalked over. "You got problems?" he snarled.

Volf straightened, arrogantly. "I spotted the meat, and I killed it." He puffed up with righteous anger. "Killers never carry."

Knowing what he was planning to do to Volf, Mikhail found it very easy not to lose his temper. "The lankers are overloaded and tired. Everyone carries—except for two guards."

"Why can't I be one of the two guards?"

"Because I am one, and Samay is the other. His back is still sore from that tumble he took yesterday, and I don't want to have to carry him back to The Home because we overloaded him."

"Pack Law says I don't have to carry."

"Pack Custom says you don't have to carry." Mikhail grinned, "but you don't have to if you don't want to." He ignored a sullen murmur of the lankers and walked over to Tev. Speaking loudly so everyone could hear, he said, "Volf doesn't want to carry—so leave his share of meat on the ground." He turned back to Volf. "If you don't want to carry, you don't have to, but it's your meat you'll be leaving behind." He winked at Tev who actually smiled back at him.

It was disgustingly easy to find and bait the field packs. Every night the young zerkers tossed them down at the entrance to the cave. The next morning, just before dawn, Mikhail picked his way carefully around the men who were sleeping well behind the barrier fire at the entrance. With a nod he dismissed the dawn guard. The man threw a couple of branches on the fire line, and disappeared to catch a few more moments of sleep. Mikhail waited patiently till the man started to snore, then raised his knife. The taboo against shedding blood on the hunt was so strong that his knife hovered trembling above his arm for several moments before he managed to nick it and rub the bleeding skin over yesterday's keld blood smears on Volf's pack. Trust Volf not to clean his pack. It made everything so easy. He finished Volf's pack, then turned to rummage for Guntor's.

"What the hell are you doing?" someone hissed right in his ear.

Mikhail jumped, dropped the pack, and had his shette out before he recognized his brother's dark outline in the gloom. "Shh." He looked behind Tev, but there was no one there.

Tev grabbed Mikhail's arm. "Blood," he whispered, hoarsely. "You're baiting packs. Whose?" He searched through the packs in the predawn light. Mikhail seethed with anger. Only one more day of putting up with Tev's righteousness, and then . . .

As the sun rose above the jungle canopy its rosy glow lit up the mounds of broken rock that extended from the mine entrance down hundreds of spear lengths to the edge of the jungle. It also lit up the wet smears on Volf's pack.

"Taizaburo, you're setting the bastard up as bait!" Tev started pacing back and forth, his shoulders hunched. "Have you lost your mind? That's murder!"

Mikhail jumped in front of his brother. "I'm just going to throw a scare into them. Nobody's going to die."

"Scare. Some scare. You can't control who responds to the smell of fresh blood. In fact . . ." He looked around, picked up the packs and heaved them back inside the cave. "We could be in danger now."

Mikhail checked the air above and then the still dark crevices of the tumbled rocks that fell away from the hillside down to the jungle. "Nothing within half a klat." Pulling out his field pack, he tore open his bandages, flooding the air with the rich smell of mirta, a smell that reminded him of his wives who wore this as a perfume, and also of desperate days on the trail when these bandages were all that saved men from the questing noses of ferts and tigrogs. His small wound had already closed, but he wrapped it anyway. Tev drew himself up to attention.

"Request permission to take the lankers back to The Home with a full load of dried meat and return later for more."

Mikhail wanted to shake him. "No need to be formal with me, Tev. You can take your lankers back tomorrow. And take Guntor, too. His wounded hand is twice the size of the other."

Tev did not relax. "Request permission to return to The Home today."

"Permission denied."

"Damn it all, Mikhail. What you're doing is zerker business. I don't want any part of it."

"No, it isn't. The zerkers and lankers are drifting apart. What we need is a little gratitude on the part of our wilder zerkers to pull things together again. Just be prepared. When Volf and Guntor get into trouble, you be there to rescue him. Then he'll owe you a blood debt."

Tev threw his arms up in disgust. "Mikhail, that could go wrong so easily. Volf, Guntor, Mariko, or one of the lankers could get killed."

"Don't be such an old woman, Tev. We have the best pack in The Home and after today we'll be a real team again."

"Team?" Tev's angry face solidified like frozen mud.

Mikhail waited, but Tev was shut off from him in a typical lanker-sullen mood. In spite of his resolve to wait, Mikhail's anger spilled over. "And don't whine to me about getting involved. If you hadn't asked for your own hunting pack, I wouldn't have been forced to pull this pack together so quickly."

Tev flinched as if a wild arrow had nearly skewered him. "Sair told you?"

"Of course he told me. He owes me more than he'll ever owe you."

"He mustn't think he owes you that much." Tev slowly packed the rest of the dressing into Mikhail's field pack and threw it at his brother. "He told *me* if you couldn't 'pull the bowstring' on this trip, I *could* form my own pack."

Mikhail lost his breath as if punched. "You're lying."

Tev walked over to one of the larger boulders on the rubble heap and sat down wearily. "Sair is playing us off against each other."

"That's dishonorable!"

"So's blood baiting."

"That's different. It'll pull the pack together and make us a fighting unit again. You couldn't offer that with your miserable lot of lankers."

"If we had higher barricades along the Waterfall Valley entrance, and enclosed more cropland, we might not need so many zerkers in every pack."

"Will you keep your voices down?" Gopa loomed out of the darkness like a giant keld. His eyes were puffy and his face still wrinkled from sleep. "I could hear you arguing halfway back into the cave. And what's this about dishonor?" He fumbled the fastenings on his tunic shut.

"Nothing," both brothers said simultaneously.

Gopa gave Mikhail a dirty look. "You're not setting up one of your tricks, are you? If you do, I'm pulling out."

Mikhail stared at his grizzled First Spear. "What's gotten into you?"

Tev shouldered past both of them, heading for the cave. "He figures the ghosts will take your soul and doesn't want to be around to be taken with you." He disappeared into the gloom.

"Are you?" Mikhail asked softy.

"No more than Tev," Gopa grumbled. "He's scared

shitless. Anyway I was thinking of transferring to my cousin's pack as ordinary spear. I'm getting too old to do double distance everyday as end man, watchman, and heel nipper."

"But, Gopa, I'll be going up to the Heights alone."

"Doesn't matter. Look at Jaspaar. After *they* took him, his whole pack fell apart and half of them died. I have to consider my family. My wives cry every night, telling me how they love me and don't want to lose me. Besides, they are too old to be taken into other quarters as wives, and I don't fancy seeing my girls becoming servants, or worse, going to steerage because they can't get any kind of a dowry together."

Mikhail's eyes unexpectedly smarted. None of his wives had shown any interest in him or his plans. He put an arm around Gopa's shoulder. "Don't worry about the Heights."

Gopa sucked in a relieved breath. "So you're not going?"

"I didn't say that."

Gopa's relief turned to a scowl. He snorted, and stomped back to join the waking men.

Bart trotted out, carrying his pack and several small strips of meat. "I saved you some new-smoked meat, Pack Leader." Norv happened to wander out behind him. Just within hearing. Mikhail chuckled. Fat lot of good it would do them soon. He took the meat and watched as Dyfid joined Bart. They murmured quietly, checking their packs and weapons in the early morning light. At least that was going well: Bart had a good pack brother in Dyfid.

Mikhail finished chewing the meat and assessed his pack's readiness. The lankers were grouped sullenly around Tev. Gopa was still angry and he took it out on anyone who drifted near. The zerkers picked up his angry emotions and started snapping amongst themselves. The whelps huddled near the cave mouth watching the closed-faced lankers and the irritable zerkers with equal wariness. The danger of the whole situation soured Mikhail's stomach. It would be a relief to put his plan into effect.

"Volf," he called, catching the zerker's eye. "Do you feel lucky today?"

Tev choked and turned away.

Volf preened. "Of course. Want me to find you another keld?"

"Think you can?" Mikhail asked. "Aren't you too tired from carrying all that meat, yesterday?"

Volf flushed. "I'm fine," he snarled.

"Good. I want you to lead out." He waved downwind. "Why not go along the river? We haven't hunted there since the first day."

Volf puffed another hand-width higher and jumped on a boulder so he could look down on the men. "Follow me. I'll find you a whole herd of keld."

The older zerkers flushed at his tone and muttered angrily to themselves. The lankers looked disgusted and turned to Tev for guidance. But Tev was sniffing the air, checking the wind.

"Don't forget the rest of the men," Mikhail called. "No running off on your own."

"I know what I'm doing." Volf pulled out his shette and set off down the rock-strewn slope. As Guntor followed Volf, he opened the buttons of his tunic and took a deep breath trying to make his chest look as muscular as Volf's.

Mikhail breathed a sigh of relief. With Volf heading downwind the blood lusters would be more likely to attack the front of the pack, but Mikhail would stay at the back, just in case. He nodded to Samay. "Tev and Norv can follow Volf, and you and Kittu can provide backup for the lankers."

Kittu tugged on his blond beard, staring at Mikhail as if he was mad. Finally he shrugged and followed Tev down the rubble slope, muttering, "Stupid, stupid."

"The rest of you take your usual places, except that I'll bring up the back with my whelps."

Gopa managed to keep his mouth shut until all the men were ahead of them. With one massive paw he waved his and Mikhail's whelps out of hearing. "Have you lost your mind? Putting Volf on point is like firing an arrow blind." Mikhail ignored him and followed his men down the slope of loose rock. Gopa hurried after him. "What's going on? You're wound up like an overtight bowstring."

Mikhail laughed and clapped his First Spear on the back. "I'm expecting lots of meat. Better move or you'll get left behind."

Gopa gave him one last angry look and padded after the line of men, his broad shoulders held stiffly as he scanned for game . . . or danger. Mikhail followed much more slowly, letting all the warriors disappear into the jungle ahead of him. As soon as he was out of sight of the field camp, he caught Dyfid's eye. "Move up." He snarled. "Close up the gap." The dark whelp started to jog. "Move it," Mikhail roared. "Do you want to split the pack?" Dyfid started to run. As Bart hurried after him, Mikhail grabbed him and dragged him to a halt. Dyfid disappeared down the trail.

A pinto hog squealed. The sound was thin and high-pitched, probably a yearling, small, but tender. In the distance Volf howled in triumph.

"All right, whelp," Mikhail snarled, his nose a finger-width away from Bart's face. "What happened to Nakano?"

Bart tried to back away, but Mikhail grabbed a handful of his hunting shirt and shook him like a dead snake. "What happened?"

"Nothing, sir." Bart was dead white; he was shrinking away inside his clothes, like Zorava, just before she was going to defy him. Mikhail shook his son harder, remembering Zorava, and her note. Bart's eyes darted sideways trying to look toward where the pack had disappeared.

"Forget about them. They'll never know you told me anything. Just spit it out, and we'll catch up."

"But Tev—"

"Tev will never know. But you'll tell me . . . now."

The "man in trouble" whistle drifted through the undergrowth.

"Shit!" Time was running out. "Tell me!" he howled.

"I can't," Bart whispered.

"So you're admitting Tev did something, aren't you?" Something stung his neck. Damn daggerjaw. Mikhail reached to grab the body, ready to crush it when it had drawn its poison, and his blood out of his neck. His hand felt no insect, but something small, smooth, and cold. He pulled it out. In his hand was a bone needle a hand-span long that thickened into a tiny plug at one end.

Bart's hunting shirt slipped from his grasp. The sounds of the jungle faded and the jumble of rocks around the trail went fuzzy. He could only focus on that strange needle.

"Pack Leader?"

Bart was watching him. Why? Where was his pack? He tried to shove the strange needle in his pocket and felt it drop. His hand fell limply to his side.

"Are you all right?" Bart sounded worried.

Mikhail started into the jungle. Must get to the

pack. The plan. Yes. The plan. The ground tilted. He stumbled and floundered into a drape vine covered in spines.

Suddenly Bart filled his vision, and worried grey eyes blocked out his view of the jungle.

"Father! What's wrong?"

A distant sense of urgency pushed at Mikhail. He had to do something. He was planning something—what? Why was Bart's face getting blurry? He put his hand on Bart's shoulder. "We must . . ." His tongue was as thick as if he had been drinking all night.

Dimly he heard Bart whistling frantically for help.

Help? Who needed help? He lurched forward and slid to his knees. The trees and vines in front of him jerked around crazily. He attempted to focus on the mold-littered jungle floor, trying to clear his head . . .

The world grew darker.

"Are you all right?"

He could barely hear his son. "Save yourself!" he screamed. He was dying; the blood lusters would know. "Leave me!" he tried to roar, but his hunt-master's bellow barely whispered from his lips. He was dying—unmarked, but dying . . .

Like Jaspaar—killed by ghosts.

With all his zerker will he shouted at his son. "Bart!" Now he couldn't hear his voice at all. But Bart answered. "I'm here."

"Like Jaspaar!" he shouted. "Ghosts!"

Klats away he could hear Bart's desperate questions. Sangir . . . slave.

He sighed and was still.

14

The Forty-first Day of the First Gifter Moon of Spring

Bart froze as the life and intelligence faded from his father's dilated eyes. He couldn't be dying, he couldn't.

But his father sighed: a long slow sigh that deflated his chest and left him a crumpled husk on the ground. Bart's back prickled. Ghosts. He shook his father, but the strong muscular body was slack. Behind him a young fert coughed. In front of him another answered. Soon others replied deep in the jungle. Death was in the air and the blood lusters were coming. "Father!" He touched Mikhail's jugular vein. Mikhail's mouth fell open. An older fert coughed, directing the pack.

A rustle behind him sent him rolling defensively away into the undergrowth. Turning, he saw a fert tear at his father's throat. Bart pulled his spear. No way it was going to tear Mikhail apart. No way. He aimed through the blur of tears.

As the fert lifted his nuzzle, Bart let his spear fly. The roar of triumph turned to one of rage when the spear buried itself deep in the fert's hindquarters. Bart's tears had made him miss the heart. The animal leaped. Bart dodged, trying to pull his bow from his back. The animal landed heavily and screamed in pain. The scream was answered, and bush crackled as more ferts tore into view. Bart strung his bow and sent an arrow into the pack. Then, with a sob of despair, he turned and ran for his life.

Tev pounded down the trail after Gopa, Guntor and Kittu. Behind he could hear Volf bringing up the rear. Damn Mikhail. Damn him to hell. If he'd gotten Bart killed, that would be it. He'd find another pack. Ontu needed a lanker adviser and at least he listened. Over his rhythmic panting his ears strained for another whistle. The "all clear," or the "stand down." But all he heard were the feeding snarls of ferts. Who was down? Why weren't there more signals? Damn Mikhail and his great ideas. So he'd saved Volf. So what? The men weren't stupid. Sooner or later they'd get to wondering why the whole jungle was attracted to Volf's pack.

He piled into Kittu who had bumped into a white-faced and gibbering Bart. He grabbed the whelp and shook him. "What happened?"

The whelp's eyes bulged, showing more white than color. He was shaking like a leaf. "Like Jaspaar. Ghosts took him."

Tev slapped him sharply. He jerked his chin to Gopa. Set up a guard. "Now, what happened?"

"We were walking and he just stopped talking; he looked sort of drunk. Then he pulled this bone splinter out of his neck, sat down and died."

"Bone splinter?"

"Yes, like a woman's sewing needle—only longer—and it had a bump on the end."

"What happened to it?"

"I don't know. I think he dropped it, but it was just a splinter, Tev, and it only had a little blood on the end, so it couldn't have done anything. But he was dead. He just sighed and was dead. Then the ferts came—dozens of them, and I ran."

Mikhail. Dead. Ghosts . . . Shit. He raised his voice. "I'm glad no one here wishes to disturb the ghosts."

"No, not us," the rest echoed as they frantically circled their breasts and muttered prayers to their Godwithin.

Tev felt as if he'd been doused with burning ice water. Now was his chance. He'd never get another. "Gopa," he snapped. "You'd better take Kittu and get back to the men with the carcasses. Tell them to avoid this area, get back to camp and be ready to move out. If they come wandering down the trail, they could be ghost bait, too."

The burly zerker blanched at the thought and took off down the trail without realizing that he'd obeyed a lanker.

Tev turned to Bart. "Now, show me where it happened."

His nephew shook his head, backing away from Tev. "There's ferts there, dozens of them, and ghosts."

"Tev. We can't go where there are ghosts!" Volf protested.

He turned and pretended to look surprised. So much rode on this. More than Volf could ever guess. "Why do you think I sent Gopa and Kittu back?" he demanded. "Because you're the only two warriors who'd go into hell itself for a good fight." He looked at them admiringly. Guntor gaped, then turned to Volf to see what he would do. Tev ignored the fear that froze his guts when he thought of the ghosts. Worry about that later. He needed the pack leader disk. He needed to know more about what had happened.

The scarred warrior grinned self-consciously. "Of course I'd fight anything—" he started.

"Good, then let's go and get Mikhail's body. Do you want it known that Mikhail's hunting pack" *—and mine if I can work it—* "left his body to be eaten?" He clapped Volf on his bandaged shoulder, to keep him from thinking clearly. "I picked you two because *we* can do it." Then he turned and pushed Bart ahead of him. Bart resisted and he had to give him a few good shoves. His ears reached for the sound of men behind him and heard nothing. Well, if they didn't come, and he found the weapons and the disk, he'd still be ahead. But what if the ghosts had taken Mikhail? He blanked the thought. Long ago he'd learned that he'd be more successful if he ordered his body to do a task and didn't think about what "might happen." Still, as they got closer to the sound of fighting, snarling ferts he found it harder and harder to press forward. It was almost as if every muscle in his body was fighting him. Was it the ghosts already?

Suddenly he heard men running hard behind him. He nearly wept with relief. He was protected. And, if they obeyed him now, it would be easier later.

He stopped when the sound of the ferts seemed right around the bend. They strung their bows and gripped their spears. All except Bart. "Where's your spear?"

"I left it buried in a fert."

"You left your weapon?" Guntor sneered. "Are you sure you didn't just drop it running away?"

"Shut up," Tev ordered softly. "Spread out and keep hidden when you shoot."

Volf drew himself up. "Zerkers don't . . ."

"Zerkers do today. Even I can smell Mikhail's blood. We've got to get in there, kill the animals and get him out and buried as fast as we can." He slipped into the undergrowth, hoping his frail control of Volf would hold. If it didn't, well, he could get along without Volf, but not easily.

There weren't dozens of ferts. Only three and they were so busy snarling over what must have been Mikhail that it was ridiculously easy to stalk and shoot them.

Tev pulled off his pack and slipped the extender cord free. They dragged the animals off Mikhail and started pushing his grisly remains into the pack. His clothes had been torn off him and so much of him had been eaten that it was easier to think of him as meat instead of as a man. His head was gnawed down to bloody bone. His entrails had been ripped out and were strewn around the dead ferts. Behind him, Tev heard Bart gag and then throw up. He jerked his head to Volf to guard him and bent to fold up Mikhail's grizzly remains and stuff him into the pack. It was a bad fit, but he refused to use his butcher knives to do a better job. When he was finished he dragged the pack over to Volf. "Get this on. Run to the iron mounds and get him buried immediately." He gestured to Guntor. "Watch his back."

Volf swung the pack onto his pack. "It's light. He's been half eaten." Bart staggered away and pounded a tree with his fists. Volf ignored him. "Are you following?"

"Yes, as soon as we find Mikhail's weapons."

"But you have no protector . . . and there's him." He gestured toward Bart.

Tev allowed himself a grim laugh. "I don't need a protector. You're the one who's carrying the smell of human blood. I'll be as safe as in The Home. Now move! Or we'll all be dead."

Volf nodded and took off at a fast jog. Guntor followed behind him, his spear ready. But he was favoring his bandaged hand. Damn. More trouble, but not now.

Tev went over to Bart and slapped his face several times. "Smarten up. Grieve later, but right now I need your eyes to find your father's weapons, especially his steel knife." He hesitated and then whispered, "and find that splinter, too, if you can." He quickly circled his breast trying to calm his heart that threatened to drum through his chest when he mentioned something to do with *them*.

Bart looked at him blankly. Tev raised his hand again, and Bart stumbled over to where Mikhail had lain. He walked as if his legs were asleep. Suddenly he straightened. "Tev, we can't mix with ghosts. We've got to get out of here."

"We'll get out of here when we get your spear and your father's knives." *And his Lieutenant's disk.*

The whelp started busily poking through the blood-drenched leaf mold on the jungle floor. He moved in a circle while Tev kept watch.

"Hurry," Tev called. He had to get back to the pack soon.

Bart found his own spear, his father's shette, and soon after that his father's small knife with the leather sheath half gnawed through.

"Have you seen his disk?" Tev asked casually.

"That? Oh, that's over there." Bart gestured across the clearing. Tev tried not to look eager as he wandered over and picked it up. The ceramic disk, a fist-sized circle with the pack's insignia: a white fert skull against a blood-red background.

Bart had stopped moving. Tev saw that the whelp was standing in a daze looking at something in his hand. Tev walked over to see Bart run his fingers along a slender polished splinter of bone. His fingers slowed and he looked thoughtfully at the needle. Then, as if tired, his legs folded and he sat down abruptly.

"Bart!"

Bart looked up. "Whas wron'?" He tried again. "What'dz ong?" He sounded drunk. He looked stupid. He blinked and squinted as if trying to see Tev clearly.

Ghosts. Jaspaar. Mikhail. Now Bart. But the needle was so small. Magic? Did magic need needles? Tev slapped the splinter out of Bart's hand.

Bart lost interest in him and let his hand drift down into his lap. His eyelids lowered. All because of that splinter. Tev raced to the edge of the clearing and pulled a half dozen leaves off a vine, put them on top of the needle and put it in his pocket. He waited, and sweated in fear. Nothing happened. But in the distance he could hear something crashing through the jungle, probably trailing the scent of blood.

He pulled his nephew to his feet and shook him. The whelp sagged in his hands like a straw doll. The animal was getting closer. He put one of Bart's limp arms over his shoulder and started dragging him down the trail.

"Walk, damn you," Tev shouted in his ear. The whelp seemed to try to move on his own, but he kept stumbling. Tev dragged him forward. Behind him he could hear something tearing at the fert carcasses they had left behind: carcasses warriors would never eat for fear of eating part of their own leader. He whistled for help, and jerked Bart forward. The whelp got his legs under him and started to stumble along with him. After a few strides he took his own weight, then began to look around. He shrugged off Tev's helping hand, and strode forward. He wobbled a bit and looked like a man recovering from a bout of jungle fever, but he wasn't dead. Like Mikhail. Like Jaspaar.

He stopped and looked at Tev. "What was that?"

"Whatever it was, don't you ever talk about it," Tev warned. He lowered his voice. "People who mess with . . ." he pointed upwards, "die."

Bart shook his head, and nearly stumbled. Tev steadied him, watching him, anxiously.

"But what are we going to do about my father?"

"What do you mean?"

"That bone splinter. It was made. It had file marks on it."

Should he trust this whelp? Although he had sworn the lanker oath of brotherhood, he was not yet a warrior and had never been tested to see if he could keep his word. Tev shrugged. "Grief's gone to your brain, whelp. Bone splinters don't kill. It was just a bit of your father." He propelled him up the slope toward the camp. "Shut up and live."

Bart turned around and walked backwards. "But what about the stranger on the Heights? What about him?"

Tev looked over his shoulder almost expecting to see another splinter heading their way. "Only your father saw him. And he's dead."

"But I saw him, too."

A rock seemed to rear out of the path and trip Tev. He stumbled. "What?"

"I saw a man in black pick up a squared log and then push it back into a crevice."

"Who have you told?" Tev put his hand on Bart's shoulder pushing him to a run as he demanded an answer. They came out of the jungle and started running up the long rock-tumbled slope to the camp.

"Nobody. That was the day I got snared by the nesters. After that nobody would talk to me. Then I realized nobody wanted to talk about it anyway. So I didn't."

Tev nodded. "Lucky you didn't, or you'd be . . ." He stopped talking and looked up the hill. Bart whirled to see Gopa bearing down on them.

"About time you got back. Find anything?" Gopa shouted.

"Yes, we have his weapons." Tev said nothing about the splinter in his pocket. Had Bart seen him take it?

"See anything?" Gopa lifted his eyebrows toward the Heights. When Tev shook his head, he heaved a sigh of relief. "We've buried Mikhail, and are almost ready to go."

"But my father," Bart cried.

"He's buried honorably."

"Ghosts didn't get him. I think someone killed him."

Shit. If Bart kept this up, they'd all be sitting down and dying. "And who would kill him, *boy*?" He smiled as Bart stiffened at the insult. "When Mikhail died we were all fighting a pack of ferts for two pinto hogs. The only one who could have killed him was you. Is there something you're not telling us?"

"Me?" Bart's grief and anguish made his voice crack.

"Who else could surprise him, but his own son?" Gopa's bulky shoulders hunched and he took a threatening step forward.

"Don't be silly, Gopa. He's just mad with grief— can't accept that his father's spirit is enslaved." Tev took Bart's arm in a vicious grip and hustled him up the hill to the camp.

"But, Tev," Bart protested.

Tev gave his arm a savage wrench as he said, "Take it easy, Bart. I'm sure you didn't mean to lose your shette."

Gopa was right behind them and heard. "Panicked,

did he? Poor Mikhail. Dying in the jungle alone, with no backup."

"But it wasn't like that."

Tev wrenched Bart's arm making him gasp. "Shut up, boy." He lowered his voice. "You're beginning to sound like Nakano." Bart's face paled to a sickly grey.

All the men were gathered outside the cave entrance, arguing. Good. No one had taken effective control. Tev pushed Bart to one side and strode into the center of the men. Bart wandered off, sunk in his own fear and misery. Tev forgot him as he gathered his wits and his energy to try what had not been done for twenty migrations.

"I've got Mikhail's weapons," he announced. He held the knives and spear up, waiting for the muttering to die down. "And I've got his disk." He held up the necklace for all to see.

All eyes swung to Gopa. Kittu walked forward to face the burly First Spear. "I will follow Gopa."

Gopa leaned on his spear and shook his grizzled head. "No. Ten years ago maybe. But not now. I've got enough troubles of my own without trying to whip this pack into shape." The men looked at each other uneasily, and started examining the remaining zerkers. Tev waited. No, they'd never consider him. Not yet.

He saw them dismiss Samay—he had a chronically bad back. Then Gopa waved to Kittu. "What about you?" Better and better. Kittu was too young, and no leader at all.

Kittu shook his blond head and rested his hands on his lean hips. "I'm out of here. This pack has gone sour, and I don't plan to be ghost bait."

"But, Kittu, we've hunted together for years," Volf protested. "How could you leave the pack now?"

Kittu's lips curled. "I've avoided you for years. Now Mikhail can't keep you in line, I'm gone before you kill someone."

Volf surged to his feet. Tev slipped in front of him talking quietly, but putting all his will power behind his words: a will power that had controlled Mikhail more often than he had ever realized. "Admit it, Volf. You were a solitary, but that's changed today, hasn't it. From now on, you'll be part of the team."

Volf looked at him as if he'd gone crazy.

Tev ground his teeth. Subtlety was out. Hit him with an axe. "After all! Since *I* saved your life, you are part of my team, aren't you?"

Volf opened and closed his mouth. Tev gave him time to think, realizing that if Mikhail had been here, this could all have been done with a nudge and joke and a shared belly laugh. Finally Volf nodded. "Well, those ferts were all over me . . . your team? A *lanker* team?" His lips parted in a sneer.

Tev ignored Volf's sneer and made his voice warm and welcoming. "Become my pack brother and my protector."

The whole pack stopped their restless movements. Even Bart surfaced from the numbness that had seized his mind. "Volf?" His astonishment and contempt were echoed by nods from the rest of the pack.

Volf wasn't that dumb. His face flushed. "Figure I can't even do that, don't you," he snarled. He whirled on Tev. "I'll be your pack brother and the best damned protector you ever saw."

Tev grinned and clapped him on the back. Volf looked absurdly pleased. Now to hold him. He put an arm over the younger man's shoulders and turned to face the stunned pack. "Well, as your pack brother the first thing I'll do is give you two salted meatcat carcasses. If you're my protector, I don't want you frantically hunting meat to trade for ship food so that you can feed your weanling son."

Volf almost sagged under Tev's arm. "Meatcats," he whispered. "Two?" When Tev nodded, Volf's face crumpled. He pulled free and turned away, his shoulders heaving silently. Tev refused to allow himself even a moment to glory in his victory. Now to get the rest of them. First the stick. He smiled humorlessly at the men as he asked. "Feel up to trimming the occasional zerker down to size, Volf?"

Volf twisted around. His eyes were wet, but they were alive. "Just point them out!"

"Let's find out if we need to." Now to gather them in—carefully. He looked slowly around the pack, assessing them. "With Volf as my zerker protector, I challenge for leadership of the pack."

"What? But you're lanker!" Kittu laughed. "That'd be rich. A lanker pack leader." His laugh died as Tev watched him grimly. "But you can't," he protested. "Lanker packs are forbidden."

"This isn't a lanker pack. It's a mixed pack."

Gopa rubbed his brow thoughtfully. "But no zerker is going to obey you."

Tev forcibly relaxed himself and gathered the confidence of a lifetime. They had to listen to him. He was the only answer to the increasing lanker anger. But he could not say that. He could only tell them what they wanted to hear. He spoke directly to Gopa, but his peripheral vision watched the stance of every zerker there, waiting for clues. "You say zerkers won't obey lankers, but think about it. Who advised Mikhail for twenty years?

Who planned the hunts? Who kept the lankers working, and mediated zerker arguments? Kittu says this pack went sour. But it went sour when Bart didn't turn. Mikhail was counting desperately on Bart's help and his disappointment turned him ugly. After being snarled at and humiliated for another tenday I quit wiping up after Mikhail. I stopped anticipating trouble and putting out the fires before they got started. I tell you. If you want a successful pack, you need me, for I won't serve as a silent partner any longer."

"It went sour when Mikhail started meddling with *them*," Gopa snarled, jerking his head toward where the Heights rose behind the dense screen of trees.

"You're right." *Always agree, it makes them easier to deal with.* "I won't meddle with *them*. With me as your leader, *they* will never have cause to bother us." His back itched. Let one bone needle sail into the clearing now, and they were all finished anyway. He waited, letting the men realize he was serious. Kittu studied Volf, clearly wondering whether or not to challenge. Gopa looked bitter and cynical.

"Gopa, you're tired of being First Spear. But you don't like the idea of becoming a junior pack member either. Stay with me. You'll be First Spear—but Volf will do a lot of the hard slugging that wears you out so much. He's been a solitary for almost a Gifter Month. He can do the long scouting trips you hate." Tev smiled at Volf. "Mind doing that? You'd be great at it, you know."

Volf shrugged as if he didn't care, but his smile escaped his control and he beamed from ear to ear.

"Samay. I know where to find some of the seeds and roots the healer is always trying to get. The pack will find them and use them to buy as much healer time as it needs to cure your back." He held up his hand. "And don't say you can handle the pain. We all know you can, but we're your pack and if we can't help you maybe we *should* break up."

Gopa jerked upright in horror. Tev disciplined his smile away. *Yes, Gopa, the pack could disperse and then where would you be?* Samay looked thoughtful as he shifted his weight to ease the strain on his back. Now for Kittu. He was young and steady—as steady as zerkers got—but he liked things done the way they were always done . . . unless . . .

"Kittu, you don't have to leave. We need you: you're a great thinker." *Complainer.* "And you often will see problems before they happen." *Or create them with your whining.* "I need you to listen to my plans and find the flaws. Stay with me and be my counselor." *And somehow I'll put up with you because I need the whole pack, not just part of it.*

Kittu tugged at his blond beard. "I can't see taking orders from a lanker. The other packs would laugh us out of the armory."

Tev showed his teeth. "Think they'll do that, Volf?"

Volf thought about it, his smile spreading to his eyes and lighting them with fire. "I could fight every day. For you, of course. Hey, Gun. Want some of the action?" Guntor, who had been sitting sullenly nursing his hand, pulled himself to his feet and swaggered over.

Tev held up his hand. Perfect. Couldn't have been better if he'd planned every word. He tried to look as grave as Sair when making a judgment. "I'm afraid Guntor can't share your fun for a while."

Guntor put his hand on his shette in the ready position. "Why not? I can fight as well as him."

"Not with one hand, you can't. I saw today. You

fought with your bandaged hand held to your side."
He walked forward. "Let's see it."

Guntor gave Bart a vicious look, then stood slowly.
When he fumbled with the wrappings, Tev used his
small knife to cut them off. He sucked in his breath
when he saw the blackened swollen hand. A stray
breeze brought a sickening smell to them. Tev lifted
the hand and turned it this way and that, taking his
time. Maybe it could be saved, and if the men obeyed
him in this they might not notice he'd taken control.
He waved Gopa over. Must keep him happy and
respected. The older zerker took one look and shook
his head. "If you don't cut off the black bit, it'll spread,
and he'll die." Mariko whimpered and clutched his
hand as if he were the one with an infection.

Tev pulled out his shette. "Well, Guntor, are you
ready?"

Guntor stared dumbly at his blackened hand. "Not
the whole hand," he whispered.

Tev shook his head. "The last finger I think. We'll
try that, and take more if we have to." At Guntor's
dazed look, he said, "Cheer up. It's not your bow
finger, and it's not your shette hand. If a warrior has
to lose something, let it be fingers he doesn't need
to stay alive."

Guntor didn't look at all cheered. His face was
getting whiter and whiter. Norv brought a log from
the fire stack as a cutting block.

Guntor licked his lips. "Are you sure . . ."

"Yes, I'm sure," Tev replied steadily. "This is something
you have to do." *And if I do it, I'll have the men
without their ever realizing it.*

Guntor swallowed heavily, and his breathing got
faster. While they waited, Tev assessed his pack. For
it was *his* pack, now. Maybe he would have a few

problems, but with Volf to threaten them, and his leadership to woo them, they'd give in. They had to.

Volf was standing at his side, still bristling, hoping someone would challenge and he could get even for his last month of misery. Samay sat braced against a log, his head in his hands. He'd do anything to fix his back. Gopa was using his shette to whittle a cutting surface for the log—already acting as First Spear even if it hadn't been consciously decided. Kittu was scowling. That was nothing new. But would he follow or run for another pack, leaving them with only four zerkers? The only people he wasn't worried about were his lankers. They were practically floating off their toes, waiting to help him in any way they could. And then there were the whelps . . . They watched in wide-eyed terror, probably wondering if they'd get home alive. Mariko, in particular, looked petrified. He was trying to cling to Guntor, terrified that Guntor might die and leave him alone. Hmm.

He caught Mariko's eye and jerked his head. Reluctantly the whelp left Guntor. Tev walked a little aside. "Mariko, Guntor could die." True. "But you can save him. I'll let you take camp duty to look after him, if you support me."

The slender whelp looked at his feet as he answered. "Why should you want my support? I'm only a whelp."

"And you'll soon be a man—a man that Guntor listens to. A man I would respect." Mariko shot him a startled look. "So I'm asking you ahead of time." The whelp stared, trying to figure Tev out. Tev met his gaze steadily and waited while the moments drifted by. Suddenly Mariko made up his mind. He squared his shoulders and faced Tev with a shrewd look that nearly took Tev's breath away.

"I'll back you," Mariko said. "I know a lot more about this pack than you think I do. And, if Guntor lives, he'll back you too—as long as you don't favor your asshole of a nephew."

Tev nodded gravely, amazed at the shrewd intelligence that he saw in Mariko's eyes. Obviously, like the other men, he'd been taken in by Mariko's fearful ways, and had not seen the mind underneath the fear. He reached out and shook Mariko's hand, surprised to find that he did respect him. But he was also worried. What else was going on in the pack that he didn't know about?

A sickening thud and hoarse scream jerked him around. Guntor was trying to claw at his hand, but Volf was holding his good hand away while Gopa was forcing Guntor's hand forward to the block again. Mariko rushed forward, but Norv intercepted him and held him back.

The sickening smell of Guntor's hand intensified. It was bleeding red, white, yellow, and black. Gopa made a few more cuts to let out the stinking fluid and Guntor started to grunt like a pinto hog. Finally Gopa stroked down the ruined arm, forcing more puss out. When he got to the hand itself, Guntor choked and fainted. Gopa finished his work, pulled the ruined skin together, fastened it with sewing thorns and wrapped the whole mess in hot fireweed. Fireweed burned out the infection, but your nerves ached with the pain for weeks. Tev felt his stomach tense—but not with sympathy. Gopa had seized the initiative and taken it away from him. Damn.

"Take him into the cave," Gopa ordered. Norv and Dyfid hurried to obey. Mariko trailed after them.

Tev jumped in. "Well, Guntor can't travel for today. We might as well hunt another day. We can head in the other direction from 'them' and stay together for safety."

Bart seemed to come out of his fog of grief. "Mikhail was killed, you know. What are you going to do about it?"

Gopa froze in the act of scraping the remains of Guntor's finger into the fire.

Shivers ran their slow way down Tev's spine. What if *they* were listening? "We know he was killed." Tev made a great show of circling his breast. "But we can do nothing against 'them.' "

"What if it wasn't 'them'? Mikhail was killed by a bone splinter that was made. I may have been spelled by it, but I could see the tiny scratch and polish marks. It was made by man." He saw the anger in Tev's face and his face drained of color. "I know you don't want me to talk about this." He gulped and continued, his voice shaky. "And I know the consequences. But he was my *father*!"

"Oh," Tev said with the interest you would give a cub who wanted to show you he could walk. "And where is that wonderful splinter now? How is it that you saw a splinter, and I didn't?"

Bart's eyes widened, "But you knocked it out of my hand." Tev snorted. Bart looked around at the men who watched warily. "You have to believe me. Maybe it was one of the other packs?" Bart said.

Oh, better and better. Tev beckoned to Mariko who had come out of the cave with Norv and Dyfid. He ignored Bart and waited until the whelp was beside him. "How is he?"

"Sleeping." Mariko tilted his head and waited, watching him from lowered lids.

"I have a job for you. We have a *boy* here, who's gone crazy with grief." He put a hand up when Bart tried to protest. "I can't trust him anywhere, so I'll leave him here as camp fetch while we hunt. Could you keep him busy?"

Mariko's eyes gleamed.

"But, but . . ." A blow cut off Bart's protest.

"Shut up when the pack leader's speaking," Norv snarled.

Tev nearly swallowed his tongue. It was too soon. He didn't need to start them arguing again: he needed action.

But no one protested. No one. Taizaburo, he'd done it!

"All right, men!" he roared, vitalized by elation. "Let's hunt. I've got a few ideas, and I'll wager all of you we come back with five man-weights of meat tonight."

"You'll get no takers," Gopa said levelly. "Haven't you noticed that we've all gotten tired of losing bets to you?" He waved to the men and they started forming up—only this time Tev stood in Mikhail's place in the line.

He pretended not to notice Bart's anguished face as *his* men formed up. The boy was dead white. He knew what happened to people who got in Tev's way. But he had still defied him. Was he really courageous, or just stupid? If it was another pack who'd killed Mikhail, Bart was as good as dead. If it was *them*, he was also as good as dead. His only safety lay in being considered a nobody whose opinion was worth nothing.

As he jogged into the jungle his thigh rubbed his pocket—the pocket that held a small polished bone needle—a needle so dangerous it could sicken someone who just touched it.

By the time they descended to the valley they

15

Day 47:First Gifter Moon of Spring:
452 Migrations After Landing

Assilla paced the room like a caged meatcat in heat. "Where is Haddim? His pack went into the armory at least an hour ago." She rounded on Sanda who was repatching the knee in one of Haddim's old trousers. "Are you sure you saw him?"

"He's the only one who lags behind in the pack. Besides, Radnor whistled the pack call until his wives came out on the deck and waved to him."

"Wonderful. They must be bringing back lots of meat." Assilla went to the storage room and came out with a couple of wooden bowls. "I'll soak some of the herbs." She laughed shakily. "I'm so hungry, I'm trembling."

Sanda swallowed. She wasn't hungry. She was terrified. She'd avoided Haddim after she came back from the barricades. Then, the next day, all the men had gone hunting, leaving a lot of disappointed girls. Now he was back. Did he still want her? Goddess Within. If only he could have forgotten . . . or come back too sick to care. No, not too sick. They needed the food.

The door scraped open.

251

Assilla pounced on Haddim. "What do you have for us?"

Haddim dropped his pack on the table. He was gaunt, his face drawn with fatigue. Assilla ripped open the fastenings, pulling out bloody hunks of meat and bone. "Ildenhorn, good, good. A treebore. Wonderful. Some keld." She sighed happily as she sorted the meat. "I'll make a stew right away, and when your whelp brings the rest up, we'll start spicing and preserving it."

"There isn't any more." Haddim stuck his chin out and his beady eyes got smaller and sharper.

"What? What do you mean?" Assilla looked puzzled. "There's not enough there to get us through migration."

"That's all I got, so shut up."

"But . . . but Radnor signaled that he had meat."

"Shut up, bitch!" Haddim roared. "Radnor did get meat. The man has luck in his veins instead of blood . . . got seven kills."

"But this . . ." Assilla sorted through the meat again. "Surely the pack got more than seven kills—they didn't give you enough."

Haddim strode around the table and backhanded his wife, knocking her down. "Get me some wine."

Assilla crept backward, keeping her eyes lowered. "We . . . we don't have any," she whispered. Sanda tried to edge into a shadowy corner of the room. When Haddim started beating his wives he wasn't above hitting his children, either.

"Then get some."

"I can't. There isn't a drop left in The Home. You have to wait for the next crop of mirta fruit."

Haddim upended the table sending hunks of meat flying across the room. "Damn you!"

Assilla crouched and bowed her head. "There isn't

any," she whispered. "I even tried the healer, but there's none left, I swear."

Haddim wiped his lips and looked over all the storage jars, along the wall to where Sanda was cowering, half hidden by the ragged pants she was pretending to mend.

"Well, what have we here, a nice new wife to greet me."

Assilla looked from Sanda to Haddim, clearly at a loss. "Husband," she said cautiously. "That's Sanda."

"I know it's Sanda, you bitch. Well, if I can't get drunk, I guess I'll have to settle for getting laid."

Assilla froze in horror. Haddim walked over to Sanda and inspected her. She tried to shrink under the ragged hide she was mending. Her head ached from lack of sleep; her mind was numb. She felt his eyes travel slowly from her head, down her body, lingering on where her tiny breasts hid under her loose tunic. She tried to shrink from him, but he snatched a handful of hair and brought her closer, turning her toward Assilla. "Take a look at my fourth wife." Sanda felt the horror turn to fear and then begin to boil. No, she screamed silently. No. I don't want to be drugged yet.

His First Wife fell back a pace, her jaw slack. Then she recovered, almost stuttering in consternation. "But she's your daughter. It's not done."

"She's not my blood and I'm doing it." He leaned forward, the light behind his eyes growing brighter. "Any objections?"

Her stepmother shrank into an even smaller bundle, seeming to be more clothes than person. "Couldn't we wait until after her guild training? She'll be more valuable to our family as a scholar."

"Forget guild training. Forget wife training. She's not going anywhere. I want her now."

"Forget wife training! But an untrained woman isn't really a wife. She'll be nothing! The women will shun her."

"Tough. Maybe a woman should find out what it's like to be shunned." He turned his back on his wife, his fists clenched. "I have to go back to the armory. We're bringing in wood for migration. I'll be back soon, and I expect Sanda to be waiting for me." His beaked nose seemed to poke across the distance into her. "Well? Are you going to be a good little wife, or should I talk to Assilla?"

"N . . . no sir, I mean, yes sir." Sanda choked out. When Haddim turned and walked out she nearly fainted with relief.

Assilla bore down on Sanda. "You little bitch!"

"I didn't do anything, Assilla, honest I didn't." She fell to her knees in front of her stepmother. "Please, don't be angry." She lowered her voice to a tense whisper. "I *don't* want to marry him."

"You're not going to. You'll just be a woman— someone with no rights at all."

Sanda kept her eyes on the weave pattern of the mat beneath her feet. The mat she had woven with Ullan so many centuries ago. No rights—like that old woman she used to laugh at when she was small— the woman who had thrown herself from the Promenade Deck when she'd been traded away from her quarters for a haunch of keld.

Pain exploded in Sanda's head as Assilla slapped her, knocking her down. "Do you know what you've done? How am I going to find a husband for Ava? The minute the men know about you, they'll assume Haddim had her, too." When Assilla raised her hand again, Sanda didn't cringe. She welcomed the pain with each blow; it gave substance to her desperate misery. Now that Haddim had spoken, her future was here: in these quarters, with Haddim who lusted for her, with Assilla who hated and feared zerkers, and with Brianna, who was dying.

Finally the blows stopped. "Get up."

She didn't want to get up. She just wanted to sink into the floor and die. Soon the rages would come and she would be a prisoner in body as well as in soul.

Assilla took her shoulders and uncurled her. "Get up." She stood Sanda up and searched her eyes. Finally she relaxed. "Well, at least you're not zerker. I had to find that out." She took a deep breath and let it out slowly. "If you'd been zerker, I just couldn't have stood it. Being First Wife to a zerker warrior is hard. Having Brianna around to set Haddim off makes it worse, but a third zerker would have been more than I could have endured."

Sanda looked at the floor. What would Assilla do when she found out?

Her stepmother grasped her chin roughly and lifted it so she could look at Sanda. "Why didn't I listen to Inara and keep you out of sight? She warned me." Her stepmother's hands dropped to her sides. "*Shikata ga nai*: it can't be helped. Haddim said something about being shunned. I think we're going to get a lot hungrier. And when he's hungry, he's mean, so you'd better get ready for him."

"But . . . but . . ." She choked on the words. "I can't bear it."

Assilla gathered up the meat, and stood looking at her. "You have to. Practice *enryo*. Put a safe distance between him and your heart. Remember. He's using your body. You can keep your mind safe behind ten meters of stone."

"How?" Sanda whispered.

"Think of other things. Make your face smile. Do as he says, and recite the maxims of Olarni." She put the meat on the table and sighed. "At least he won't be drunk." She waved to the meat. "You might as well take some of this and make a hunter stew for tonight. Add lots of jungle greens for bulk. Cut the rest in strips and pack it in spice pods. I can preserve it tomorrow." She went into the bathing chamber, to rinse the blood from her hands.

Sanda sank against the cool rock, still holding Haddim's tattered trousers. Tears blurred her vision as her dreams of Bart walking her back from their marriage feast were ripped to pieces like smoke in a winter storm.

"And when you're finished, you might see if you can get any of the stew into your mother, though I don't know why we try any more." Assilla went toward the outer door.

"Where are you going?" Sanda dropped the leathers and ran to her stepmother. "Don't leave me alone. Please don't!" She grabbed Assilla's skirts the way she had when she was a child and unexpectedly burst into tears. Assilla didn't hit her, but she didn't stroke her hair either. Instead Sanda heard her muttering "*Gaman*: Bear up, endure." She pulled away. "I have to warn Inara, and send Ava to her aunt's until her Thirteenth Sort. We still might keep Ava looking pure enough to get her a husband." Her stepmother finally reached out and smoothed Sanda's hair back gently. "It comes to us all, child."

The closing door echoed like a sprung trap.

❖   ❖   ❖

Sanda numbly cooked the stew, terrified of what would happen that evening, and dreaming of dozens of impossible escapes: that Bart turned zerker and challenged Haddim for her; that Haddim got into some wine and fell down the armory stairs and broke something; that Assilla would find a way to stop her service; that . . . Meanwhile she automatically chopped and stirred, frugally using just enough wood to heat the stew.

If only she could talk to someone, anyone. But Ullan was watched constantly. Assilla would just tell her to endure, and her mother . . . her mother would say nothing. She was almost dead. She filled a bowl with a little broth and headed for her mother's bolted bedchamber.

She swung open the door. For a split second she saw a figure standing on a storage chest, looking out the window. Then her mother was on her and fingers pressed into her throat.

"Momma, please!"

Bony fingers dug painfully into her shoulders, and Sanda was dragged over to the window where the late afternoon sun made a golden patch on the floor. "It is you. Finally I can talk to you."

Sanda backed away from her mother. "Momma. You can talk!" The sour smell of sweat, stale Peace, and mildew threatened to gag her. But her mother's appearance was even more frightening. Her body was bone overlaid with sinew, and not much else. Only her stringy hair gave her face volume, for it sprang straight out from her head.

"No Peace. It's all gone. Of course I can talk . . . is anyone in the wardroom?"

Sanda shook her head and edged backward. But her mother's bony hand reached out, and for the second time today she felt the unsettling touch of a disturbed zerker. Only behind the gaunt figure, and the desperation, she felt an overwhelming love.

Blindly she took the stinking rack of bones into her arms, for the love was the same love that had surrounded her and protected her, until the day Haddim had married her mother—and quadrupled her dose of Peace. "Momma, Momma, I can't stand it any more. I can't."

Her mother stroked her with hands that were more bone than flesh. "Poor Sanda. Poor zerker."

Her muscles jerked. "I'm not," she protested automatically.

"Of course, you are. I've seen it coming. Why do you think I pretended to get sick? Why do you think I continued to starve myself after they locked up the storage room?"

"You! You were stealing the food!"

"Of course." Brianna gave Sanda a fierce hug. "Now listen. There's a way for you to be safe—to hide."

Sanda pulled free of her mother's arms. "There's no way out. Haddim knows, and Ullan knows, and Bart knows."

"Forget Haddim."

"How can I forget Haddim? He's coming back at the first evening bell, and he wants me in his bed! I'm not even going to go for wife training. I'll just be his *woman*."

"The bastard!" Brianna knocked Sanda aside. Weak as she was, the zerker rage reached out and caught up her daughter. Sanda leaped to her feet, wondering how she'd ever agreed to service Haddim. She'd kill him first.

But her mother caught her arm and pulled her into a hug. "No, little one. No. Not now. You must listen first. Then we'll plan." She looked significantly toward the still-open door. Sanda ran to close it.

"Listen carefully. We may not have a lot of time." She sat down on her bed and visibly gathered her strength. "Sanda, you don't need to be drugged. You can hide."

"Hide! Where?"

"Not where. How. Like Nystra."

Sanda blinked, caught off stride. "Nystra? But she's the Mother General."

"She's also zerker."

"She can't be." Sanda visualized the calm Mother General who glided through The Home ministering to the women. "There, there," she said soothingly, bitter disappointment souring her stomach. "You're mistaken, that's all."

Her mother interrupted her soothing litany. "No, I'm not. Nystra is zerker. I was there when she turned, but I told no one. When I turned, my father was there, and he had me drugged. But Nystra is zerker— and no one ever knew."

"She really turned?" Sanda couldn't believe it.

"She was sewing and when her shoulder seam was wrong for the fourth time, she ripped it up and ripped every other seam out. She'd have ripped the leathers apart, too, but they were full-butt keld backs." Brianna pulled Sanda close so she could look directly into her eyes.

Sanda shivered. Brianna's body might be wasted, but her eyes showed more fire than Haddim's.

"Learn to hide, Sanda. Learn to hide the way Kayella did. She became a stonemason and worked herself into exhaustion every night." Her eyes narrowed. "Kayella. What happened to her? Nobody will tell me. Did they drug her? Is she all right?"

"Oh, Momma. The Daughters of Olarni have taken her."

"The Olarnites. But she isn't old enough. What would those withered up old bitches want with her?"

Sanda took her mother in her arms as if she were the parent. "I'm sorry, Momma. She was too old for the medicine. It drove her crazy. The Olarnites agreed to take care of her."

Her mother clutched her stomach as a wail of anguish tore out of her throat, quickly muffled by the dirty rag she stuck in her mouth. Sanda clutched her and they both rocked in grief for the young woman they would never see again.

With a mood change characteristic of zerkers, Brianna suddenly lifted her head. "Now. Let's plan. We must save you. Will Ullan tell?"

"She begged me to find out how the ancients controlled their zerkers without drugs. That was the price of her silence."

Her mother started to say something and stopped. "But . . ." She frowned, then pushed the thought away. "So she'll stay silent, and in a few years no one will believe anything she says anyway." At Sanda's startled look she said, "Believe me I know. When my husband Jaspaar came home dead and without a mark on him, I tried to tell them he wasn't sick. We used to play in bed all night, and he'd hunt all day, and he loved every minute of both. The ghost must have . . . No. Stop. Don't ramble. Ullan won't tell. What about this Bart? Who's he?"

"He's a lanker whelp who wants to marry me." Sanda looked down and felt self-pity almost overwhelm her. "That is he *wanted* to marry me. And he doesn't care about my being zerker."

"If he's lanker, that's good. You have to stay away

from zerkers from now on. Become a guild wife so you can work away from zerkers . . . and work hard."

"But Ullan . . . how can I stay away from her? I'm her only friend."

"Ullan will understand. Just sing the song."

"What . . . ?"

Her mother's eyes glazed and she sang in a slow harsh voice.

> *"Zerkers see and zerkers feel*
> *Every slight and every weal.*
> *Words and gestures must be healing*
> *Or their rages you'll be feeling.*
> *Watch your words and soothe your tones*
> *And remember in your very bones*
> *That ZERKERS SET EACH OTHER OFF."*

"Oh that."

"That!" Her mother jumped to her feet and paced up and down the room. "Never forget *that*. If I'd remembered *that*, maybe I'd be standing beside the Mother General, helping her with the guilds instead of being trapped in this drugged body. *She* had her children normally. When I became pregnant they took away my Peace and chained me to my bed." She grabbed Sanda by the shoulders. "You must hide. You must. The Peace. It calms you, sure. But it only calms your body. Not your mind. You can still see everything, hear everything."

"But, Momma . . ."

"You see a shuddering wreck. But I'm not. I can think. Just like you. I weep when I drool. *But I can't do anything about it!* I suffer. But I can't even scream with frustration." She wrung her hands. "If only I'd paid attention that day! But my father was zerker, and he was in a bad mood to start with. But I could have gone up to the children's gallery. I could have found something else to do. But no, I had to show him that I could cook as well as a woman. And when the clay cooker broke in the fire, my father lost his temper. Oh, Goddess Within, why didn't I leave the room that day? Why didn't I?" She burst into tears and buried her face in her hands.

Sanda approached her mother cautiously. She wanted so much to comfort her, but her mother was frightening.

Brianna dropped her hands. Tears still shone in her eyes, but they were obviously forgotten. "Now, this is what we'll do about Haddim."

Sanda supported her mother as they walked into Haddim's bedchamber. Apart from that one time Haddim had dragged her in against her will, Sanda had never been in here. The square chamber was dominated by a huge bed made of burl oak timbers, longer than a man, and as wide as it was long. On it a stuffed cat-hair mattress was covered by a thick chicken-feather duvet. Behind, a faded tapestry covered one whole wall. On it men lined the barricades, fighting ferts during the full migration. To one side of the tapestry a long recessed shelf held extra blankets, cushions and folded winter coveralls. Above it, hooks wedged into the rock held Haddim's tunics, night robe, and old leathers. At the foot of the bed was an old blackened chest.

She kicked back the coverlet with one foot and eased Brianna onto the bed. As she covered her mother, she couldn't help but compare the two of them. She didn't know much about men. But she knew instinctively that Haddim would be furious when he found this wasted wreck in his bed. Her mother's head lolled. She was asleep again.

"Momma, wake up." Sanda lifted her mother's head back up on the pillow. "Momma, it isn't going to work. You're exhausted, and weak."

"Get me some of that stew you're making for *him*." Her voice grated with hatred.

"But he'll know it isn't me and he'll be furious."

"Leave Haddim to me. You just keep your mouth shut and lock yourself in your bedchamber up on the children's gallery." Her eyes closed and she started to snore.

Sanda hurried to the wardroom and, hands trembling, stirred up the stew and took a bowl of the broth into her mother. As she walked the aroma of the stew raced up to her brain making her mouth water. She took a large mouthful before fear of Haddim sent her hurrying in to her mother.

She woke her mother who greedily drank the broth.

"Not so fast, Momma. You haven't been eating for a long time. I have to feed you slowly."

"No, more stew. I need the strength."

Sanda pulled the bowl away. They'd had lessons on this. She stepped back out of reach. "We must wait, Momma."

Her mother heaved a long slow breath, but her eyes did not close. Instead they sharpened. Sanda shivered.

Brianna pointed to the chest warped by age and split along the grain lines. "While you're waiting, I want to get a package out of that chest. It's wrapped in red shimmer cloth."

Curiously, Sanda opened the trunk. It contained an old cracked bowl. She lifted it aside, and in doing so, saw men and women dancing around its side, wearing long flowing robes of red, gold, green and blue.

"Hurry up, he could be coming."

She saw the red cloth and lifted it out. "What's in it, Momma?"

"Just something for lovemaking, child. Something wives do. Give it to me."

Sanda handed it over, wondering what it was that women did. The package felt as if it were encased leather. She waited to see what was in it, but her mother just shoved it under the covers.

"More broth."

The wardroom door crashed open. Sanda jumped up, spilling the rest of the bowl. How could she have fallen asleep? She shook her mother awake.

"Oh Sanda, where are you?" Haddim sounded like a cub before he ate his birthday pie.

"Answer him," Brianna hissed, "then hide."

"Here," Sanda croaked, frantically looking for a hiding place.

"Under the extra blankets." Her mother was fumbling under the covers for something.

Sanda dove for the linens and burrowed her way under.

The bedchamber door creaked open. She froze, praying that she was totally covered.

Haddim took a gusty breath. A rustle of leather marked his approach. "Don't hide under the covers." Sanda nearly jumped. He was right beside her, facing the bed. "Love isn't that bad, you know." He grunted as he sat down. "Now give me a kiss, and I'll be nice to you. Otherwise . . . yeow!"

Sanda jerked; the blanket slipped and she saw him falling backward, dragging the duvet with him. He

landed crouched, facing her mother who knelt on
the bed, with a long, narrow, and exceedingly thin
dagger held in front her. Her naked chest heaved,
and her thin pendulous breasts trembled over the
knife.

Haddim put his hand inside his tunic, felt his chest,
and then stared at the blood that glistened darkly in
the gloom.

"Take my daughter, will you—just try." Brianna
took a firmer grip on her knife and slid her bony
legs apart, bracing herself.

Instead of shrinking from the dangerous blade,
Haddim stood up straighter and laughed. "Want a
fight, do you? Well, this time we'll fight to the finish.
There are no wives around to throw water on us or
call the guard." He stepped back, pulled his tunic
over his head and wrapped it around his left arm in
one blinding motion.

Brianna remained crouched, shielded by the thin
knife. She pulled her lips back from strong yellow
teeth in a ghastly grin. "It doesn't matter if I win or
lose this fight, I've still won." She got up on one
knee, turning to follow Haddim as he shifted around
the bed, looking for an opening. "If I win, you die.
If you win, your pack mates will despise you for raping
your daughter on the body of her mother. They'll
expel you for sure." At his startled gasp, she chortled
triumphantly. "Don't think that because I'm frozen
I can't hear. I sit by my open window for hours. The
men call you 'The Drunk' and wonder why . . ." She
dodged as Haddim lunged, and slashed at his open
chest.

Haddim drove his leather wrapped hand at the
dagger and howled as the leather split open. But
the force of his blow knocked the knife across the

bed and onto the floor below Sanda's hiding place. Brianna lunged for the knife, but Haddim kicked her full in the chest, knocking her against the tapestry-covered rock wall. "Now you're going to pay," he said softly. "But you're right about killing you. I can't do that. But I can beat you half to death. Then I'll find Sanda even if I have to drag her out of the children's quarters." He laughed softly as Brianna moaned. "You'll watch, Brianna. Yes, you'll watch. I'll rip her open. I'll make her scream for mercy."

"No!" Brianna shrieked and reached blindly for his throat. He knocked her aside easily, then gave her a back-handed slap that knocked her away from Sanda, across the bed and off onto the floor. She got up and ran for the door. Sanda slid out from her hiding place ready to run for the outer door and get help. But Haddim jumped after Brianna, caught her hair and swung her back into the room. As he did so, he saw Sanda.

"Great. Two at once." He kicked Brianna, doubling her up, and started for Sanda who was diving for the knife. His foot welded it to the floor. "Come on. Fight. Kick. Scream." His beaked nose bore down on her. She tried to wriggle away, to bite him, to kick him, but he held her easily and brought her to his mouth. His hands crushed her body against his and he started grinding his lips against hers. His mouth forced hers open.

He gasped. His grip slackened. He dropped her and whirled. Sanda had one glimpse of a bloody slit in his back before she dropped for the floor—and landed on the knife. She rolled up, knife in hand to see her mother holding an identical knife.

"I'll kill you." Haddim gasped. He was in agony, and berserker. He kicked aside the knife, grabbed

Brianna by the neck and started to throttle her. Sanda threw herself on his back stabbing for his neck, trying for the killing slash women used on meatcats. Never had her knife been so true. He choked. Blood sprayed out of his mouth and he deflated like a limp bellows.

"Momma, are you all right?" Sanda tried to wipe the blood off her mother's face, but she only smeared it.

Her mother's eyes fluttered; they sought Haddim and her mouth curved in a grim smile. "Bastard." She pushed weakly at his body trying to get out from under his weight. Sanda shoved him and he rolled away, his head flopping and his eyes looking vaguely surprised.

Brianna grabbed the dagger. "Find the other one, Sanda. They're a matched pair." Sanda found the other one on the floor by the door. Her mother pushed herself upright. "Help me to the door. I have one more thing to do."

With Sanda supporting her, Brianna staggered to the outside door. Now that the danger was over, her step was halting and her breath came in exhausted gasps. "Open the outer door."

"But, Momma, you're naked, and you're covered with blood. You can't go out there. We can't go out there." The stark reality of what she'd done suddenly hit her. "They'll kill me."

"No. You did nothing." Her mother clung to Sanda for balance. "I killed Haddim."

"But . . ."

"I killed him. Not you. You watched. Two zerkers fought to the death. Understand? If they suspect you, they'll test you to see if you're zerker. And you'll be locked up—like me." She leaned forward, her grey hair hanging half over her face, and kissed her daughter. "I killed him. Now you can be trained as a wife. You can become a scholar. *You can hide!* Don't you see? Haddim is dead. Ullan will keep your secret if you try to help her, and that lanker boy will probably not survive initiation. You're safe!"

When Sanda stood there, frozen, Brianna gave her a savage hug. "Remember. Cry when they question you. Cry as hard as you can. They'll think you're a lanker-weak woman, and leave you alone." She jerked away and staggered to the door. She was so weak she had to put her whole weight behind her attempt to get it open. Then she lurched into the Promenade Deck, stark naked, drenched in fresh blood, and with daggers in both hands.

"No!" Sanda rushed after her. But it was too late. Three women working on planters along the edge turned, staring.

Brianna raised the daggers in both hands. The late afternoon sun picked out the wet sheen of blood that bathed her ribs, her pendulous breasts and the sad grizzle between her legs. "I claim sanctuary," she shrilled. The women turned to stare at Sanda. Suddenly she was aware of the blood on her tunic. Two more women rushed up, then shrank back, recognizing Brianna. Sanda stood by helplessly, wringing her hands. She should do something. But what? Confess? Die?

Her mother took another step into the Promenade Deck and shouted. "He tried to rape my daughter. I killed him. I claim sanctuary with the Olarnites."

The two knives fell from her hands. Sanda darted forward and caught her mother as she slowly crumpled to the ground.

16

Day Fifty of the First Moon of Spring

As the Assembly Bell rang its summons, each new chime mingled with older ones, swelling in volume like a river in spring flood. On the Promenade Deck, Bart hurried toward the Assembly Hall, straightening his whelp-green formal tunic. It was the day of the Thirteenth Sort—the day Sanda had planned to run for steerage. But now that Haddim was dead, Bart wondered what she was going to do.

Dyfid strode ahead of him, his feet keeping pace with the pealing bells. He was wearing a tunic of warrior red. Bart lengthened his stride, envious. Dyfid had survived his initiation and was a full warrior. Already Tev's wives had offered to arrange his marriage in place of his mother—who was steerage.

As he overtook the new warrior, Dyfid gave him a sour look. "Did you ask Tev about your initiation?" Dyfid shouted over the volume of the bells.

Bart shook his head. "I haven't gone near Tev since he became the pack leader. And he didn't even look at me when he arranged for your initiation. I just don't know where I stand."

The bell ceased tolling, leaving only the echoes to chase each other back and forth across the cliffs.

269

When the last hollow clang dwindled away, Dyfid spoke more quietly. "Well, you can't expect Tev to let you be initiated when you accused him of lying about your father."

Bart's gut tightened as they began the old argument. "But my father was murdered. And Tev was lying. How could I keep silent about that?" He gave a fearful glance around and whispered. "Do you think Tev will . . ." He made a tiny throat-cutting gesture. After all, Dyfid was in thick with the lankers. He'd know what they were thinking.

Dyfid shook his head. "Of course not. You're my pack brother, remember? He needs me. If he attacks you, he attacks me and he doesn't want to lose me. I'm his ear in steerage as well as one of his most loyal supporters." When Bart started to talk, Dyfid held up his hand. "He doesn't want to lose you, either. But he's getting impatient, waiting for you to see sense. He told me today that if you didn't shape up soon, he was booting you out."

Bart stumbled. Dyfid reached out to steady him. "I don't know what happened when your father died, Bart. But I do know what will happen if you don't come to terms with Tev." He gripped Bart's arm. "Think about it." Then he turned and hurried off.

Bart stood stunned, his eyes on the rock deck. Gradually he began to hear murmurs around him as people passed. "Says his father was murdered . . . can't accept it was *them* . . . wants to blame us . . . wasn't another pack within three days' travel . . . he's trouble . . . caused young Guntor to lose his finger . . . yeah, bit him . . . wouldn't want him in my pack . . . should be sent to steerage."

Steerage! He'd rather die than go there. He trudged on, wishing the ceremony were over so he could hide under his bed fur and seek the oblivion of sleep. If only he could talk to Sanda. Somehow talking with her helped him sort out his own thoughts.

He nearly collided with Ontu as he entered the Assembly Hall.

"Out of my way, whelp." Then Ontu paused, recognizing Bart. "Your poor father. Imagine his pack becoming a lanker pack."

A low voice growled behind Bart. "You got any complaints about Tev's mixed pack?" Bart didn't have to turn around to recognize Volf, or know that he was grinning viciously. As Tev's protector, Volf had gone looking for fights, challenging anyone who objected to Tev's new position.

Ontu flushed and backed off. "Better watch yourself," he blustered. "If I really cared about this, I'd beat you silly." He walked off hastily. Volf looked after him, disappointed.

When Bart took another step, a tremendous blow sent him sprawling. Guntor's cruel chuckle followed him down.

"Stupid whelp. Don't know why Tev keeps him. Can't hunt, can't fight, can't even protect a sick man."

Bart got to his knees. He could still see the red of Guntor's warrior tunic, and the white of the bandage on Guntor's left hand. He refused to look higher. He was afraid Guntor might goad him into a challenge.

Guntor laughed cruelly. "He should be taught a lesson, but I promised my new wife I wouldn't fight during the ceremony." He swaggered away.

As Bart walked down the long rectangular hall toward the dais, he looked straight ahead, not wanting to know who had seen him thrown aside.

A friendly hand touched his shoulder. "Don't take it so bad." He turned, relieved. Lars, the steerage foreman, stood smiling at him. Steerage! Did the man think Bart was his next recruit? Bart slapped the hand off and almost ran away.

Already the room was darkening into night. Usually torches were placed in all the brackets, but tonight there were just a few around the dais. Wood of any kind was in short supply—and migration was near. Bart sat in the gathering gloom at the back of his own pack. Only last Midwinter Feast he had bet his father he would be Second Spear within a migration. Now he wondered if Tev would let him stay. Jarret, the young whelp, edged away from him as if he were bad luck.

Bart looked at Tev's broad shoulders. Why had he lied, saying there was no splinter? Was Tev worried about ghosts? Was he covering for the murderer? Was he the murderer? He'd killed Nakano. Why didn't he kill Bart? He shook his head, confused. It made sense that Tev would want to kill Mikhail to be pack leader. But everyone had been a half-klat away helping Volf—or so they said. His mind went round and round in circles. Every warrior in The Home was accounted for.

So what should he do? Be a true warrior and try again to convince people of his father's murder? *And probably die, like Nakano.* Or be a coward. Everything in his warrior training urged him to lay Mikhail's murder before all the warriors—but—a shiver ran down his spine. What if the Sangirs had taken his father? Maybe Tev was right. Maybe he should have kept his mouth shut.

When the warriors were seated, the women drifted into the hall with their cubs and girl children, drowning out the warriors' baritone with women's chatter, children's shouts, and babies' cries. The crowd startled Bart.

He'd never realized how many women there were, and how few men.

The women swayed aside and Edgar ushered his boys—trainees of six to twelve—into the empty space behind the whelps. The boys outnumbered the whelps and the warriors. Edgar separated the eighteen boys who were to celebrate their Thirteenth Sort and took them to sit beside the dais. Bart remembered when he'd sat there. He, and Guntor, and Nevor and the others. Nevor had broken his leg. The break had become infected and he'd died. Tardo had gotten jungle fever. Vair had died of pneumonia. Borth had . . . He suddenly realized how many had died, and looked for those still alive. Seven. Only seven. Twelve had died in three years!

The boys settled, a guildswoman led in the girl's Thirteenth Sort. Bart searched for Sanda, but she was not there. Unease crawled down his back. Where was she? Had she already run for steerage?

The gong sounded; the door behind the dais opened, and the Elders who had survived to sixty entered. Slowly and with great dignity nine men in long red tunics climbed stiffly down the four steps from the dais, some favoring old wounds, others reduced to using canes and crutches. They settled themselves in front of the warriors. Of the nine only one was zerker.

Behind them, Sair limped into the room. He wore the red tunic of a warrior, but where the warriors' belts were black, his was gold, and on his neck hung the large blue and gold sun disk of the Supreme Guardian. In his hands, wrapped in white shimmer cloth, he carried the original sword of Taizaburo.

Next, Radnor strutted through the open door. Bart started. That was his father's place and in spite of

everything it was a shock to see Radnor where his
father had always been. Behind Radnor came Korv,
the new second Lieutenant of The Home. As he entered
the Hall his pack rose from their seats and cheered
him. He smiled and waved to his pack, and then to
the others. More and more men cheered him. Radnor
scowled.

When the men finally quieted down Sair gestured
for them to sit, then raised his arms signaling for
silence. The men sat immediately, but the undisciplined
women took a long time to settle down. When their
chatter finally died away Sair spoke. "Tonight is the
Ceremony of the Thirteenth Sort, but before we begin,
we have a judgment for the murder of Haddim."

That brought total silence. Everyone, including
the warriors, craned their necks looking back toward
the main entrance. A baby cried plaintively, and the
cry was instantly muffled, probably by his mother's
breast. Bart knew without looking that all the nurslings
were either sleeping, or drinking. The weanlings,
those four and over, knew better than to make a sound
once Assembly started.

The door opened at the back and everyone turned
to watch as two strong-armed guildwives carried Brianna
in on a stretcher. Sanda walked alongside holding her
mother's hand. Her walk was jerky, her eyes unfocused.
Had she turned? Was she already drugged with Peace?
When they reached the dais the women halted. Sanda
blundered forward another step, then stopped.

Bart hoped Sanda would look his way so that he
could give her some kind of comfort. But what could
he do across a room?

Her mother looked ghastly. She was a pile of
parchment-covered bone decorated with a hank of
grizzled hair. The penalty for killing a warrior was

abandonment in the jungle. She looked as if she'd die before they got her there. The guildswomen helped Brianna to her feet and held her up.

Sair stared at Brianna, then addressed Nystra. "This killed Haddim?"

"She is drugged, Honored Warrior. At the time of the murder she was not."

"Not drugged! Then the First Wife is also responsible. Get her up here."

A low murmur rose among the women, then hushed as Assilla slowly walked down the center aisle to the front and took her place beside Sanda.

Bart could hardly recognize her. She was no longer the officious First Wife who had dragged Ullan off the dactyl netting less than a Gifter month ago. She looked like a grannie, her skin slack, and her face lined with worry and fear.

She lifted pleading hands. "Honored Guardian . . ."

"Shut up. We know *your* guilt." He limped to the edge of the dais. "Why must there be a judgment? Why was she not killed at once?"

Nystra curtsied to Sair, then turned so her voice could travel across the packed rows of the men, women, and children.

"People of The Home. Brianna married Haddim honorably. He promised to care for her, and her children. But he tried to force his own stepdaughter to service him. He could have given Sanda wife training and married her. But he wouldn't wait. When Brianna came upon him trying to rape her daughter, she attacked him, as any mother—lanker or zerker—would. For killing a warrior she deserves to die. For protecting her daughter she deserves to live."

An angry murmur rose from the women, then broke into a babble of furious whispers.

Beside Brianna, Sanda looked down at her feet. Slowly, with tremendous effort, Brianna put out her hand and managed to touch her daughter's wrist.

Nystra raised her arms; her quiet voice carried into every shadowy corner. "Women of The Home, Brianna only wanted her daughter to have a decent life. Will you support her?"

In the middle of the hall, sunk in the shadows, a woman started a piercing trill. It was answered from the back of the room, and in an instant, hundreds of trills filled the hall, sending chills down Bart's spine.

Sair gestured angrily. Radnor hit the gong, but the sound was drowned by the shrill, angry protest. Nystra raised her arms. Silence crashed down on the hall as over five hundred women were obedient to her will.

Sair flushed. He picked up the Sword of Taizaburo. "So be it. She shall not be sent to the jungle. Since she killed a warrior, let her learn to live without warriors. Let her be alone, forever." He lowered his voice, almost chanting the sentence. "Let her be taken to the Daughters of Olarni, and be deprived of her Peace. Let her go crazy without her drug." He pointed to Assilla. "And let you be the one to look after her. You allowed her to go without Peace. Pay the price."

"No!" Assilla ran to the edge of the dais and fell on her knees. "Send me to the Olarnites, but don't make me look after her. She'll kill me!"

Sair smiled, cruelly. "I expect she will. . . . Now, get out!"

Nystra had to call two more women to half carry, half push Assilla out of the hall. As she passed, Bart could hear her pleading with the women. "What about my daughters? Who will look after them?"

But the women pushed her on. Behind them came

Brianna on her stretcher. Nystra took Sanda over to the girls waiting for their Thirteenth Sort. Bart wondered if she even knew where she was. He longed to comfort her.

He felt someone's eyes on him and glanced around. Tev was twisted on his knees, watching. Then his uncle looked at Sanda and then back at him before nodding thoughtfully.

What now? Nothing good: he'd wager his life on that.

The gong sounded again and Sair raised his arms and fell into the Invocation. "In blood were we born. In knowledge will we prosper. In purpose will we endure. Let Godwithin aid our survival." He lowered his hands.

Radnor stepped forward. "Our ancestors fell from the stars."

"Goddess Within aid us," the women chanted.

Korv's deep rumble chanted Mikhail's part. "Olarni founded and built this Home."

"Goddess Within strengthen us." The women were starting to sway.

The warriors chanted with their hands over their hearts. "When Olarni gave up her throne, Taizaburo became our First Guardian."

"Goddess Within protect us." There was a rustle like a thousand flyers and every woman in the home circled herself.

Sair turned toward the boys waiting for their Thirteenth Sort. "Know our story well.

"When our ancestors fell from the skies, it was Taizaburo who went back into the burning ship to rescue the wounded. When half the camp turned zerker it was he who warned the Mother General Olarni, and it was he who held the camp for Olarni while she struggled with her demons. When Olarni returned from her forty-day quest, it was Taizaburo who stood by her side until The Home was safely built. And finally, it was Taizaburo who ruled for her when she gave up her weapons. By his loyalty and service he saved us from our zerker fires. For it was he who set up the hunting packs that gave structure to our lives. It was he who gave us our warrior code. In the end, he died fighting on the barricades during migration so that The Home might be saved."

Sair looked over to the boys who were to make their choice and then toward his warriors and whelps sitting directly before him. Sair continued, "His life is our model. We serve. We fight. And we die—for The Home."

"We serve The Home," the warriors repeated firmly in a steady baritone murmur.

The words struck Bart to his core. *We serve The Home*. He'd repeated that so proudly during his Thirteenth Sort. And what was he doing now? Would finding Mikhail's murderer help The Home? If the ghosts did take Mikhail, he should be silent. If Mikhail was killed by warriors, he could start a pack war. But a warrior had to do something, didn't he? A warrior *acted*. That was his life. His head started to ache. Deliberately he turned his mind back to the ceremony.

Sair had finished with the legend of Taizaburo, Salahmn, the Second Guardian of The Home, the splitting of the peoples, and the building of the Waterfall Home—every story bathed in the blood of dead heros.

"Now we gather to see our children choose how they will serve The Home." He nodded to Edgar, and the boys of the Thirteenth Sort rose.

The first boy came forward, his eyes shining. He

came to a halt in front of Sair. "I am Indo, son of Radnor. I wish to serve The Home as a warrior."

Sair looked behind the boy to the assembled packs. "Is there a pack who wishes to train this boy?"

Radnor came from behind Sair, smiling. Unlike Guntor, who was his stepson, Indo was a child of his own body, and he wore his feelings proudly like a new knife. "I, Radnor, will accept this boy and make him a whelp in my pack."

Sair stood straighter and eased his sore leg. "Do you, Indo, promise to obey your Pack Leader in all things, and serve him faithfully as long as there is breath in your body?"

Bart looked at the back of Tev's head. He hadn't obeyed Tev. A fire of shame swept through him. He hadn't obeyed; yet Tev hadn't killed him, nor had he sent him to steerage—yet. *But what if Tev had somehow been involved in Mikhail's murder?* The man was so tricky his bow never knew where the arrow was heading. He groaned aloud, causing Norv to look over his shoulder and hiss him into silence.

Sixteen of the boys chose to be warriors. Only two chose steerage. One had the panting sickness, and Bart knew no pack would take him. The other boy looked healthy enough. After he chose, he sat to one side beside Lars, the Foreman of Steerage, and looked fixedly at his feet.

As the new whelps sat proudly with their packs, Sair looked back into the gloom where the women were sitting. "Let the cubs who have seen six migrations come forward."

There was a shuffling behind Bart as mothers with cubs rose and approached the dais. After the discipline of the boys, the disorder of the women and children reminded Bart of leaf beetles staggering this way and that seeking food. Although there were only about thirty women and cubs, they seemed like twice that number.

Sair raised his left hand. "Do you give up your cubs so that they may serve The Home?"

"We give our sons to The Home so that we may live." The response was ragged: some women were hugging their sons, others were crying.

"Let these boys be accepted for training." Sair signaled to Edgar who hitched himself forward to face the boys.

"Go with Edgar. Work hard. Learn. Survive."

The boys followed Edgar to where the Thirteenth Sort had been, and sat down, their eyes shining and their chests bursting with pride. The women drifted back into the gloom, wiping their eyes. Their sons had left home. From now on they would live in the dorms on the armory deck, and their mothers would only see them on Assembly Day.

The hall began to heat up. The odor of male and female sweat mingled together. In front the zerker warriors stirred restlessly. They'd been sitting for too long. Wives would have to walk carefully tonight.

Sair straightened his tunic, looking carefully at each girl in the Thirteenth Sort. Could it be he was looking for another wife—number ten? The harsh lines on his face softened and he smiled. Most of them smiled back, enjoying his attention. Only Sanda's face remained blank. She still looked ahead—as if she were on a cliff staring at a flower two klats away. When the other girls got up, Ullan had to reach down and tap her on her shoulder. Sanda jumped to her feet, looking bewildered. Her eyes swept the room— and fixed on him. Life leaped into her face and she mouthed a word. He frowned. She mouthed it again.

"Mirta!"

Mirta. That scraggly pet of hers. He nodded and she looked relieved. She turned back toward the dais.

He held his breath. Would she choose steerage now that Haddim was dead? And, if she did choose steerage, would he be responsible for her? Could he be responsible for anyone when he was in so much trouble in his own pack?

Suddenly he realized that he too had a choice to make. For if he got himself killed, Sanda would be stranded. He had to choose. Be a warrior. *Be cast out or killed.* Or obey Tev. Forget his father. Lie.

A groan rose from the women. One of the girls had chosen steerage. The girl was olive-skinned and had long hair that waved in kinks. As she went to stand beside the steerage women she shot a look of pure hatred and triumph at the mass of warriors.

Sanda approached the dais. "I, Sanda, Jaspaar's daughter, stepdaughter of . . . Haddim, choose to apply to the guilds to become a scholar."

A scholar! She wasn't going to steerage! But what if she lost control? Then she'd be married to a zerker. Didn't she want to marry him? And if she became a scholar, could he ever afford to pay her relatives her marriage price? A scholar would be expensive. Then the rest of her words hit him. He hadn't known she was Jaspaar's daughter! So her father had died just like Mikhail. Somehow it made him feel even closer to her.

As Sanda crossed to stand beside Bassarra, Officer of the Guild Council, she looked longingly in his direction. He knew she considered themselves promised in marriage. But how could he carry that out now? Once she turned, she was out of his reach. Unless . . . Did she really think she could hide being zerker?

He dropped his eyes and saw Tev, watching. So what? There was nothing Tev could possibly use in that. He ignored the rest of the ceremony. Only when his father's name was mentioned did he look up. The ceremony was over and Sair was announcing . . . what?

"And Radnor has taken Tekiri, the widow of Mikhail, into his home as his fourth wife."

So soon? It was as if his father hadn't lived. He waited miserably until the ceremony finally ended. When the women got up, stretching to relieve their cramped muscles, babies wailed in protest and children started shrieking and chasing each other.

Sair limped through the crowd, bearing down on him.

"What are these stories I hear you're telling?"

The men around them fell silent and turned to watch. Out of the corner of his eye Bart could see Tev drifting up behind Sair.

This was it. Loose his arrows or put away his bow. The black centers of Sair's pale blue eyes drilled into his. "Sir." He tried to think fast and, of course, couldn't. "Sir, I guess I was crazy with grief." He was a liar. Not a true warrior. But a safe one. Now Tev would have no reason to kill him.

Sair relaxed fractionally. "So what did happen?"

"He fell down and died." He felt light-headed with relief.

"You saw no bone splinters, no warriors."

"No, sir."

"The healer said it sounded like his heart stopped," Sair said. Bart remained silent. Sair waited. Finally Bart nodded. So that's the way Sair wanted it. A nice *natural* death. "When are you going to be initiated?" Sair asked.

Shame made it impossible to meet the Guardian's

eyes. But Tev pushed forward. "He's being initiated tomorrow. We'll see him off at dawn."

Dyfid descended out of nowhere, whooped, slapped him on the back, and disappeared.

Relief, fear and excitement battled with Bart's surprise. Excitement won out. The fear would come later— when he waited for the dawn and wondered if he'd ever see another one. But for now he was excited. Tomorrow the waiting would end. Tomorrow he would become a man.

Sair nodded. "Good." He waved to Tev and limped away.

His pack leader—he had to think of him that way now—pulled him away from the crowd of men and led him toward an empty space near the dais. "I'm glad you finally came to your senses."

Bart said nothing.

"You were starting something. The older men were remembering a few unsolved deaths during the Pack War. Then Movich and Nakano's names came up."

He looked stubbornly at Tev. What did his uncle expect him to say?

Tev looked around and drew closer. "I still want to find out how your father died, but we have to do it my way."

He looked so convincing, but then Bart remembered Nakano. "Yeah, sure," he said tonelessly.

Tev looked at him intently. "You don't believe me, do you?"

He shrugged.

"Bart, you have a lot to learn. Stick with me and we'll get around to trying out some of those crazy schemes of yours."

"What?"

"You know, capturing baby keld. I think it could

work. Not one keld, of course. Too many people would have to look after it, and that would be more trouble than it would be worth. But four or five might work."

Four or five! Bart could only gape at his uncle.

Tev grinned. "I also might help you marry Sanda."

"Sanda!" Bart almost shouted, then looked around guiltily. But no one seemed to have noticed. The dais torches had been moved to the door. They stood in deep gloom, while the crowd slowly pressed out into the night.

Tev chuckled. "It's all right. Once you're a man, you must think about marrying. I know you like her, and I'll help you to pay the guild her bride price." He stabbed a finger into Bart's chest. "Because she can help us, too."

"Help us do what?" Godwithin, was Tev going to use how Bart felt about Sanda for his own purposes?

"Sanda is Jaspaar's daughter. Maybe she can remember something about what happened to him when he was killed by the Ghosts. Besides, she's going to become a scholar. She can get into the old records. She likes you . . . maybe loves you. I'm sure she'd want to find how her own father died. She could learn whether deaths like those have happened before. If we look for patterns, Bart, we'll eventually find out what happens to men who challenge the Sangir." He made a tiny circle with his finger. "Either that or we'll all be dead."

Bart stood there with his mouth open. Realizing how stupid this looked, he asked. "But why don't you ask Jihanee, the scholar?"

"Women talk. And anyone who gets interested in the Heights dies. The only woman I'd confide in would be someone who wouldn't talk. A wife who is bonded to me by love. But because my two wives trust me, I can't marry Sanda. It would upset them,

and . . . well . . . they might talk about a lot of things."
He grinned ruefully. "Trust is a delicate herb. Bruise
it once and it dies. Anyway, if I help you with your
keld scheme and with Sanda, will you help me find
out about the Heights?"

Bart could only nod. Tev confided in his wives?
Wives were for cooking and giving you sons. You
confided in your pack brothers. Still . . . he'd talked
pretty freely to Sanda.

"Bart!"

Tev looked over his shoulder and laughed. "Looks
like you won't have to wait long for your first marriage."

Bart whirled to see Dyfid walking forward, carrying
a lighted taper and leading a young woman—a woman
with his dark skin. But where his skin was nut brown
and hard, hers glowed with the richness of health.
Where Dyfid was short, burly and powerful, she was
curvaceous. Her breasts were the heavy breasts of a
nursing mother, and her hips swelled richly under
her robe. But her waist. Her waist was firm, and
tiny. He stared, realizing that this could be his.

All he had to do was survive initiation.

17

Day 1:Second Gifter Moon of Spring:
452 Migrations After Landing

"Sanda!" The blurred image of a guildwife loomed closer. "Sanda! Pay attention."

She retreated further into numbness. She was so ashamed. Why had she let her mother take the blame for killing Haddim? But she knew why. She was afraid. Her fear was stronger than her love for her mother.

Cold water shocked her to attention. Bassarra, the tough acne-scarred officer of education, stood holding a bucket. They were in the large wardroom of the wife-training quarters. Near the hearth, pots, pans and dishes for two dozen girls were hanging from roof hooks or stacked in recessed pottery slots. Around Sanda the girls of her sort watched her avidly from their cushions on the floor. She rubbed her eyes. She was exhausted; her sleep had been jarred by echoes of her mother's screams. Her mind had been tormented by memories of her own joy of killing, her endless cross-examination by the hard-eyed women who guarded her mother, and her shame that made her cry her eyes red every night. Strange how crying like a demented grannie was all right, but anger on the same level would have condemned her forever.

287

Bassarra shook her. "Don't go away on me again. I know you've been through a lot, but it's over now."

Sanda lowered her eyes. *It's over now?* It was just beginning. She'd lost her mother. She'd lost Bart. Except for Assembly Days—where she'd be watched every moment—it would be three years before she'd be allowed on the Promenade Deck. So she'd even lost Mirta Blossom. Now she was trapped in the upper decks, ringed by women who'd turn on her with all the venom of a milk snake taking a cave mouse.

Bassarra gave an exasperated sigh. "I think you'd better go to healer Leeorah."

Her body jerked her erect on the cushion. Healer Leeorah had treated Kayella—and driven her mad. "I'm fine," she lied. "I was just tired." Fear sharpened her senses; she saw Ullan slumped beside her and, across the room, Ava sat primly. Her rich brown hair was hanging in soft clean waves, and her dark skin glowed as she leaned over to whisper to Jessance.

Bassarra gave Sanda one sharp warning glance then addressed the group. "It's time for your tour of the upper decks. The guild apprentices will be seeing where they will train, and those who are going to be wives will get a chance to find their way around." She rubbed her hands briskly. "We'll start with the potters and stonemasons." She paused. "You can stay here if you want, Ullan."

The young zerker flushed. "I want to see it," she said stubbornly. "It'll be my only chance." Bassarra nodded, her face set against sympathy.

Ava raised her hand. At Bassarra's nod she wiped her eyes dramatically. "Do I have to go, Bassarra? I'm so unhappy, I can hardly breathe." Jessance leaned over to put her arms protectively around Ava. When she met Sanda's gaze, her narrow almond eyes slitted in anger. In response, Sanda felt the old hatred stir in her guts. Damn Ava. It wasn't enough to be a bitch. She had to take all of Sanda's friends away, too.

"No, you can't stay here," Bassarra snapped. "When you're a wife, you'll have to come up here to buy things or make contracts. So pay attention."

Ava sniffed. She lowered her head, letting her wavy brown hair fall over her face like a grieving widow.

"*Gaman*." Bassarra responded, not unkindly. "Bear up. Endure. You've both been through a lot."

"Yes," Ava sniveled, "but it wasn't my fault." All the girls turned and stared at Sanda. Sanda raised her chin and pretended she didn't see, but she could feel their morbid curiosity.

"It wasn't anyone's fault," Bassarra said briskly. "A zerker went mad. *Shikata ga nai:* it couldn't be helped." She turned and led the way out.

Ava followed, leaning on her friend's arm. As they passed, several girls reached out and touched her before they followed her through the twists and turns of the tunnel. Sanda walked behind the giggling, whispering girls. She tried to tell herself she didn't care. But she did. Already she was an outcast. And if they ever knew she was zerker . . . Her mother said to hide. She had to hide—for her mother's sake. She padded along the smooth-worn path in the center of the tunnel, wondering how Kayella had ever managed to hide. If she wasn't so tired, she'd be wanting to take a chunk out of Ava. Then the scent of Peace trickled past the pervading wet-rock smell of the tunnel and someone squeezed Sanda's hand.

Ullan. Her mother's words drifted through her head. *Zerkers set each other off.* She should stay away from Ullan—walk faster—keep safe. She returned

Ullan's squeeze and didn't pull free from her friend's hand. She knew she was like a meatcat offering its neck for the cleaver. She knew it, but couldn't pull free from the only comfort she had.

They entered another room—a huge room with large windows. Under one of the windows, several pottery wheels sat idle. Under another, two women were squaring a block of stone—measuring and chipping in a slow timeless rhythm. Along the wall were wooden racks filled with logs, wooden wedges, tool boxes, sand screens, and mallets. Several women sat companionably about a large, low table looking at parchments. Ullan dropped Sanda's hand and plodded ahead for a closer look. "Aren't we going to see any potters?" she asked, disappointed.

One of the women heard her. "Sorry, dear." She got off her cushion and came toward them. "We're out of charcoal for the kiln; we have to wait till after migration."

Ullan's mouth drooped with disappointment, but she cupped her hands at her tiny waist and bobbed a little curtsey. "Do you think I could watch you then? I'd even help." She stood quietly, like a little wife, only her loose black hair and brown tunic proclaimed her youth.

The woman frowned. "Aren't you the Mother General's daughter, the one who turned?"

Sullen now, Ullan nodded.

"Sorry. Rules, you know." The woman went back to her low table and sat down with her back to them. Ullan looked at the floor, but Sanda could see a tear glisten on her cheeks. She wanted to console her friend, but backed away instead. Ullan's feelings were too strong. They were driving away Sanda's fatigue and rousing her anger. She looked around, hoping that someone else would help. Only Jessance seemed to have noticed. The pretty girl carefully smoothed her hair back, watching Ullan with heartless interest.

When they went to sickbay, Ullan caught up to her. "All I ever wanted to do was make pretty things," she whispered. In spite of her resolve, Sanda put her arm around her friend's tiny waist. Immediately a lump formed in her throat, followed by sullen anger. How could women speak of sisterly love and then condemn Ullan to a life without any kind of happiness?

"Don't," Ullan whispered. "Don't make me feel you. They'll strengthen my dose." She pushed Sanda ahead of her toward sickbay—the place where Kayella had gone mad.

She smelled the gallery before they arrived. Mirta, lenpic, spice pods, burl root, comfort nuts, woman heart, and dozens of other scents mingled, making many of the girls sneeze. The sickbay was full of chests, pottery urns, and the ceiling was festooned with drying herbs, roots, baskets of nuts, and filled and stoppered gourds. At regular intervals, along the back wall—just like in the children's gallery of every home—doors opened into small bedchambers. Because of the cost they were only used for warriors, but this was where they'd taken Kayella.

She looked for Leeorah, so she could fix her hatred on something concrete. The healer bustled forward. She was a tall, slender woman with a long neck and sharp bright eyes—like a snake, Sanda thought.

"Welcome to sickbay," Leeorah said briskly.

Gena, who habitually stayed quietly in the background, pushed her square body forward; her usually sullen sunburned face was eager. "My mother says you can cure worm rot. Couldn't you tell us what you use?"

Leeorah looked sympathetic. "Is that breaking out in steerage again?"

Gena nodded worriedly. "My little brother has it bad. He has sores all up and down his legs. Is there a simple way to cure it? It has to be simple because you know my family has no cards for a healer."

Ava snorted. "But they have enough cards to pay for your education, don't they?"

Gena's back stiffened as she met Ava's eyes. "No. *Steerage* has enough cards. People have gone hungry so I could study and bring my knowledge back to them."

Bassarra, the Officer of Education, smiled cynically. "But as a healer, you will be claimed by a warrior, and he will forbid you to go to steerage."

"I will beg him to let me. Besides, as a healer, I will be claimed by an old warrior, and he'll die, leaving me a widow, with the right of choice. Then I'll go home."

Leeorah shook her head. "That's very noble of you, but a lot of water can fall over the cliff before you'll be free to help your people. However, I'll show you the leaves you can grind up for a poultice to put on your brother's legs. But you'll have to find someone to get them from the jungle. Meanwhile, stop him from sleeping on the damp, earth floor. As you'll soon learn, that's what causes worm rot in the first place."

Gena's lips turned down in a bitter scowl. "And how can we get off the damp floor when we've used all our wood to keep us warm last winter?"

"You could dig slots out of the rock wall, and sleep as we do," Leeorah suggested.

"With what, our bare hands?"

"Don't be rude," Bassarra snapped. "Apologize."

Gena turned white. Her face looked like bone against her nut-brown curls. "I'm sorry," she whispered. "Please don't hold it against me. Please." She fell on her knees before the healer.

"I won't. But you know I demand obedience, and respect, from my apprentices."

Gena nodded.

Sanda seethed. Why should Gena have to apologize for stating the truth? Who did Leeorah think she was? Telling Gena to treat her brother with jungle leaves she couldn't get, and a bed slot they couldn't pay to have made.

Bassarra stood by the open door, ushering the girls on. "It's time to go up to the Scholars' Gallery."

Sanda banked her anger and wormed her way to the front of the line of girls. Finally!

From behind, Bassarra called out directions. "When you get to the first opening go up the companionway."

Her heart beat faster as she started to climb the stairs that angled directly into the cliff. She could hardly keep from racing up into the gloom. Just when it got too dark to see, there was a landing and the companionway turned and climbed back toward the light of another slit on the cliff. Twice more she climbed into the darkness, then turned back again to the rock face. Used to climbing the cliffs, Sanda soon outdistanced the rest of the girls, who fell behind, panting. Sanda knew she should stop and pretend to be tired, too, but she was too excited. She'd heard about the Scholar's Gallery all her life. It held the records of The Home, the chronicles of each year, and the files of all the guilds. But what she wanted to see were the manuscripts from the days of Taizaburo and Olarni. In the last years of her life, Olarni had ordered each colonist to write down everything he or she knew about the worlds they came from and the skills they knew. Those records drew Sanda like a starving meatcat to spilled stew.

She burst through the entrance to a wide gallery lit by a larger window than those of the countants. Every corner of the room was as bright as the Promenade Deck. The center window was hinged, like a door, and had been pulled back letting the fresh spring breeze in and spreading brilliant sunlight on the page Jihanee was reading.

Jihanee. The tiny mistress of all the knowledge in The Home. From her hair, which was an indeterminate color of dark blond or early grey, to her rumpled gown, she looked uncared for and uncaring. All except her eyes. Like polished stone they were. Brown, with green flecks that raked everyone with piercing intensity— and dulled as her mind turned inward, as it did most of the time. Because of that, Jihanee was the only woman warriors gave way to on the Promenade Deck. It was too undignified to constantly knock down a tiny woman who didn't know where she was going.

The Mistress of Scholars smiled up at her. "I expected you'd be the first." Sanda bobbed a curtsey toward her and headed for the rack of leather-bound parchments. "Wait, you can't read those files until you're an apprentice," she said, putting her hand up to stop Sanda.

"Please, mistress, just one?" She continued walking toward a rack of leather-bound parchments. Real books. Finally! "Where are the ones written by Olarni and the other first people of The Home?"

"Oh, they're in the Archives."

"The Archives. You mean they're not here?" Disappointment was tinged with desperation. "Where are the Archives?" Any day she might lose control in public. She had to see those books now! She might never get another chance.

"You're blocking my way," Jessance complained, lifting her snub nose as if she smelled something bad. Sanda bit off a sharp retort and moved into the center of the sun-lit gallery.

Scholar Jihanee pointed to an iron-bound wooden door at the end of the chambers. "The Archives are through there."

Sanda strode over to the door, then stared. It was small, just high enough for her to walk through, was made of ironwood, and was braced with grey star metal. But what made her guts twist with frustration was the lack of a handle, or latch string. A chill solidified her roiling frustrations into bile. There was only one door in The Home like that.

Bassarra bustled by her. "This is the Scholar's Gallery and, of course, you all know Scholar Jihanee." She waved to the inner side of the room where there were stacks of leather-bound parchments and scrolls, shelves of slates, piles of unused or old hides, and racks of bottles used for inks or preservatives. "There," she pointed toward the small door beside Sanda, "is the Olarnite Gate. This is where you can come if you have served The Home and find yourself without a husband, or quarters to live in or wish to ease the burden on your family." She looked at Jihanee. "I think about twenty have gone through in the last two months, haven't they?"

"Twenty-four," Jihanee said precisely. "This has been a lean spring."

"At least it's almost over." Bassarra walked toward a rope that hung beside the door. The rope seemed to disappear into the rock ceiling. "Another Gifter Month and the keld and ildenhorn will be migrating, then, we'll feast." Grasping the rope she gave a mighty pull. The girls listened, but could hear no summoning bell.

The Officer of Education laughed. "There is a bell—up about five or six levels."

Ava pushed forward. "Will we see an Olarnite?" The older woman nodded.

Sanda cleared her throat. "But how can the Archives be up there if the Olarnites allow no one out?"

Jihanee spoke from behind her. "Scholars don't go all the way up to the Olarnites' Deck. They just go one level up, to the Archives. They're behind the Gate so the Olarnites can guard our files. In times of pack wars—" she made the holy circle, "Goddess Within prevent—we can be sure that no one will ever destroy the records."

Sanda was aghast. "Who would ever want to do that?"

The heavy sound of a bolt came from the small door. Suddenly a ten-centimeter slot appeared at her chest level and an ancient face looked out at them.

"Who calls?" she quavered.

Bassarra bustled forward. "The Thirteenth Sort is here."

The woman disappeared, and they could hear the sound of bolts being thrown. One, two, three, four, five. The girls looked at each other. None of their homes had more than one stout bar. Finally, centimeter by centimeter, the door creaked open. Thin and bent, her chin covered with feathery granny whiskers, the Olarnite sidled through the narrow opening resting her gnarled and crooked body on a stout cane. Finally she got through the door, and stood blinking in the stronger light. Her white hair was plaited neatly and the braids were wrapped around her head. Because she was so bent, she had to crane her neck and look up to see the girls.

"Every year they look younger," she mused. "Their skin is so soft." Her gaze passed slowly over the girls who watched her just as avidly.

She was dressed like a man! Her plain black overtunic with its long sleeves and high neck ended at midthigh. Below that she wore straight loose black trousers and felt slippers.

Sanda edged forward. "How's my mother?" she blurted. The woman squinted and moved closer to see her better. "Your mother?"

"Yes, she came through here last night—she was on a stretcher. How is she?"

The sister clucked sympathetically. "Once a woman crosses the Olarnite Gate she is as dead to those below." When Sanda made a pleading gesture, she shook her head. The girls stood uncomfortably silent; Ava snuffled into Jessance's shoulder. Sanda dropped her hand, stung. What did it matter to the old crone if she told them how Brianna was? Rules, rules. The Home strangled you in them and then shrugged off the pain with platitudes.

The old woman surveyed the other girls. "I wonder how many of you will come up here—in another thirty years." One of the girls murmured in disbelief. The Olarnite peered around till she found her. "You think you'll never be old, but the time will come all too soon."

"What do you do?" Gena asked. "I know you make ship bread and sell it, but what else?"

The old woman laughed. "We pray for The Home, or seek perfect union with the Goddess Within." Sanda ground her teeth. How could her mother ever seek the Goddess Within if she was crazy from being locked up without Peace? She glared at the old woman who continued to talk. ". . . guard the Archives, and recopy files that are decomposing or fading with age."

Recopy the files! Sanda would cheerfully starve to be able to do that. But who did it? Withered-up old crones! Ullan cleared her throat and shot Sanda a warning look. Sanda shrank away from the group. How was she ever going to hide when, even as tired as she was, everything upset her? She frantically looked for something to calm her mind. Her eyes fell on the title of the top book on the nearest rack.

Drainage Maps of The Home.

She took it down silently and opened it. The first page showed a map of all the levels of The Home. Her anger seeped out of her as she looked at the plans. The dam that provided fresh water, even when the Waterfall River was barely a trickle, was marked in heavy black. Clean water drains were marked in blue, and like a spice root they divided and multiplied as they descended from level to level. Sewage drains were marked in red and were an upside-down reflection of the water drains, starting with dozens of tiny tendrils on the artisan decks and ending with two main exits into the fertilizer ponds. What amazed her, though, was that even steerage had clean water.

"All in good time," Jihanee said, taking the book out of her hands. "Once your wife training is out of the way, you'll be up here every moment of daylight whether you want to or not."

Sanda went numbly back to her Sort. *Once your wife training is out of the way.* That was five Gifter months away—250 days. Could she possibly hold her temper until then? It was all right for her mother to tell her to hide. But even now, when she was almost too exhausted to think, she could feel her rage glowing like a well banked fire.

Ullan put a hand on her shoulders. "*Gaman,*" she whispered, then added, "please!"

Sanda shrugged her off. How long did Ullan think she could remain hidden?

But Nystra had hidden for years! Did Ullan know that? Or had Nystra not told her daughter. *For the good of The Home.*

For a second she considered telling the girls about Nystra, then rejected it. No one would believe her. Nystra was the calmest woman in The Home. Yet Brianna had starved herself to tell Sanda that Nystra was zerker. Should she tell Ullan her own mother was zerker? No. If Ullan got upset, then she might set Sanda off. No, she could do nothing.

Bitterly she followed the other girls down the companionway to the next gallery. The click of abacuses drifted down the tunnel, and soon the girls were blinking again in light that flowed through five puddle-glass windows, and reflected off polished metal plates that covered the opposite wall. In the room nine women sat cross-legged in front of tilted tables that held parchments, quills, ink pots and abacuses. A thin woman with shining jet-black hair looked up and called cheerily to the girls. "Be nice to me, girls. When you're wives and guildwives, I'm the one who'll keep your counts. If you make a contract, I'll write it up for you, and keep the records of your private and family wealth."

Ava edged forward. "What if a family dies? What happens to their cards?"

The woman peered at her. "Aren't you Assilla's daughter?"

Ava wiped her eyes with her sleeve and nodded.

"I just wanted to know about my dowry," she said in a little-girl voice. "My mother had over a hundred cards set aside for me, but . . ." She let her voice trail away.

The woman looked toward Bassarra who shrugged and nodded. She put her hand on her table and pulled herself to her feet. "Let's look in your family's counts." She turned to the rest of the girls. "All families have counts. We keep track of wealth so you don't have to keep cards lying around where . . . ah . . . where they might get lost."

Sanda snorted. She knew why Assilla never kept cards in quarters. Haddim would use them for drink.

As the countant took down a large, wood-framed slate, Ava rushed to help. Together they brought it back to the countant's table and the guildwife settled down to read the tiny rows of figures.

"Let's see. This column is the individual portions, and here's the family total. But that was split three ways for his three wives when your father . . . er . . . died."

"Three ways! But Brianna killed him. She shouldn't get any cards." Ava looked to Bassarra to back her up. "Besides, why should a zerker get any cards at all? They don't work in the guilds and they don't do any family work either. They just sit around waiting to get pregnant."

Sanda seethed. Ullan jerked as if stung. "Do you think I want that?" she cried. "I want to be a potter. I want to earn my way. Nobody asked me if I wanted Peace."

The girls fluttered nervously, even though they knew Ullan was soothed by her Peace. Again Sanda wanted to comfort her friend, but she was afraid. *Zerkers set each other off.* Finally Gena slipped over to Ullan and put her arm around her. "There, there," she said soothingly.

Ullan threw the girl's hands off with a wide sweep of her arms. "Don't do that! I'm not raging. I'm upset. How would you feel if someone suddenly told you that you could never be a healer?"

Gena backed off, and Ullan's tortured eyes met Sanda's. The pain sliced through the air and into her. She looked away and the pain eased—a little.

The countant was bent over the family slate again. "Here's Assilla's counts." Sanda watched with grim satisfaction. She knew what was coming, and waited to enjoy it.

"Assilla had one hundred and forty-two gold cards and sixty green cards." Ava practically rubbed her hands with anticipation.

"Of that sixty gold cards go to the Daughters of Olarni as an acceptance fee."

"But they take all!"

Sanda warmed to the conversation. For once Ava wasn't getting her way.

"Yes, but those who can pay, must," the countant said firmly. "Your mother's portion will be split three ways for your and your sisters' dowries. You have twenty-seven gold cards and thirty-three green ones."

"But . . . but that's not enough!" Ava grabbed the woman's arm.

Sanda grinned nastily at the whining bitch.

The woman freed her arm. "At least you have a dowry," she said icily. "And you're very beautiful . . . in a pouty sort of way. Pity the poor girls who have neither looks nor cards." She bent over her work. "I'm busy."

"But you don't understand. I promised Guntor over a hundred gold cards . . . enough to buy a blister-steel blade for his shette." She stopped, realizing what she'd said. When Bassarra stopped to talk to another countant, Ava moved out of earshot of the guildwives, giving significant looks over her shoulder, letting her friends know that she had something dramatic to say. After a moment Sanda followed them. She wanted to be there to stop any lies Ava might tell.

Ava had gathered her friends around her, as if she were the actress in a myth play, and they the audience. She raised one hand, dramatically, but Ullan interrupted her.

"What makes you think someone like Guntor would ever want you?" she sneered.

Ava simpered. "We're promised. Of course he couldn't ask for me, right away. But now that he's married the widow Malawi, he'll be asking as soon as I finish wife training."

"No, he won't." Ullan smiled viciously. "He won't ask for you, and with your poor dowry, you'll probably end up as the wife of the poorest lanker."

"What do you know, you, you zerker?" Ava snarled. "I'm promised. So there."

"So am I," Ullan laughed. "Guntor is ambitious. Now that he's married to Malawi, Sair's daughter, what better match than the zerker daughter of the Mother General. Ava, when I'm trained, he's going to marry me. It's all been settled and Malawi has signed the contract to pay my mother the bride price."

"No," Ava whispered. Her face paled and she lifted a trembling hand as if shielding herself from the truth. "No, he promised me."

Ullan laughed. "When? He never walked you to the Barricades, so you had to be seeing him alone. Guntor's a lusty man. I don't expect he was content to hold your hand. Besides, we know all about your

father. Did he have you before he tried to force Sanda?"
The girls hissed at this and Jessance drew back from
Ava, smoothing her skirts.

Ava glared at Ullan then put her hand to her forehead,
like a tragic myth heroine. "A tenday ago I had a
father, a mother, and a big dowry. Now my father is
dead. Tempted by that," she said, pointing at Sanda,
"and killed by her mother. My own mother has been
sent to the Olarnites, Ullan has stolen Guntor, so
I'm all alone." She broke down and cried, her face
in her hands. Jessance and several other girls forgot
their earlier shock and rushed to her side, holding
her and patting her back.

Sanda clenched her fist until her hands hurt. Nobody
cared about her life; about her sister, mad in some
Olarnite cell; her mother, locked up without the comfort
of Peace; or herself, wanting to be a scholar, but
facing a future as grim as her mother's. She glared
at the other girls who were soothing her stepsister.
Ava would probably manage to choose her own husband,
and get her new First Wife to do all the work as
well.

Ava lifted her head and pointed at Sanda. "She's
evil. She destroys everything she touches. If I've lost
Guntor," she spat, "I'll never forgive you, and I'll
hold a feast when you turn zerker."

No. Not that. Let her say anything but that. "I'm
not, and I won't turn!" Sanda snapped. She put her
arms around her body and hugged herself so she
wouldn't hit Ava. Calm down, she told herself. Calm
down. Nothing would make Ava happier than to see
you turn.

"Look at her, she's already hugging herself. Next
she'll start rocking—just like her mother." Sanda bit
her cheek. Pain stabbed through her mouth, driving

her hatred on. Ava continued, happy for the audience. "Zerker," she taunted. "Murderess's daughter. Seductress. Harlot." She rolled the words from stories and legends around her tongue with great relish.

Bitch. Energy flowed into Sanda's body, making her strong, fearless. Her fingers itched to rip the smooth skin from Ava's face. She bore down on her stepsister.

Ava grabbed a slate and held it up in front her. "Bassarra," she called. "Help me. Sanda is turning."

Ullan got in front of Sanda and shoved her face to within a centimeter of Sanda's. "Remember the Peace . . . your mother . . . your promise."

Sanda stood, shaking, ripped apart by her hatred and her fear.

Ava pulled Ullan aside with one hand, and lifted the slate in her other.

Stupid lanker. So slow. Sanda raised her hands to block the bitch. But Ullan had grabbed both her wrists. They locked eyes. Ullan pleaded silently from her very soul.

Pain blinded Sanda and she sank into blackness.

Pain.

She tried to get up; agony pulsed across her hairline. She flopped limply back and that brought more pain. Cautiously, she opened her eyes. Light filtered through a tiny window in her cubby.

Gena rose from beside the bed. "How do you feel?" she asked, then before Sanda could answer she went on. "You're my first patient. They let me stay with you and I'm to give you water when you come to."

"What happened?" Sanda asked, careful not to move her pounding head.

The other girl sat on her bed slot. "It was terrible," she confided. "Ava hit you over the head with a slate and then Ullan grabbed her and tore her hair out, kicked her, and bit her before Bassarra and the countants could separate them. Then Ullan started in on Bassarra. Finally the countant, Daintry, Jessance and I grabbed Ullan and sat on her long enough for Bassarra to pour some Peace down her throat."

Sanda groaned. More Peace. Ullan would soon be labelled as one of the crazy zerkers, and they'd dope her senseless, like they had Brianna. And all because Ullan had been trying to protect her.

Gena slid to the floor and picked up a beaker of water. She carefully lifted Sanda's head—as Sanda had so often lifted her mother's—and gave her a drink. Sanda's soul writhed in shame. Was this her future, too? Tears came to her eyes. All because of her demon stepsister.

"What happened to Ava?" she asked.

Gena put down the beaker and settled comfortably on the bed. "Well, to start with she was badly beaten up. She's going to have a black eye; Ullan's bites on her hands and shoulder were pretty deep. I wanted to go to sickbay and help fix her up, but Bassarra said somebody should be with you."

"So is Ava in sickbay?" Sanda prompted.

"Oh yes, you see," Gena's eyes grew large, "maybe Ava is zerker. After all, she did attack you. So while she's being fixed up, Leeorah will test her. If she's zerker, she'll be drugged, of course. But if she isn't, we're going to have an assembly, and we're going to learn how to judge, just like the women do. Isn't that exciting?"

Sanda knew Ava wasn't zerker. She felt Ullan, even through her Peace, but she'd never felt Ava, even at her nastiest. "I hope they sentence her to steerage," she said harshly.

Gena's face closed, and Sanda remembered too late that Gena was steerage.

"You think you're so good, don't you? Just because you have pretty hair, a slender figure and untanned skin." The stocky girl got up and reached for the door. "I may be steerage, but I'll never be zerker." Sanda sat up, sending pain flashes through her eyes. She fell back, but Gena didn't move to help her. Instead she opened the door. "You have water and you have a chamber pot for tomorrow," she snapped.

"Tomorrow?"

"Oh, I didn't tell you, did I? Jessance said that you had your fists clenched and were going to meet Ava. She said Ullan stopped you from fighting. Bassarra said we couldn't test you to see if you were zerker because the testing drug was dangerous for someone with a head injury. Instead of testing you, they're going to lock you up for two days." She looked around the room. "Bassarra said, if you were zerker, two days in this cubby would drive you crazy." She stepped through the door. "And if you turn, we'll see how high and mighty you are." She slammed the door behind her. Seconds later, Sanda heard the sound of a bar sliding through the grip of the door handle.

Damn Ava. She looked around the tiny room. Two days. In here? Is that what they'd done to Kayella? Is that why she'd gone crazy? She rolled over, and jagged needles of pain swept across her head and down her neck. She lay there fighting nausea, tears streaming down her face. Sooner or later they'd get her. Sooner or later she'd be drugged and all her dreams of being a scholar, of helping Ullan, or marrying Bart, would be shattered. She might as well face it.

But she couldn't. She lay in bed wrestling with her depression. But as the day waned, and her head began to clear, she saw no way out. Today she'd been almost too tired to lift her head, but she'd still gone berserker. Bart's advice just didn't work when you were locked up with the likes of Ava.

When it got darker, the walls seemed to press in. She got up gingerly and tried to pace. Two steps, turn, two steps, turn. *Two days in this cubby will drive you crazy.*

She paced again, trying to think of something she could do. But always she came up against Peace. Except that she couldn't accept being drugged. She'd rather die. Yes, like Zorava. But there was no dactyl net here to hang from. Well then, she could jump. Yes, she could jump. One second of discipline, one moment of push off, and it would be all over. No drugs. No Ava. *No Bart. No Archives.* Well, that couldn't be helped. Both of those were beyond her reach anyway.

She looked toward the window. It was dark. No one would see her in the gloom. No one would stop her.

She pulled herself up to the window and wriggled through into the cool spring air. Fee had not yet risen and the valley below was plunged in unfathomable darkness. Overwhelming despair swept her. All that struggle—her mother's sacrifice, Ullan's attempts to protect her, Bart's promise of marriage—it was all for nothing. She had to push off, and fall down, down into the valley, or she had to face slowly turning into someone like her mother.

She looked down. She could see the cliff for about twenty meters and then darkness closed in. Only the migration lamps along the barricade winked like the stars in first dark. She braced herself. Now. End it. She pushed.

But when she started to slide headfirst out of the window, her body automatically reacted. Her legs spread, and stopped the slide.

Damn you. She pulled her legs together, then tried to take her hand off the cliff. As she did, her legs braced again. She was panting with the effort, with the body fear of falling, and with shame. She was nothing. She couldn't even commit suicide. But she couldn't face Peace, either. Somehow she had to find a way. If she could only fall off.

That was it! She could climb until she was so tired her body couldn't save her! She wriggled out of the window, clinging to crevices and knobs of rock, and started climbing.

Somehow, she'd kill herself. As she felt her way up the dark cliff, her eyes filled with tears. She grieved for the Archives she was leaving behind, for the promises she was breaking to Ullan and to her mother. But most of all she grieved for the life she would never have with Bart.

18

Bart's initiation didn't start till dawn, but he was up when the Gifter was still high in the sky, wasting precious lamp oil as he checked his weapons and packed and repacked his field pack. Just before dawn Dyfid joined him. He sat in companionable silence while he watched Bart check his arrows yet again.

"You'll be all right; you can see anything coming before I even notice a blur. I always envied you for that, and for your place in the upper decks."

Bart gave Dyfid his full attention. "But now your place *is* on the upper decks."

"Is it? My father and mother are still in steerage, and my friends are there, too."

Bart felt uncomfortable. "And I'm not your friend?"

Brown eyes regarded him unblinkingly. "I really hope so. I've bet my future life on our partnership. But you've always treated me like a steerage slave and we can't live that way when we are warriors."

Bart gaped at him. "I never did!" he protested.

Dyfid shook his head. "Don't think I didn't see you looking over the whelps and deciding that I would make the best servant for you because I was such a hard worker. Well, now that we're both lankers, I'll be your pack brother, but not your servant."

Bart's face flamed, but honesty made him realize that Dyfid was right. He stared at the dim armory,

ashamed of the way he had treated the only man
who had remained his friend throughout this whole
mess. Suddenly he stood up and stuck out his hand.
"Can we start again," he asked, "as equals?"

Dyfid grinned and stood to grip his wrist. "I knew
I chose well." He slapped Bart on the back. "Once
you come back, we'll find ourselves the same protector,
and life will get back to normal."

"If I survive," Bart said levelly. "Vantor from Ontu's
pack went out four days ago. He hasn't come back."

"Don't even think about that! It's bad luck." Dyfid
looked toward the window slits that were changing
from Gifter-grey to dawn-blue. "And another thing.
All steerage knows that most blood lusters strike moving
objects. If you think you're prey, stand still."

"That's crazy. You've got to run, or fight!"

"No, *zerkers* have to run or fight. They'd go mad
if they had to stand still—and they control all the
packs, or did until a tenday ago."

The door to the upper decks creaked open. Tev
walked slowly down the stairs. "Ready?" he asked.

Bart nodded.

"I'm going to say the usual things at the parting
ceremony, but I wanted to catch you alone." He looked
at Dyfid, and jerked his head toward the outside.
Dyfid nodded and left, at the trot.

"You know the men don't think too much of you,"
Tev said bluntly.

Bart shifted uncomfortably.

"They could understand you being upset about
not turning zerker, or the way you got caught with
Guntor, but what you said after your father's death
worried them." He placed a hand on Bart's shoulder.
"The men think you're a whiner, a troublemaker, a
liar, or worse, unlucky." As Bart stiffened, Tev's hand

pressed down, forcing Bart to listen. "If you want to start changing their minds, you've got to do more than just survive, you've got to bring something back to The Home."

"Meat? You mean bring home meat, like the zerkers do?"

"More. You have to bring back something that will help each man in the pack. Find the location of a new stand of mirta, or an undiscovered thicket of mellow root—anything to gain you some form of respect."

Bart just grunted. Wasn't staying alive enough? He longed for his father. Mikhail had a simple straightforward attitude. *Fight, hunt, and trust your pack.* He wished Tev were not so complicated, that his every word or action didn't have to carry one open and one hidden purpose.

The door to the Promenade Deck opened again; Volf and Gopa clattered down the stairs, clearly angry. Beside him, Tev sighed.

Gopa stormed up to Tev. "Volf is accusing me of blood doping his pack. I heard you and Mikhail fighting about something before he died. And I heard you swearing about blood doping." He glared at Tev. "Now I'm being blamed for it, so it's my right to demand that you tell us what was going on."

Volf shoved between Gopa and Tev. "I got to thinking. After you pulled that pack off me all the ferts in the jungle went after the pack, not me. Mikhail wasn't even there, so it had to be Gopa."

"It wasn't Gopa." Tev put his hand on Volf's arm, forcing him to look at his pack leader. "Gopa knew nothing about it. It was one of Mikhail's schemes to bring you into line."

"He wouldn't," Bart protested, but no one paid him any attention.

Volf demanded, "Why didn't you tell me?"

"There was the little matter of my life. I couldn't stop him, so I made sure I was right behind you on the hunt."

"The bastard."

"Yes," Gopa agreed.

Tev relaxed, then saw Bart staring at him, horrified. "Sorry, Bart, I didn't want this to get around." He grabbed the two men and squeezed their arms. "And I don't want it to get around. Our pack should never know Mikhail broke their trust."

"Hell, Bart already knows that. Mikhail let him nearly die among the nesters," Gopa said.

"If Volf hadn't left me, I wouldn't have been alone," Bart shouted.

Volf surged forward, but Tev caught him. "Volf was crazy with fear that his weanling son would die. He made a mistake, but it won't happen again, will it?"

Volf half grinned. "No."

"And how is your son?"

A huge smile banished the brutal ugliness of Volf's face. "I gave him a cub bow two days ago and he's already skewered a grunkle, two spiders and my wife's best Assembly gown."

Bart listened in shock. They believed Tev.

Tev clapped Volf on the shoulder. "I think we have to have that cub in our pack, don't you?" He put his other arm around Gopa and they walked toward the exit tunnel.

"Come as soon as you're ready," Gopa called over his shoulder.

If his father had blood doped Volf, he deserved to die. Or did he? But whatever he did, it was not what Bart should be thinking about right now. He inspected his equipment for the fifth, or was it the sixth time. His shette and small knife were honed. He'd checked his arrows twice. He pulled up his spear and checked the lashing that bound the iron tip to the spear. The original rawhide had been covered with resin and lacquered to metal hardness. Everything was ready. It was time to go. He shouldered his pack and entered the tunnel. When the guard opened the fortified door, Bart straightened his shoulders and put his father out of his mind.

"Look at him. All ready to feed the ferts," Guntor sneered.

Beside him Mariko laughed softly. "No. He won't get that far. I bet he rings the steerage bell within a hundred heartbeats."

Bart ignored them and pushed past. Behind him Guntor and Mariko laughed uproariously.

His face flamed as he walked down past steerage and onto the river path to the barricades. He'd die before he rang the steerage bell. By the time he reached the valley floor the dawn light brightened the sky to a pale yellow. The silvery notes of a flute drifted toward him. Jarret, their youngest whelp— no, their third youngest whelp, they'd taken Kreigor and Dald into the pack yesterday—sat on a stone by the river rapids, playing his flute to the accompaniment of the water bubbling over the stones. When the boy saw him, he scrambled to his feet and joined the group of warriors.

Beside the men was a woman—Wahiri! He tried to look casual as he strode forward. She left the group, bringing him a package. Dyfid trailed behind, grinning from ear to ear. When she got within four paces of him, she lowered her eyes, and dropped a deep curtsey.

"Rise, woman." Bart lowered his voice, and tried

to sound commanding—the way a warrior should when dealing with women.

She rose. A flame of desire licked up his spear as he admired her figure, so round at her hips, so tiny at her waist, and so heavy with milk in her breasts. He tried to remember how many children she had, and couldn't. He inhaled her woman smell of crushed lenpic and visualized them together.

She held out a package. "Since your family is no more, I offer you cooked food for your initiation."

Cooked food. One half of the marriage ceremony. The other half was up to him—to provide her with meat for her pot.

"What would you like," he asked, feeling strong and powerful, "some keld, or some ildenhorn?" Behind her Dyfid choked with laughter. Bart blushed, and grinned—and was thrilled to see her smile back. Such lovely brown eyes. Soft and gentle.

"Anything you bring me will be welcome." She curtsied again and stepped back. They were formally betrothed now. Once he brought her meat, they would be married. He tucked the food into his pack, then strode forward, trying to look like the warrior he desperately wished to be.

The men were gathered just inside the gate. Tev beckoned impatiently. Guntor and Mariko hurried past him, looking innocent.

Bart barely heard the traditional words, urging him to be brave, to survive and to serve The Home, he was already planning what he would do. He couldn't climb a tree. Tev and Wahiri had seen to that. If he came back empty-handed after promising Tev knowledge and Wahiri meat, he'd be the butt of watchfire jokes for the rest of his life.

With a start he realized that Tev had finished and

was stepping forward with the bell. He shook his head. "I don't need the bell."

"I'm sure you don't," his uncle said evenly. "But every whelp must carry it. We want to test you, not kill you. If you get into difficulty, it is your duty to ring the bell."

Bart took the brass bell that would summon help from the roving packs—and condemn him to life as a steerage field worker. Tev stepped back and raised his hand.

"Go out a whelp. Come back a warrior."

Bart saluted smartly, turned and jogged through the open gate of the barricades. He felt tremendous relief that the endless waiting was finally over. Alertly he scanned the sky, the cliffs, and the brush on either side of the trail. Nothing. There rarely was anything moving at dawn. The night prowlers were sleeping and the day hunters still kept to their lairs and nests.

Down he went, keeping a steady sensible pace. As soon as he was out of sight of the barricades, he imagined himself coming back, loaded with meat, meeting men on the trail who nodded to him, and slapped his back. *His father's torn body flashed in front of his eyes.* He broke out in a sweat and started jogging faster.

The light strengthened, but soon dimmed again as storm clouds hid the sun. Good. It wouldn't be that hot in the jungle. As he passed the place where Mikhail had seen the stranger on the Heights, he examined the spot. Nothing. But Mikhail was dead because of what he'd seen. And Bart was alive, because no one but Tev knew he'd seen the stranger, too.

The air became warmer as he descended. Warmer and more moist. A lone dactyl drifted over the Heights and started riding the warm air above the jungle.

He watched it closely, and continued to jog, feeling exposed, and missing the spears and arrows of his pack brothers. Luckily his eyes could track what the dactyl was looking at, and for the moment, it was looking upslope.

The neck swivelled down. Bart skidded to a stop, braced his spear under his arm and strung his bow. If it dived, he wanted to be ready. Then he remembered Dyfid's advice, and froze. The dactyl circled above him, its neck angling, to keep him in view. When it passed behind him, Bart lived several days of fear until it drifted into sight again.

It folded its wings and dove—upslope.

Bart clutched his bow and spear and ran downslope toward the jungle.

He arrived in the jungle out of breath. Stupid, he told himself, and paused in the shade of the first trees, protected from the dactyl, but not yet facing the dangers of the jungle. As his breath eased—he shouldn't have run that last klat, it was cowardly—he listened to the jungle, sorting the sounds. Animals grunted, chattered and called. Insects whined. Water plopped drop by drop from leaf to leaf. Treebores gabbled in the distance. The wind sighed down from The Home and rustled the leaves of the trees bordering the jungle.

Resolutely he entered the wide hunter's trail into the jungle. He had to get as far from the following packs as possible, for if he was seen, he would be shamed. And he knew that Guntor and Mariko would be looking for him. He resumed his steady jog. The jungle closed in around him. The light dimmed. The humidity increased. Leaves that could hide daggerjaws or fire spiders brushed his leathers. His ears strained.

Every sound could mean food, or death. He constantly scanned remembering his father's chant: Danger above; danger to the left; danger to the right; danger in front and behind.

The hunter's trail divided. He took the one that went right down the widening valley into the main jungle. It was further, but he would be more likely to get meat. Thank Godwithin, Wahiri didn't ask for anything specific.

A klat drifted by. And then another. He wiped his forehead, keeping the stinging sweat out of his eyes. The air got hotter and he seemed to be breathing half water. His feet squelched in the mucky mold as the trail skirted Killer Swamp, a place no one went, not even for food. Swamp raft trees could split without warning, dropping man or animal into liquid mud.

Something screamed in the swamp. Bart moved faster. He could feel a thousand eyes on him.

Finally the ground rose, and became drier. He came to another split in the trail. It was midmorning—still most of the day left to find game. He took a swallow from his water gourd, trying to decide which way to go. The clay pits were nearer the edge of the cliffs where numerous canyons supported ildenhorn and sometimes keld. But the other trail went down into the deep jungle. More dangerous, but the home of the pinto hogs, and the sword-backed plate horn, both easy kills, if you knew their weaknesses. As he stood there, he could almost hear his father yelling. "Move on. Don't be an easy target." But his father was dead. And Tev had shown him stealth.

Which way? His whole life depended on getting meat—and finding a mirta stand or a mellow root thicket. Damn. He'd forgotten about that. He wandered a little way into the jungle, then laughed at himself.

Anything this near the trail would surely bear a pack ownership marking. The pungent scent of a spice bush tickled his nose. Maybe Wahiri would like some spice pods? He plunged into the center of the huge thicket and started examining the pods, looking for whole pods that were unmarked by leave mange, or center worm. These were last year's pods and most were spoiled. It took him ages to find a healthy fistful.

Suddenly, near the trail, a bush rat emerged from his burrow and started to groom his long hair. It was barely a meal, but meat was meat. Bart slowly shifted to grasp his spear.

His eyes caught another movement. A tigrog tail had twitched above a shield fern. He froze. Just his luck. But how many were there? His body remained still. He held his breath to hear better. Another bush rat hopped onto the trail. A leaf twitched. The tigrog slid into view. Its molting fur looked rotten: it left strands of its wool on the undergrowth, but it moved silently. The bush rats continued to sniff the ground for seeds.

A streak of mottled wool lanced through the air. The tigrog's jaws crushed one rat. The other rat jumped straight up—into the mouth of a female tigrog who rose from her hiding place not a spear length from Bart. He waited for others to join the feast. When none did he slowly raised his spear. If he could get the near one, he'd have his shette out before the other one charged.

Animals exploded into the clearing: lean, snarling ferts as high as his waist, winter-thin and scarred. The tigrogs yelped, tried to run and were ripped apart in seconds.

Bart nearly fainted in sheer terror. The world greyed for a second then steadied. Ferts! Not a family of ferts, but five studs! When males gathered like this it was to guard the females during migration!

Agonizing with each minuscule movement, Bart slowly sank to his heels in the spice bush. Godwithin. He might as well commit suicide. Caught in the jungle— in migration! In hours this whole area would be crawling with ferts. He crushed a whimper before it could find its way out of his throat . . . and sank deeper into the spice bush. The pungent odor of the pods, savaged his nose. He ground his finger along his upper lip. He couldn't sneeze. He couldn't. The itch in his nose became a burn. His body started to convulse. He opened his mouth, trying to breathe another way. The spice burned his tongue. He curled up silently, fighting the sneeze. But the burning in his mouth and nose overcame him. He exploded in a throat-ripping sneeze. All five adult ferts jumped a man height straight up in the air . . . and landed facing him!

He ripped his shette out, but stayed crouched, praying to Godwithin that another male would challenge for leadership—now!

But there was no challenge and the ferts *did* see him, but although their noses were questing, they didn't rush him. Instead they trotted forward to investigate, almost like meatcat kittens looking at a new twist of leather on their floor.

His back! He was unprotected! The nearest tree was a spear length away, but draped by lianas. While he chopped his way through, he'd be defenseless. The first fert reached the spice patch and stopped as if he'd run into a wall. It sat down and looked at him. Bart stopped breathing. The fert got up and trotted around the bush. The others followed. Bart twisted slowly, trying and failing to keep all of them

in sight. The jungle disappeared and all he could
see were the five ferts, circling, and sniffing. Their
noses were raised into the air, but they didn't come
any closer. Finally, they lost interest and went back
to tearing the tigrogs and bush rats to pieces.

Bart was left shaking in the spice bush. They'd
seen him, but they hadn't smelled him! The spice
pods had masked his scent! He waited till they had
ripped the carcasses apart and carried them off. That
convinced him that it was truly migration time. Females
hunted with males—except in migration, and then
the males herded them together and fed the hugely
pregnant females.

The second the males were out of the clearing,
he started ripping pods from the bush, shoving them
into his pockets, and his pack, rubbing them into
his hair, his skin, his clothes. He sneezed and laughed.
His eyes were running; his nose dripped as if he
were coming down with pneumonia; his mouth ran
with saliva that absorbed the scent and burned his
throat. He ignored his pain and ripped whole branches
off the main plant to stick them in his belt.

Then he broke every bit of training he had ever
received and ran, full speed, back along the trail.
He ran like an ildenhorn, bounding over fallen logs
and racing mindlessly forward. He had to get back
to warn the hunters. If they got caught by migration,
The Home would die! He tried to estimate the time,
but the huge trees totally obscured the sun, making
the world a shifting interplay of green, dark green,
green-brown and brown-black. Still, it had to be past
midmorning; the men would be well into the jungle
and the pack would soon spread out too far to hear
the warnings.

He ran faster—speeded up past the pace he could

maintain all day. Too fast to keep watch. The trail dropped away. He passed the swamp. Behind him he could hear the coughing roars of the male ferts. From the tales of the older warriors he knew that when packs met, the leaders would fight. The winner would herd the new females into the center, and all other males would become guards. That was the only thing that slowed them down, and Bart sincerely hoped that they'd meet another twenty groups today.

As he ran out of the swamp, he filled his lungs, put his fingers in his mouth and sent out a whistle he had never used; the migrating ferts warning. Usually it was used only on the barricades, but now Bart sent the bone-piercing call into the undergrowth, praying that it would penetrate far enough to be heard.

Something fell on the path behind him. He didn't even look around. He shouldn't be running, like an animal in flight, leaving a trail of noise and fear. But migration . . . He tried to run faster; his breath became labored and he slowed down. He had to last another few klats. He had to reach the men before they spread out too far.

The jungle behind him was silent. The ferts had settled their differences and the first migration group was on the move again. He knew how fast they traveled in migration. Last year he'd been allowed to watch from the safety of the armory door. The ferts moved as fast as the heaviest pregnant female—about a slow warrior's jog. So he was making time—unless there was another group ahead of him!

He stumbled, almost fell, then pushed on. If he didn't make it to The Home, he wouldn't survive. You can't spend three tendays in a tree. Sooner or later you have to come down. He whistled the migration warning so hard his eyeballs bulged.

Distantly he heard an answering whistle. It was so far away he couldn't make out the message, he stopped and used every bit of breath he could muster for another warning, then listened. Over the pounding of his ears, the jungle calls, chatters, grunts and shrieks, he heard the migration warning being repeated.

Relief gave him strength. He ran the last klat toward the edge of the jungle like a cub, scampering after a harvest sweet. When he burst out of the jungle, he found Sair waiting with his pack.

"Good lad," Sair said. "You can wait and go up with the next pack." He wrinkled his nose. "You stink like a demented wife."

Men could be heard crashing through the jungle. Seconds later Tev came running heavily into the clearing. His face was flushed and when he stopped he rested his hands on his hips, lifting his shoulders and panting. "Who warned us?" he asked Sair.

"I did." Bart walked forward, ready for his praise.

Guntor groaned. "You mean we ran two klats—away from game—just because some stupid whelp panicked?"

"I didn't panic. I saw five studs together."

Guntor sneered. "Yes, and you survived. What did you do? Scare them with your ugly face?"

Tev put a hand on Guntor. "Remember his eyesight."

"*You* could have seen them; they were only two spear lengths away."

Volf snorted. "He's lying. No lanker could ever survive that."

"But I did," Bart protested. "They saw me, but they couldn't smell me. So they left me alone."

"I can smell you and you smell like a woman." Guntor hooted, but Tev and Sair were looking at each other.

Sair walked quietly forward and waved the other zerkers back. "They saw you, but didn't attack?" He stepped back as the fumes hit him. "I can see why." All the men laughed.

A fert battle erupted in the jungle behind them, dousing the laughter like a quenched flame.

Sair closed his eyes. "Godwithin. Ontu is still out there. Thirteen men. Five whelps." He made the sign of the Holy Circle. "Let's go."

"Wait," Norv pleaded. "My brother, Ians, is in that pack. Couldn't you wait? We'd have more of a chance together?"

Sair lifted his whistle and sent the migration call slicing into the jungle. The men listened, and listened. Sair shook his head. "Ontu said he was heading up Nidoee Canyon. He can't hear."

They all listened to the struggle in the jungle. When the winner howled in triumph, silencing all the jungle noises, the men turned pale. The ferts were moving again.

"We just got out in time," Sair said. He jerked his head. "Move out!"

"Wait," Tev grabbed Bart by the shoulders. "Did the ferts really pass you by? " Bart nodded. Tev turned to Sair. "Then we'd better send him off to warn Ontu. Maybe Bart could get through."

Bart nearly gabbled in fear; Sair nodded. "It's worth a try. If we lose all those men, women and children will starve next spring no matter what the harvest."

Pulling Bart aside, Tev whispered fiercely. "Ontu needs someone to tell him what to do."

"What?"

"Shut up and listen. Ontu's a good leader as long as everything is straightforward. His dead lanker pack mate always used to give him ideas on how to handle the unexpected. You have to help him lead that pack back."

"He'll never listen to me."

"He might if you pretended to admire him. Whenever you have an idea, say. 'I bet you're going to do this,' or 'I guess you've already decided to do that.' "

"But what will I tell him to do?"

"The ferts come up the center of the trail. Leave the trail, find lots of spice, put it on all of you and come up along the cliff. You'll have rock behind you and a chance to fight back. Now get."

The two packs trotted off. Every few strides a warrior would look anxiously over his shoulder.

Nidoee Canyon. It was at least three klats to the cliff wall and then another to the entrance. Well above him, Tev turned and waved him into the jungle. Sure. Easy for him. He was on his way home.

Instead of entering the jungle Bart started running along the edge of the trees. It was further this way, but he could see any attacker long before they leaped.

A dactyl warning whistle drifted down from the mountain. Bart looked up. The dactyl was already diving. He sprinted for the trees. The warning came again. *Danger of Death.* He threw himself headfirst toward the nearest tree. The dactyl screamed. Air buffeted him. The scream turned to a shriek. He looked up; it had come too close to the tree and was thrashing itself free of a branch. Before it was free, Bart was into the jungle running for his life—and looking out for more spice bushes. Enough for a whole pack. When he saw a thicket he plunged in, emptied his pack, loosened the extender string and crammed it full of hastily stripped pods. No sooner was he on the trail again, than he heard a fert cough. He leaped off the trail and hid. Not that it would do him any good, but he felt safer crouched under the blanket fern.

Seconds later the pack leader ranged past, nose questing, ears twitching, and eyes seeking prey. Meat. Him. But the animal traveled right on by, and so did ten other males. When the females started coming by, other males padded through the jungle beside the trail—once almost a hand span from Bart. But, even though his shaking should have alerted the whole jungle, the ferts ignored him.

When they had passed, he started off again. He didn't see any more ferts, but the jungle was now silent. They—the tree dwellers and the ground dwellers—knew it was migration.

He reached the cliff and ran to the canyon entrance. Nidoee Canyon was a long twisting canyon that penetrated klats into the cliffs. He sent out the migration warning, and started jogging up the canyon. The ground climbed steeply and soon he was out of the jungle and into the needle forest. He turned another corner in the canyon, and whistled again.

Immediately it was answered. In moments the pack jogged out of a fold in the ground and surrounded him, demanding to know what had happened.

"Shit. You mean they're ahead of us?" Ontu rubbed his long yellow teeth as if cleaning them would help. "Taizaburo! What are we going to do?"

His First Spear looked up the canyon. "Couldn't we hole up here until it's over?"

Norv's brother, Ians shook his head. "They need us at the barricades. Without us there are too few warriors to protect The Home."

Ontu rubbed his teeth with a stubby forefinger.

You have to lead that pack back. Bart took a deep breath. "There's another way. I got here by wearing

the spice pods. Fert packs passed me three times,"
he lied, "and they ignored me."

"Three times!" Ians shuddered. "Not me!"

"I doubt Ontu would make you do that," Bart said.
All eyes swung toward him. "I'm sure he will just
cover you with spice and take you along the cliff
wall, away from the main migration route. Then the
ferts won't smell you and, if they do, you have the
rock at your back."

"Uh . . . sure. Yes, of course." Ontu straightened
his spine. "Come on, let's get home."

Bart emptied his pack. The men grabbed the pods
and rubbed. Soon they were all choking and sneezing—
and glaring at Bart.

"This better work," Ians said. He rubbed his eyes
and swore when the scent on his hands made his
eyes tear.

Ontu ignored the complaints. Once he knew what
he was doing, he was a good pack leader. He assigned
Wiar, a hardened warrior with an overshot jaw, to
protect Bart, organized the men and started back.

Ians trotted up beside Bart. "Get up there and
keep giving him ideas," he hissed, softly, so that Bart's
protector could not hear.

Tev's plan worked. It was slow. Once they got on
the Migration Trail there was no cover, and whenever
a pack of ferts passed, Ontu ordered them to stand
motionless, something that drove the zerkers crazier
and crazier. When they crossed the stone bridge,
Ontu set off at a dead run to get them to the other
cliff. When they arrived he looked at his zerkers.

"Better?"

They nodded and Wiar growled. "Let's fight them
anyway. I'm tied in knots with all this creeping around."

Ontu just looked at Wiar and then looked significantly at Bart, reminding the zerker of his sworn duty to protect Bart. Wiar flushed. Ontu nodded approvingly. "Just another klat to go." He looked at the sun that was directly overhead. "If we hurry, we'll get there just before most of the ferts even get to The Home. Then they will settle down for the night, and we can get organized for the rest of migration."

Ians scratched his short beard. "Why don't we just wait for dark and travel while they're sleeping?"

"And trip over sleeping ferts?" Ontu inquired sarcastically.

The men froze as another pack loped into sight around the bend. In the front was a huge male. Where most ferts lived until they were half a man height, this one was shoulder high, his muzzle silvered, and his ears tattered. Bart hoped the warriors on the barricades were ready for him. Behind the leader came at least twenty forward guards, followed by forty or fifty females. The side scouts ranged from one end of the cliffs to the other, looking for food. Not that there was any now, the previous packs had killed or driven off all but the insects.

When the last rear guard disappeared over the rise, Ontu jerked his head. "I have a bad feeling about this one. Let's follow right on their heels." The zerkers sighed with relief and urged their lankers into a fast trot, eager to be home, and eager for a fight to release all their pent-up energy.

They heard the fight long before they came in sight of The Home. Men howled orders or shouted their pack fighting yells. Ferts coughed and roared. Bart pushed ahead with the rest, around the last bend.

The barricades were under siege. The old male

had bunched his females in the center of the pack and all of them were charging the walls.

Wiar surged forward, only to be stopped by Ontu. "But we've got to help them," Wiar protested, his overshot jaw emphasizing his alarm.

His grizzled leader shook his head. "Look at the gates. They're closed. Once we start fighting, we have no escape."

The ferts hit the wall. Without Ontu's pack, the men were spread thin along the barricade. Tev's pack got the brunt of the attack, and used their spears to push the ferts off. The other warriors leaned over the barricades trying to pick off more with their arrows. As they watched, three ferts climbed on the living bodies of their pack mates and ran lightly up to within a snout of an empty section of wall. Volf and Guntor threw themselves forward, stabbing with their lances.

Wiar groaned. "We have to do something. I can't stand here. I'll go crazy." He started forward.

Ontu blocked him again, but he was clearly wavering.

Ians kicked Bart forward. "Yes," Ontu said, hopefully.

"Isn't this great?" Bart chattered. Yes, sure. Think of something. "Why don't we try to sneak up on them, and shoot them from behind?"

Ontu shook his head. "That'll leave us with our backs to any other pack that comes up the trail. Think of something else."

Think of something else—of something Tev would do. Think of how he would use the spice, and the battle to get us *in*.

"Hurry up." Wiar looked as if he wanted to shake an idea out of him.

Bart's eyes scrambled over the trail, the cliffs, the area in front of the battlefield, desperately seeking an idea. Tev would make Ontu look great. Ontu could fight; he just didn't have a lot of ideas. If only they had another barricade. But they didn't need another barricade. They were invisible to the ferts! All they needed was somewhere to fight where their backs would be covered. He scanned the fighting area until he saw it. A waist-high ledge along the Starboard cliffs.

That was it. "Just think, we're invisible to the ferts. All we have to do is line up on that little ledge, near the Starboard side of the barricades and shower the ferts with arrows. We've our backs to the Starboard cliffs, and we'll be high enough to look down on the fight." And if the ferts saw them they could climb that ledge with one leg chopped off.

Dead silence greeted his suggestion. To get across the valley they had to cross the river that flowed out of their home valley—and rivers held nurls. Finally Ians said, "You first."

"No." Ontu put his arm on Bart's shoulder. "We'll go first."

Wiar shoved his square jaw forward. "Count me in, too."

The rest of the pack backed into the safety of the cliff. Bart and his two protectors slunk across the open valley floor. From the barricades they heard shouts as the men saw them, and waved them back, away from the battle. The ferts rushed the barricades again, and the men on the wall were too busy to even shout.

Bart and his group edged forward. The river was shallow here and bubbled over stones. The really big nurls could live in deep water, but enough small nurls could still bring down the unwary ildenhorn— or man. Bart scanned the fight at the barricades. But none of the ferts so much as looked their way.

Wiar sucked in his breath. "Maybe if we run, they won't get any more than our boot soles."

Bart looked along the bank. "Couldn't we take rocks from the edge and form stepping stones?"

Before the words were out of his mouth Ontu and Wiar were down at the edge of the water grabbing huge boulders and heaving them with manic ferocity into the stream. "Get flattened ones," Bart called when a particularly large boulder landed and rolled.

He heaved his spear as a flat grey nurl as big as his arm tried to use its flippers to push itself toward the tantalizing prey at the water's edge. The spear caught it square on the head and impaled it. Instantly every nurl in the river converged on it. "Now!" Bart screamed. "Run while they're eating." He leaped on the first three rocks and came to the end of the stepping stones. The next leap took him into the water. He could hear Wiar screaming behind him and leaped for the shore. Once safe he ran for the ledge on the Starboard side of The Home, the men pounding behind. They scrambled up the ledge. One climbed and two guarded his unprotected back. From the ledge they could look down on the fight. "You owe me a set of boots," Ians grated.

Bart looked down. Part of the insole of Ians' boot was gone, his trousers were ripped and . . . "Ians, you've been bitten." Before Ians could move, Wiar had his field pack out and was masking the smell of blood with the sweet perfume of mirta.

Ontu strung his bow. "Let's kill." He loosed his first arrow. A large male who was clawing his way up the stones of the barricades yelped and fell back. Bart picked his own target. He shot. A yearling twisted in midair, biting his hip. On the wall, Tev screamed and pointed. Bart followed his arm. Of course. The females. He sighted and shot. A young female flopped over and started to keen. The other females picked up the keen and pressed forward harder. Well, that didn't work.

"Move over," Ians grunted. Bart gave him room, and the rest of the pack scrambled up on the ledge.

Bart picked another female. A gust of down-valley wind fouled his shot, but it hit a yearling in the paw, and it screamed in rage.

"Watch out for the leader!" Ians hissed. "He's looking at the dead ferts behind him."

He was doing more than that; he was also calling to his females. A cough, a snarl and a frontal rush knocked the ferts away from the wall. Then he led them toward Ontu's men, raising his nose high in the air.

"Freeze," Ontu snarled. "If we don't smell and look like a spice bush, we're dead." The men froze on the ledge, smelling of spice—and fear. The ferts trotted back and forth, seeking the enemy. Again and again they lifted their noses, but the air seemed to bring them nothing. Finally the old leader snarled again. The pack left off their hunt.

"It worked," Ians whispered.

"Of course it worked," Ontu snapped.

Ians leaned over and put his mouth to Bart's ear. "Want to join our pack?" he asked, watching the ferts.

Some of the pack turned toward the up-valley trail. Others headed back to the wall. The old leader shouldered them back up the valley, snarling, and slicing viciously with his teeth.

"Let's run for it before the next group comes," Bart suggested.

No one needed a second invitation. They practically fell down the cliff, then ran in huge leaps and bounds.

Behind them Ontu roared his orders. "Grab a carcass, men. We need the meat."

The men swerved and each lanker-zerker team grabbed a carcass and started dragging it frantically back to the gate. Bart found himself heaving on the hind legs of a pregnant female. "Love kitten stew," his partner grunted. They reached the gate and found Ontu already there.

"Throw it in and get another," he ordered. "The way is still clear."

Back they ran twice more. The men on the barricades cheered themselves hoarse. Each fert was heavier than the last, and Bart felt as weak as a cub. But the food! More food than any of them had seen in months. The pile of bodies inside the gate blocked the entrance, and Edgar brought his whelps in to move them away.

As Bart and Wiar carried in their third carcass, Sair whistled the warning from the barricades. The next pack was rounding the bend.

"One more," Ontu urged his men. "One more."

Bart ran, his back still bent double from the last load. Soon they were sweating and straining with a yearling. "Now I know why we always make the lankers carry," Wiar grunted.

The men on the barricades picked up the warning whistle. Bart and Wiar started to run. Every step wrenched at his back; his partner started to pull him forward. "Come on, don't stop now," Wiar rasped.

Bart forced his tired body to go faster, but Wiar was almost dragging him. He looked up to see that they were going to be the last in. Already the large door was bolted shut, and only a tiny war hole in the door remained open, a hole large enough for a man— or a very stretched-out fert.

"Hurry," men screamed above them. "Drop the fert."

"Don't you dare," Wiar grunted. "My family needs the food." Bart could hear the ferts snarling as they charged the barricades, but he kept on running, and he held onto his meat. Wiar dragged him through the bolt hole after the fert. Ontu slammed the war hole shut. Bart sagged with relief, only to stiffen as Tev's voice screamed down at him.

"Get your ass up here, we need all the warriors we can get."

Warrior! Tev called him a warrior!

Ontu slapped him on the back. "Good man! Without your warning we would never have made it home before migration."

When he started for the barricades, Ians hurried over to Bart. "Remember what I said."

As he climbed to the top of the wall, Bart basked in the warmth of that request. It was the first time anyone had wanted him—*really wanted him*—since the nesters. He walked along the wall past the other packs. Men took a second or so to reach out and playfully punch him, or tug his hair, before turning back to face the trail. Bart's face split in the first happy smile in months. As he reached his place beside Dyfid, the ferts hit the wall.

19

Day 1:Second Gifter Moon of Spring:
452 Migrations After Landing

It was pitch black; not even the tiny moon, Fee, eased the darkness. As Sanda felt her way up the cliff, her injured head pounded and her stomach turned acid with self contempt. "Coward," she told herself each time she reached for a new handhold or wedged her foot in a new crack in the rock. "Some zerker you are. Can't even force yourself to take one tiny step off a cliff?"

She passed the second artisan deck and detoured around the windows of the scholars' gallery and climbed upwards. She kept hoping she'd slip, but her fingers and toes seemed to be like steel hooks. She felt a window slot with her hands and pulled herself up. The window was barred. Within the bars glass panes were wedged into the rock, and behind that, more bars. As she peered into the blackness Fee slowly rose and by the light of the moon she could dimly see a row of book shelves near the window.

The Archives!

Frustration and a terrible sense of loss started her head pounding again.

Tough. You deserve to hurt, coward. She stood

on the window slot and reached for another handhold and slipped her fingers into a ribbon of darkness. Reaching for knobs and bumps on the rock face she edged upwards and toward the waterfall. Soon its spray dampened the rocks. Yes. Good. Maybe the rocks were slippery. Soon she'd fall.

A shadow covered her. A shadow! She cringed under an overhang. Claws scraped the rock millimeters from her exposed shoulder, and a nightglider hovered by the cliff, its membranous wings sounding like flapping bedcovers. Its eyes were like jet beads and its long snout was armed with a row of sharp fangs that seemed to drip with anticipation. With a blast of wind, it was gone, climbing into the dark sky. She looked up. The overhang had protected her. If she moved, the glider would get her. "So move," she muttered. "*Let* it get you. That's what you want." She shifted her weight to move out of the protection of the overhang. A rock fragment shifted under her hands. She jiggled it. The rock grated free as she edged out from under the overhang. Mentally she cowered on the cliff. But physically she turned to meet the glider.

"Fool," she yelled at herself. "This is your chance. Let it kill you. Isn't that what you want?"

The nightglider saw her and folded its wings for another dive. When it snapped its wings open she threw the sharp rock right at the membranous skin flap between the wing bone and body.

The stone hit with a solid thunk, and the wing folded around it; the glider screamed as it luffed to one side and fell from view. She braced herself and looked down. Far below her, the glider was flopping awkwardly. He tried to perch on a rocky outcrop, missed and slowly flapped out of sight in the darkness.

And she was still alive! Damn, she couldn't do

anything right! Well, at least she could still climb. She edged sideways until she found a vertical crack that disappeared into the gloom, and started up again. Wedging her feet on one side, and her back on the other, she climbed until her legs and thighs started to burn. Good. Keep climbing. Soon it'll happen. Then no more fear, no more shame, no more Peace.

Her breath began to come in pants, and even though the wind was cold, perspiration sheathed her. Her body cried out to stop, but she sternly drove herself on. "Coward," she snarled. As Fee came further out over the valley, she could see more and more around her. Insects scuttled away from her hands. For once she wished a poisonous snake was lurking in one of the crevices. Still she climbed on, almost wishing the ghosts were out. Almost. Tonight she wanted an end to everything, not to begin it—as a soul slave to a Sangir.

Light penetrated deeper into the crevices in front of her. The Gifter was rising, sending its silvery light through the valley. She paused and looked around for one last time.

The bone-burnished face of the Gifter hung over the waterfall, and was reflected in the pool on the valley floor at the foot of the falls. Beyond it the Waterfall River was a silver-black ribbon that lay along the valley, disappearing under the barricades, and becoming crumpled at the rapids along the Migration Trail. Her breathing eased.

"Stop putting it off," she hissed, and started to climb again. This time she was *not* going to stop— ever. She climbed until her legs and thighs trembled. Good. Keep climbing. Soon it'll happen. Soon.

Suddenly she found herself climbing stone blocks. The blocks were huge, but fitted together without mortar, giving her easy finger and toe holds. She looked to either side. The wall extended as far as she could see into the darkness. She must be in Olarnite territory!

Curiosity gave her strength and she pulled herself up, looking for windows. Instead she climbed over a wall. And found herself looking at a small river valley that extended deep into the cliff. The valley was totally covered with dactyl netting that was bolted to the cliff and draped down to rings set into the wall. She swung her feet over the wall. Her reaching toes touched metal, not rope! A dactyl net made of metal! And so much metal! The valley had to be at least thirty by fifty meters deep. There must be thousands of gold cards worth of metal here. Haddim would drool. No. Haddim was dead. She pulled her feet back and sat on the wall, looking.

The valley was filled with ship fruit trees, in bloom. Between the trees, the darker ground showed ploughed furrows. Between the furrows irrigation ditches from the creek glittered black with water.

Sanda took a deep breath, drinking in the scent of the durapple blossoms . . . and a door opened on the cliff wall, spilling light into the garden. A woman appeared against the light. Sanda flattened herself on the wall.

Another woman followed the first, and they both walked into the garden and sat on a stone bench facing the waterfall. Curiosity forced Sanda toward the two women. She lay on her belly and wriggled along the wall till she was about ten meters behind them. Then one of the women turned and the Gifter's silver light outlined her profile.

Nystra!

What was Nystra doing in Olarnite territory? Had

she gone through the Olarnite Gate? Was there going to be a new Mother General in The Home?

The light from the Gifter reflected off the tears that streaked down Nystra's face. She spoke to the other woman, but the waterfall muffled her words. Suddenly Sanda knew she just had to hear what they were saying. She wriggled down onto the metal netting. It creaked but she was sure the sound was lost in the roar of the waterfall. Her skirt caught in the weave of the net; she jerked it free, pulled it up between her legs and tugged the loose end through her sash. Then she wriggled forward again. Soon she could distinguish the words.

"Sometimes I don't know how I can go on." Nystra's voice was broken with misery. "I tried so hard with Ullan. I told her the tales of the ancients, hoping she would model herself on Olarni. If only I could have told her the Olarnite tales. But I didn't dare tell her. I mean, if I had told her that 'native' foods and ship food have different structures that we digest differently, she might have begun to talk to the wrong people."

Bassarra half shrugged, half nodded. "If she had, I don't think anyone would have understood her. I'm the Officer of Education, and I barely understand the old records which explain why so many of our people turn zerker. All this talk of *amino acids* and *nerve receptors*. How can we have acids in our body without it burning? And how can it affect our nerves so that a person goes zerker? Unless the acids burn our nerves, but that's not what the records say." She patted Nystra's hand. "No, you did the best you could."

Nystra nodded. "I tried everything. I made sure she didn't get any jungle food—especially the meat eaters, even though I went into debt to pay for the ship food she ate. And it worked—just like the old records said. As long as Ullan only got ship's food, she was her old bubbly cheerful self. And I didn't leave it at that. I also tried to get her interested in meditating, because I know that helps me when I am struggling for control—in the spring when even I can't get ship food." She wiped her eyes.

Sanda hung riveted to the net. Of course! Suddenly the Song of the Ancestors rang in her ears.

> But the battle had given them kills right at
> hand
> And they feasted all through the night.
> And awoke to a world where half of the band
> Were berserker with strength and might.

It wasn't because the Goddess Within was punishing them. It was because they had eaten jungle meat—and for the first time! She edged closer. Why was that knowledge held secret? Why didn't all zerker women, and men, know this? Think of how many women could hide, if they knew!

The other woman—Bassarra—put her arms around Nystra and drew her down onto her shoulder. "You did everything you could. How were you to know that your sister-wife would want to save the ship food for migration and feed Ullan grunkle pie and tigrog stew when you weren't there to watch?"

Sanda squirmed even further forward, driven as much by a desire to understand as to hear.

"I should have been around! I knew she was ready to turn. But with the ship food, she seemed so normal. I even dared to hope that she was lanker." Nystra pulled a rag from her pocket and blew her nose. "If I hadn't been so busy, I would have made sure she didn't eat anything that would make her condition worse. I would have insisted that she join me for morning and evening meditation so that she'd be calmer. And I'd have worked her so hard, she'd have been too tired to rage."

"But we don't know for sure that those things allow zerkers to hide," Bassarra protested. "Remember, there are disciplined zerkers, and there are wild zerkers. Maybe Ullan is a throwback to the wild ones who started so many pack wars."

Sanda wanted to rip the mesh open and pound the two women to pulp, to find out more. How did you tell a wild zerker from a disciplined one?

Nystra relaxed against Bassarra's shoulder. "I guess I was fortunate to be called to the Goddess Within when I was so young. About a week before I fell into my first rage, I entered 'The Silence.' It changed my whole way of looking at life."

"You still turned."

"Yes, but luckily the first time, I was with Brianna, and she didn't tell."

"You're lucky she didn't tell later," Bassarra said.

"No, not lucky at all. I ordered Leeorah to put muscle waste in her Peace. I promised myself I'd make it up to her by helping her children."

Muscle waste! Sanda didn't know what it was, but the name said it all. Brianna's halting speech, her inability to string a sentence together, her horrible smell—heavier and different than the Peace Sanda had smelled on Ullan. Thank the Goddess Within, she'd never told anyone about Nystra. And she never would either. The woman was a demon!

Bassarra pushed Nystra back to look at her. "I didn't know you'd been using muscle waste on Brianna.

No wonder she looked so bad. It's a miracle she hasn't died."

"I'm not proud of it." Sanda clutched the wire, dizzy with the hatred that roared through her. Not proud of it. They'd nearly killed her mother, and they weren't proud of it! Damn them. She glared at Nystra who continued, "But I did make it up to her. I knew Kayella needed hard work so I got her into the stonemason's guild at a time when they really didn't need any more apprentices. But I never realized that she knew I was zerker. I thought I was going to lose everything when she cut loose in sickbay, and started naming the hidden zerkers in The Home."

"I know. Leeorah said her eyes flashed like summer lightning and her power actually spread her hair around her like a billowing cape."

"She was all of that. When she said, 'Kill me now; I won't take Peace,' I didn't know what to do. I know my predecessor would have killed her, but you can't experience the Goddess's love and be able to kill."

"You could have fooled me. By the time I got there, she was threatening you—saying she'd tell the men who the hidden zerkers were—you, Tekiri, and Grannie Akeydn. When you grabbed Leeorah's surgery knife, I thought for sure you were going to kill her."

"Bluff, dear, bluff. I do it every day of my life." She rubbed her head tiredly. "At least she believed me, and we made our deal."

"That reminds me. Now that Haddim's household has broken up, what *have* you done about Reena."

"She went with Inara to her new household. I'm paying the cards to keep her, and when Sanda finishes her training, I'll tell her that Kayella willed her child to Sanda."

"Are you going to keep the rest of the bargain—telling Sanda about the hidden zerkers?"

"No. And I don't intend to. We have to go back to the old way of testing zerker women. The experiment with Ullan didn't work. No, that's not true; it was working until Ullan got jungle food in her diet. But we have so little ship's food. We can't give it to women without drawing attention to them. I only got away with it because of who I am. But my sister-wives were angry with the way I 'spoiled' Ullan, and in the end they ruined all my plans. No, it boils down to one thing. Zerkers have to be fired like a ceramic vase. We helped Kayella, and what happened? She lost her edge. She wasn't on guard. If Sanda is to survive as a hidden zerker . . ."

They knew! Sanda started to shake as she pressed closer, listening.

"She has to be tried, and transmuted into a warrior among women. A woman who watches and fights for survival with every breath." She patted her friend's arm. "That's why your idea of locking her up for two days without food was brilliant. It'll give her a chance to face her raging storms, and quell them."

They knew. They'd known all along.

"Or go mad," Bassarra said

"No, I don't think so. Without jungle food to fire up her rages, she'll manage just fine. I have great hopes for that girl."

Sanda's vision blurred. She bit her cheeks as hatred and gratitude warred with each other in her body. Hatred won. If she'd known about the food, and the meditation, she'd have had some hope. She wouldn't have been driven to suicide. She clenched her fists in rage, missing Bassarra's next words.

". . . succeed. Enough women suffer or die without any help from us."

"If only we could figure out how to avoid increasing Ullan's dose as she ages," Nystra said.

"Don't worry about her. She's marrying a zerker— a young zerker. She'll douse her fires on his seed. Good sex and lots of babies will keep her placid. And speaking of fires. You're dangerously upset." She pulled Nystra closer and kissed her ear. Her hand caressed Nystra's shoulder and dropped to cup a breast.

Sanda stuck her nose through the mesh, watching. Was this the women's love that the girls giggled and wondered about?

Nystra sighed and swept Bassarra up in a desperate hug. Bassarra laughed and pushed her back.

"Let's go in and find a comfortable bed. A little bit of love will quench your fires and make the world much brighter." She got up and pulled Nystra to her feet. "Come on, my little lenpic blossom."

Nystra nodded, glanced up—and froze.

"Look!" she yelled pointing at Sanda.

With a roll, Sanda was at the wall, and scrambling over it. Behind her she could hear screams. She started climbing down, and practically fell the first ten meters. A bell clanged above.

Other voices joined Nystra's, and a warm torch glow flickered above the wall. Hide. She had to hide. She'd never get down before they climbed the wall. Frantically she craned her neck looking for something, anything.

There. Over there by the corner of the garden, an overhang. She dug her toes into the cracks of the walls and crabbed sideways as fast as she could.

"I don't see anything. Are you sure you saw someone?"

The voices were clear above the waterfall. It was a woman, but unlike any woman she had ever heard. It was loud, sharp, and commanding. Who was up there? She moved faster, missed her grip and nearly fell. Shaking from fatigue, and terror, she made it to the overhang and pushed herself as far into the cliff as she could.

"Who was it?" The voice was now directly overhead.

"I don't know. All I saw was the silhouette of a figure in a tunic and loose pants."

Pants! Sanda felt her gown. It was still pulled up between her legs and tucked in her sash.

"A man!" The unknown voice strengthened with anger. "Who do you think it might be? If he saw the wire, the men will be demanding it for weapons, and then how will we protect our food?"

"It might not be a man," Bassarra said. "Olarnites wear pants."

There was a long silence and the strange voice said, "I'll check."

The cliffs around Sanda flared, lit by a warm glow from above. Suddenly a lamp drifted down past her, bringing the brown banding of the rock into warm color and illuminating several beetles who scuttled for safety. The glow faded as the lamp descended further and further.

"I don't see how anyone could have gotten up here. It's got to be five hundred meters down to the Promenade Deck," Nystra said.

"But it's only half that distance to the scholar's deck," the strange voice said, "and didn't you mention that Priestess Donu was pushing to replace you so that the position of First Priestess and Mother General could be combined? Could it be she's looking for ways to get rid of you?"

"Donu? Donu couldn't climb up here," Bassarra said. "She's fat and arthritic."

"Does she have daughters?" the stranger asked.

"Jessance," Nystra said. "She's in training, but she couldn't . . . Bassarra, get down to training level and check Jessance."

Sanda couldn't understand. Women who went up to the Daughters of Olarni never came down again. How could Nystra or Bassarra talk of going to the Promenade Deck? They were forsworn . . . forever.

"No," the stranger snapped. "Bassarra, go to the Promenade Deck and see if any man goes home late. Nystra, you stay here with me."

Sanda gasped. Who would dare order Nystra around? She was the *Mother General!*

"Yes, Sister."

Sister! And Nystra was obeying her, instantly, the way a wife had to obey her husband. A sister. An Olarnite. But not like the old grannie who guarded the Olarnite door. The strong voice was that of a much younger woman.

"Whoever was on the net moved zerker fast," Nystra said.

"Damn. Well . . . I can't see anything, so I guess you'd better get down to the main decks. Lock every access tunnel and companionway as you go through. Then check Jessance, and every other girl on the training deck. We've got to find out who that was. And shut them up."

Sanda's stomach muscles clenched till they burned. This was no Nystra who couldn't kill because of her Goddess union. The lamp was drawn up silently. She waited in terrified silence but heard nothing.

Now, climb for your life.

But just as she was edging out of her crevice she

heard someone cough. Then nothing. She looked out. Clouds were coming down the valley. Would it be dark enough? She had to leave! She watched the clouds edge closer. Was the woman above still there? She had no way of telling.

A feathery wisp of cloud drifted across the Gifter, then another. The silvery light bathing the opposite cliffs dimmed. How far had Nystra gone by now? Down one companionway? Two? As it got darker, she eased forward, and pulled herself slowly out from under the overhang.

There was no one above. She turned and then swarmed down the cliff. Every finger seemed to have eyes that saw and reached for a handhold. Every toe had feelers that brushed the cliff face and found the best purchase. Down she went. Never had she climbed so fast. Spiders scuttled out of her way, and night gophers chattered at her as she almost landed on them. She came to a dead end—crabbed sideways and continued her rush. Her feet felt emptiness. She traced the outline of a window.

Archives!

Her muscles burned, and her breath came in pants. Too bad. Ignore it, she screamed to her body, and it ignored fatigue that would have felled her only moments before. Her feet found another window. The Scholars' Gallery. She crabbed sideways, for what felt like hours trying to find the edge of the huge windows.

There! Her toes found a rough crack, and she started down again. A creak warned her of an open window; she scuttled back above the gallery. Looking down past her body, she could see a warm glow coming out from behind the opening window. *Look down*, she urged the searcher. *Look down*.

A dark head leaned out—and looked from side to

side, and then down. Eventually the head withdrew, the window closed and the lights behind it went out. She climbed down again. Were the searchers ahead of her?

One more deck to go. Goddess Within give me strength. Her heart poured into her prayer and somehow she had the strength to get down past the artisan deck. Finally her feet found a window on the training deck. But which one was hers?

She wanted to sit down and cry. But there was nowhere to sit. She wanted to rage. But had no breath or energy left.

As she hung by the window she heard someone crying inside. That was all she needed. A girl to report her. She started to edge away. But which way? If it had been the cliff outside her family quarters, she would have known every crack and tuft of windgrass, but here . . .

Light flooded out of the room, and Sanda ducked. They were searching already!

"Gena," Nystra said softly. "What's wrong?"

"I can't stand it," Gena sobbed. "I can't stand being treated like dirt. I'm smart. I work hard. I'm going to be a healer, but everyone acts as if I'm covered with slime."

Gena. She was three doors down from Sanda. But which way? Left. Yes, left. Cry, she silently urged the sobbing girl. Cry your heart out and *keep her there*!

The rest had given her a bit more energy. It had also given her body time to complain. Her fingers hurt. Her toes stung with dozens of cuts. Both knees felt as if they'd been scraped raw.

One window. One to go. Sweat trickled off her eyebrows and stung her eyes. As she passed the last window, light bloomed in the tiny hole!

When she got to her own window she wriggled through like a snake in its death throes . . . and fell on the floor with a crash that knocked sparking lights into her head. Thank heaven the room was so small, so easy to find her bed. She threw back the covers and slid under—just as the door creaked open.

She closed her eyes and hunched up. Beyond her closed eyelids, light turned her world red. Footsteps came close to her bed.

Don't pant. Breathe slowly. In—two—three. Out—two—three. Her lungs screamed for more air. Her heart hammered in her chest.

The footsteps receded and the door closed. She gasped for air. Safe!

And she was going to stay safe! Bart was right. Hard work was part of the answer. But only part of it.

Meditation? She could feel a conversion experience coming on. The high priestess would be thrilled to have another contemplative in The Home.

Food. Meat, especially the meat of carnivores, set zerkers off. Well, fasting was the answer to that.

Sex? She giggled as she settled herself more comfortably. Her breathing eased naturally. She was so tired. Her exhausted muscles slowly unknotted as the bed warmed to her body. There was a way out. She had a chance to help herself, and maybe even Ullan—someday. She took another deep breath as her hammering heart slowly eased its pounding.

And to think that this was the day she had decided to die.

20

The Migration Trail was alive with early spring flowers. Where only a tenday ago Bart had struggled in crackling dry grass, now redheart buds, keld cabbages, yellow bowl flowers, white spring roses, and orange baby slippers competed with the emerald spring herbs and shrubs. Behind him, the ship crops were covering the fields with tiny heads of tender green, filling the air with their scent, and drawing the ferts even more strongly toward The Home.

Sair clapped him on the shoulder. "You really should get more sleep at night." He guffawed, laughing at the blush that climbed up Bart's neck. "Oh, to be young and first-married again."

Bart tried to look dignified, but he could feel his face soften as he thought of Wahiri. She was the perfect wife: beautiful, soft, gentle, and obedient. That she was also a wonderful cook was an added bonus.

Sair laughed again. "If you win any more nights with her, she'll get pregnant with triplets. But I sure hope they don't smell like you." He waved toward the crushed spice pods that Bart carried around with him in anticipation of another dash outside the barricades for meat. Twice he'd been caught outside, and had

351

been forced to freeze, couched in a fold in the ground, praying his spice would work. Fert had screamed and died all around him, but they had never attacked.

". . . some spice pods." Sair looked at him expectantly.

"Yes, sir," he said brightly, wondering what he'd missed.

"Good, the Mother General went around to all the women this morning, and she said she'd leave The Home's supply of pods with Leeorah, the healer. You can pick it up now, while there's a lull in the fighting."

"Yes, sir." Bart was not enthusiastic. Guntor had gotten a ripped shoulder muscle, and was the door guard to the armory. He headed for the stairs, his legs feeling leaden. He'd never been so tired in his life. They'd been fighting for twelve days and, because he had the most spice ground into his clothes, he'd been constantly sent out, with Ontu's pack, to pull down the mound of ferts near the wall, and bring in fresh meat. In all he'd won six glorious, but sleepless—well, almost sleepless—nights with Wahiri.

"Going back up to see that new wife of yours?" Ontu growled as Bart passed. Bart shrugged. After all, women weren't supposed to be as important as fighting.

Wiar pounded him on the back. "Watch the cliffs. The barricades reek of death. Some of the fert stragglers have been sniffing around trying to find another way into The Home."

Bart nodded and headed for the stairs, feeling like a crippled elder. On the ground Edgar was supervising his whelps who were sorting retrieved arrows, carrying water and food for the warriors, and replacing the used mirta bandages that were stored along the cliff.

"Water, sir," one of the whelps said, respectfully.

Bart took the water and drank, looking up at the warriors on the wall. Only one man from each pack actually stood guard, the rest were sleeping, or sharpening their shettes and spear heads. All looked exhausted, and many wore bulky mirta bandages from close fighting. But, according to Tev, it was better than last year. Because of Bart and Ontu's pod-smelling pack, the pile of bodies at the foot of the wall never rose high enough to provide an easy stepping stone to the top.

"Hurry up, Bart," Sair urged. "And get down here if you hear the warning."

Bart nodded and saluted, wishing Sair would send a whelp, and knowing why he didn't. He was showing Bart favor by letting him visit the armory and have a quick visit with his new wife. He trudged up the path, feeling as if he were carrying a double load.

The fert packs were further apart now as the migration eased. Yesterday there had been only six. In less than two tendays, the fert migration would be over, and the keld would start up the trail. Keld were easy prey after the ferts, and carried a lot more meat. Already the men were looking forward to the keld feast at the end of migration.

He stopped to rest three turns above the river level. From here he could see over the barricades; the Migration Trail was still empty. His eyes drifted over the ploughed fields in the valley. Now that he was a man, one plot and four field hands had been assigned to him, but he hadn't had time to find out where the plot was, or who the hands were.

His eyelids started to close. He jerked awake and plodded on. What he needed was a whole summer to sleep. He could hardly wait till the keld feast. After that the men rested and speared their wives for a tenday before starting the summer hunts. He labored up a set of stairs that he usually never noticed. Godwithin but he was tired. Still, he braced himself to meet Guntor, the only warrior who refused to recognize that he was a man. Whenever they were alone, Guntor pointed out that Bart had never stayed a day and a night in the jungle, and called him a pod-stinking whelp, trying to provoke a fight. Well, not today, he was too tired. When he saw Wahiri, he was going to sleep until the next alarm.

His stomach tightened as he rounded the last turn before the armory entrance and carefully arranged his face in a lanker-blank expression. After all, what could Guntor say to hurt him? Even Sair had personally thanked him that first day, and every day that he and Ontu's pack had ventured outside the walls.

He looked toward the door, wanting to know Guntor's mood.

But Guntor wasn't there! No one was there and the door stood ajar. Ajar! In migration! The barricades stopped most ferts, but occasionally they climbed the talus slopes near the entrance and got around the walls. His fatigue vanished and he ran to the door and threw it wide. The light streamed into the tiny guard room. Guntor lay half-naked on the floor on top of a woman—Ava—who writhed and moaned, her face flushed with pleasure.

"You stupid asshole!" Bart forgot his fear of zerkers. He reached the pair in a bound. Ava saw him and screamed, but Guntor was too far gone in his pleasure. Bart jerked the man off. Guntor roared in pain. His face darkened with rage, but his body hunched and his hands protectively cradled his spear.

"You . . ." He looked beyond Bart. "Godwithin!"

Three long lean ferts bounded through the open door and into the gloom.

Bart threw himself forward against the door, but more ferts hit the door and he could not shut it. Then Guntor was beside him, and Ava. They sweated as finger-width by finger-width the door was pushed open. Four more shapes slipped through; the weight eased. Guntor slammed the door and held it while Bart dropped the massive beam across the brackets. Behind the door ferts howled in frustration. He and Guntor raced for the armory.

Sanda stirred the poultice mixture slowly. The armory unsettled her. Along the far wall, under the windows, hundreds of steerage field hands were camped in little family groups, filling the cave with their chatter, their smells, and their children. Around her, near the infirmary, the girls in training worked for Leeorah and Nystra, caring for the wounded warriors in the infirmary, or making new bandages, poultices and medicines.

A shriek ripped the air. She whirled. Another screech tore through the center of the steerage camp. Then everyone was screaming. Children ran, looking for their parents. Parents raced about, grabbing children and sprinting for the stairs, the dorms, the infirmary.

By the door a grey fert—not a fert pelt or a stuffed target fert, but a real fert—tossed a child in the air, and leaped under it to pounce on another. Sanda backed against the wall. The scramble became a terrified struggle to get away from the two, no three, ferts who were ripping through a family, killing, then playing with the bodies of children, women, and men, before rushing off to kill again.

"Jont, Jont." A frantic woman screamed and dashed through the flow of people. "Jont, where are you?"

Ullan grabbed her arm. "Run," she yelled. Sanda

suddenly remembered Kayella. This was just like Kayella and the wall snake. She stood rooted to the spot.

Steerage crammed the armory stairs; those on the outside were being pushed to the edge—and off. As she watched, a child tumbled screaming to land with a sickening thud, and lie still. At the other end of the hall, the entrance to the whelps dorm was a howling knot of at least a hundred people. Ullan dragged her toward the infirmary. She followed, holding back. *Slow,* her mind screamed. *Slow.*

Four more animals leaped into the armory, roaring with blood lust. And there was blood aplenty. Sanda could smell it. Ferts pounced on another eight to ten people who were almost instantly torn to pieces. A woman carrying two children blundered into Sanda, knocking her down. Ullan came back for her. As she got to her feet, the rush of people pushed her against the wall. She felt something at her back. A spear. She grabbed it. Ullan saw her and grabbed another. The rush of people surged toward the stairs. *Slow,* Sanda screamed to herself, glad through her terror that hunger had so weakened her. Better to be a dead lanker than a drugged zerker. They reached the foot of the stairs. People were jammed all the way up to the top and the door was wedged shut by the panic-stricken crowd whose screams were now underlaid by sobs.

Bart and Guntor raced into the armory. Bart shot arrows as he ran. Guntor, dressed only in his leather shirt, roared a challenge, threw his spear and then charged the nearest fert, his shette a blur. Two ferts jerked in their death throes, then a third. The other ferts never noticed. They were greedily bounding toward the mass of humanity on the stairs, drunk on human blood.

"Brace your spears," someone yelled.

Sanda braced her spear. Energy flowed into her hunger-weakened body. The ferts tore forward. The people behind them no longer screamed. Some whimpered, some prayed, some cursed softly. They waited—helplessly.

Another fert fell thrashing in his own blood, but three were left. Sanda braced her spear against the stone steps. Beside her Ullan charged a fert, screaming. *"Slow,"* Sanda whispered. *"Slow."* Another fert came directly at her. Its teeth gleamed red. Blood dripped from its mouth, its chest and its claws. It crouched; it sprang. She closed her eyes in terror. The spear was yanked out of her hands. Pain slashed through her arm. Her eyes flew open. The skewered fert still tried to wade up the spear past its cross piece to get to her. She pressed against the people behind her. The whole crowd wailed and surged upward. Women screamed as their children were pulled from their grasp. People shrieked as they fell off the unguarded edge of the stairs.

A blade slashed into the fert, nearly severing its head. Bart tossed the animal aside and bent down to her. "Sanda, are you all right?"

"The ferts?"

"All dead."

Her famine weakness overcame her. She fainted.

Bart found he was loath to leave Sanda. He picked her up and took her to a quiet corner. Ullan followed, her eyes satiated with bright happiness. She was also drenched with blood. Fert's blood. Guntor had killed the fert she had wounded.

"I'll look after Sanda," she said, "while you call the men."

Bart reluctantly put Sanda down. She was so different from Wahiri. Even though she was thin, starving almost, he'd seen more life in her eyes in the moments before she fainted than he'd seen in Wahiri in their twelve days of marriage. And what a zerker! She was one of the powerful ones—like Olarni. Power obedient to will. Think of the sons she would bear!

At the window he paused. There was no signal for this. Finally he sent the migration warning down the cliffs to the men in the barricades, followed it with "danger of death," and ended with "stand down." He grinned as he saw frantic men waving and yelling before about twenty separated from the others and raced for The Home.

By the time they had run up the thirty turns to the armory, steerage had laid their bodies in family groups, and the survivors sat numbly beside them. One of the bodies was apart from the others—steerage without family. He recognized the boy who had chosen steerage, the one with the panting sickness.

The warriors piled in through the tunnel. Lars, the steerage foreman, met them, angrily shouting about warriors and broken promises. Sair swept him aside, and limped over to Bart.

"What the hell happened?"

When Bart explained, Sair's lips thinned. He bore down on Guntor who had found his pants and was cleaning his shette. Bart followed and found himself beside Radnor, Ontu, and Tev. Sair was flushed with anger. "You should be sent to steerage for this."

"No! Kill him!" a woman shrieked. The rest of steerage took it up and chanted. "Kill him, kill him!"

Sair chopped with his hands. Steerage shrank back as if from a naked blade and quieted down.

"But it wasn't my fault!" Guntor yelled. "She came

to me and offered herself. I was into her before I knew it."

"Where is she?"

Leeorah and Nystra pushed through the crowd and shoved Ava into the circle of men.

"He raped me," Ava shrieked. "He raped me."

"Why were you down there in the first place?" Nystra's calm question sliced into the knot of warriors.

"Yes," Sair grated. "Why?"

The frightened girl widened her eyes and sniffed. Not one warrior looked impressed. "He promised to marry me," she whimpered pathetically. "I just went to ask him when. Then he raped me."

"Nobody could rape you," Guntor said brutally. "You're easier than a steerage whore. I only took your father's leavings."

"Shut up!" Sair looked at Bart. "Was it rape?"

"Godwithin, don't ask him!" Guntor shouted. "He'll lie."

The Guardian's eyebrows rose. "That's right. You tried to rape Bart, too, didn't you?" He shook his head. "So it was rape. With her father dead, and no one to protect her, you raped this innocent girl."

Ava sniffed and wiped her eyes, looking carefully down, like a dutiful wife. Bart wanted to let it rest there. But he was a warrior, and damn it, Guntor was from his pack.

"She wasn't raped," he said. Guntor gave him an incredulous look.

Sair shrugged. "It doesn't matter. The Home was breached. Guntor's caused too many deaths today. Steerage won't want him. He should be cast out of The Home forever."

"Wait!" Tev rushed forward and whispered in Sair's ear. Sair listened, shook his head, and finally nodded.

Bart tried to listen, but steerage was making too much noise. What was Tev up to now? He watched, fascinated, as Sair beckoned to Mariko. Mariko's slender good looks were jarred by the jerky anger of his walk. *Aha. Jealous*. Tears glinted in his eyes. *And hurt, too*.

Sair raised his hand, signifying a judgment. Steerage stilled their angry rustling. "Guntor, you have proved that you are no warrior of The Home. But Tev has begged for your life. He reminds me that these steerage families may starve without their wives, husbands and children to work in the fields. So I give you your life. But you must pay ten times the blood price to each family for each death."

Guntor didn't look any happier. It took a long time to pay off a blood debt. Bart scanned the bodies, figuring. There had to be at least thirty bodies scattered around. At ten man weights of food or meat per blood price, times ten. . . . He got lost and turned to listen to the rest of the judgment.

"That pays for the deaths, but not your appalling discipline. Lucky for you Tev has promised to train you all over again. From this day until you pay off all your blood debts, you are to be treated as a whelp and will be under the orders of Mariko. You will feed your wife, but you will not be allowed to leave the armory level." He stepped forward and ripped Guntor's pack insignia off each shoulder.

Guntor rocked, as if from a blow, his eyes widening in shock. Mariko looked equally surprised, but his lips curved in delight. The men chuckled. Everyone knew Guntor treated Mariko like a cub, cuffing him and loving him as the mood struck him. And Mariko put up with it, because he needed Guntor's protection—desperately. Sair continued, "You will follow his orders and if he at any time complains to me, or if he dies, you will be cast from The Home to die in the jungle."

He looked at Ava. "What do you suggest I do with *that*?" he said to Nystra. "Steerage?"

The field hands hissed. "We'll give her Elrida The Crazy's old quarters," one woman screamed.

Sair frowned. "We don't kill children, especially future breeders. She has zerker blood running in her veins. She could bear zerker sons." He looked questioningly at Nystra. "She's yours. You judge."

Nystra stepped forward. "When this happened you were already being punished for starting a fight with Ullan." She raised her hand in judgment. "You are hereby judged unworthy to become a woman of The Home. We will not train you as a wife. You can choose to go to steerage or the jungle—if you want to die. Otherwise, you will always be a child—a breeding child. But a child. If your children survive weaning, they will be given to other women. You will never be welcome in the Gathering Rooms, and when your service to The Home is over, you will not be allowed to go to the Olarnites. When you die, your body will be tossed in the fertilizer ponds to nourish The Home."

Ava clenched her hands and raised them, screaming at the top of her lungs, "You can't do this to me! I was raped! He's lying."

Nystra ignored Ava and looked over her shoulder to the men behind. "If any of you want a servant, take her away. I will have none of her, ever."

There was a long silence, and then Rossu, a crinkly-haired, flat-nosed lanker pushed through the men and stood before Ava. "I walked you to the barricades. I treated you well, and you shamed me." His lips curved. "I think I'll enjoy this." He grabbed her arm roughly.

Ava screamed, and tried to scratch him. "You can't do this. If my father were alive, he'd kill you."

Rossu cuffed her, and sent her stumbling past Sanda who had recovered from her faint and was watching, wide-eyed. Ava saw her stepsister.

"Bitch!" she screamed. "Look what you did. You and your stinking mother." Rossu grabbed her long hair and nearly jerked her off her feet. Her screams of anger changed to shrieks of pain. She scrambled to keep up with him as he climbed the stairs.

Sanda watched Ava trip. Rossu yanked, and a handful of her hair came away in his fist. Ava clapped her palm to her scalp, shocked speechless. Rossu opened the door and kicked her through. As the door slammed Sanda dropped her eyes and kept them on the sand floor. She practiced *enryo* for all she was worth—not to shield herself from pain, but to hide her savage satisfaction and to cherish Ava's incredulous expression.

21

The Betrothal

Bart tied the sash of his red warrior's tunic, and sneaked a look at the shiny lacquered medal of Taizaburo on his chest. "Now I can wear this comfortably."

His wife looked up from stirring a sauce over the huge hearth that covered the whole wall of their tiny quarters. "But why? Everyone cheered when they gave you that medal after you saved The Home from starvation with your spice pods. Why, after Sair, you are the most respected man in The Home."

"Maybe, but now that I've spent my day and night in the jungle alone, I feel a lot better about wearing both the medal and warrior red."

Wahiri went back to her three little sauce pots beside the roasting keld that filled his whole hearth and dripped rich fat onto the bed of coals. While she cooked, Bart looked around *his* quarters. They were small, to be sure. But both rooms were his. And, as older warriors died off, he and Wahiri would move to better quarters. He sneaked another look at his medal. It was sky blue with a black sword painted on the disk. The only other one in The Home belonged to Sair, and he had won it when he ended the last pack war and united the lanker and zerker packs.

363

Wahiri put down her spoon and checked her roasting keld. Bart laughed. "Take it easy. The keld is cooking nicely." And it was. His first contribution to the annual keld feast that celebrated the end of migration and the beginning of summer was a fat female. Young. Tender. Tasty.

"But it's the first time I've been in charge of a keld feast. I want it to be just right." She looked at him worriedly. "After all, every one of your friends *and your friend's wives* will be visiting and tasting it—and comparing it with others."

Bart breathed in the succulent smell of a delicious keld basting in its own fat, and the fragrant accompaniment of jorlwood smoke and smiled fondly at Wahiri. "It's almost time to go."

Wahiri took some more wood from the stack by their door and laid it carefully on the fire. "I hope everyone likes my sauces. It's so hard to make them without spice pods. But there isn't a pod to be had in The Home." She carefully turned the crank, rotating the animal over glowing coals.

Bart grinned. Wives were going to find it very hard to keep their pods. All the men took them on the hunt. As long as they were motionless, the smell of spice protected them from almost all predators. If they moved, however, the ferts and tigrogs still attacked.

Bart watched Wahiri bustle about, feeling an overwhelming sense of contentment. Everything was perfect . . . except . . . Sanda. If only he could claim her. With Sanda, everything would be perfect . . . well, almost. There was still the chilling mystery of his father's death. He looked out of his open door toward the Heights. Nothing stirred on their bleak cliffs.

"I'm ready." Wahiri stood there, eyes lowered, the

perfect wife. But Alna, her daughter by Ludde, and her little son, Faior, were nowhere in sight.

Bart looked at Wahiri in surprise. Then he saw that although her eyes were properly lowered, her hands were twisting endlessly at her sash.

"What is it?" When she said nothing Bart took her chin in his hands and forced her to look at him. "Is there something wrong with the children?" Her face, trapped in his hands, twitched a slight no. "What is it then?" Bart urged. "Spit it out. You know I don't believe in *enryo*."

Wahiri somehow managed to meet his eyes. "I have a favor to ask of you."

"Well, don't be afraid of me. Just ask." Bart backed off from her, and relaxed—the way he might back off from wary game. But inside he was alert. This was the first time Wahiri had ever said anything on her own.

"You brought in so much meat during migration that we had more than enough for our needs, so I sold the surplus. People came to me from almost every family, and I have saved over a hundred gold cards and twenty-three green ones." Her hands disappeared into her pockets and came out with a fistful of golden cards. "See!"

Bart stared, amazed. He had never seen so much wealth in one place. He was rich, probably richer than half the pack leaders.

He was rich enough to claim Sanda! Of course he couldn't marry her till her training was completed, but he could claim her now.

Wahiri smiled back at him and he realized that he was grinning from ear to ear. Then her nerve seemed to fail her and she looked down again.

"Come on, woman," Bart said agreeably. "A hundred

cards is wonderful news. So, what's the problem?" Over a hundred gold cards! He couldn't wait to claim Sanda!

Wahiri finally looked up. "Will you take in my five-migration-old niece from steerage?" she blurted. "She's a good girl, really she is, and with this wealth I could train her and give her a good dowry and you wouldn't have to worry about her at all."

Bart stopped smiling. A steerage brat. In his house. He knew that some of the men sneered at him because Wahiri was steerage born. Another steerage born in his home would only increase that.

"We have enough cards, really we do, and Cara will work very hard," Wahiri begged.

Bart scratched his head to give himself time to think. The cards were his to do with as he pleased. He could just take them from her. But he liked Wahiri. And she was a good wife.

"Are you sure this is what you want?" he asked her. "You know if you draw attention to your steerage background the women will shun you."

"The women already shun me," Wahiri said bitterly. "Besides, a little shunning counts nothing against saving a girl from the winter hunger in steerage."

"Well," he said, still thinking furiously. "I suppose I might take her in." Wahiri's face lit up like a summer morning flower. "But," Bart went on, "I am going to have to balance her with someone else—someone from a warrior family, someone with status, someone who can earn more money for a larger family."

Wahiri froze. The mask of *enryo* slammed into place on her face. "Sanda," she said woodenly. "You want Sanda." Her eyes dropped again, and Bart knew that her feelings were no longer even in this room.

"How did you know?" Bart demanded. "I never told anyone."

Wahiri shrugged. "Dyfid told me you were always looking at her. He warned me that you would try to bring her into your home." She heaved a long sigh and held the cards out to him. "Can I bring my niece into our house today?" she asked in a cool polite voice.

Bart nodded. He felt unbalanced at the speed in which she had masked all her feelings, yet overjoyed that Sanda would really be his. When she gave him the cards, he trapped her small calloused palm in his hands. "You won't be sorry," he promised her. "Sanda is a good girl and she will be a great help to you. She will bring a lot of wealth and status to this family."

Wahiri raised her voice. "Alna." Her daughter appeared immediately, as if she had been waiting. "Go and get Cara," Wahiri said. "We will want her in our family before the feast."

Alna whooped with joy, and shot out of the door and out of sight before she finished talking.

Bart stood stupidly, the cards in his hands.

"Go on," Wahiri said with perfect politeness. "If you hurry, you can have her by your side as your claimed wife, when we go to the feast." As she spoke the bell started to toll the call to the Keld Feast. Bart gave her an awkward pat on her shoulder and hurried out.

He knew just where to go. With Haddim dead, Sanda's rights were owned by her uncle, Kysill, a lanker warrior. Kysill had three girls of his own to provide dowries for. Besides, Bart knew he needed a new shette, and these cards could get him one of the finest Olarnite steel. His quick walk shifted to a jog and his spirits soared into the sunlit sky.

As he passed Dyfid's quarters his friend came out
with his family. His wife, Bordah, was old, over thirty
for sure, and his oldest stepdaughter was twelve, almost
ready for wife training. She led Dyfid's four-year-
old stepson by the hand.

"Aren't you coming to the feast?" Dyfid asked.

Bart nodded. "I'll see you there. I have to do something
first." He hurried on before his pack brother could
say anything more. He really should put this off, and
wait until after the feast. But, with Sanda so close
to being his, he didn't even care if he was late for
the celebration.

As he strode across the swaying bridge to the Port
side of The Home, spray from the waterfall frosted
his beard and his face. Then he was hurrying through
the crowds of The Home. He took a deep breath of
the air, warm with summer winds, fresh with waterfall
spray, and laden with the scent of roasting meat, and
he laughed out loud.

People smiled back at him, and warriors saluted
him respectfully. Women curtsied, looked at the
medal of Taizaburo on his chest and whispered to
each other behind their hands. Bart straightened
and walked more slowly, more in keeping with his
new dignity.

The crowds thickened. Everyone except the birthing
or dying headed for the celebration. Warriors, wives,
and children mingled with boys, whelps and steerage
hands. The decks had been empty for so long, the
number of people amazed him. Women called to
children, and children, already losing their winter
leanness, were tumbling on the deck with pregnant
meatcats who were so full of food and kittens, they
could hardly move. And the laughter. It bubbled off
the wall and soared into the sky where it chuckled

off the cliffs. A cub ran full tilt into Bart and bounced off to land with a plunk on his backside. Bart paused, bent down and set him on his feet, feeling a remarkable tenderness toward the child. He was the same age as his own son, Faior.

"Get home." The harsh command sliced through the merriment. A dark-haired woman pushed Ava toward them and away from the Assembly Hall. Bart hardly recognized her. She was still dressed in the brown of childhood, but already she looked old. She seemed to have lost half her weight. There was a huge bruise on her cheek and she cringed like a beaten field hand.

"Please," she whimpered, "just for the celebration?"

"No." The woman appealed to the crowd around her. "She breached The Home. Should I let her celebrate with decent people, or with the families of those she killed?"

One of the elders was walking by. He spat at Ava's feet. "You're all too soft. In my time, they would have thrown her off the Promenade Deck, and good riddance."

The woman nodded grimly, boxed Ava's ears and pushed her out of sight.

Bart bumped into someone. "Sorry."

Tev laughed. "Has the medal already gone to your head?"

Bart flushed, then laughed. "Nobody ever admired me before," he confessed. "I can't help liking it." He grinned. "You know, I thought that when I didn't turn zerker, my life was over." He edged away from Tev. He had to get to Kysill before the older man left for the feast.

Tev kept pace with him. "I figured you'd snap out of it sooner or later, but not like this." He paused.

"Speaking of snapping out of it. There's a man who might take years to snap out of it."

Bart turned to see Mariko and Guntor coming toward them. Mariko strode head high through the crowd glorying in his new status as a man. The young lanker was freshly robed in a new red warrior's tunic. Behind him, Guntor once again wore whelp green. He walked behind his warrior as was proper, but his hands were clenching and unclenching with sullen rage. As they passed, he looked up and his eyes met Bart's. For a second, unspeakable hatred flared across to Bart and froze his breath solid in his throat, then Guntor dropped his head and marched angrily on.

"I'm glad that you and Dyfid are joining Ontu's pack," Tev said quietly. "That kind of hatred could rip a pack apart."

Bart nodded. "Sorry," he said, "I still have something to do before the feast." He hurried off.

Bart's heart hammered as he handed over the one hundred gold cards. Kysill took out seventy, handed the rest to his wife, and told her to send for Sanda. The wife, obviously disappointed at not getting more, hurried out. Bart edged toward the open door and looked out at the Promenade Deck that was awash with women and children gathering in family groups before they wandered toward the Assembly Hall. Beside him Kysill made small talk that he barely heard.

Then the world faded as he saw Sanda hurrying toward him. Her face was flushed and her eyes alight with the same joy that made him want to shout and do cartwheels down the length of the deck. In seconds she was facing him, breathless with emotion.

"Is it true?" she demanded. "Are you really claiming me?"

"Lower your eyes, girl," the wife ordered in shocked tones. "You're acting like a steerage slut."

Sanda gave a startled look around as if suddenly realizing where she was.

Be calm, be meek, Sanda ordered herself. *Look like a lanker. Act like a lanker.* She took a deep breath and slowly released it. But while she looked at the ground her heart hammered against her rib cage with joy. It was a dream come true!

Her Uncle Kysill took her hand in his. "We don't have time for a betrothal feast, because of the Spring Keld Festival, but you are claimed by Bart, Mikhail's son, warrior of Ontu's pack." He slipped her slender hand into Bart's hard warm one. "We'll have the proper ceremony after the festival. Meanwhile, you may spend the festival with him." He waved to his wife. "See to her supervision." Turning to Bart he said, "Sanda will be a good wife to you." He clapped Bart on the back and turned back into his quarters. As he went inside, one of Kysill's younger wives hurried out carrying a small child. Sanda took care to keep her eyes lowered.

Bart took her hand and drew her across the deck to the dactyl net. Seeing that they were not going anywhere, the young wife settled down in the sun by the door and started to nurse her child. Sanda relaxed a little. The wind was blowing strongly down the valley and its ceaseless moan would cover their conversation and give them some privacy.

Both of them stood looking into the valley, suddenly too shy to speak. Down below the fields stood black and empty. All the field hands were climbing the long path to come to one of the five feasts a year when they were freely given meat.

"I couldn't believe it when you didn't lose control

during the fert attack," Bart said. "You showed discipline worthy of a warrior. Ullan went crazy, but not you."

"I was too weak from hunger," Sanda admitted. She shivered, remembering the hot foul breath of the fert as it fought its way down her spear.

"I'll feed you up," Bart said, grinning. He reached over and took her hand. Sanda darted a look over her shoulder and saw that the young wife was watching her wistfully. Bart gave her hands a little squeeze. "I have more meat than I know what to do with. I'll send it up to the upper decks for you."

A vision of Ullan's rage made Sanda clutch his hand. "No, Bart, don't do that." She lowered her voice to a whisper. "That will only set me off." Bart turned a startled look on her. Sanda nodded. "I've learned from . . . from the old records that if zerkers eat jungle meat they get worse." As she looked up at him, feeling solid comfort from his steady grey eyes, the ideas that had been whirling in her head all during migration tumbled out one on top of the other. "Bart, I want to help the zerkers in The Home. I want to find out how the ancients learned to control their rages without Peace. I want to change the way the zerker women are treated and help the crazy old zerker men who destroy their lives and their families when they get old and out of control. I keep thinking that if Haddim had been able to control his alcoholic rages, he would never have alienated his pack brothers and . . . and . . . driven my mother to murder him. I already know that eating ship food, or eating meatcats is the answer. The song of the ancestors clearly tells us that we had no beserkers when we came to this world. It was the jungle meat that drove us wild."

"But I was taught that the Godwithin turned men zerker to give us warriors to save us from this world," Bart protested.

"Yes," Sanda agreed. "I was taught the same thing. But the Song of the Ancestors was composed by Olarni herself. It hasn't been changed in all these generations and *it* says:

> *"But the battle had given them kills right at*
> *hand*
> *And they feasted all through the night.*
> *And awoke to a world where half of the band*
> *Were berserker with strength and might.*

"Think about it, Bart. It really sounds as if the feast of animal food turned them zerker. Since I . . . figured this out, I've been avoiding meat as much as possible. I find that my temper is the worst not after the meal, but the morning and day after the meal. It's the food, Bart. The food of this land. It is somehow different from ship food."

"But we don't have enough of that food to soothe all the zerkers in The Home," Bart said reasonably. "Though Godwithin knows I would dearly love to see that happen."

"No," Sanda agreed, "But there has to be another way. There just has to be." She met his grey eyes and put all her will and all her passion into her request. "Will you help me, Bart? Will you tell me what happens to the men—the way you did in the cave when we were building Mirta a cage? Will you help me somehow change the curse of the zerker nature in our lives? I'm going to study the old records, the zerker women and men in The Home. Somewhere, somehow, I want to be able to change what happened to Ullan, what happened with Haddim, and what still might happen to me." She stopped, out of breath.

"It won't happen to you," Bart said. "I'll never tell,

and my First Wife is indebted to me for taking in her niece. You'll be safe with us." He smiled at her. "I love you too much the way you are to ever want to see you change."

"Even if I should lose my temper?"

Bart met her gaze. "Even then. I've been around zerkers all my life, and you're the best of the lot. Go ahead, study. Help Ullan. I'll tell you everything I know about zerker men—particularly Guntor who is well on his way to becoming one of the crazy zerkers you spoke about." His face darkened. "Guntor was my best friend before he turned. But since he became a zerker, I've watched him turn into my worst nightmare. When I talk about it to other lankers, they just shrug and say that they had the same experience with one of their friends, or that they had to watch that happen to their brother, or cousin. So, if you can help the zerker men, I know that the lankers will be grateful, because we're the ones who have to watch out for their rages and clean up after they are over."

Sanda raised her eyes to his. She didn't care what Kysill's wife thought of her. "Thank you, Bart. We'll manage something, I know we will."

Bart nodded, grinning. He turned toward the valley and murmured. "One thing you should know is that lanker-zerker brothers or lovers are the most powerful combinations in any pack." He smiled. "And we're a lanker-zerker marriage. We'll make a great team."

Sanda nodded, feeling herself blush.

"But there's something else that's as dangerous to The Home as any wild zerker," Bart said. "And that's the problem of the Heights."

Sanda drew the sign of the holy circle on her breast. "Don't even speak of it," she warned. "The ghosts might get you."

He put his hand on her shoulders. "Sanda, I saw the person on the Heights. He was so far away I almost couldn't make him out, but I did. There was a man dressed in dark brown or black, dragging a log."

"A log? But there are no trees on the Heights. That's one of the reasons why we came down here," Sanda said. "There was no firewood. So you couldn't have seen a log."

"You know how good my eyesight is, Sanda. I saw him struggling with a log. It looked as if someone else was on the other end of it. My father saw him, and he died because if it. But he was killed by something real and solid—by a polished bone splinter. I don't know how it killed him, but it nearly killed me too even though I only touched it."

"Bones are a sign of death."

"Bones are a sign of tools," Bart insisted. "Look at steerage. When they need tools, they make them from bones, and they sure aren't ghosts." He reached to take her hand in his. "It's not as if I'm asking you to face a ghost. I'm only asking you to quietly find out about the Heights."

"I could ask Scholar Jehanee."

"No, I don't trust anyone but you. If you ask her, word will get around, and I'll end up dead, just like my father."

She could feel the blood drain from her face.

"Think about it," Bart urged. "All that game goes up on the Heights for the whole summer. And we never follow it. Why?" He crossed his arms, brooding. "Since my father died, I've been talking to all the old men and listening to their tales. It comes up again and again. Men who try to go up to the Heights die in strange ways. Did you know that your father was one of them? Then there was Iduaor. About a hundred migrations ago he wanted to follow the keld to the Heights and salt enough food up there for the whole winter."

"Oh, the Lost Pack," Sanda said.

Bart nodded. "The Lost Pack. They passed the line of stones by the Totem and were never seen again."

"Yes, the next winter over two hundred children and old people starved," Sanda said. "But the warriors were warned. The old songs said that ghostfires burned for days before they went up. The Priestess foretold their death, and said they would be punished for ignoring the God and Goddess Within."

"In hunting, if we come to an area where there are no beasts of prey, warriors know there's something dangerous there," Bart said, "We walk carefully. We look for it. And we usually find it. Sometimes we leave it alone. We've learned to stay out of the swamps near the sea where the tides can rush in and crush a man. But at least we know what it is. Think, Sanda. If we could raise keld like meat kittens and take what game we want from the Heights, there would be no more starvation in The Home."

"No more starvation!" Sanda was transfixed by the idea. "No more crying children who can't eat the food adults eat because it isn't ship food. No more spring funerals for babies and toddlers." She hugged herself as a thought hit her. "If we had more jungle meat, we could keep more meatcats over the winter. Then there would be lots of ship food in the spring. In fact we could feed most of the jungle meat to the cats and let them turn it into ship food for . . ." She stopped in mid-thought. "But ghosts. . . ."

"Not ghosts, Sanda, people. I saw him. If I'd been

beside him, I'm sure I could have heard him grunting with the effort."

Sanda stood silently, a thousand ideas rushing through her mind. A man dressed in black? A polished bone splinter that killed? The Lost Pack? Her own father's death?

That is what had started all her mother's problems. When her father had been alive they'd all been happy. Her life had only gone crazy when her father had "died" and her mother had been given in marriage to Haddim.

"Will you try, Sanda? If you do, I will do everything I can to help you."

Slowly, she nodded. "What I need to do is to make a secret climb up the Heights and look around. It'll take more than one night, though, and I'll need you to somehow hide my absence," she said thoughtfully. "But if ghostfires start burning, I'll be coming back— fast," she warned.

"Climb?" Bart stared at her in amazement and wonder. "Are you still climbing?"

"Once or twice a week. I've even got up as far as the Olarnites."

Something furry rubbed around her ankles. She looked down. A very ragged bony meatcat looked up at her, then rubbed his cheek against her calf.

"You did save him!" Sanda swooped her old pet into her arms and hugged him until he squawked.

Bart grinned. "He's tough. But then you're tough too—and smart. I like to talk to you about my ideas and my plans."

Sanda looked happily up from scratching Mirta's ruff. "Olarni once said, *Give me men and women with intelligence and courage, and I will build you a new life*." She tilted her head thoughtfully. "Do you think we can make a difference?"

"Only if we stick together." He grinned. "And I plan to stick you in my home as soon as your apprenticeship is over, and we'll make a great team—all of our lives."

In her arms, Mirta Blossom started to purr.